Charlotte gasped.

"What are you *doing* here?" she whispered harshly, her face burning with anger. "What's *happened* to you?"

"I *need* you, Charlotte."

"God damn you. God damn you. What did you do? For Christ's sake, what did you do?"

Charlotte was speaking to her estranged husband, the C.I.A. analyst Charles Stone. Except for her, everyone Stone loved was dead or threatened. Everyone he trusted had betrayed him. Stone had nothing left to lose but his life. And what he had to save was the future shape of the world as they closed in on—

THE MOSCOW CLUB

"SUPERB . . . Finder has a jeweler's eye for the mechanics of terror and intrigue."
—Robert Moss, author of *Moscow Rules*

"Real, and wise, and scary as a night with the secret police."
—Justin Scott, author of *The Nine Dragons*

"COMPELLING INTRIGUE AND ACTION . . . from the catacombs of Paris to the inner sanctums of Washington to Lenin's tomb."
—David Morrell, author of *The Fifth Profession*

"AGILE CLOAK AND DAGGER . . . PULLS OUT ALL THE STOPS . . . lively prose and action . . . marvelous at showing us Moscow itself."
—*Detroit Free Press*

JOSEPH FINDER

THE
MOSCOW
CLUB

A SIGNET BOOK

SIGNET
Published by the Penguin Group
Penguin Books USA Inc., 375 Hudson Street,
New York, New York 10014, U.S.A.
Penguin Books Ltd, 27 Wrights Lane,
London W8 5TZ, England
Penguin Books Australia Ltd, Ringwood,
Victoria, Australia
Penguin Books Canada Ltd, 10 Alcorn Avenue, Suite 300,
Toronto, Ontario M4V 3B2
Penguin Books (N.Z.) Ltd, 182–190 Wairau Road,
Auckland 10, New Zealand

Penguin Books Ltd, Registered Offices:
Harmondsworth, Middlesex, England

Published by Signet, an imprint of New American Library, a division of Penguin Books USA Inc. This is an authorized reprint of a hardcover edition published by Viking Penguin, a division of Penguin Books USA Inc.

First Signet Printing, January, 1992
10 9 8 7 6 5 4 3 2 1

PUBLISHER'S NOTE
This is a work of fiction. Although real people appear in their natural settings, none of the events depicted in the story really happened and are entirely fictitious. Any actions, motivations, or opinions attributed to or about real people in the book are purely fiction and are presented solely as entertainment.

For my parents
and, above all, for Michele

ACKNOWLEDGMENTS

Quite a few people with far more important things to do provided generous help in the writing of this book. I thank, particularly, Doe Coover, Peter Dowd, Ami and Varda Ducovny, Lisa Finder, Randy Garber, Diane Hovenesian and Dr. Robert Berry, Justin Kaplan and Anne Bernays, Bob Lenzner, Gil Lewis, Jan Libourel, Paul McSweeney, Ray Melucci, Detective Paul Murphy of the Boston Police Department, Richard Rhodes, Robie Macauley, Randi Roth, Ranesford Rouner, Rafe Sagalyn, Charlie Smith, Harry Stoia of Boston Lock & Safe, Joe Teig, Rick Tontarski, Jerry Traum, Joe Walker, Tom Wallace, and, for invaluable assistance on the mechanics of terrorism, Jack McGeorge. I thank, too, my friends in the intelligence profession, who of course bear no resemblance whatsoever to the more odious types contained herein.

For medical expertise, I thank Dr. Stan Cole, Dr. Ann Epstein, Dr. Jonathan Finder, C. George Hori, Dr. David Jablons, Dr. William Kasimer, and Lynn Swindler.

For specialized wisdom in matters of Sovietology, in these peculiar times when the Soviet Union seems to metamorphose by the day, I'm grateful to many friends and colleagues, including Nick Daniloff, Susan Finder, the nationalities expert Lubomir Hajda of the Harvard Russian Research Center, Elena Klepikova, the Lenin scholar Nina Tumarkin, the encyclopedic Kremlinologist Sidney Ploss, and the incomparable Priscilla McMillan. For the textures of life in Moscow, I was helped by many here and during my visits to Russia, including Maria Casby, Ruth Daniloff, Andy Katell, Alex Sito, and Misha Tsypkin.

Working with the people at Viking Penguin has been a pleasure, particularly my splendid, astute editor, Pam Dorman, who was enthusiastically involved at every turn.

And of course I must thank the indispensable Danny Baror of the Henry Morrison Agency.

Finally, there are three people without whose generous and patient encouragement I couldn't have done it: Henry Morrison, the most dedicated agent I know, adviser and champion; my brother, Henry Finder, brilliant editor and brainstormer; and my wife, Michele Souda, for devoted editorial attention and constant loving support, who was there from the start, in a hammock on Martha's Vineyard.

They were too deeply entangled in their own past, caught in the web they had spun themselves, according to the laws of their own twisted ethics and twisted logic; they were all guilty, although not of those deeds of which they accused themselves. There was no way back for them.

—Arthur Koestler, *Darkness at Noon*

PROLOGUE

Moscow

At ten minutes past midnight, the chauffeur neatly maneuvered the sleek black Chaika limousine up to the main entrance of the yellow brick residential building on Aleksei Tolstoy Street and put the car in park. Hastily he opened the door for his passenger, an extremely highly placed member of the Central Committee, who emerged with barely a grunt of acknowledgment. The chauffeur saluted, because he knew his boss enjoyed such signs of respect, returned to the driver's seat, and prayed that the anxiety in his eyes had not been visible.

When the car was sufficiently far from the building's front door, he popped a Bruce Springsteen tape that his wife, Vera, had bought on the black market into the tape player and turned up the volume so loud that Springsteen's raspy voice rattled the limousine's instrument panel, the *thump thump* of the bass no doubt audible even outside the heavy armored car. He needed the music's raw power, the familiar tune, to calm his nerves.

As he drove, he thought of Verushka, who would be asleep in the warm bed when he returned, her swollen breasts tight against the silk of her nightgown, her belly already beginning to protrude because of the baby that was growing inside. She would be sleeping deeply, blissfully, as she always did, unaware of her husband's secret disloyalty. When he slid into the bed, she'd awake, smelling faintly of the Moscow Nights perfume she always put on before bed on the evenings he worked late, and they'd make love.

Then he slowly drove down the steep incline into the underground garage, where the Chaikas and Volgas that belonged to the building's other residents—all of them members of the Soviet ruling elite—were parked in their assigned spots. The headlights illuminated the garage's dim interior; the chauffeur noted with some relief that no one else seemed to be there. That was good.

He backed the limousine into the reserved space and glanced around the garage again, his fingers drumming nervously on the padded steering wheel, not quite in time to the music. He switched off the engine but let the song play to the end, then turned the key and sat in absolute silence while his heart hammered with fear.

For an instant, he thought he saw a silhouette of a man against the far wall, but it was only the contorted shadow of a parked car.

He got out and opened the rear door on the driver's side. The interior stank of cigarette smoke. A few hours earlier, it had been opaque with the smoke from the Dunhill cigarettes his boss favored. He and one of his comrades were returning together from a secret meeting on the outskirts of Moscow, and on the way they had shut the glass panel so they could talk in privacy.

The chauffeur, dutifully watching the road, had pretended to be unaware that anything peculiar was going on, but he knew that his boss was involved in something dangerous, something frightening. Something he did not want anyone else in the Central Committee or in the Kremlin to know about. Something that was, that *had* to be, wrong.

Several times in the last few weeks, the driver had been ordered to take his boss to a secret rendezvous with other very powerful men, late at night and always via a circuitous route. The chauffeur knew he was trusted implicitly; among all the drivers he was universally considered the most discreet, the most reliable. Not for a moment would the men in the backseat think him anything less than absolutely loyal.

He rolled down the windows and then, with a small portable device, vacuumed up the cigarette butts. The boss smoked like a fiend, but hated when his car smelled like stale cigarettes in the morning. It was relaxing to do something as safe and routine as this.

Then he glanced around the garage again to make sure he was unobserved and felt the surge of adrenaline. It was time.

He reached under the well-padded, tufted leather seat, his fingers touching the metal springs until he felt the cold metal oblong. He slid it carefully off its bracket and pulled it out.

To anyone else it would have appeared nothing more than a curious black metal object, perhaps part of the seat's undercarriage. It was not. He depressed the tiny lever on one side, and a microcassette tape was ejected into his open palm.

Quickly he pocketed the tape and replaced the disguised West German tape recorder beneath the seat. Then he got out, closed and locked the car doors, and began to whistle softly as he walked up toward the street.

The chauffeur had scheduled the drop in the customary manner: Around noon, while his boss was at work at the Central Committee building on Staraya Square, he had strolled out to the liquor store on Cherkassky Boulevard and asked the bald salesman for a liter of vodka. If the man had handed him a bottle of pepper vodka instead of the plain stuff, that would have meant trouble. But today it was plain vodka, which signaled all clear.

Now the streets were dark and deserted, wet with the rain that had come a few hours earlier. He walked out to the Ring Road and headed south, toward Vosstaniya Square. A cluster of young women, probably students, laughing excitedly, quieted as they passed him—perhaps confusing his crisp uniform, with the blue epaulets of the KGB's Ninth Directorate, for that of a militiaman—and then burst into giggles.

After a few minutes, he came to a public restroom down a flight of concrete stairs. The acrid smell of urine got stronger and more overpowering as he descended. The granite-and-concrete facility was lit by a bare bulb on the ceiling, which cast a yellowish glare over the fetid interior, its urinals and broken porcelain sinks and splintered wooden toilet stalls.

His footsteps echoed as he entered. The restroom was empty. At half past midnight, who but drunks and vagrants would be in this vile place? He entered a stall and closed the wooden door, fastening the latch. The smell here was oppressive: the chauffeur gagged. Goddamn filthy Muscovites. He held his breath and spotted the graffiti-covered patch of wall where the bricks and mortar were especially uneven.

He grasped the edge of one of the bricks and pulled at it. Slowly it came out, the loose mortar crumbling onto the discolored concrete floor below. He hated this location more than the others—much more than the bakery or the shoe-repair place or the poster shop, for it felt so much more deserted and exposed—but he supposed there was some logic behind their choosing such a loathsome drop site.

It was there, of course; they never failed.

He drew out the small, newspaper-wrapped package and opened it quickly. Enveloped in a wad of rubles, which there was no need to count since they never cheated him, was a new, cellophane-sheathed cassette tape.

He noticed that his hands were trembling. He put the package in his front coat pocket, placed the recorded tape in the crevice, and then nudged the brick back into place.

Which was when he heard something.

Someone had walked into the restroom.

He froze for a moment and listened. The footsteps weren't crisp, they were somehow *soft,* as if made by a pair of felt boots, but that was ridiculous: no one wore those anymore, except old men and peasants and vagrants.

There is nothing to worry about, he told himself. This is a public place, and ordinary people will be coming in here, and it has nothing to do with you, it's nothing to worry about. It's not the KGB, you're perfectly safe.

He flushed the toilet and almost retched when he saw that it would not flush, and he stood there for a moment, listening, dizzy from fear. The footsteps had ceased.

He slowly, casually unlatched the door of the cubicle and saw who it was.

An old drunk. A pathetic old drunk, standing huddled in a corner in his felt boots and lousy worn pants and cheap nylon jacket, bearded and disheveled and desperate.

The chauffeur felt a wave of relief. In a quarter of an

hour he would be in Verushka's arms. He gradually let out his breath as he nodded brusquely at the drunk, who looked at him and spoke.

"Give me a ruble," the drunk said, his words slurred.

"Get out of here, old man," the chauffeur replied as he walked toward the door.

The vagrant shuffled closer, stinking of booze and sweat and tobacco, following him up the stairs and out onto the street. "Give me a ruble," he repeated, but his eyes seemed alert, oddly out of place on his dissipated face.

The chauffeur turned to say with exasperation: "Get out—"

But before he could finish, his head exploded with ineffable pain as the unbelievably sharp wire cut into his throat—a garrote, it had to be—and he could hear the old vagrant, who was no mere drunk and was suddenly upon him, hiss, "Traitor," as he pulled the wire tight.

The chauffeur was unaware how beet-red his face had suddenly become, how his eyes bulged and his tongue was forced outward, but in the last few seconds of his life, delirious from oxygen deprivation, he felt a wild and illogical pleasure, sure that he had made the drop undetected, that one final mission was accomplished: a false and wonderful sense, before everything darkened and then bleached to utter white, of odd and soaring victory.

PART ONE

THE
TESTAMENT

In Moscow he went to his office in the Kremlin. . . . Silently, with hands folded behind his back, Lenin walked around his office, as if taking leave of the place from which he once guided the destinies of Russia. That is one version. Another has it that Lenin took a certain document from his desk and put it in his pocket. This second story is contradicted by a third: he looked for the document; not finding it there, he became furious and shouted incoherently.

—David Shub, *Lenin* (1948)

1

The Adirondack Mountains, New York

The first hundred feet or so had been easy, a series of blocky ledges rising gently, rough-hewn and mossy. But then the final fifty feet rose almost straight up, a smooth rock face with a long vertical crack undulating through it. Charles Stone rested for a long moment at a flat ledge. He exhaled and inhaled slowly, with a measured cadence, glancing up at the summit from time to time, shielding his eyes from the dazzling light.

Rarely was a climb as perfect as this: that trancelike serenity as he pulled and pushed with his hands and feet, laybacking up the tiered rock, the pain of physical exertion overwhelmed by the sensation of unbounded freedom, the razor-sharp concentration. And—only other climbers wouldn't consider it corny—the feeling of communion with nature.

He was in his late thirties, tall and rangy, with a prominent jaw and a straight nose, his dark curly hair mostly obscured by a bright knitted wool cap. His normally olive-complexioned face was ruddy from the chill autumn air.

Stone knew that solo climbing was risky. But without the carabiners and the rope and the pitons and the chockstones and all the customary apparatus of protection, climbing was something else altogether, closer to nature and somehow more *true*. It was just you and the mountain, and you had no choice but to concentrate utterly or you could get hurt, or worse. Above all, there was no opportunity to think about work, which was what Stone found most refreshing. Luckily, he was so valued that his employers permitted him (though reluctantly) to climb virtually whenever he wanted. He knew he'd never be another Reinhold Messner, the master climber who had solo-climbed Mount Everest without oxygen. Yet there were times, and this was one of them, when that didn't matter, so much did he feel a part of the mountain.

He kicked absently at a scree pile. Up here, above the tree line, where only shrubs grew out of the inhospitable gray granite, the wind was cold and biting. His hands had grown numb; he had to blow on them to keep them warm. His throat was raw, and his lungs ached from the frigid air.

He struggled to his feet, moved to the crack, and saw that its width varied from about an inch or so to half an inch. The rock face, up close, looked more perilous than he'd expected: a vertical rise with little to hold on to. He wedged his hands into the crack and, fitting his climbing shoes into toeholds in the smooth rock, he hoisted himself up.

He grabbed onto a cling hold, pulled himself up again, and managed to wedge his hands into the crack. Finger-jamming now, he edged up slowly, inch by inch, feeling the rhythm and knowing he could continue climbing this way clear to the top.

And then, for a brief instant, his reverie was interrupted by a sound, an electronic bleat he could not place. Someone seemed to be calling his name, which was impossible, of course, since he was up here completely by himself, but—

—then it came again, quite definitely his name, electronically amplified, and then he heard the unmistakable racket of helicopter blades crescendoing, and it came again: "Charlie!"

"Shit," he muttered to himself, looking up.

There it was: a white-and-orange JetRanger 206B helicopter hovering just above the summit, coming in for a landing.

"Charlie, Mama wants you back home." The pilot was speaking through an electric bullhorn, audible even over the deafening roar of the helicopter.

"Great timing," Stone muttered again as he resumed finger-jamming his way up the crack. "Some fucking sense of humor." Twenty more feet: they could just goddamn wait. So much for his day of climbing in the Adirondacks.

When, several minutes later, he reached the top, Stone bounded over to the helicopter, ducking slightly as he passed under the blades.

"Sorry, Charlie," the pilot shouted over the din.

Stone gave a quick, engaging grin and shook his head as he clambered into the front seat. Immediately he put on the voice-activated headset and said, "Not your fault, Dave." He strapped himself in.

"I think I just broke about five FAA regulations landing here," the pilot replied, his voice thin and metallic as the helicopter lifted off the mountaintop. "I don't think you can even call this an off-site landing. For a while there, I didn't think I'd make it."

"Couldn't 'Mama' wait until tonight?" Stone asked plaintively.

"Just following orders, Charlie."

"How the hell'd they find me out here?"

"I'm just the pilot."

Stone smiled, amazed as always by the resources of his employers. He sat back, determined at least to enjoy the flight. From here, he calculated, it would be something like an hour to the helipad in Manhattan.

Then he sat upright with a jolt. "Hey, what about my car? It's parked down there, and—"

"It's already been taken care of," the pilot said briskly. "Charlie, it's something really big."

Stone leaned back in his seat, closed his eyes, and smiled with grudging admiration. "Very thorough," he said aloud to no one in particular.

2

New York

Charlie Stone mounted the steps of the distinguished red brick townhouse on a quiet, tree-lined block on the Upper East Side. Although it was nearly afternoon rush hour, it was still sunny, the sensuous amber light of a fall day in New York. He entered the high-ceilinged, marble-floored foyer, and pressed the single door buzzer.

He shifted his weight from foot to foot while they verified his identity by means of the surveillance camera discreetly mounted on the lobby wall. The Foundation's elaborate security precautions had annoyed Stone until the day he caught sight of the working conditions over at Langley—the cheap gray wall-to-wall carpeting and the endless corridors—and he almost got down on his knees and shouted a hosanna.

The Parnassus Foundation was the name given, by a CIA wag no doubt enamored of Greek mythology, to a clandestine branch of the Central Intelligence Agency charged with the analysis of the Agency's most closely held intelligence secrets. For a number of reasons, chiefly the belief of one former Director of Central Intelligence that the Agency should not be entirely consolidated in Langley, Virginia, Parnassus was situated in a graceful five-story townhouse on East 66th Street in New York City, a building that had been specially converted to repel any electronic or microwave efforts to eavesdrop.

The program was enormously well funded. It had been set up under William Colby after the Senate Select Committee on Intelligence (the so-called Church Committee hearings of the 1970s) tore the Agency apart. Colby recognized that the CIA needed to attract experts to help synthesize intelligence, which had traditionally been the

Agency's weak spot. Parnassus grew from a few million dollars' worth of funding under Colby to several hundred million under William Casey and then William Webster. It engaged the services of only some twenty-five brilliant minds, paid them inordinately well, and cleared them for almost the highest level of intelligence. Some of them worked on Peking, some on Latin America, some on NATO.

Stone worked on the Soviet Union. He was a Kremlinologist, which he often considered about as scientific a discipline as reading tea leaves. The head of the program, Saul Ansbach, liked to call Stone a genius, which Charlie privately knew was hyperbolic. He was no genius; he simply loved puzzles, loved putting together scraps of information that didn't seem to fit and staring at them long enough for a pattern to emerge.

And he was good, no question about it. The way baseball greats have a feeling for the sweet spot of the bat, Stone had an understanding of how the Kremlin worked, which was, after all, the darkest mystery.

It had been Stone who, in 1984, had predicted the rise of a dark-horse candidate in the Politburo named Mikhail S. Gorbachev, when just about everyone in the American intelligence community had his chips on other older and more established candidates. That was Stone's legendary PAE #121, the initials standing for Parnassus Analytical Estimate; it had gained him great renown— among the four or five who knew his work.

He had once casually suggested, in a footnote to one of his reports, that the President should be physically affectionate with Gorbachev when the two met, as demonstrative as Leonid Brezhnev used to be. Stone felt sure this sort of gesture would win over Gorbachev, who was far more "Western" (and therefore reserved) than his predecessors. And then Stone had watched, gratified, as Reagan threw his arm around Gorbachev in Red Square. Trivial stuff, maybe, but in such small gestures is international diplomacy born.

When the Berlin Wall came tumbling down, almost everyone at the Agency was caught by surprise—even

Stone. But he had virtually foreseen it, from signals out of Moscow he'd parsed, communications between Gorbachev and the East Germans that the Agency had intercepted. Not much hard data, but a lot of surmise. That prediction sealed his reputation as one of the best the Agency had.

But there was more to it than seat-of-the-pants instinct. It involved pick-and-shovel work, too. All kinds of rumors came out of Moscow; you had to consider the source and weigh each one. And there were little signals, tiny details.

Just yesterday morning, for instance. A Politburo member had given an interview to the French newspaper *Le Monde* hinting that a particular Party secretary might lose his post, which would mean the rise of another, who was much more hard-line, much more stridently anti-American. Well, Stone had discovered that the Politburo member who'd given the interview had actually been cropped out of a group photograph that ran in *Pravda*, which meant that a number of his colleagues were gunning for him, which meant that, most likely, the man was just blowing smoke. Stone's record of accuracy wasn't perfect, but it was somewhere around ninety percent, and that was damn good. He found his work exhilarating, and he was blessed with an ability to concentrate intensely when he wanted to.

Finally, there was a buzz, and he stepped forward to pull open the inner doors.

By the time he passed through the vestibule's black-and-white harlequin-tiled floor and walked up the broad staircase, the receptionist was already standing there, waiting for him.

"Back so soon, sweetie?" Connie said with a dry cackle, immediately followed by a loose bronchial cough. She was a bleached blonde in her late forties, a divorcée who dressed, unconvincingly, as if she were twenty-five; who chain-smoked Kool menthols and called each of the men at Parnassus "sweetie." She looked like the sort of woman you would meet sitting on a barstool. Hers was not a difficult job: mostly, she sat at her desk and received top-secret courier deliveries from the Agency and talked on the phone with her friends. Yet, paradoxically, she was as discreet as they came, and she oversaw the Foundation's connections to Langley and the outside world with an iron discipline.

"Can't stay away," Stone said without breaking stride.

"Fancy outfit," Connie said, indicating with a grand sweep of her hand Stone's dirt-encrusted jeans, stained sweatshirt, and electric-green Scarpa climbing shoes.

"There's a new dress code, Connie—didn't they tell you?" he said, proceeding down the long Oriental rug that ran the length of the corridor to Saul Ansbach's office.

He passed his own office, outside of which sat his secretary, Sherry. She had been born and raised in South Carolina but, having ten years ago spent one summer in London when she was eighteen, she had somehow acquired a reasonable facsimile of a British accent. She looked up and raised her eyebrows inquiringly.

Stone shrugged broadly. "Duty calls," he said.

"Indeed," Sherry agreed, sounding like a West End barmaid.

Saul Ansbach, the head of the Parnassus office, was seated behind his large mahogany desk when Stone entered. He stood up quickly and shook Stone's hand.

"I'm sorry about this, Charlie." He was a large, beefy man in his early sixties with steel-gray hair cut *en brosse* and heavy black-framed glasses, the sort of man usually described as rumpled. "You know I wouldn't call you back if it weren't important," Saul said, gesturing to the black wooden rail-backed Notre Dame chair beside his desk.

Ansbach had been a quarterback at Notre Dame, and he had never quite fit in with the proper, careful Ivy League types that once dominated the CIA. Perhaps that was why they had sent him to New York to run Parnassus. Still, as with most CIA men of his generation, his clothes were more Ivy League than the president of Harvard's: a blue button-down shirt, a rep tie, a dark suit that had to have come from J. Press.

Ansbach's office was dominated by a marble fireplace almost four feet high. It was suffused by the orange light of the late afternoon, which sifted in through the double-glazed, soundproof windows.

They had met when Stone was in his last year at Yale.

Stone had been taking a seminar in Soviet politics taught by a large brassy woman who had emigrated from Russia after World War II. He was the star of the class; here, studying the very thing that his father had once done for a living, he had found his natural milieu, the first subject in college he really cared about, and he began to shine.

One day after class the teacher asked him whether he'd like to have lunch the next day at Mory's, the private club on York Street where the professors ate Welsh rarebit and complained about Guggenheim fellowships they hadn't received. She wanted him to meet a friend of hers. Charlie showed up, uncomfortable in his blue blazer and the Yale Co-op tie that was threatening to strangle him.

Sitting at the small wooden table next to his teacher was a tall crewcut man with thick black glasses. His name was Saul Ansbach, and for much of the lunch Charlie had no idea why they'd invited him. They chatted about Russia and the Soviet leadership and international Communism and all that sort of thing, but they weren't just talking; later he realized that Ansbach, who at first said he worked for the State Department, was actually testing him.

When it came time for coffee, Stone's teacher excused herself, and then Ansbach tried for the first time to recruit him for an intelligence program about which he remained vague. Ansbach knew that Charlie was the son of the infamous Alfred Stone, who'd been condemned as a traitor in the McCarthy hearings, but he didn't seem to care. He saw instead a brilliant young man who had demonstrated an extraordinary flair for international politics and Soviet politics in particular. And who was also the godson of the legendary Winthrop Lehman.

Charlie, who considered the CIA vaguely sinister, said no.

Several times before he graduated, Saul Ansbach called, and each time Charlie politely told him no. A few years later, after Stone had embarked upon an illustrious career as a scholar in Soviet politics, teaching at George-town, then M.I.T., Saul asked again, and this time Stone finally gave in. Times were different; the CIA seemed far less odious. Intelligence work increasingly appealed to him, and he knew that now, with his reputation, he could have things his way.

He set down his conditions. He'd work when he wanted to (and climb mountains when he wanted); he wanted to work at home in New York and not have to move back to Washington, whose government buildings and white pedestrian "malls" gave Stone the shudders—to say nothing of dreary old CIA headquarters in Langley. And—since he was giving up the security of academic ten-ure—they'd pay him very, very well. For work he so en-joyed that he'd do it for free.

You never know, he later thought, how one quick decision can change your life.

Now Saul walked to the heavy mahogany double doors and shut them, emphasizing the gravity of what he was planning to say.

"It *better* be important," Stone said with false gruff-ness, about to observe that being plucked from the moun-taintop was a little like being interrupted during sex before you're finished. But he held his tongue, preferring not to have Saul ask when Charlie had last seen his estranged wife, Charlotte. Charlie didn't want to think about Char-lotte right now.

If you tell yourself, Don't think about white elephants, you will. The last time he saw her.

She is standing in the hallway. Her bags are packed for Moscow. And her eyes, unforgettable: too much makeup, as if her sense of palette had left her. She'd been crying. Stone is standing next to her, tears in his eyes, too, his arms half outstretched to touch her once more, to change her mind, to kiss her goodbye.

Ah, now you want to kiss me, she says sadly, turning away, a beautiful doll with smudged eyes. Now you want to kiss me.

Saul sank into his own chair, exhaling slowly, and picked up a dark-blue folder from his desk. He waved it and said, "We just got something in from Moscow."

"More garbage?" Most of the intelligence the CIA receives from the Soviet Union consists of rumor and unsubstantiated gossip; the Agency's Kremlinologists spend much of their time doing close analysis of information that is publicly available.

Ansbach smiled cryptically. "Put it this way: this file has been seen by exactly three people—the director, a transcriptionist cleared straight to the top, and me. Is that sensitive enough for you?"

Stone nodded appreciatively.

"I realize you don't know much about *how* we get the intelligence we do," Saul said, leaning back in his chair, still holding the file. "I like to keep collection and analysis separate."

"I understand."

"But I'm sure you're aware that since Howard we've had hardly any assets inside Russia." Ansbach was referring to Edward Lee Howard, a CIA Soviet Division case officer who defected to Moscow in 1983, rolling up virtually all the CIA's human sources in the U.S.S.R.—a devastating blow from which the Agency had never fully recovered.

"We've recruited another," Stone prompted.

"No. One of the few we had left was a driver in the KGB's Ninth Directorate. Code-named HEDGEHOG. A chauffeur assigned to various members of the Central Committee. We got him early, with steady money, paid in rubles, since hard currency would be too risky."

"And in return he listened to what was going on in the back seat."

"We gave him a recorder, actually. He concealed it under the back seat."

"Clever fellow."

"Well, he'd been noticing that one of the people he was assigned to had been having an awful lot of late-night meetings outside Moscow with a number of other high-powered people, and his ears pricked up. We got several tapes from him. Unfortunately, the poor shmuck didn't know how to operate a tape recorder. He kept the volume dial all the way down, so the sound quality is lousy. We've been trying to run a voiceprint ID on the speakers, but the rumble is too loud. We managed to transcribe most of it, but we have no idea who's involved, who's doing the talking."

"And you want to figure out what's going on," Stone concluded. He was looking not at Ansbach but at the framed prints of mallard ducks and botanical oddities that hung on the wall above the wainscoting. He admired Saul's attempts to make headquarters resemble a baronial estate more than an office. "But, Saul, why me? You've got others who can do this." He crossed his legs and added studiedly: "Who were already in town."

Ansbach, by way of reply, handed him the blue folder. Stone opened it, frowned, and began reading.

After a few minutes of silence, he looked up. "All right, I see you've highlighted the parts you want me to pay attention to. So we've got two guys talking here." He read aloud the yellow-highlighted fragments, skipping as he read, conflating them into one long string.

" 'Secure? . . . The Lenin Testament . . . Only other copy, Winthrop Lehman has . . . the old fart got it from Lenin himself . . . the tin god . . . can't do anything to stop it . . . ' "

Stone cleared his throat. "This Winthrop Lehman—I assume they're talking about *the* Winthrop Lehman."

"You know another one?" Ansbach asked, spreading his hands with his palms up. "Yeah. *Your* Winthrop Lehman."

"No," Stone said softly. "Now I see why you wanted *me*."

Winthrop Lehman, who would become his godfather, had been national-security adviser to Franklin Roosevelt and Harry Truman. In 1950 he had hired a brilliant young Harvard historian named Alfred Stone—Charlie's father—as his assistant. Later, even during Alfred Stone's disgrace, the so-called Alfred Stone affair, when Senator Joseph McCarthy had successfully branded Alfred Stone a traitor on a trumped-up charge of passing secrets to the Russians, Lehman had stood by him. Lehman, the statesman, aristocrat, and whom newsmagazines had dubbed "philanthropist" (which simply meant he'd been passingly generous with his vast fortune), was now eighty-nine years old. Stone was aware that he would not have been recruited to Parnassus were it not for some behind-the-scenes power-brokering on the part of the enormously influential Lehman.

Saul Ansbach steepled his large, knobby hands and placed the point under his chin as if he were saying a prayer. "You recognize the reference, Charlie?"

"Yes," Stone replied tonelessly. "The phrase 'Lenin Testament' came up during my father's hearings before the McCarthy Committee. It was never explained; it was never mentioned again." In spite of himself, he found his voice growing steadily louder. "But I'd always assumed—"

"Assumed it was just some mistake, is that it?" Saul asked quietly. "Some glitch, some shoddy piece of research done by some young whippersnapper on the Committee's staff?"

"No. The 'Lenin Testament' that *I* know about is no mystery. It was a document written by Lenin in his final days, in which, among other things, he warned about Stalin's getting too powerful. Stalin tried to suppress it, but it came out a few years after Lenin's death." He caught Saul's half-smile. "You don't think that's what they're referring to, do you?"

"Do you?"

"No," Stone agreed. "But why don't you have HEDGEHOG find out more?"

"Because he was killed two days ago," Saul said.

Stone's eyes widened somewhat; then he shook his head slowly. "Poor guy. KGB got on to him?"

"We assume it was KGB." He shrugged broadly. "Apparently, the hit was professional. As for *how* he was blown—well, that's another troubling thing. We don't know."

"So you want me to find out what they meant by 'Lenin Testament,' if possible, right? Talk to my father, try to worm the information out of him, maybe? No, Saul. I don't think I'd like that very much."

"You know your father was set up. Did you ever ask yourself why?"

"All the time, Saul."

All the time.

Alfred Stone, professor of twentieth-century American history at Harvard, had once been one of the stars in his field, but that was years ago. Before *it* had happened. Since then, since 1953, he was a broken man. He had published almost nothing. In recent years, he'd begun to drink too much. He was—it was a cliché, but in this case it was accurate—a husk of his former self.

Once, before Charlie was born, Alfred Stone had been a young, fiery lecturer and a brilliant academic, and in 1950, at the age of thirty-one, he was asked to join the Truman White House. He'd already won a Pulitzer Prize for his study of the United States and the end of the First World War. The president of Harvard, James Bryant Conant, had asked him to serve as dean of the Faculty of Arts and Sciences, but he decided instead to go to Washington. Winthrop Lehman, one of Truman's assistants, and a holdover from the Roosevelt administration, had heard about this rising star at Harvard and had asked him to the White House, and Alfred Stone had accepted.

He should have gone on to become some sort of minor national celebrity. Instead, he returned to the Harvard campus in 1953 shattered, kept on at Harvard's sufferance, never again to produce anything of any worth.

Charlie Stone had been ten years old when he first learned about his father's tortured past.

One day, after school, he found the door to his father's book-crammed study open and no one inside. He began poking around, exploring, but finding nothing of interest. He was about to give up when he found a large leather-bound scrapbook on his father's desk. He opened it. His heart started pounding when he realized he had made a *discovery,* and he pored through the book with guilty pleasure and complete absorption.

It was a collection of clippings from the early 1950s concerning a part of his father's life he had never heard about before. One article, in *Life* magazine, was titled "The Strange Case of Alfred Stone." Another headline, in the New York *Daily News,* called his father "Red Prof." Rapt, Charlie went through one yellowed clipping after another, as the mildewy, vanilla smell of the scrapbook enveloped him. Suddenly various bits of overheard conversation came together, things he had heard people say about his father, quick, nasty things, and arguments between his parents in their bedroom. Once someone had painted a large red hammer and sickle on the front of the house. A few times, he remembered rocks being thrown through the kitchen window. Now, finally, it made sense.

And of course his father had returned to his study suddenly and caught him at the scrapbook, whereupon he strode to the desk in a dark fury and snapped it closed.

The following day, his mother, the willowy, dark-haired Margaret Stone, sat Charlie down and gave him a brief, sanitized account of what had happened in 1953. There was a thing called the Un-American Activities Committee, she said, which was once very powerful before you were born. There was a terrible man named Joseph McCarthy who thought America was overrun with communists and who said they were everywhere, even in the White House. Your father was a very prominent man, an adviser to President Truman, and he was caught up in a battle between McCarthy and the President, a battle that the President wasn't able to fight on all fronts. McCarthy dragged your father before his Committee and accused him of being a Communist, a spy for Russia.

Lies, all of it, she told him, but our country was in a very difficult time, and people wanted to believe that our problems could be solved just by rooting out the spies and the Communists. Your father was innocent, but there was no way of *proving* his case, you see, and . . .

Charlie replied, with the unassailable logic of a ten-year-old, "Why didn't he say anything? Why didn't he fight them? Why?"

"But did you ever ask your *father*?" Ansbach lifted an earthenware mug from the top of a stack of green-and-white computer printouts and took a swallow of what, Stone felt sure, had to be tepid coffee.

"Maybe once, when I was a kid. It became immediately clear that that was none of my business. You just didn't ask about that stuff."

"But as an adult . . . ?" Saul began.

"No, Saul, I haven't. And I won't."

"Look, I feel funny even asking you. Exploiting your relationship with your father, with Winthrop Lehman, for Agency business." Ansbach removed his black-framed glasses and polished them with a Kleenex he took from a box in one of his desk drawers. When he resumed speaking, he was still hunched over the glasses, polishing busily. "Obviously, if our agent hadn't been killed I wouldn't need to ask you, and I know it's outside the realm of the pure analysis you're hired to do. But you're our best hope, and if it weren't important—"

"*No*, Saul," Stone said hotly. He itched to light a cigarette, but he had quit smoking the day Charlotte had left. "Anyway, Saul, I'm no field operative, in case it slipped your mind."

"Damn it, Charlie, whatever this 'Lenin Testament' is all about, it's clearly a key to why your father was thrown in jail in 1953." Ansbach wadded up the Kleenex and replaced the glasses on his face. "If you don't want to do this for the Agency, I should think at least you'd—"

"I wasn't aware you cared so deeply about the personal lives of your employees, Saul." The appeal to family: Saul was a master manipulator, and Stone felt a surge of resentment.

Saul hesitated for what seemed an eternity, examining the cluttered heaps atop his desk, running his fingers along the desk's worn edges.

When he looked at Stone again, he spoke with great deliberateness. His eyes, Stone noticed, were bloodshot;

he looked fatigued. "I didn't show you the last page of the transcript, Charlie. Not because I don't trust you, obviously . . ." He took a single sheet of paper that had been facedown on the desk in front of him and handed it to Stone.

It was stamped "Eyes Only/Delta," which meant the need-to-know requirements were so stringent that no more than a handful of people at the very top of the U.S. government would ever be permitted to see it. Stone glanced at it quickly, then read it again, more slowly. His jaw literally dropped in astonishment.

"You see," Saul said, dragging out his words as if it pained him to speak, "Gorbachev has been in trouble in the Politburo since the day he was named General Secretary. You know that; you've warned of that for years." He pressed the heels of his hands against his eyes, massaging them wearily. "Then all this turmoil in Eastern Europe. He's a man with enemies. And with the summit coming up in a matter of weeks, the President heading for Moscow, I thought it was vital—"

Stone was nodding, his face flushed. "And if we can figure out what this reference to a 'Lenin Testament' means, we can determine who's involved, what their motivations are. . . ." His voice trailed off; he was lost in thought.

Ansbach was peering at Stone now with a fevered intensity. He asked, almost whispering: "You read it the way I do, too, huh?"

"There's no other way to read it." Stone could hear the faint sound of typing from down the hall, which had somehow managed to penetrate the massive doors, and for a long moment he watched the pattern of sunlight and shadow on the wall, a neat geometric grid cast by the slats of the window blinds. "These people—whoever they are—are about to pull off the first coup in the history of the Soviet Union."

"But nothing *inside* the Kremlin," Saul added, shaking his head as if he didn't want to believe it. "Nothing like that. Something much, much worse. You with me on this?"

"Look, Saul, if that report is accurate," Stone said, his glance still riveted on the wall, "we're talking about the fall of a government. Massive bloody chaos. A dangerous upheaval that could plunge the world . . ." He shifted his gaze back to Saul. "You know, it's funny," he said softly. "For years we've wondered if this exact thing could ever happen. We've speculated about the terrible notion that someday the power that's now held by the Kremlin could ever be seized by another, much more dangerous clique. We've talked and talked about it, so much that you'd think we'd get used to the idea. But now—well, the thought of it scares the hell out of me."

3

Moscow

The word "dacha," which means "cottage," was a laughably modest designation for the palatial three-story stone structure tucked away behind a grove of pines in the town of Zhukovka, eighteen miles west of Moscow. Zhukovka is the enclave of some of the most powerful figures in the Soviet elite, and this particular dacha indeed belonged to one of the most powerful men in the Soviet Union.

He and eleven other men sat around a dining table inside, in a low-ceilinged room whose walls were covered with religious icons that gleamed in the amber light. The table was set with Lalique crystal and Limoges china, caviar and toast points, an abundance of fresh baby vegetables, chicken tabaka, and French champagne. To all appearances, it was nothing more than the table of one of Russia's privileged.

In fact, the room itself was swept regularly for electronic listening devices with a spectrum analyzer, which could monitor any transmissions on any frequency. Several small speakers mounted high on the walls emitted the steady, high-pitched hiss of "pink sound," sure to foil any devices that had somehow escaped detection. Nothing said within this room would ever be overheard.

The twelve dinner companions, each of whom occupied or had occupied extraordinarily powerful positions in the government—from the top rank of the Central Committee, to the Red Army, to the military-intelligence agency GRU—were the leaders of a small, handpicked group that called itself by the singularly undramatic name Sekretariat. Informally, sometimes, they called themselves the Moscow Club. They shared a fierce but secret zealotry: an unshakable devotion to the Soviet empire, which was, it seemed, crumbling day by day. And so they all nurtured a hatred of the Kremlin leadership under Gorbachev, and of the fearful direction in which the nation was headed.

At dinner, the conversation was as it always was. They spoke of the decline of the Russian empire, of the unconscionable chaos introduced into Russia by Mikhail Gorbachev. These men, ordinary Moscow bureaucrats of reasonable temperament, collectively incited one another to heights of pique and alarm. It didn't take much.

The Berlin Wall had been bulldozed. The Warsaw Pact was little more than a name. East Germany was gone. One by one, like a house of cards upset by a puff of breath, the Soviet-ruled, pro-Communist governments of the Soviet-bloc nations were toppling. From Prague to Budapest to Vilnius to Warsaw itself, the lunatics really had taken over the asylum. Citizens were marching, demanding the abolition of Communism. Lenin and Stalin were no doubt spinning in their graves as they witnessed how Mikhail Gorbachev had given away the shop.

And the republics *within* the Soviet Union were, one after another, pulling out, raising a defiant fist at Soviet rule.

The whole empire, once so strong, a world power forged by Stalin, was disintegrating. It was a nightmare.

One of the Sekretariat's leading members, an economist named Yefim S. Fomin, had been ousted from the Politburo for his outspoken views, and he was one of the most outspoken tonight. He was a member of the Central Committee in charge of industrial planning, and he spoke with some authority.

"Gorbachev's economic schemes are disastrous," he remarked. Fomin was a heavyset man with a thick shock of white hair who had a peculiar knack of speaking almost without moving his lips. "Our economy is falling apart, we can all see that. The Communist Party is no longer in control! The man is destroying our nation from within."

When dinner was over, the first to speak was the Sekretariat's coordinator, Colonel Gennadi Ryazanov, a pale, thin man of forty-five in charge of the GRU's foreign-intelligence section. Ryazanov looked weary; he had been working himself almost nonstop in the last few weeks. He had four children and a wife, all of whom kept asking when he was going to spend some time away from the office. He had a boss at the GRU who knew he wasn't working especially long hours there and wondered what the hell could be wrong—marital problems, a sick kid? No one but the men in this room and one other—the leader of the Sekretariat, who could not be seen with them—knew what was absorbing so much of his time and nervous energy: the very plans they were discussing tonight.

Ryazanov was a high-strung perfectionist who abhorred mistakes and miscalculations. He had awakened every morning for weeks with an acid stomach. He hadn't touched his dinner tonight.

Now he spoke extemporaneously, occasionally consulting a sheaf of neatly typed notes, which he placed beside a glass of water. "It is generally accepted in the West— in fact, throughout most of the world—that the Soviet leadership is, to coin a phrase, coup-proof." He turned up his lips in a small, tight smile. Ryazanov was not a natural speaker, and some of the men in this room, who knew him well, realized he had been working on this presentation for some time. "After all, we've now got some democracy here. Our Supreme Soviet routinely vetoes laws that the Kremlin demands. I think that perception will help us."

He looked around the table to engage everyone's

eyes, paused a moment, and continued, tapping a pencil on his sheaf of notes. There was uncomfortable stirring; he had dilated too long.

"Your point?" the economist Fomin inserted between rigid lips.

"My point," Ryazanov said, casting him a dyspeptic glance, "is that the reality and the perception do not coincide, and that will help us. I think we all agree that we can no longer wait. Extreme measures are called for. But there's simply no logic in assassinations any longer. Such an act would create a backlash within the government— would make the Soviet Union even less governable. There are those who will tell us that if you cut off the head the body will die. But the head is not just Gorbachev; it's all of his supporters within the Politburo, within the leadership. And the death of one man will not silence them. Quite the reverse."

His pencil rat-a-tatted on his notepad. He was clearly still lobbying the few who weren't fully convinced. Silently, he wished he could just go home and have supper with his family and play with his youngest, three-year-old Lyosha, who was probably asleep by now anyway. He felt a wash of stomach acid surge up toward his throat, but he continued gamely. "Our plan is difficult, but quite clever. Assassinations rarely work, and 'accidents' are rarely believed. But the world does believe, and believe firmly, in the presence of terrorism in all walks of life. Even in Moscow."

"Is everyone in this room satisfied that there is no possibility any of our intelligence organs—KGB, GRU— will learn of our plans?" The question came from Ivan M. Tsirkov, another Sekretariat plant in the GRU, who was short and round-faced, with small eyes and a high tenor voice. He looked a little like Lenin, but without the beard.

Ryazanov's eyes widened as he frantically tried to answer, but before he could do so, Igor Kravchenko, the head of Department Eight of the KGB First Directorate, cleared his throat. "There has been a breach of security," Kravchenko said softly. He was tall and stocky, with an air of great complacency, his eyes calm behind his rimless glasses.

The shocked silence was almost palpable. Ryazanov himself shuddered inwardly.

"You, Comrade Morozov," the KGB man said, extending a finger toward another of his colleagues, Pyotr L. Morozov of the Central Committee. "One of my people learned that the man who was serving as your driver was in the employ of the CIA."

"*What?*" breathed Morozov, a plain-faced man of about fifty. Gentle and blond-haired, Morozov was descended from generations of Russian peasantry, and boasted of it regularly. "But you assured us all the drivers were cleared!"

"The matter has been taken care of," Kravchenko said implacably. "The man has been executed. But did you discuss anything in front of the man that—"

"No, of course not," Morozov protested, his thick hands flailing, hands that had never done work more menial than shuffling papers from one desk to another. "When Yefim Semyonovich"—he indicated Fomin the economist, who in response compressed his lips involuntarily—"when we spoke in the car, we closed the compartment. We knew better than to trust anyone outside this room."

Colonel Ryazanov could feel his face redden with a prickly heat. He contained his anger, because he knew you never gained anything by venting anger. He gesticulated with his pencil and objected as mildly as he could: "Executed! But you can't interrogate a dead man!"

"Yes," Kravchenko agreed placidly, "that was a botch." He used a vulgar Russian expression that referred to a whorehouse. "Our people screwed up. Too eager. But I didn't want the agent interrogated by anyone at the Lubyanka, and better he was killed than that our existence becomes known. In any case, I am quite satisfied that the Sekretariat remains absolutely secret."

"And the Americans?" Tsirkov persisted, his voice almost a chirp. "If there is even one leak from the American side, we are all endangered."

Kravchenko answered. "Our American friends were the ones who notified us that this chauffeur was in their bag. They, after all, have more reason than anyone," he said solemnly, "to keep their relationship with us an inviolable secret."

"But what guarantee is there that the plans have not already been breached?" came an angry voice from the far side of the table. It was Morozov.

Kravchenko's reply was, once again, calm. "That is being taken care of. Even as we speak, it's being handled superbly. That will not present a problem."

"*Mokriye dela?*" asked Tsirkov, using the Russian tradecraft term that means "wet affairs," or killing.

"Of necessity. Nothing that will be detectable in any way."

"Then what is the exact nature of the plan? What will happen on Revolution Day?" This came from Mikhail Timofeyev, the blustery, compactly built Red Army commander. "Our forces will be on maximum alert. But on what pretext?"

Colonel Ryazanov sighed nervously, wishing he didn't have to present the carefully worked-up plan in so abrupt a manner, wishing he hadn't been interrupted by this disconcerting news, disliking to set things out so plainly, without preface. Slowly and carefully he explained, and the room was absolutely silent. Finally, one voice came from the end of the table. It belonged to the economist Fomin. "That is brilliant," he said. "Horrifying, but brilliant."

4

New York

Everything about Stone's apartment reminded him of his wife, Charlotte. It consisted of eight spacious rooms in a prized old cooperative building on Central Park West, a building whose potentates—a surly co-op board of three attorneys, a once-famous matinee idol, and two sisters who had inherited a fortune and lived in this building almost since time began—took pride in turning applicants away.

Stone had never been sure why he and Charlotte had managed to get past the board's scrutiny, except maybe that they were a nice, respectable-looking couple, he an esteemed young State Department employee (or so the board believed), she a highly regarded television correspondent, and both of them (thanks to the Parnassus Foundation, though no one knew it) quite well off.

The place had a lot of Victorian detail, but it was obscured by hideous flocked wallpaper and kitchen appliances in Harvest Gold: the previous owner had had money but no taste. Charlotte, while looking for a job, had it entirely redecorated. Now it was plush and comfortable, eclectic and vaguely Edwardian. There was a paneled entrance with a floor of green Italian marble, and a pleasantly crowded sitting room where piles of books sat beside Lord Melbourne and Louis XV chairs. The bedroom was furnished with a Flemish rosewood armoire and a Queen Anne oak chest of drawers she'd spotted at a flea market in western Massachusetts. The kitchen, with its high-gloss black cabinets, bore Charlotte's unmistakable imprint.

The library had walls of a deep wine color, recessed bookcases that held a complete set of Nabokov first editions, an eighteenth-century Russian traveling desk of ebony and mahogany with ormolu mounts, an immense Agra carpet, and a Regency library armchair with tufted leather seat that had been a gift from Winthrop Lehman. Lehman had been given the chair by Winston Churchill during the war, in gratitude for Lehman's assistance in the Lend-Lease business; he had given it to Charlie on his wedding day.

Sixteen years of marriage, and then all of a sudden—what was it? a year and a half ago already?—she'd moved out. Since then the apartment had seemed ludicrously empty.

Sometimes, late at night, burying his face in the pillow in the bed they had shared for so long, he could smell her perfume, gardenia-scented, light and erotic, and he would remember the number of nights they had slept together— 5,980 nights; he had figured it out—and for a long time he would stare up at the ceiling.

He still dreamed of her often, which felt unhealthy and vaguely shameful.

There was something about her, an indomitability of spirit mixed with the vulnerability of a child, that Stone had recognized when he had first met her, during senior year in college. She had been sitting at one of the long dark wooden tables in the dining hall, her elbows resting on the overwaxed, uneven surface, holding a book. Everyone around her was talking and laughing, and she was sitting alone, reading, but not with the pensiveness or detachment you often saw in someone sitting apart from a crowd. She seemed to be enjoying her solitude, lost in it.

She was beautiful. Her blond hair was wavy and unruly; crinkly golden waves sprouted from the part at the middle of her head and just touched her shoulders. Her eyes, which were a spectacular hazel-blue, were spaced a little too far apart, beneath a prominent arched brow. Her jaw was strong and jutted a little, especially when she looked at you skeptically, which was often. When she smiled, which was just as often, long deep dimples emerged in brackets around her mouth. When she sat in the sun, her strong nose freckled.

She was in the dining hall, reading a book on Winthrop Lehman. Charlie could not resist interrupting her— with all the subtlety he could summon—"I wouldn't put much stock in that biography. I know the guy, and he's far nicer than that writer makes him out to be." A cheap line, a cheap tactic, and it didn't work. She looked at him blandly and replied, "That's interesting," and went back to reading.

"No, really," Stone persisted. "He's my godfather."

"Hmm," she said, politely disbelieving, not bothering to look up this time.

"Are you writing something on him?"

She looked up again and smiled. "A political-science paper. I'd rather not hear anything personal about him. I'm writing a critique."

"What's your angle?"

"I think his reputation is overblown. I don't think he's a great man at all. I think he was a perfectly ordinary diplomat and wheeler-dealer who happened to have a lot of family money and be in the right place at the right time." She flashed a smile; there was a space between her front teeth. With impeccable timing, she added, "So you say he's your godfather?"

A few days later, he managed to talk her into going out for pizza. She arrived in her Yale sweats, thereby wordlessly declaring that it was not *really* a date, just a study break. They bantered, argued. Each of Stone's confident proclamations she met with an equal and opposite response, as if deliberately trying to provoke—and then she'd soften it all with a wonderful, heart-melting, endearing demi-smile.

Stone, nervous, found his heart racing. He chipped away at the foil label on the cold wet beer bottle with his thumbnail. He was fixating on, of all things, her *complexion*, which was milky-white with permanently blushing cheeks, the healthy flush most people get walking outside on a frozen winter day, only she had it all the time.

He walked her to the Gothic archway outside her dorm room, and they stood for a long moment, awkwardly. "Well," he said, "good night."

Suddenly she seemed as awkward as he, one long leg turned in front of the other in an unconscious ballerina's stance. Once again the vulnerable little girl. "Good night," she said, not moving.

"Thanks," Stone said.

"Yeah, thanks."

His heart now hammering, Stone asked, "Can I see your room?" and immediately felt foolish.

"My room?" Her eyes wide.

Stone gave an exaggerated shrug, a goofy smile. He couldn't stand to leave her.

She took a deep breath, and Stone was startled to see her smile shyly and say in a small, hopeful, *knowing* voice: "Really?"

And then Stone was in over his head. In a haze of anticipation and amorousness, he leaned forward and kissed her. It took a few seconds, but she kissed back, with a passion that surprised and delighted him.

Every other college student listened to Jefferson Airplane or Strawberry Alarm Clock, but Charlotte put on a scratchy old Bessie Smith record, and they danced in the darkness of her cramped bedroom to the insinuating lyrics of "I Need a Little Sugar."

They made love several times that night. She craned her soft white neck, twisting her head from side to side, eyes closed, back arched. Her lovely florid cheeks glistened with tears and triumph and sweat, and when she began to come she looked right at him, the first time during their lovemaking that she had had the courage to open her eyes, and right then, at the most intimate moment.

Afterward, in the first months, they made love constantly, it seemed, obsessively. They were inseparable; they lost touch with their friends. In the mornings, they would wake up late, too late for breakfast in the dining hall, and they'd lie nude on her narrow bed and drink instant coffee made in an aluminum hot-pot, scrape butter on English muffins unevenly toasted in the toaster oven she kept under her bed, and make love again.

They spent almost all their time in her dorm room, always in sweatpants, which could drop to the floor with a simple tug of the waist cord. Underneath, Charlotte's blond triangle was always moist, excited by just his glance.

Stone studied her, majored in Charlotte Harper, intent on learning everything about her. He discovered that she was from a small town in Pennsylvania near Iron City, and both her parents worked in a plastics factory. They were second-generation Poles; "Harper" had been changed from something much longer and unpronounceable. They weren't poor, but they were always struggling, and they didn't understand their daughter Charlotte, who insisted on going to college, when her older sister, Martha, was perfectly content to go right to work after high school in the Department of Motor Vehicles, where she met her husband and immediately produced three children. Charlotte had gone to the University of Pittsburgh but then decided in her sophomore year that she wanted to study history. All the professors she hoped to work with were at Yale, and so she transferred.

He couldn't stand the idea of being away from her. Even the similarity of their names seemed a happy coincidence, a good omen—although she demanded he never call her Charlie.

She was one of the kindest, yet most fiercely independent people Stone had ever met. When he nervously took her to New York to have lunch with Winthrop Lehman at the Century Club—in effect, introducing to his godfather his girlfriend and the woman he planned to marry—she got into an argument with the living legend about American foreign policy—and then later told Charlie that she actually liked the old fart. Lehman, it was clear, was charmed by this lovely, feisty woman. As they left the club, Lehman took her hand and planted a dry, mandarin kiss upon her cheek, something Stone had never seen him do to anyone else.

At graduation, her parents met Charlie's father. There were long silences at lunch. Her parents, simple people, were intimidated by this Harvard professor. But Charlotte had a way of drawing people into exuberant conversation, making them connect. She took to Alfred Stone instantly, and after maybe half an hour they were laughing and telling jokes, and Charlie sat there watching, amazed. Sometimes Stone felt that Charlotte's magnetism was like the pull of a planet whose gravity is a hundred times ours.

Leaving the restaurant, Alfred Stone put his arm around his son's shoulder and muttered, "You'd better marry this girl before someone else does."

The next night, Stone asked her to marry him. She looked at him with that same you-can't-possibly-mean-me, little-girl look Stone had first seen under that Gothic archway near her room, and said, "Really?"

They were married three months later, and for years, almost until the very end, neither one could imagine ever being without the other.

Now, as Stone packed a small overnight bag, he found that he could not help thinking of what Saul had told him the day before. He thought about the Alfred Stone affair, and he wondered how something so long past could have anything to do with what was now happening in Moscow. He walked over to the stereo and switched on the radio, which was set to his favorite FM classical station.

A piece by Mendelssohn—the Italian Symphony— was just ending, and then the portentous, gravelly voice of the announcer came on, giving an interminable synopsis of Mendelssohn's life, then continuing, in annoying detail, about Mendelssohn's E-flat Octet and how it prefigured the *classical* themes he would later develop, and how *restrained* his romanticism was, and how—

Stone snapped the radio off. He zipped up his suitcase and ambled over to the tall windows that looked out onto Central Park West. He watched a young woman walk by with a foolishly manicured poodle, then a couple with matching hooded college sweatshirts. He could not stop thinking about the Alfred Stone affair, and he realized suddenly that he dreaded going to Boston.

Alfred C. Stone, professor emeritus of history at Harvard, lived in a comfortable three-story clapboard house on Hilliard Street in Cambridge. It was the house Charlie had grown up in, and he knew all the odd corners, the places where the floorboards creaked, the doorknobs that didn't quite turn. And the smells: lemon-oil furniture polish, wood fires, the not unpleasant mustiness of a hundred-year-old house.

The house was in a part of Cambridge where academics lived next to old money, where you never flaunted your wealth and you drove dented old Volvos and Saabs and wood-sided station wagons. The neighborhood was at once proper and Cambridge-informal, far enough from the punks and the riffraff of Harvard Square, but close enough so you could walk in and go to the right bank and shop at the right grocery store and maybe pick up an unstylish shirt at the Andover Shop.

Alfred Stone was seated behind his desk in his study, wearing his customary tweed suit, when Charlie arrived. He had been retired for four years, but he always wore a suit, as if he might suddenly be called upon at any moment to teach an emergency class on the New Deal and the Roots of Postwar Liberalism or some such thing.

He had been a handsome man, before his arrest and imprisonment had turned his life upside down, before he had begun to drink too much. His auburn hair was mostly gray now, and his cheeks were webbed with the fine broken capillaries of a heavy drinker. His horn-rimmed glasses, habitually smudged, had carved deep red ridges on either side of the bridge of his nose.

Beside the desk, in a loose heap on the floor, was Alfred Stone's labrador retriever, Peary. Charlie had found him in the pound and given him to his father as a birthday present two years before. Peary sleepily raised his head, acknowledging Charlie's presence with a slow wag of his tail.

"I think he has a real soul," Alfred Stone said. "I'm convinced of it. Look in his eyes, Charlie."

Charlie looked. Peary returned the look quizzically, gave another wag, exhaled noisily, and sank slowly to the rug.

"He's a good influence on you," Charlie told his father. "Why 'Peary,' by the way? I never asked."

"This dog just loves being outside. So I named him after the polar explorer Robert Peary."

"Peary's a great name."

"You know you're putting on a little weight?"

"Just a little." Charlie instinctually pinched his waist. "Too much sitting in front of the computer, and not enough climbing."

"Maybe that's it. Also, you quit smoking. Drink?" Alfred Stone got up from his desk and walked over to a small bar he'd arranged on top of a glass-fronted bookcase. He lifted a two-liter bottle of cheap Scotch, the liquor of a serious drinker, and turned to Charlie questioningly.

"Not in the afternoon, Dad."

"Don't get moralistic on me."

"I'm not," Stone said, although he knew he was doing precisely that. "Alcohol fogs my brain in the afternoon." He added archly: "I need a clear head to fathom matters of national security."

"Well, I don't," the elder Stone muttered, pouring his drink. "Lord knows, nobody's asked *me* to do that in almost forty years. Anything interesting these days?"

Stone knew that his father rarely asked about Parnassus, respecting the supersecrecy, and when he did he expected his son not to answer. Charlie replied with a rumor that was all over Moscow and therefore not at all secret. "I think one of the Politburo members has got a bad heart."

Alfred Stone returned to his desk chair and leaned back slowly. "They've all got bad hearts."

Charlie grunted as he sank into a leather club chair. He liked the light in his father's study at this time of day. The sun came in at a slant, casting a warm hue over the highly polished hardwood floor, the ancient Oriental rugs, the brown tufted leather couch, its surface scarred by hairline cracks, where Alfred Stone took his naps.

And the floor-to-ceiling built-in bookcases, painted white. The shelves of history books that revealed Alfred Stone's interests: Robert Sherwood's *Roosevelt and Hopkins,* Churchill's history of English-speaking peoples, Acheson's *Present at the Creation*, Truman's memoirs, *The Secret Diary of Harold L. Ickes*, Carl Van Doren's *Benjamin Franklin*, Walter Lippmann's *A Preface to Morals*, Lytton Strachey's *Eminent Victorians.*

The walls were cluttered with framed pictures: a black-framed photograph of the young Alfred Stone, beaming with excitement, with Harry Truman (and autographed "with fond regards"); a photo of Alfred and Margaret Stone with Winthrop Lehman, taken at some formal dinner; a silver-framed picture of Margaret Stone, her hair done up in large Mamie Eisenhower curls, smiling knowingly.

"What?" Alfred Stone asked.

Charlie realized that he had muttered something aloud. The sunlight had shifted now, and it was shining directly in his eyes.

"Nothing," Charlie said hastily, turning his head. "Listen, when was the last time you saw Winthrop?"

"Winthrop? Oh, it's been years. I know he's having some party in a couple of days, a publication party for his memoirs or something. I was invited. Weren't you?"

Stone remembered the invitation, which he'd filed away, planning not to go because he expected to be up in the Adirondacks. "Yes, I was, come to think of it. Are you going?"

"Probably some very high-toned affair. No, I don't especially want to, but I wish you would."

"Maybe I will. I . . . ." He shifted again, then moved the armchair, putting a ripple in the carpet as he did so. "There's something I want to ask Winthrop about, actually."

His father was still leaning back absently in his chair. "Aha."

"I ran across something that I think has to do with, you know, with what happened to you. The McCarthy stuff and all that."

"Oh?" His father involuntarily hunched his shoulders. A nervous tic began in his eyes, the old tic, which afflicted him whenever he was tense.

"I know you don't like digging all this up. I realize that. But did you ever hear the phrase 'Lenin Testament'?"

Alfred Stone stared at his son a beat too long, his face frozen, except for the old tic in his left eye, which was now wildly out of control. His reply, when it came out, was hushed: "*What?*"

"You've heard of it, then."

The elder Stone removed his glasses and massaged his eyes. After a while, he spoke again, this time much more nonchalantly. "You're the Russia expert. Didn't Lenin leave some sort of testament behind, criticizing Stalin and so on?"

"Not that. Some other 'testament.' It came up at the McCarthy hearings, didn't it? Didn't McCarthy mention something about it?"

Alfred Stone spread his hands, palms up, a dismissive gesture that said, I don't remember. He replaced his glasses, got up, and went over to the bar. "I got a card from your wife," he said, pouring some Scotch, straight, into a crystal tumbler.

"Dad . . ."

"She said she's coming back to the States on leave, sometime around now."

He was transparently avoiding the subject, but Charlie knew that his father had always liked Charlotte, that they had always been close, and he replied: "I don't think she likes Moscow too much, Dad."

"I trust she's having a better time of it than I did there." He spoke gently now: "You want her back, don't you? But you're too much of a man to admit it, is that right?"

"I can't be very specific about why I want to know, but it's important. Please."

"Charlie, I'm not interested," Alfred Stone said, his voice betraying his alarm.

"There was some state secret involved, wasn't there?"

Alfred Stone shook his head, his eyes wide and glistening. "I don't know what you're talking about," he said angrily.

"Would you mind if I asked Winthrop?"

"*Don't*, Charlie," Alfred said too sharply. Peary, startled, looked up and barked once, warningly.

"Why not?"

"Please, just do me a favor. I don't want you reminding him of that whole nightmare."

"I very much doubt he'd mind. He and I've talked plenty of times about his role in history, his meeting with Lenin, that kind of thing. I doubt he'd—"

"Charlie, I don't know how much he stuck his neck

out for me in those days. More than anyone knows, I suspect. I don't know what he had to lie about to save my skin. Please, don't ask him." He leaned over and began massaging the loose skin at Peary's nape. Peary uttered a low, throaty growl of contentment. "There's a lot I've never told you about—this whole thing. About Winthrop, and my situation." He looked up. Charlie had never seen him so shaken. "I realize you want to . . . I suppose 'vindicate' is the apt word . . . vindicate me, but I really don't want you opening that can of worms again. I mean, it—means a lot to me. Genuinely."

"What do you mean by 'can of worms'? You've seen a reference to this testament, haven't you?"

After a long pause, Alfred Stone replied, "Yes. Yes, I have." He didn't look up as he continued to speak. "Winthrop asked me to go through his personal files at the White House one day for some reason, I forget what. We all had central files and personal files, and these were the personal ones, the ones you can take with you when your White House service is over."

"You saw something."

"A mention of it, yes. I remember it catching my eye, because it seemed so peculiar. Something to do with Stalin."

"With *Stalin*? Did you ever ask Winthrop?"

"No, and I wish you wouldn't, either."

"But for you—"

"*Don't*," he said. His face was even more flushed now; he was visibly disconcerted.

Charlie hesitated a moment. "All right." No, he thought: he wouldn't have to *ask* Lehman a thing. There were the famous Lehman archives, in the subbasement of Lehman's New York townhouse. Surely the answers would be there.

"You never would have gotten a security clearance without Winthrop, you know that. Because of me—"

"I know."

"Charlie, did you come to see me expressly to ask about this thing?"

"And to see you."

"What's past is past, Charlie."

Stone nodded contemplatively, not replying, knowing his father was wrong. The past had become the present.

The sun was setting now, and the room had grown suddenly dark. Charlie thought of the young Alfred Stone in the photo with Truman, the excited smile, and then he looked at his father now, and he thought: Whatever's happening in the Kremlin, I'm in this for you. You've always deserved the truth.

Later, even just a few days later, he would desperately wish he had dropped the matter then and there.

5

Washington

Since there weren't any significant parties in Washington that conflicted that night, Roger Bayliss decided to put in an appearance at the Italian Embassy's gala. Bayliss, the chief Soviet expert on the National Security Council and an aide to the assistant to the President for national-security affairs, secretly enjoyed donning his white tie and tails and attending these affairs, bantering with the other Washington powers. Publicly he bemoaned having to drag himself there.

Bayliss had reason to be pleased with himself. Not yet forty, he had already carved out an enviable position in the government. He'd been selected by the NSC directly from the prestigious Soviet section of the National Security Agency, the group of one thousand analysts privy to the highest-quality intelligence from the Soviet Union and around the world. A handsome, jut-jawed man, he radiated a gladiatorial self-confidence that turned a lot of people off (but turned a lot of not very bright but very ambitious Washington women on). In the last few years, he had formed alliances with some extraordinarily powerful people, from the director of the CIA to the director of his own alma mater, the NSA—alliances that, he felt sure, would soon push him to the very top.

It was during cocktails that the peculiar incident took place. He had been chatting up a prominent Washington hostess when he happened to collide with a man he recognized as Aleksandr Malarek, the first secretary of the Soviet Embassy, who was talking with the French ambassador.

Although they'd never met, he knew who Malarek was, just as Malarek no doubt knew who he was. Malarek was not a handsome man, but something about his manner—the fluidity of his movements, the well-tailored American suits—made him seem elegant, and disguised the fact that his legs were somewhat too short for his body. He was slender, with a swarthy complexion. Unlike quite a number of Soviet diplomats, Malarek had good teeth. His eyes were brown and, as more than one writer for *The Washington Post* Style section had observed, seemed sincere. His hair was prematurely gray, actually silver. He was smooth, a witty conversationalist, a charmer, and a favorite at Washington parties.

"Pardon me," Malarek said, grinning and shaking his head self-deprecatingly. "You're Roger Bayliss, aren't you?"

"Aleksandr Malarek," Bayliss returned, just as jovially, and added wryly: "Nice to bump into you."

There was the customary minute or two of mindless small talk, and then Malarek said something that disturbed Bayliss for the remainder of the evening.

"I hear you bought a new car," the Russian said.

He was right—Bayliss had recently invested in a turbo Saab, obsidian-black—but how did Malarek know? Later Bayliss understood.

He left the party an hour and a half later, still faintly puzzled by the strange encounter with Aleksandr Malarek, and walked the two blocks to where his new Saab was parked. He unlocked the driver's seat and got in, and then he saw it.

Wedged between the passenger seat and the car door was some kind of card. It looked as if it had been slipped into the car from the top of the window.

Bayliss reached over to retrieve it. The card was a postcard of the tacky variety you often see for sale on spinning racks at tourist sites. This one was of Miami Beach, Florida, and it bore no message on it at all, just an address in Washington, D.C.

When Bayliss recognized the address, his heart suddenly began beating very quickly. This was it. At last, after all these decades. This was it.

Gingerly, he placed the card into the breast pocket of his dinner jacket and, actually trembling from excitement, started the car.

6

New York

For over an hour, Stone had been staring at the luminous green computer monitor in his Parnassus office. Anyone watching, unfamiliar with Stone and the kind of work he did, might have reasonably supposed the man had gone into a catatonic trance.

He sat, immobile, in the comfortable old suit he wore to work most days. His office was considerably plainer than Ansbach's, the furniture purely functional, the bookcases jammed with the standard reference works.

On the screen was a list of the members of the Soviet Politburo. Next to each name was a highly classified synopsis of the man's medical record. Something was nagging at the back of his mind about the rumor circulating around Moscow, that one of the leaders was in poor health and had been recently treated for a serious heart-related illness in the Kremlin Clinic. The Agency wanted some good, informed speculation as to which one it was and had put it to the brain bank at Parnassus.

A Politburo member was ill. Okay. Which one?

He stretched his long legs, folded his arms, and leaned his head back all the way. After a moment, he sat up and accessed the CIA's records of each man's travels in the last three months. The screen went blank for a few seconds, and then a complex chart came up. Stone scanned it for a moment and got to his feet.

Nothing.

Sometimes he thought Kremlinology was like putting a ton of carbon under intense geological pressure: eventually you'd get a diamond, if you waited long enough.

What happens to a Soviet leader when he gets sick? Stone asked himself.

Well, sometimes nothing. He gets sick and he dies. Or he gets sick and he recovers.

But in an unstable political system—and, God knows, the Politburo was unstable these days—sometimes it wasn't a good thing at all to get sick, to stay away from the Kremlin for very long. Sometimes when the cat's away the mice will . . . usurp his power.

The brainstorm—or brain squall, as Stone self-deprecatingly called the aleatory flights of inspiration that had helped him out of many a logjam—came several hours later.

Khrushchev had been overthrown when he chose a bad time to take a vacation on the Black Sea. Gorbachev had almost been ousted in 1987 while on holiday. If you happen to have the misfortune to be one of the Kremlin's rulers and you want to hold on to your power, the rule of thumb is: Don't take vacations. And don't get sick.

Whoever was ill might well have lost some modicum of power. And power in the Kremlin is measured, in part, by the number of your cronies you can drag up the hierarchy with you.

Stone keyed in a code to access a roster of recent promotions and demotions within the Soviet bureaucracy. The list, when it came, scrolled on and on: a lot of action within the Kremlin's ranks. Not at all like the Brezhnev years, when things were static. Moscow these days was hopping, the leadership constantly in flux.

Then he accessed a program he'd designed himself specifically to spot patterns of hirings, firings, and demotions and the common thread among them. Stone called it KremWare, and regretted that it wouldn't have much of a sale.

After another hour or so—the software was complicated, after all—he began to see a pattern.

A diamond. Yes.

In the past few weeks, there had been a marked pattern of demotions of officials whose careers had in some way crossed paths with the new head of the KGB, Andrei Pavlichenko. There it was.

A number of ambitious Moscow bureaucrats who thought that by knowing the head of the KGB they would rocket to the top of the heap suddenly found themselves pushing paper in small, badly heated offices in Omsk or Tomsk.

Unconsciously he reached for a cigarette, remembered for the millionth time that he no longer smoked, and said, "Shit."

Yes, Pavlichenko was almost certainly the one who was ill. Stone was quite sure of it; the pattern was there. You couldn't be one hundred percent certain, but the odds were excellent that it was Pavlichenko.

He rewarded himself by reheating a third cup of coffee in the microwave, then stuck his head out of his office door. "Sherry?"

"Yes, Charlie."

"I'll have a PAE ready to go out in an hour or so."

"All right." She'd have to get it into presentable form, hard copy—the people at Langley didn't like working with their computers if they didn't have to. Many of them, especially the old-line types, favored Underwood manual typewriters and Parker fountain pens. Which was of course decidedly ironic, since their daily work relied for the most part on some of the most advanced technology in the world.

"What the hell are you doing in today?" It was Saul.

"I thought you'd be out. . . ." He glanced at Stone's secretary and gestured toward his office. Charlie followed.

"Did you find me the holy grail?" Saul asked, shutting the door.

"I'm working on it," Stone said, sitting on the edge of Saul's desk. "In the meantime," he continued, "I think I've got one nut cracked." He explained his deduction.

Ansbach's face lit up in a grin. "Jesus, you're good."

Stone gave a slight bow.

"Sounds right," Saul said. "In fact, I'd be inclined to be more certain about it than you seem to be."

"Okay, you see the connection to the—the HEDGEHOG report, don't you?"

"What do you mean?"

"Pavlichenko's losing his grip on power, right? So KGB suffers. Which means diminished party discipline."

"And?"

"Just a theory, Saul. Pavlichenko is Gorbachev's man, brought in personally by Gorby—partly so Gorbachev can get a handle on the KGB, partly to guard against any attempts to oust him, since if anyone would have their ears to the ground it's the boys at Dzerzhinsky Square." Stone was pacing the room now, as he usually did when he was excited. "The same folks, after all, who helped get Gorby in there in the first place—"

"Right," Ansbach said, infected by Stone's enthusiasm. Like most of the Agency's old guard, he relished the delicious irony of Russia's most progressive leader's ever being supported by one of history's most repressive agencies of control.

"Okay. So"—Stone whirled around and pointed a finger at Ansbach—"if Pavlichenko weren't in failing health, maybe there wouldn't be any conspiracy."

"So how does that help us?" Ansbach asked, shaking his head.

"When was the last time there was a coup in the Soviet Union—after the Bolshevik Revolution, I mean?"

"Never," Ansbach replied, good-humoredly playing the model schoolboy. "Hasn't been one."

"Well, not quite. Sixty-four." In 1964 Nikita Khrushchev was ousted by a hard-line, neo-Stalinist coalition made up of Leonid Brezhnev, Aleksei Kosygin, and Mikhail Suslov.

"That was hardly a coup," Ansbach objected. "That was a good old orderly palace revolution."

"All right. In '64 you had dissatisfaction with the chaos Khrushchev was wreaking."

"Like Gorbachev."

"So maybe it's conservative hard-liners."

"Maybe," Saul said. "And maybe it's one of the many nationalities that now openly hate Moscow—the Latvians or the Estonians or the Lithuanians. Or maybe it's people who are pissed off with the way Gorbachev dismantled the whole fucking Warsaw Pact."

"Possible."

"*Possible?*" Saul shot back, but he was interrupted by the buzz of one of his telephones. He picked it up, listened for a moment, then said, "Jesus Christ. All right, thanks."

When he put down the receiver, he gave Stone an ominous look. "A bomb went off in Moscow a few minutes ago."

"A bomb? Where?"

"In the Kremlin, Charlie. Right inside the fucking Kremlin."

The Nite & Day Restaurant was a small place below street level on East 89th Street, with dark wooden booths and Formica tables, steel napkin-holders, bottles of Heinz ketchup. It had been "discovered" when *New York* magazine called it the best "retro diner" in the city, an "unpretentious little spot." Stone, who had been having lunch there for years, considered it a little more akin to a dive, which was why he liked it.

He was having lunch with Lenny Wexler, one of his Parnassus colleagues who worked on Japan, especially the Japanese intelligence services. Wexler was small and bearded, with wire-rim glasses, a holdover from the sixties who often took time off from the Foundation to drive to Grateful Dead concerts in his van. He was quiet and reflective, undoubtedly brilliant, and had a weakness for endless obscene shaggy-dog jokes, one of which he was just now finishing.

" 'I'm keeping an eye out for you, too,' " Wexler concluded, and laughed uproariously. Stone, who normally enjoyed Wexler's jokes but now found himself distracted, laughed politely.

Wexler tucked into his bacon cheeseburger with a side order of macaroni and cheese. He was watching his cholesterol, he had announced as he blithely ordered; three oat-bran muffins every morning, he explained, allowed him to eat whatever he wanted during the day.

"Did I tell you Helen and I have been trying to get pregnant for the last six months?" Wexler asked.

"Tough job," Stone said, and took a bite of his burger.

"Yeah, well, it takes the fun out of it."

"I imagine. Go out there and win one for the Gipper," Stone said as he put down his half-eaten hamburger. He was thinking of Charlotte again, and Wexler sensed that.

"Oh, sorry. Well, you're better off without her. Anyway, I've got a girl for you. She works with my sister."

Stone smiled tightly. He had always liked Lenny. During the difficult period after Charlotte had moved out, he'd been a steadfast friend, a rock.

"What the hell," Wexler asked with alarm, "you still thinking you two're going to get back together, is that it?"

"Possibly. I'd like that."

"Yeah, well"—Wexler swallowed a large forkful of Day-Glo–yellow macaroni and cheese—"lot of fish in the sea. Guy like you with money and looks," he managed to say through the macaroni, his words muffled, "don't sell yourself short."

"I don't."

"So what do you make of this thing about the bomb in the Kremlin?"

"I'm not sure yet." They usually didn't talk about work, almost never in public places.

Wexler nodded slowly and went back to the macaroni and cheese. "Did I tell you one of our assets in Tokyo was caught?" he said *sotto voce*.

"I don't think so."

"Oh, yeah. They arrested him, interrogated him. Solitary confinement for three days. They probably got him to spill everything."

Stone suddenly stopped eating, holding his burger in midair.

HEDGEHOG. The KGB hadn't arrested HEDGEHOG, or interrogated him, or anything of the sort. They'd killed him.

Why?

Why was HEDGEHOG simply killed?

"Something wrong?" Wexler asked.

"Nothing," Stone said, his mind spinning. "Hey, how's the old cholesterol count doing there?"

Wexler looked up, his eyes wide, his mouth full. "Goob."

"That's nice. Ever try their Boston cream pie here?" Stone asked silkily, a wide grin on his face. "I hear it's excellent."

"Really?" Wexler said, glancing over toward the dessert case.

Saul Ansbach leaned back in his chair, waiting for the secure connection to Langley to be completed. Absently, he cleaned his fingernails with an orange stick, thinking. After a minute, his secretary's voice crackled on the intercom.

"Okay, Mr. Ansbach."

"Thanks, Lynn."

He leaned forward, picked up the phone, and listened for the voice of Ted Templeton, the Director of Central Intelligence. The secure connections were free of the usual noise or static, and as a result Templeton sounded eerily close. The DCI's voice was always confident, a resonant baritone; over the phone it was even more so, almost operatic.

"Saul, good morning." His *What's up?* voice.

"Morning, Ted. Say, what do we have on this bomb in the Kremlin?"

"Not much, unfortunately. The Russians cleaned it

up before anyone could get anything. A terrorist, evidently a Soviet citizen, tossed a pipe bomb in the Kremlin Armory. Really did a lot of damage. American girl killed. Some Fabergé eggs got scrambled."

Ansbach gave the half-smile he wore whenever life began to approximate a Kremlinologist's wildest madcap imaginings. The Kremlin Armory was where the Soviets stored, in proud disdain, all the czarist treasures, crown jewels and whatnot. "The Russians get the guy?"

"The shmucks shot the alleged perp dead," Templeton said, his ungainly imitation of cop-speak. "Good old Kremlin guards. What's up, Saul?"

"Listen, we're a little closer to understanding what that HEDGEHOG thing is all about—"

"Saul, I want this thing to go no further."

Ansbach furrowed his brow. "In what—"

"We're dropping it, Saul."

"What do you mean, 'dropping it'?"

"NFA, Saul. No further action."

A few minutes later, after they discussed other matters, Saul hung up the phone, puzzled and alarmed. He took off his glasses and massaged his eyes. He had begun to develop a throbbing headache.

Outside, it was starting to rain.

One of the small privileges of being the godson of Winthrop Lehman was that, when you went to his townhouse, you never had to suffer a New York taxi ride. Lehman's Rolls-Royce Silver Shadow picked Stone up in the early evening, in front of Stone's apartment building on Central Park West, to take him to the party.

The rain that had begun that afternoon had become a dark, howling torrent, the sort of downpour that, in New York, with its skyscrapers and concrete canyons, always seems like the end of the world.

The chauffeur, a ruddy-faced red-haired man in a yellow rain slicker, opened the car door for Stone.

Stone smiled as he got in. "You'd think Mr. Lehman could arrange a nicer day than this for his publication party," he said as he got in.

The chauffeur was not to be outdone. "He knows a lot of people, sir," he called out, "but I don't know if he's got any strings to pull up there."

Stone chuckled politely.

Once behind the wheel, the chauffeur said nothing; that was the way Lehman preferred it, and Stone did not try to make small talk. Driving through Central Park, the Rolls's suspension so good that he could scarcely feel the uneven streets below, Stone felt as if he were in another world. The car's interior was immaculate, its leather aromatic of some kind of oil, the air cool and dry. Outside, the unfortunate pedestrians struggled with ruined umbrellas and gargantuan puddles and powerful gusts of wind.

He sat, absorbed by his thoughts. He recalled Lehman, the rich and distinguished man in his expensive bespoke suits, the skin of his head like speckled parchment stretched tight over his cranium. As a child, an adolescent, even a young man, Charlie had felt somewhat elect because of his family's connection to Winthrop Lehman. If his family had been besmirched by his father's jail term, the unfair but unmistakable aura of disrepute that surrounded his father—the whispered allegations that Alfred Stone really *was*, after all, a spy, once—things were almost put right by their association with Lehman. Almost.

Lehman was the man whose portrait had several times been on the cover of *Time* magazine, whose photo had hundreds of times been on the front pages of newspapers. He was the man who had gotten Alfred Stone out of jail.

Stone remembered the first time he had met Winthrop Lehman.

It was 1962, during the height of the Cuban Missile Crisis, air-raid shelters, and duck-and-cover. Most of the fourth-graders, marching silently through the halls of the elementary school with the terrifying air-raid-drill siren whooping, believed the bomb might drop at any minute, without warning. Anticommunism was rampant: the sort of grave, vacuous politics at which nine-year-olds excel. Charlie's mother had just died, a few days earlier; he had suffered the funeral, and the burial at Mount Auburn Cemetery, in silence.

A kid named Jerry Delgado had grabbed him in the cloakroom outside of Mrs. Allman's chalk-dusty classroom and whispered for the hundredth time a quick, biting insult about Charlie's father being a commie spy, and Charlie, unable to hold it back any longer, took off after the boy with a brute force he didn't know he had. A gaggle of nine-year-olds watched, thrilled and fascinated, as Charlie knocked Jerry Delgado to the floor and pummeled him with tightly clenched fists. When Mrs. Allman broke it up, punishing both parties equally by sending them to the principal's office, Charlie felt a warm, pleasurable glow: being strong was after all so much more effective than being smart.

After school, Charlie returned home to find, parked in the driveway, a long black Chrysler limousine. His first, scared thought was that it was someone official, the police or the FBI, come to tell his father about Jerry Delgado, or maybe it was even Jerry Delgado's parents.

But it was Winthrop Lehman, the famous Winthrop Lehman, about whom his parents had spoken so often. He and Alfred Stone were in the study talking, and Lehman came out in a dark-blue suit to say hello. The great man shook Charlie's hand with rapt concentration, as if Charlie were some world leader. Lehman was in town for the day— something to do with giving his collection of Impressionist paintings to the Fogg Art Museum—and after he and Alfred were finished talking, Lehman asked Charlie if he wanted to go for a walk. Charlie shrugged and said sure.

They walked into the square, had ice cream at Bailey's, and then walked around the Fogg. Charlie had never been inside, wasn't much interested in painting, but Lehman pointed his favorites out, telling him about van Gogh and Monet. Lehman noticed a scrape down Charlie's face, and he asked what had happened. Charlie told him, not without pride. Finally, Charlie brought himself to ask Lehman: "If my dad didn't give documents to the Russian government, why did they put him in jail?"

Lehman stopped in the echoey stone courtyard of the museum, leaned over slightly as he placed a large hand on Charlie's shoulder, and replied: "Your father is a terribly brave man." He did not explain what that was supposed to mean, and Charlie didn't pursue it.

Later, intrigued by his godfather, Charlie went to the library and looked up everything he could find on Winthrop Lehman. He learned that Lehman was an heir to a railroad fortune; that he'd survived two wives and had no heirs; that in the early 1920s he had lived in Moscow for several years, doing business with the Russians, as had Armand Hammer and Averell Harriman; that Franklin Roosevelt had asked him to come to Washington and help guide the country through the New Deal and later to arrange Lend-Lease assistance to the Soviet Union during the war; that Harry Truman had asked him to stay on as a national-security adviser. A cover story in *Time* in 1950 estimated his wealth at over a hundred million dollars; a picture caption described him as "America's pre-eminent statesman."

Knowing he was connected, even in a small way, with such a famous and powerful man gave Charlie something certain to cling to, at a time when he didn't have a whole lot else.

By the time Stone arrived, Lehman's party was in full swing, if ever a party at Winthrop Lehman's august townhouse could be said to swing.

A servant took his coat; Charlie stood for a moment before the mirror in the foyer, smoothing the lapels of his charcoal-gray business suit, straightening his tie, running his hand quickly through his hair. From the other rooms, he could hear the energized babble of cocktail-party conversation, the laughter and the clinking of glasses. A black-and-white-liveried waiter went by, carrying a tray of caviar canapés. Stone smiled: Winthrop Lehman did not skimp. As he entered the main room, he passed a table on which were displayed several copies of Lehman's memoirs, *A Lifetime*.

The interior of Lehman's endless apartment had been built, in the nineteenth century, to resemble an eighteenth-century French château: deep-brown mahogany paneling with elaborately carved pilasters, mammoth fireplaces of black marble, Venetian crystal chandeliers, gold fixtures, sconces, and escutcheons, Empire furniture upholstered in the original beige silk, several large Aubusson rugs. Portraits by Sargent hung on the walls; porcelain Oriental vases mounted in centuries-old ormolu adorned the Baroque giltwood side tables.

The room in which the party seemed to be centered—where Winthrop Lehman sat holding court, in an overstuffed gold-striped wing chair, surrounded by admirers—was the immense library: high cathedral ceilings, oak wainscoting, floors of rich green marble partly covered by sumptuous Kirman rugs; great swags of heavy pale-green silk drapery dominating the tall windows.

Stone spotted a few faces he knew and quite a few more he recognized. The senators from New York and Connecticut were speaking with an elfin real-estate mogul; the Vice-President seemed to be deep in colloquy with the Speaker of the House and the anchorman of a national evening news program.

The crowd was glittery, old New York society consorting with investment bankers, a handful of fashion designers, the heads of Citibank, ITT, and General Motors, a sprinkling of university presidents, the directors of the Metropolitan Museum of Art and the Cooper-Hewitt (both of which had benefited handsomely from Lehman's contributions over the years). There were a number of very thin-armed, very rich dowagers, including one society matron who had brought her two miniature Chinese dogs, which snarled and snapped at anyone unfortunate enough to brush by.

"Charlie Stone!"

Stone winced inwardly at the approach of someone he didn't particularly like, a terminally dull and self-important investment banker he had met once, a few years earlier.

The investment banker, who was holding aloft a glass of wine as if he were Madame Curie displaying her first test tube of radium, clasped Stone's hand heartily, and began to say something tedious about the International Monetary Fund.

"How's tricks, Charlie?" he asked solicitously. "Pensions, is that right?"

Very few people even had an inkling of what Stone did for a living. He told anyone who asked that he was a private consultant. No one knows exactly what a consultant does, and most, Stone found, ask no further. He learned, too, that when he gave the plausible-sounding lie, "pension-fund actuarial analyst," he could see, with great satisfaction, eyes begin to glaze over. At parties, anyone who asked him out of politeness to explain would receive a stultifying explanation that dampened any curiosity, provoked quick desperate smiles and the sudden urge to excuse oneself and get a refill.

Stone said something indeterminate about a new development in the pension funds of a Hartford insurance company.

"Hmph," the investment banker said. "I suppose anything can seem interesting if you do it for a living, right?" He meant it sincerely.

"Exactly."

The investment banker took another sip of his wine and began telling a story about the Saint-Emilion he was drinking and how it was the favorite wine of Julius Caesar. Stone, who knew that Lehman never served anything but burgundy, smiled and nodded. No reason to puncture the poor man's affectations, Stone thought.

Lehman was seated as if on a throne, nodding deliberately in response to something one of the surrounding throng had said. He wore a beautifully tailored dark-gray English suit, but it looked as if it had fit him beautifully decades ago. Now he had shrunk within it.

Lehman's eyes were a cool, even chilling, gray. They seemed watery, and they were grotesquely magnified by the lenses of his glasses, whose frames were a pale fleshtone. His nose had once been what was often called aquiline, but now it seemed merely sharp and protruding. As he spoke, Stone could see the off-white of his too-perfect false teeth.

Suddenly he saw Stone, and he extended a liver-spotted hand. "Charles. How good to see you."

"Congratulations, Winthrop."

"My godson, Charles Stone," he explained to a dowager at his left. "Come closer, Charlie. It's good to see you."

"You're looking well."

"Don't lie to me," Lehman responded lightheartedly, in a reedy voice. He added, with a raised eyebrow: "Your clients are treating you well?"

"Quite well."

"Your clients are lucky to have you."

"Thank you."

Stone came close to asking about the "Lenin Testament," but he restrained himself.

"Is Alfred here?"

Stone's attention was momentarily distracted by something he glimpsed out of the corner of an eye, a familiar silhouette.

"Excuse me?" he said, and turned to see a lovely blond woman in a white low-necked dress with high taffeta shoulders, huddled in intense conversation with Saul Ansbach, in the adjoining foyer.

"No, he's not, Winthrop. Excuse me for a moment, please," he said, feeling his stomach constrict.

It was Charlotte.

At about that time, roughly 150 miles to the north, a young seminarian at the Russian Orthodox monastery in Maplewood, New York, packed a small valise and got into a car that belonged to the seminary.

After an hour's drive, he arrived in Saratoga and pulled into the parking lot of the De Witt Clinton Rest Home, a graceful nineteenth-century stone structure, rough-hewn and yet symmetrical, in the architectural style of H. H. Richardson. He found the set of keys secreted exactly as he had been told they would be—magnetically affixed under an iron staircase at the back of the building— and he made his way in.

When he found the correct room, he checked his bag once again. The 5ml vial of atracurium besylate was there.

The moonlight illuminated a shriveled figure in a

wheelchair, an old man who sat dozing. He had no legs.

The seminarian recognized the man immediately. He was named Alden Cushing, once one of the most important industrialists in the country. At one time, he had been the business partner of the industrialist and statesman Winthrop Lehman, going back to Lehman's years in Moscow. The seminarian had studied the file on Cushing and knew that Cushing's name was usually paired with Lehman's in old issues of *Fortune* magazine from the twenties and thirties. He was often seen in photographs with William Randolph Hearst and John D. Rockefeller the original, playing golf at San Simeon, hunting in West Virginia. The seminarian wondered what could possibly have reduced such an extraordinarily powerful man to such a state, from San Simeon to a small, grimy nursing home in upstate New York, a room that stank of medicines and salves and bad institutional food.

"Mr. Cushing," he said quietly in English, opening the door and switching on the light.

Cushing awoke gradually and seemed disoriented. He shielded his eyes from the light. "Who . . . ?" he demanded weakly.

"I'm a priest," the seminarian said. "We have some mutual friends."

"A priest? What—it's the middle of the night!"

"Everything is all right. You will be all right." The seminarian's gently accented voice had a hypnotic quality to it.

"Leave me—!" Cushing croaked.

"Everything will be all right."

"I kept my promise to Lehman!" Cushing's head shook involuntarily. His voice was high and cracked. "I never said a word." His eyes filled with tears, which gathered at the corners of his eyes and then spilled onto the mottled cheeks in odd rivulets.

Within a few minutes, the seminarian had found out everything he wanted to know. Then he placed a soothing hand on Cushing's mottled arm, smoothing back the pale-blue cotton pajama sleeve.

"You're obviously very upset, Mr. Cushing," he said.

"I've got something to calm you down a bit." His voice was soothing.

Cushing's eyes were large and round with terror.

The seminarian held up a small syringe, which he fastidiously knocked against his hand. "This is to keep any air from getting in your bloodstream," he explained. He tightened the tourniquet on Cushing's upper arm, deftly located the vein, swabbed the spot with an alcohol pad, and inserted the hypodermic needle.

Cushing was now looking at him furiously. His mouth worked, opening and closing, but no sound emerged. He could see a slight backwash of his own blood enter the syringe just before the priest injected.

Cushing's limbs had gotten heavy. He felt his eyes close.

"You'll be feeling fine very soon," he could hear the priest saying. What kind of accent was that? Nothing made sense. He wanted to shout, to push him away.

But Cushing could not have replied, or moved, much as he wanted to.

He was completely alert—he could hear every word the intruder spoke, every sound in the room—but he realized with a steadily dawning terror that he could not breathe. Or speak. Or move. Or scream.

A minute later, he began to lose consciousness. Everything darkened, until slowly the room was completely black. Cushing's body had gone flaccid. Anyone passing by would have thought he had fallen fast asleep.

The atracurium that had been injected into his bloodstream—a muscle relaxant that is metabolized by body temperature and body pH—acted quickly. Within a very short time, it would be entirely metabolized. There would be no trace, and the presumptive cause of death would be cardiorespiratory arrest. Even if Cushing's body were subjected to a routine pathological examination—which it would not be, because of his age—the metabolite of atracurium would not be detected. If they found the needle mark in his arm, well, he had asked for a sedative the day before. Cushing, everyone knew, was a very high-strung man.

7

New York

Stone approached Charlotte and Saul noiselessly, careful not to be noticed. He wanted to see her, hear her for a moment, without his wife's knowing he was there.

They were speaking in hushed voices in the dark alcove, Saul shaking his head, Charlotte beaming at him.

She had changed. Her hair was different, shorter, but it was becoming. She had aged a bit, too; you could see it around her eyes, but they were laugh lines, and they suited her. She had lost a little weight. She looked spectacular. If she wanted, she could look unnervingly like Grace Kelly, and tonight she must have wanted.

Stone realized with a flash of anger that she wasn't wearing either her diamond engagement ring or her wedding ring. He was embarrassed by the rush of his feelings for her. He considered turning around, not greeting her.

Instead, he watched, and listened, for the moment unobserved.

"But how do you *know* it's Russian?" she was saying with a toss of her head.

Saul's voice, barely audible, came back: "I didn't say that."

"But you implied it."

Saul shrugged. "True, but—"

Charlotte, urgently whispering: "Then, if a bomb went off in the Kremlin—"

"I can't talk about it."

"But you've just admitted your people are looking into it. Which means I have a story."

"Come on, Charlotte. Go easy on me. What about journalistic ethics?"

"Ain't no such thing."

Stone smiled to himself, and shifted his weight from one foot to the other.

Saul muttered, "Charlotte, I've been with Langley, on the Soviet account, for thirty-five years. Thirty-five years of studying Moscow. Thirty-five years of infighting at Langley. Thirty-five years of never being sure whether what we know about Russia is right."

"That's—that's a hundred and five years, Saul," Charlotte said, giving Saul's shoulder a quick squeeze. "You don't look half that."

"You're a doll."

"Don't worry, Saul. I won't use it—yet. Professional courtesy, let's call it."

"Thanks, kid. And if I can ever—Well, it looks like you have an admirer."

Charlotte turned slowly and saw Stone.

Her face registered in a split second a range of emotions—surprise, love, sadness, a flash of anger—all melding, in barely a second, into a look of defiant poise.

"Hello, Charlie."

"Hey, Charlotte. I hope you're not surprised to see me here."

She paused and smiled wistfully. "I knew you'd be here. Excuse us, Saul."

Saul, nodding, departed with a broad smile.

They each stood frozen for a long moment, until Charlie slipped one hand around to the small of her back and said, "Need a little sugar?"

He leaned slightly and touched his lips to hers. She responded almost imperceptibly.

"So?" Stone asked.

"So?" she repeated, shy, awkward, the girl on a first date.

"Been here long?"

"You mean the party, or the country?"

"Both."

"I just got here, to the party. I've been in the States four or five days. Visited my parents, and I happened to be in the city yesterday when I heard about Lehman's—"

"Were you planning to give me a call?" Stone tried

to smile, but couldn't suppress a note of accusation. Several other men nearby were noticing her, the way men always did. One important-looking older man was giving her a lecherous once-over. Stone shot him a menacing, proprietary glare, followed by a swift deflating smile.

Charlotte sighed and looked down. Stone had never seen this dress on her, and he wondered if she'd bought it for the occasion. How many new outfits had she bought in the last year or so, and what were the occasions at which she wore them? "Yes, I was," she said at last. She flushed and looked up again.

"You want a drink or something?"

"I've given up alcohol. And coffee."

"Coffee? You were the caffeine queen of Central Park West."

"Yeah, well, no more. I hate instant, and that's all you get in Moscow. Nescafé."

"I like your lipstick."

"Thanks." She pursed her lips in a burlesque of Marilyn Monroe. "Diane Sawyer recommended it." She gave a quick, only-kidding laugh. "Do you still smoke? I don't smell it on you."

"I gave it up."

"Really? When?"

"I don't remember," Stone lied.

When you left, Stone thought.

Right after their marriage, they moved to New York, where he attended graduate school at Columbia's Russian Institute and she worked at a series of temporary jobs. They lived in an awful, dark studio apartment in the Village, but they didn't mind. After he got his Ph.D., he was asked to join the Georgetown faculty, and they moved to Washington—a move neither one relished. Charlie, whose dissertation on power in the Kremlin was widely lauded, gained immediate recognition as one of the finest Soviet scholars of his generation, and Charlotte, none too happy about not really having a career to speak of, found a job doing rewrite at a Washington newspaper.

Then Charlie was lured to a tenured job at M.I.T.,

in Cambridge, and they moved again. And there Charlotte's career began to take off. She talked her way into a job at a local Boston TV station, rewriting AP newswire copy, and in a matter of months they offered her the position of "weather girl," which she turned down flatly. She became a reporter, assigned to the lowliest of stories—Cops & Cadavers, she called them—but she learned fast. She learned how to do "cutaways," reaction shots during interviews, without nodding, which always looked bad. She learned how to look right into the camera with her direct gaze and project sincerity and strength.

Once in a while, she'd wish aloud that someday she'd have a chance to use the Russian she, too, had learned in college, which was even better than Charlie's (Stone attributed that to her Polish blood). Someday she would. In the meantime, she became first a good reporter, then a terrific one. But of course, since this was television, it was her poise and her looks that attracted all the attention. In the era of Barbara Walters and Jessica Savitch and Diane Sawyer, stations were searching for female anchors, and Charlotte had not only the looks but the *authority*. The station asked her to anchor a morning news show—grimly early, from six to six-thirty in the morning, a show called "Boston A.M."

After a network executive happened to be in Boston for a business meeting and happened to be up early one morning watching the news, he called Charlotte and offered her a network news-reporting job on the spot. In New York.

Which was right around the time that Stone had decided to take up Saul Ansbach's offer to join Parnassus, to leave the academy for the murky world of intelligence. And so they returned to New York, apparently in triumph.

Stone remembered this as the happiest time of their marriage. Both of them, finally, were doing work they loved. Stone plunged himself into the top-secret Kremlinology with a zeal he hadn't known he possessed. Charlotte applied to her reporting that bulldog tenacity, fierce intelligence, and warmth that had carried Stone away the first time he met her back at Yale. She propelled herself through the large pool of network general-assignment reporters until she was getting a story on the news almost every night. A rising star.

They settled into the easy, old-shoe routines of marriage. They watched TV together, cooked once in a while, went out with friends. Charlotte began to learn photography; Charlie became a weekend "gearhead," teaching himself everything about how cars worked, working under the hood of his old BMW 2002 more for relaxation than anything else.

There were squabbles, of course. Things didn't always go smoothly. The feverish, obsessed passion of the early years had settled into something steadier, richer. Stone's love for Charlotte had, if anything, deepened. From time to time, they spoke of having kids, but never seriously; or it would be serious for a week and then one or the other would back away from it. That would come, when they were ready. Older parents were better anyway, weren't they?

And then everything came crashing down.

One day late in 1988, the CIA received reliable indicators that Gorbachev was about to be ousted. There was no time for the Agency to put together a courier package for him, so they flew Stone down to Langley and put him up in a nearby hotel to do an emergency analysis, pore over the files at headquarters. No visitors allowed: Agency rules.

The project went on for weeks. Stone and Charlotte called each other every night. Every night Charlotte would ask when he was coming back; every night Stone would say he didn't know.

Then Charlotte's sister, Martha, committed suicide.

Charlie immediately flew to Pennsylvania for the funeral, then went back to New York with Charlotte to comfort her. She didn't sleep, and hardly cried; she sat in a chair in the bedroom, and stared at a Jane Austen novel without reading it. She seemed inconsolable. After a few days, believing he'd done all he could, he returned to Washington.

That was his mistake. Later he realized he should have

stayed on with Charlotte. At first he called her every night, but after a while he was working night and day and he didn't call but once or twice a week. Perhaps he should have known then how desperate she was for companionship.

He returned to New York at the end of the month to surprise Charlotte.

He did.

She was coming out of their apartment building arm in arm with a man he'd seen before. He was an executive from another network, a pretty-boy in an Armani suit with a flashing, perfect smile, who made TV miniseries or some such thing.

The affair had been going on for two weeks, Stone later learned. He confronted Charlotte wildly, furiously, late that night, after letting himself into their apartment. Then he stormed out, got drunk, and called a woman friend who was divorced, a sensuous, bosomy redhead. They spent the night together.

And the golden bowl had cracked.

The next morning, Stone returned to their apartment, his anger cooled, ready to talk. He was just in time to see Charlotte packing her belongings in boxes and suitcases, sloppily and hastily, weeping all the while. She refused to talk. That afternoon, she moved out to a friend's vacant apartment, and she refused to take Stone's calls.

A few weeks later, she returned one more time, to gather a few last things. They didn't talk about what had happened; there was an air of finality that was terrifying.

She said that the network was sending her to Moscow. Not exactly a widely sought-after position, since it was considered off the traditional career track. But someone at the top of the network had made a decision to "glamorize" coverage of the Soviet Union, and she was certainly glamorous enough.

"I'm taking the job," she said.

Stone, who knew this was coming, felt his stomach turn inside out, but he didn't plead with her, and later he wondered whether he should have. "Don't, Charlotte," he said. "You're making a mistake."

"If we don't take time off from each other, this marriage won't survive," she said.

Charlie went to kiss her, moving slowly, as if through water, and she turned away, spilling tears.

"Ah, now you want to kiss me," she said cruelly. "*Now* you want to kiss me."

For the first time in his life, Charlie, who was never without an apt retort, could think of nothing to say.

Stone held out a hand to Charlotte. "We need to talk," he said. "Alone."

"Can't it wait until after the party?"

"No." A servant passed by, on her way to the kitchen.

When she was gone, Stone continued. "You remember the story about my father?"

"Which story?"

"*The* story, Charlotte. The prison, all that."

"What the hell does that have to do—"

"There's a document in Winthrop's personal archives. Down in the subbasement. I think it might explain something about what happened to my father."

"Charlie, I don't understand—"

"I need your help. I need you to get us in there."

Charlotte hesitated, her insatiable curiosity already threatening to overwhelm her. "Winthrop's your godfather. Why don't you ask him?"

"I can't. He'd be suspicious. But you're a journalist, and Winthrop is a man of considerable ego. You see? Do it for my father, at least. For him."

"Unfair, Charlie."

"Winthrop," Charlotte said to Lehman a few minutes later, placing her small shapely hand atop his large knobby one. "I'm leaving the country tomorrow, but I'm thinking of putting together a television profile on you, your legacy in Russia today." She watched as Lehman's vanity took him over. "Charlie's offered to guide me around."

Oak wainscoting gave way to plainer oak paneling as the two walked down the narrow corridor. A copper-haired middle aged woman, probably an employee, passed by and smiled deferentially. The noise of the party grew fainter.

Winthrop Lehman's archives were located a long walk away, behind a steel door that locked electronically. They comprised some ninety filing cabinets in a temperature- and humidity-controlled environment, and in those green steel cabinets were some of the most fascinating documents Stone had ever seen—a veritable inside history of twentieth-century American diplomacy.

He had visited Lehman's personal archives a few times before, as an undergraduate, when he was working on his senior thesis on the formation of American foreign policy toward the Soviet Union. Stone was one of the very few people ever allowed to see the archives. There was a historian from Stanford whom Lehman permitted to browse, but most scholar-squirrels and packrats, as Lehman called academics, were politely but firmly turned away. Lehman had decreed that the files were not to be opened to the public until after his death, when they would be given to the Library of Congress. Some of the papers would probably not be declassified for years.

"You're not really leaving the country tomorrow, are you?" Stone asked. They passed a supply closet, then a dumbwaiter that was filled with dirty dishes.

"I am."

"*Christ*, Charlotte. What are the terms of this separation, anyway? Complete and utter exile, is that it? We never see each other?" They passed a room that exuded the strong odor of chlorine bleach. He spoke with a quiet, cool anger. "You know I'd visit you in Moscow if the Agency allowed that. But they don't."

Charlotte nodded, her face a mask of neutrality. She scratched at her chin.

"Do you want to just throw our marriage away, is that it?" Stone asked.

She didn't reply. They walked down a creaky set of wooden stairs.

"How's your love life?" he asked. His voice echoed in the stairwell.

"Uneventful," she said. Her tone was too airy, too offhanded.

The walls were concrete now; the floor was some kind of hard gray institutional stone. He pulled open a door, held it for her, and saw that her blush had still not gone away.

She said, "I don't know what you're—"

"Just *tell* me, Charlotte. Make it easy."

"Look, Charlie." They stopped for a moment in front of a small service elevator. "I've seen people. You have, too. But there isn't anyone now. For one thing, there isn't any time."

"Or anyone."

"You know that's not true."

"You're right," Stone conceded. "You never had a problem attracting men. So why haven't you?"

"Did it ever occur to you, Charlie, that I might want to be alone for a while?"

He flashed for an instant on the last vacation he and Charlotte had taken together, before she first went off to Moscow. They flew to Barbados, to a rustic, secluded resort on the rock-strewn east coast of the island, where they drank rum and ate flying fish and made love. He remembered her greedily grinding her pelvis against his for more, just once more. He remembered the wind blowing the front door of their bungalow open so that the Canadian woman who lived next to them, who was sunning herself on the deck a few feet away, could suddenly see into their room, see them making love, and she turned away, hotly embarrassed, scowling; and Charlie and Charlotte, after an instant of mortification, both laughed until they thought they'd be sick.

"What's our arrangement, anyway?" Stone said, pressing the button to summon the elevator. "When are we going to get back together? Not to put too fine a point on it."

"I don't know," she said.

The elevator arrived with a muted click, and they got in.

"Let me be even clearer." He wanted to shout, *I love*

THE MOSCOW CLUB 71

you, but he said merely, rationally, "I *want* us to get back together. We both made stupid mistakes. But that's the past. We can undo them."

Charlotte didn't know how to answer. She turned away from him, staring dumbly at the steel wall of the tiny, close elevator, and she felt a great bloom of feeling, like something physically rising in her, compressing her throat, bringing tears to her eyes. She was glad he couldn't see her.

But he suddenly grabbed her shoulders and, with an unexpected forcefulness, kissed her. She suffered it at first, warily, as if receiving a vaccination shot.

Her arms stayed at her side; her eyes remained open, alert.

"Don't—" Her protestation was barely audible.

Her lips, trembling, barely moved in response. They parted slightly, almost not at all, and then closed tightly, for punctuation.

The elevator door opened in front of Lehman's archives.

The archive room was small, with a low ceiling and a highly polished, tiled floor. Its walls were lined with filing cabinets. The chamber went on for fifty feet or so, its rows of cabinets so close together that the place felt uncomfortably cramped.

At the back of the room, in gloomy darkness, was one row of locked cabinets, which contained the classified material. Stone remembered from years ago that you could not turn on the lights in that area without setting off an alarm somewhere upstairs in the main house. The fluorescent lights embedded in the ceiling gave off a bluish glare, their faint buzz the only sound in the chamber's absolute silence.

"How do you know where to look?" Charlotte asked. She was nervous; they both were. They were poking around areas of the archives where they hadn't any business, and at any moment someone might come in.

"I remember these drawers are organized by year, and month, and then by subject."

It was possible, certainly, that Lehman might send a servant after them to make sure things were going all right. To summon them up to the party, perhaps, for a toast. Anything was possible. And if he discovered . . .

But Stone didn't want to think about it. He quickly went through the drawers, looking for that slip of paper his father had seen years ago, while just inches away Charlotte sat on a small steel table, next to a dusty old Canon copying machine, her legs dangling. She was keeping watch on the door.

"Won't Winthrop think it's odd, you rooting around down here while upstairs the party is in full swing?" she asked tensely, watching Stone open drawer after drawer.

"He thinks it's *you* rooting around. Anyway, I think it strikes him as perfectly plausible that someone might want to do a TV retrospective on him. He's never been a shy man." A long silence passed, while Stone slid open metal drawers and glanced at the tab indexes.

A half an hour passed, then an hour. "Getting close," Stone said. He could sense her staring at his back, and turned to confirm it. She was. "You doing okay?"

"I'm okay." Charlotte seemed pensive. "What are these lights for?" She pointed at a small square panel next to the brushed-steel door, on which were rows of pinpoint lights.

"The alarm system," Stone replied. "Marjorie used the key to admit us, so the primary system was deactivated." Marjorie was Lehman's secretary.

"But why so many lights? I don't get it."

"You see those cabinets back there?" He pointed without looking, his left hand moving quickly through the files.

"Where it's dark?"

"Right. Those two rows back there are alarmed. Marjorie explained it to me once."

"What's in them? The locked cabinets, I mean."

"She said they're mostly confidential, boring documents—records on Lehman Shipping, legal papers, that sort of thing."

"Which is why they're alarmed."

"I didn't say I believed her."

"But if they—"

"Bingo," Charlie said.

"What?"

"We're on our way."

It was a small, yellowed slip of paper, a memorandum on FBI letterhead, dated April 3, 1953, addressed to Lehman, badly typed:

BIDWELL, HAROLD.
CUSHING, ALDEN.
STONE, ALFRED.
DUNAYEV, FYODOR.

Of possible suspects we've discussed only above 4 appear to have any knowledge of "Lenin Testament."

Enclosed, security-classified dossier.

Warren Pogue
Special Investigator,
Federal Bureau of Investigation

At the bottom of the note was a pencil scrawl: "File to 74."

Charlotte looked up when she'd finished reading it. "That's drawer 74, right?"

"Right."

"Over there." She pointed at the dark row of locked cabinets.

"That's it."

"One of the locked ones."

"I'm not surprised."

There was a metallic click.

"What was that?" Stone asked.

Charlotte didn't reply. Her eyes were wide. She watched Stone as he glanced around the chamber.

"Oh," he said. "The ventilation system just switched on. That's all." The chamber's silence was now intruded upon by a distinct, almost but not quite subsonic whine, a hum, the white noise of finely calibrated instruments filtering the air, removing the moisture, maintaining it at precisely sixty degrees Fahrenheit.

He reached into his breast pocket and withdrew a small square dark-blue velvet case and a tiny black Mag-Lite flashlight.

"What's that?"

"Just an old trick I picked up."

He walked over to the dark end of the archives.

"Can you see what you're doing over there?" Charlotte asked.

He switched on the Mag-Lite in response. "No sense alerting Lehman's people. They've got their hands full with the party."

The small bright-yellow circle from the flashlight located cabinet number 74. It was an old-fashioned filing cabinet painted in somber dark green; very likely it dated from the late 1940s or early 1950s.

He inserted the two instruments into the lock. One, the torsion wrench, was about six inches long and was shaped like an elongated L. The other, the feeler pick, resembled a wig pin or a dental probe. He held the torsion wrench at the bottom of the lock to keep the tension and, with the feeler pick, raised each tumbler pin, one by one. He had practiced on other locks, but this one was his first serious attempt, and it was a little more difficult than he'd anticipated. He felt a slight give on the torsion wrench as each pin lined up. Finally, the lock popped out with a satisfying click.

"Charlie, what the hell are you doing?"

"Picking the lock. I had a feeling the good stuff might be locked up."

"If anyone sees you—"

"Charlotte," Stone said patiently, "Winthrop Lehman is a very stuffy, very old-fashioned man with some very old-fashioned notions of what state secrets are. For God's sakes, the stuff in here has got to be *decades* old. Whatever he did to help my father, whatever behind-the-scenes help he gave, I'm sure he considers the matter a closed chapter. . . ."

His voice trailed off. For a long time, he was silent.

"Where'd you learn to pick locks, anyway?"

"That detective friend of mine," Stone murmured, but his mind was elsewhere. "Sawyer."

"Great," she said unenthusiastically.

It felt as if a great mass of ice had suddenly welled up in his stomach. All he could hear was the thudding of his heart, the sibilant rush of his breath.

"What is it, Charlie?"

"Oh, Jesus," he managed to say hoarsely. "Here it is."

"What?" She got up and walked over to where Stone was standing in darkness, his flashlight beam illuminating a yellowed piece of paper. Looking over his shoulder, she read.

"Oh, Charlie," she said two minutes later. Her voice shook. "Oh, my God." She put her arms around his waist and hugged him. "Oh, God, Charlie, I'm sorry."

"There's a phone in here, Charlotte," Stone said tightly. He had to reach his father at once: a brief phone conversation was all that was required, a cryptic exchange that would signify nothing to anyone else. "I need to make a call. I want you to switch on that copying machine and make two sets of copies of each of these pages. I need to make a call."

In a small rented studio apartment on East 73rd Street, at precisely the same time, a man with a swarthy complexion and dark hair—anyone familiar with the various Soviet nationalities would have noticed the hint of Asiatic in his face—sat monitoring a radio transmission, which was being recorded on a small cassette machine. He listened with the resignedness of one who has been doing a monotonous task for a very long time and resents the monotony; he chain-smoked Marlboros.

The man was far from good-looking. His face was pitted with the tiny deep round scars of childhood smallpox. He looked out the window, which was grimy with the foul city air, and watched the rain on the slick black streets. The neighborhood was a peculiar mix of well-dressed young people and more-settled-in older ones; he watched them scurrying. Someone walked by with a giant radio blasting rap music, if you could call that music, and the man was suddenly filled with great irritation.

He worked as a security guard at a Russian-émigré newspaper in lower Manhattan. The job was, of course, largely a fiction—the newspaper had no need of security—but he put in enough time to earn a declarable, if pitiful, income. He was known as Shvartz, which sounded Jewish, although it wasn't his real name; he had been given the name as well as a false career and family background a few months before he had left the Soviet Union, and even a record—fictional as well—of past anti-Soviet activity.

Shvartz listened to the transmission with little interest. He had been at work since early this morning, nonstop, and after eight hours of this he was close to fed up with what he felt sure was a pointless exercise.

The radio transmission emanated from a telephone in a house a few blocks away. So clear was the signal that it was as if he were listening in on an extension in the same house—which in a sense he was. The system before him was equipped to monitor as many as sixteen telephone lines, but it was now monitoring only three, and each of them came from the same house. Clearly the project was a priority.

He crushed out a cigarette, lit another, and continued listening.

Then the man noticed that a call was being made on the rarely used third line, and from then on he paid very close attention to the conversation.

A man was speaking to a woman.

Frankly, Shvartz had not expected any calls on that line at all. When the decision had been reached a few months ago to place the rich man's home under telephonic surveillance, the men who took turns sitting in the uncomfortable apartment, listening, knew they were in for a bad time of it, a long dull stretch. An endless, achingly routine assignment.

Placing a bug or a tap on someone's premises or telephone requires access, at least in some way, to either the home or the telephone lines. Breaking-and-entering the subject's townhouse had been rejected immediately as too risky: the man was too rich, too well guarded.

So the organization had obtained, by means of an untraceable payoff, a NYNEX phone-company repair van and a set of uniforms and hard hats. The two men designated by the organization located the correct telephone switching box behind 71st Street; one of them opened the fixture and began to test the pairs of wires. He used a piece of equipment familiar to telephone repairmen: a handset with a dialer attached to a miniature computer.

Tapping into each pair of wires, he repeatedly punched in the code, and the computer's LCD readout displayed the telephone number of the wires he had selected. After a few trials, he had isolated the three desired lines. Across each line he installed a small high-frequency transmitting device, each of which emitted signals up to a thousand feet away. They relied on the same sophisticated, if now common, technology employed in car telephones.

Of course, the tap was detectable, by someone using anti-eavesdropping equipment, or by the telephone company, should it be inclined to investigate, but it was highly unlikely that either event would occur. The rich man had not ordered a sweep of his telephone lines in many years, since the time he stopped working for the government. Careful surveillance had confirmed this. Although, as a matter of habit, there may have been subjects he didn't speak about openly over the phone, he had no reason to suspect a tap on his line.

Shvartz had no idea what this business was all about. He was never told; that was a necessary precaution. He knew that the operation was carefully concealed from the KGB, the GRU, and every other Soviet intelligence agency.

The long dull stretch was over. The man glanced at the digital readout and copied down the numbers. The call was going to area code 617. Boston area. Interesting. He picked up his own telephone, punched out the number of a local telephone, said a few brief words, and hung up.

He took the last cigarette from the pack, lit it, then rewound the cassette.

* * *

The dark-haired man thought for some reason about the crude wood-and-iron rattraps he had designed as a boy, remembered watching with dispassionate curiosity as the rats, who knew nothing except the most primal fear, struggled furiously. You could watch a rat die with, not pleasure exactly, but *distance,* the same sense of distance you felt watching, from a New York skyscraper, the ant-sized pedestrians.

His job, he now realized with some pleasure, was no longer going to be quite so routine.

The apartment buzzer sounded, and he got up and walked over to the panel by the door and pressed the button. "Yes?"

"A package," came the voice from downstairs over the speaker.

"Where's it from?"

"California."

He pressed another button to open the door downstairs, and then watched through the spyglass. About a minute later, the blond Russian stood before the door. The dark-haired man released, one after another, the three locks that had been specially installed by the organization, and let the Russian in.

The Russian was out of breath; his suit was wet with rain. He had been running.

"So we've caught ourselves a fox," he joked.

We've caught ourselves a rat, the dark-haired man thought, as he pulled the cellophane off a fresh pack of Marlboros.

8

"The answering service didn't know where he was," Stone said.

Charlotte looked up and said, puzzled, "Doesn't he always tell them where he is, where he can be reached?"

"It's unlike him," he conceded. He picked up the papers and read them again, numb with shock and anger. For some reason, he didn't want Charlotte to know how deeply this discovery affected him, how it was turning his insides to ice. As he read, his face was impassive.

The file was seven pages long, no more. It consisted of one letter, from an FBI agent to Winthrop Lehman, and one report, filed by this agent—originally, it seemed, for the House Un-American Activities Committee. The Joe McCarthy committee; the witch-hunters, as Alfred Stone always called them.

Suddenly it was clear—almost clear—why Alfred Stone had been imprisoned so many years ago.

DEPARTMENT OF JUSTICE
Federal Bureau of Investigation
Washington, D.C.

PERSONAL AND CONFIDENTIAL

Memorandum

To: Mr. Winthrop Lehman
From: Special Agent Warren L. Pogue
Date: May 20, 1953
Subject: Alfred Stone

Reference is made to ALFRED CHARLES STONE, 33, who presently serves as Assistant to the National Security Adviser to the President.

Conclusion
Investigation discloses sufficient evidence to warrant concern about possible knowledge by subject of matter we discussed.

Bureau laboratory analysis of fingerprints on the security report (attached in glassine envelope) confirms that ALFRED STONE has handled report.

I have personally seen to the destruction of all photographs and surveillance reports of ALFRED STONE during his most recent stay in Moscow, as per your request to the Director. The Bureau will pursue no further investigation.

Mr. Hoover has asked me to convey to you his sentiments that the House Un-American Activities Committee, with which he has a close working relationship, is nevertheless not under his control, and will most likely not rest until Stone is jailed, if briefly.

He shares your concern that, as STONE hand-carried the Lenin Testament to the Russian woman whom our agents have identified as SONYA KUNETSKAYA, he should be kept from any questioning by the Committee. Although he appears to know nothing of the M-3 operation, there is grave danger, Mr. Hoover feels, that under sustained questioning he may inadvertently reveal the asset's identity, which will gravely endanger the operation.

Mr. Hoover recommends that an arrangement be made with the Committee such that STONE is imprisoned without further public questioning, until such time as he can be compelled to accept our terms.

The attached security report is the only extant copy, for your records.

FBI File No. 97-8234

"Jesus *Christ*," Stone could not help murmuring.

He reread the memorandum several times, still unable to believe what was so clearly there.

In effect, Winthrop Lehman had cooperated with the FBI to put Alfred Stone in jail.

Why?

Because he knew something about an extremely secret intelligence operation, was that it?

Because he had taken this Lenin Testament to a woman in Moscow named Sonya Kunetskaya?

It had always been an item of faith to him that the spy charges leveled against his father were laughably false. But now . . . was it possible that they were true? Stone had seen countless documents from the McCarthy furor,

and this memorandum was archetypal. The stilted language, the undercurrent of ominousness, the shred of substance served up into a banquet of allegation.

But might there be some truth to it?

"The alarm," Charlotte said. "Let's get out of here."
She stood so close to him that he could smell the faint
traces of her perfume, which was called Fracas. He remembered: he had always been the one to buy it for her.
He could feel her warm breath on his neck as she spoke,
and wondered if she, too, sensed a sexual charge, even
now, at this tense moment.

Stone nodded absently.

He turned next to the photocopy of the "security report" that had been clipped to the memo. It was a three-
page, stapled, single-spaced report, also filed by Warren
L. Pogue. The original had been encased in a brown-tinged
glassine envelope that felt as if it might crumble beneath
even the most delicate handling.

This was even more remarkable. It told of a meeting
several Americans— among them Winthrop Lehman—had
had with none other than Joseph Stalin, in 1952:

DEPARTMENT OF JUSTICE
Federal Bureau of Investigation
Washington, D.C.

TOP SECRET

Office Memorandum

To: Director Hoover
From: Special Agent Warren L. Pogue
Date: February 2, 1952
Subject: Stalin Meeting

Following is a transcript of the recollection of Al-
den CUSHING, former staff associate of Winthrop
LEHMAN, of meeting with Joseph Stalin in Moscow,
January 16, 1952:

Q: Tell me about the trip.

A: I was asked to accompany Winthrop Lehman to a meeting with Joseph Stalin early in 1952. The occasion was one of official business, although the exact purpose was never made clear to me. I make it my policy not to poke my nose where it doesn't belong. I was curious as to what sort of official business this might be, since there were no negotiations going on to my knowledge. But I was only there to—

Q: Who else was there, of the Americans?

A: Myself, and Harold Bidwell from State. That's all.

Q: Who was there besides Stalin?

A: Quite a number of Russian officials, as I recall. A fellow named Poskrebyshev, if I have his name right. Malenkov, who was . . . Beria, the, you know, the Minister for State Security, the secret police. And [M-3]. May I consult my notes?

Q: Of course.

A: Oh, yes, the head of Stalin's bodyguard, a fellow named Khrustalyov. And one of Stalin's aides-de-camp, named Osipov, a young guy obviously very much trusted by Stalin. Someone else, too. A guy named Trofimov, Viktor Trofimov. The one who defected a few years back? He was there.

Q: How did Stalin look?

A: Much better, much stronger than I had expected. I heard he had had several operations by then, and of course he's, what, seventy-one or seventy-two by now. But he looked old all the same. Short fellow. I was surprised at how short he was. Pockmarked face. Very sharp eyes, always watching you.

Q: Mentally how was he?

A: Hard to say. Sometimes he was so sharp it was scary. Other times he drifted in and out of what I'd say was senility. He forgot my name, kept forgetting it. I don't mean that there's any reason in the world why he should know my name, but he kept looking at me and saying, "You never told me your name." Like that.

Q: You met at his dacha?

A: That's right. Earlier in the day, Winthrop went out there to meet with Stalin alone. He also met with Beria. Didn't bring me or Hal with him. But we were all invited to dinner at the dacha in Kuntsevo. People called it Blizhny; that was the name of the villa.

Q: You had dinner?

A: I was getting to that. You said you wanted all the details. Yes, we had dinner there. Fancy spread, lots of dishes. Stalin sleeps late, past noon, and eats lunch around three in the afternoon, and then he doesn't eat dinner until around ten at night. So it was late by the time we were driven there, and it was awfully cold. Below zero. We were brought right into the dining room on the ground floor and introduced to Stalin. He told us he lived in that very room. Slept on the sofa. He showed us where. He had a log fire going. But before we could eat, he wanted us to watch a movie. We all went into another room, almost as large, and watched a Charlie Chaplin movie. *Modern Times*.

Q: Stalin likes Chaplin?

A: Oh, yes. He thought *Modern Times* was terribly clever. Great fun, he thought; really poked fun at capitalism and assembly lines and all that. Ten of us sitting in the room, watching the movie. And then we went back to the dining room and ate and drank. This was somewhere after midnight.

Stalin said, "Let's eat. Everyone's hungry." Well, of course, no one was hungry at all at that hour, but no one dared to contradict him. Stalin wouldn't eat anything unless someone tasted it first. He was deathly afraid of being poisoned, I surmise. He kept pointing at food and saying something like, "Lavrentii Pavlovich"—Beria—"the herring looks delicious." And then Beria would have to eat some of it before Stalin would. Oh, yes, and even before we ate Stalin made us all drink. Quite a bit, actually.

Q: Stalin drank a lot?

A: No, not at all. He mostly sat there, smoking his pipe, watching us. He made us guess how cold it was, how many degrees below zero, and for each degree we were wrong we'd have to drink a shotglass of vodka. Lehman, who must have checked the thermometer before he left his hotel, was almost right on the nose. I didn't fare so well.

But he'd turn surly and suspicious all of a sudden. He turned to one fellow, I think it was Osipov, who he'd been quite friendly to all night, and he said, quite coldly, "I didn't invite you here!" This fellow, you could see him shaking in his boots. He said, "Yes, sir, you did." But Khrustalyov got up and dragged Osipov out. We never saw him again.

Stalin was exceedingly unpredictable. He got up suddenly during dinner and went over to his gramophone and put on a record of someone playing the trumpet badly and a woman laughing. Mostly the record was of this woman laughing uproariously. I remember it was called "The Okeh Laughing Record," because when I was younger that was quite the big thing. Stalin found this terribly amusing. And—

Q: Do you think Stalin suspected anything about Beria and [M-3]?

A: No, sir. No reason to believe that.

Q: And how did Stalin happen to bring up the subject of Lenin and the Testament?

A: Well, it was quite natural, actually. Rather far into the dinner, Stalin raised his glass to a portrait of Lenin that hung on the wall and said, "Let us all drink to the memory of our great teacher, our great leader. Vladimir Ilyich!" And we all stood up and toasted the portrait and drank. And then he turned to Hal Bidwell, who hadn't said a word the whole evening—his function was just to take notes—and said, "You have seen Vladimir Ilyich?"

And Bidwell seemed at first not to know what to say. And then he figured it out—Stalin meant, Have you been to Lenin's mausoleum? Bidwell said, "Well, sir, I have been to the mausoleum, if that's what you mean."

Q: And that was when Stalin lost his temper?

A: Oh, yes. Oh, it was fearsome, I must say. Stalin understood at once what Bidwell was hinting at. You know, that old tale that the body in the mausoleum is made of wax. Stalin pointed a thick finger directly at Lehman and said, "You joke about that. You joke that our Lenin is a wax doll. You have told your people about that, haven't you?" Lehman just shook his head, and I've never seen him so frightened. Stalin said, "Maybe you told your friends why." He looked at Bidwell, pointing his finger, and shouted, "Has he told you why he knows it is wax? Has he told you?" We were by now all trembling with fear. He pointed the finger at Lehman again and said, "Have you told them about the Testament, too? Have you told them? The Testament belongs here, Mr. Lehman. His *Testament* belongs in the Kremlin, Mr. Lehman." He said this with—with contempt, I remember.

Q: But Stalin spoke in Russian, didn't he? How did you know exactly what he said?

A: Bidwell told me afterward. He speaks Russian quite well, you know. He used a Russian word, *zavyet*, which means "testament." As in "last will and testament." He said, "The Testament must not be in the West. It must be destroyed."

Q: And you said Lehman then responded.

A: Yes, but first Beria said something. It was an old
Russian proverb. Something like "The paper is patient.
The paper never forgets." Or some such thing. And
then Lehman said, "You know it must not be
destroyed."

Q: And what did Stalin say then?

A: He didn't say anything. He got up and went over
to his gramophone and played "The Okeh Laughing
Record" once again.

"Charlie," Charlotte said, "did you notice one of the
row of alarm lights is flashing?"

"Hmm?" Stone was not listening.

"One of the rows of lights is blinking now. The blue
row. It wasn't flashing before."

"What?"

"Do you think it's possible that the drawers themselves are alarmed, too?"

"That's impossible," he said suddenly. He glanced
away from the file. "I didn't see any . . . Unless the floor
. . . Sometimes they put pressure-sensitive plates on the
floor." He groaned.

"I think you set off an alarm, Charlie," she said.
"You'd better get away from that area."

He glanced up at the flashing blue lights in the alarm
panel. She was right; any moment, someone might decide
to investigate. He'd explain that it was an accident, that
he'd forgotten about the alarmed section.

But Stone could not take his eyes off the document.

"Charlie, can we *please* get out of here?"

"We'll be all right, I'm reasonably certain. I want to
look further, now—"

Charlotte gave a long anxious sigh. "Your father was
set up by Winthrop, wasn't he?"

Stone didn't reply.

"Charlie, what's 'M-3'?"

He peered into the copying machine's dusty works for a long while before he answered. "Probably just some routine FBI designation. Nothing terribly interesting."

But he was lying. He knew that M-3 was a mole, a penetration agent. The "M" series, he knew, was nomenclature from the early 1950s for penetration agents. The fledgling CIA had more code labels prepared than actual moles to be coded: it wasn't a very successful program.

Apparently, Alfred Stone had come upon evidence of an American mole in Moscow, and someone or some group of people—who?—was or were afraid that he would reveal the secret.

"I don't follow this," Charlotte said, tugging at a strand of hair and tucking it behind her ear. "The FBI interrogated everyone who was at this dinner with Stalin and heard Stalin mention something about a Lenin Testament, which probably meant nothing to anyone there—do I have this right? But clearly it was urgent that word of this document not get out, right? *Why?*"

Stone shrugged and compressed his lips. "I can only guess." He hesitated a moment. "I want to ask you to do me a favor. I want you to feel free to say no."

She looked at him, her face open, inquiring.

"This—this Sonya Kunetskaya that the document mentions. Do you think you might be able to—"

"To track her down, see if she's alive, right?"

"Right. But if you don't want—"

"I'll take a stab at it, sure." She tucked a lock of hair behind her left ear. "But I'm puzzled about something. If Winthrop betrayed your father, sold him out, why did your father put up with it? Why did he take it?"

"Well, I see you two are still down here." The voice, high and reedy, yet strong for a man who was almost ninety, startled them.

Winthrop Lehman, supported on his left side by a powerful-looking bodyguard, stood in the door of the archives. The light caught his glasses so that they couldn't see his eyes. The bodyguard, who had a short, neat haircut and the build of a linebacker, glared menacingly.

"Winthrop," Charlotte began, and got up quickly from the table.

Lehman advanced slowly toward them, aided by the bodyguard. "You know, the party's long over," he said. "Everyone's gone home. I think it was a success, don't you?" He came closer, his voice echoing metallically. He seemed short of breath. "When Marjorie told me the blue alarm had gone off, I told her I'd go investigate for myself. I knew it wasn't a burglar; I knew it was just you two. Always good to see people hard at work."

The documents lay on the table beside the copying machine, in Lehman's line of vision. But he was an old man, after all, and it was unlikely he would be able to see them.

"I hope you're planning to say nice things about me, Charlotte," Lehman said. "What's that?"

He was looking at the documents. The red stamp on the folder had attracted his attention, the mark that indicated the file was top-secret. He walked closer, the bodyguard helping him along.

"What's this?"

He waved a hand weakly at the documents, and then bent over slightly to get a look.

"*Where did you get this?*"

He snatched them up from the table with a suddenness that startled Stone.

"I may have set the alarm off by mistake," Stone said blandly, hoping to divert the old man, but Lehman cut him off.

The elderly man's voice trembled with fear—or was it anger? "I never said you could go into the locked drawers!" With a shaking hand he handed the sheaf to his bodyguard. "How dare you invade my private files!"

"You did him in, didn't you?" said Stone fiercely. "After all these years, I guess I misunderstood your motives. Guilt—is that right?" Stone quietly slipped the dossier into his back pocket. Lehman had grabbed the photocopies that Charlotte had made while he was on the phone.

"Get out of here," said Lehman. His voice quavered with anger. "I did everything I could to help your father. What you think you're doing, breaking into the locked cabinets with the tools of a burglar, I can't possibly imagine. You have no business . . . What do you think you're doing?" Now his voice rose to a shrill, horrifying shout, and Charlotte put her arm, which was shaking, around Stone's waist.

"Get out of here," Lehman rasped. "Get out of here! Damn you! Get out of here!"

He clutched on to the bodyguard. "Get them out of here!" he hissed, with the ferocious, white-hot anger of a man with a great deal to hide.

They spent the night together.

She refused to go to their apartment; he went to her hotel. They talked late into the night, sharing a bottle of wine they'd ordered from room service. They wanted to dance, but there wasn't a radio, so they put the TV on and found one of those endless late-night ads for cheap-imitation polka records, and they danced distractedly to the lousy music and talked, more honestly than they had in years.

"There isn't a day goes by that I don't think how stupid I was to do what I did," Charlotte said. "But I was crazy. I was out of my mind. I needed someone, and you were off in Washington."

"I understand. I forgive you. Do the same for me."

"Have you been faithful?"

"No," Stone admitted. "Have you?"

"No. Whatever 'faithful' means."

"Then we're even." He shrugged and turned his palms up. "All right . . . ?"

"All right what?"

He exhaled and shook his head, feigning annoyance to mask his nervousness. "Look, do you want to try again? You know, love among the ruins? Piece it back together?"

Charlotte didn't know how to answer. She only knew

that she'd been changed by what had happened between them, that part of her would never be hurt again because it would never again be accessible. She thought of those sea creatures that scuttle about the ocean floor, naked and vulnerable, until they lodge themselves in a protective shell. Well, she'd grown herself a shell.

Confused now, she was pensive, even tender. Charlie kissed her, first lightly, then with growing passion. Charlotte let him kiss her, let him stroke her breasts, but she felt nothing. Or, more accurately, she wouldn't allow herself to feel anything. She was immensely attracted to this man, her husband, but some toggle switch inside her had gone off. He was her real love, the man she was convinced she'd love forever, and now she didn't know if she could trust him or anyone else. All she wanted, even a year and a half later, was to be left alone. Was that so crazy?

She wouldn't make love with him. Charlie was hurt, confused, but soon they both fell asleep, next to each other in the big hotel bed, their bottoms touching, and she cried softly as he slept beside her.

Very early the next morning, they said goodbye at Kennedy Airport, at the Lufthansa terminal, where she was catching the first flight to Munich. A few days visiting friends there, she said, and then back to the Soviet grindstone.

Both of them were tired, worn out from the night before. There were long, silent pauses in their conversation, which neither one rushed to fill. The terminal bustled around them, its frenetic pace a counterpoint to the slow melancholy they both felt.

"Send my love to your father," Charlotte said, lifting her green leather carry-on bag to her shoulder.

"Charlotte—"

"Thanks for seeing me off. I should go. They're announcing my flight."

"Charlotte, this is crazy—"

But she continued briskly, unable to talk about feelings she didn't understand. "I'll try to find that Russian woman for you. That Sonya Kunetskaya."

"Not for me, Charlotte. For my father."

"Okay. For your father." She shook her head slowly, sadly. "You know, we had something wonderful. . . ."

"Jesus, Charlotte, we still do."

Now, suddenly, she was sobbing, as if she'd been holding back for hours. Probably she had. Stone put his arms around her, squeezing hard. She nestled her chin in the hollow of his shoulder. He felt her tears, burningly hot, run off against his neck, into his open shirt collar. "Be careful, Charlie, will you?"

"I was going to tell you the same thing."

The amplified voice announced the last boarding call.

Making his way languidly out of the terminal, Stone passed a bank of telephones, and he stopped short. Impulsively, he picked up one of the handsets, dropped a quarter in the slot, and dialed his father's number.

Three minutes later, he hung up the phone and began to run for a taxi.

Alfred Stone had been rushed to Massachusetts General Hospital.

9

Moscow

The killing of an American girl within the very walls of the Kremlin shook the Soviet leadership to its core, and an urgent session was called at once.

President Mikhail Gorbachev spoke with quiet anger. His fellow Politburo members were used to his flashes of anger, but even his enemies knew that, when he lowered his voice in this way, he was not to be interrupted.

"A bomb thrown by a Russian," he said tonelessly. "Who was shot dead on the spot. And therefore cannot be linked to any subversive organization."

He removed his steel-rimmed glasses. He looked around the table, but there was only silence, furrowed brows, here and there a bemused shake of a head.

"Gentlemen, this incident has attracted the attention of the world. This, on top of everything else. We are perceived as a regime that is spinning out of control."

The silence was unbroken, tense. Gorbachev waited, then gave an acidulous smirk. "Are we?"

The room in which the small group of men who rule the beleaguered Communist Party of the Soviet Union—the Soviet Politburo—meets has rarely been seen by Westerners. In fact, the inner sanctum is disappointingly plain. It is located on the third floor of the Council of Ministers building in the Kremlin, a baroque yellow-fronted structure, topped with green domes, known as the Old Senate Building, built in the late eighteenth century by the Russian architect Matvei Kazakov. One can approach it by means of an ancient elevator, down a parquet hallway carpeted with a pink-and-green runner. The ornate door behind which the Politburo meets is ten feet high.

The room is a long barren rectangle, its walls covered in light-yellow silk, devoid of hangings. The molding and trim are painted with gold leaf. The only clock in the room is located on the conference table, a long highly polished wooden table whose top is covered in green baize. Around this table are fifteen chairs, enough for the entire Politburo and the rare invited guest; against the walls are dozens more chairs for candidate members, ministers, assistants, and others, although today only the full members were present, a portent of the seriousness of the discussion.

Disconcertingly, the chairs around the table have cushions upholstered not in, say, silk damask, but in green vinyl. They had been re-covered during the reign of Brezhnev, who was opposed to anything either too regal or—because he disliked long meetings—too comfortable. But no one wanted to return to the chaotic, arbitrary days of Khrushchev, when Politburo meetings might be called in the Kremlin dining room, or even around some vodka bottles at his dacha.

Contrary to much that has been written, there exist

no full transcripts of Politburo meetings. This is a custom that goes back to Lenin's time—as is the day on which the Politburo invariably meets, Thursday, and the hour, almost always three o'clock in the afternoon. The minutes reflect only what has been decided, which resolutions made, and copies of these resolutions are sent to all Central Committee members in maroon envelopes. Of course, the top-secret resolutions do not circulate.

Soon the Politburo would be entirely phased out, its chief governing duties transferred to a similar, non-Party body known as the Presidential Council. There were those in Moscow who wondered whether members of the present Politburo would sit idly by and watch their power ebb.

The business on the agenda of this particular Politburo meeting was what is known among its members as "yellow-priority," a designation just short of emergency.

The first to break the silence was one of Gorbachev's allies, Anatoly Lukyanov, chief of the Central Committee's General Department. He was to Gorbachev what a White House chief of staff is to an American president.

"If I may suggest something," Lukyanov said, "I think the problem lies with security." He did not have to elaborate; he turned to look at Andrei Dmitrovich Pavlichenko, the head of the KGB, who sat several places away. "It is almost unthinkable to me that a KGB chairman who's doing his job properly wouldn't know of an underground network of criminals with the resources to accomplish such a thing. For there must be a network."

Everyone present understood the import of Lukyanov's charge. Such things had never happened under Yuri Andropov, the head of the KGB throughout the 1960s. Even Pavlichenko's predecessor, Vladimir A. Kryuchkov, had been more vigilant. Terrorism was virtually unheard of in Moscow—and within the Kremlin walls? Unfathomable.

Pavlichenko was, Gorbachev knew, probably the brightest man in the room—but he was far easier to control than his predecessors at KGB, largely because he owed his position and his allegiance entirely to Gorbachev. He was also known to have suffered recent heart trouble, which meant that he was even less of a threat to his colleagues. One could not ignore such human frailties; they had their uses.

To everyone's surprise, Pavlichenko's reply was temperate, not at all defensive. "It is, indeed, unthinkable," he said evenly. "This has been an embarrassment both to me and to my people." He shrugged and spread his hands, seemingly casual, but tension creased his face. "Ultimately, it is *my* responsibility, as you all know."

"Perhaps you could use a medical leave." The suggestion, put icily, came from Eduard A. Shevardnadze, the foreign minister, a vociferous Gorbachev supporter.

Pavlichenko paused, visibly restraining a less temperate response. He gave a polite smile. Sometimes he thought that every Politburo meeting was like entering the lions' den. "No," he said. "The moment my health begins to interfere with the performance of my job, I'll resign at once. You can be assured of that. We are digging very deep, questioning widely, making whatever arrests are appropriate." Pavlichenko was now addressing not only the President but the entire conference table. "And I shall not rest until we are all satisfied."

The KGB chairman knew, as did everyone else in the room, that in a very real sense Gorbachev owed his political survival to KGB. Wouldn't, in fact, be here without KGB. A lot of people who didn't think much of KGB called it Gorbachev's Faustian bargain. But it was true: Gorbachev would have been long gone without either KGB or the army behind him, and the army boys felt queasy about the man, who made no secret of his intention to slash military spending. But the people at KGB, infinitely more cosmopolitan than their military comrades, saw the sense in Gorbachev's plan, saw that he wasn't weakening Russia but (in the long run, anyway) strengthening it, and so they stood behind him throughout the turmoil.

Pavlichenko did not have to vocalize what was on everybody's mind: the delicate negotiations that were about to bring the President of the United States to Moscow for a summit meeting might easily be wrecked by the bomb in the Kremlin Armory—the President could easily, and justifiably, cancel on the grounds of security.

The American President was to arrive in early November to observe Revolution Day, the date of the Bolshevik Revolution. As a bit of propaganda the occasion was unmatched: it legitimated the Bolshevik Revolution, placing it, in the eyes of the West, in the same category as the French and American revolutions. No question the White House hadn't taken the decision easily, and the President was as aware as anyone that this was an important gift to Gorbachev, more than just a simple reciprocation of Gorbachev's previous visit to the United States.

There was more.

Two months earlier, the Politburo had voted to convey a private invitation to the American President: to observe, with his wife and the American secretary of state, the anniversary celebration of the Bolshevik Revolution. This was an honor the Politburo usually accorded to foreign Communist leaders of the highest rank. Some in the Politburo had opposed the invitation as a form of ideological pollution, but they had nevertheless voted to extend the invitation.

And the President had accepted.

Gorbachev now looked up. His theatrical timing was, as usual, impeccable.

"Well, I received a communication from the President last night. He expressed his regret as well as his firm belief that we were as angered and disturbed at the death of the girl as he was. He also said he looked forward, once again, to meeting with me in Moscow on November 7. And standing with us together on Lenin's tomb."

Several of Gorbachev's supporters smiled at the cleverness with which he had played his hand. The opponents, though similarly impressed, were more reserved.

"The question remains," came the querulous voice of Yegor K. Ligachev, Gorbachev's most outspoken opponent, almost shouting, "how was this incident allowed to happen? Who is behind this? Is it true—*are* we not fully in control? Are there elements that threaten not only the summit but *our very existence*?"

"We will meet again in a few days—" Gorbachev began, but then he noticed Pavlichenko's raised index finger. "Yes?"

Pavlichenko spoke softly. "The President may not be fully in control of his own government."

"I don't understand."

"The results of the forensic analysis of the bomb were brought to me this morning," the KGB chairman continued gravely. "The bomb was no Molotov cocktail. It was not dynamite. It was a C-4 plastique explosive." He paused for emphasis. "This particular type of plastique is manufactured only in the United States."

The faces of the men around the table were visibly shocked. There was a long, electric silence.

The President finally raised his eyes from his legal pad. "This meeting is sealed," he said, meaning that not even closest aides were to be informed of what had just been discussed in the room. *Yes,* he thought, *something is going on.* He shook his head slowly; his instincts rarely failed him. *Something ominous.* He passed a handkerchief over his damp forehead, and rose to call the meeting to a close.

10

Boston

The hall outside Alfred Stone's hospital room in the coronary-care unit rang with the insistent, irregular beeps of a dozen cardiac monitors, all at different pitches: a discordant, jangled electronic chorus. His room was small and bare, furnished with an intravenous stand, a beige telephone, a television mounted high on the wall opposite his bed, and, directly above the bed, a monitor on which a jagged green line traced his heartbeat across the screen. The ledge beside the plate-glass window was bare as well;

it was too soon for it to be cluttered with flowers. The customary hospital smells wafted through the corridors, the vague odors of tomato soup and rubbing alcohol.

Alfred lay asleep on the bed, under a light-blue blanket. He seemed to have aged twenty years: his face was drawn and chalky-white. A clear plastic tube ran from a tank behind him to his nose and up around his ear, carrying humidified oxygen. Three wires, affixed to his chest, were connected to the monitor.

"Your father awoke from a nap yesterday afternoon with heartburn and a crushing pain in his chest," the nurse explained wearily. She was tall and mannish, somewhere in her fifties, her gray-flecked black hair pulled back into a bun so tight Stone wondered whether it hurt. "He wisely called an ambulance. In the emergency room they determined he'd had a mild heart attack."

"How soon will he be well enough to go home?" Stone asked. "Tomorrow?"

"I should say not." She tugged at some loose skin at her jawline. "A few days here at the very least. He's been admitted for what we call a rule-out MI. That means we'll be following his blood chemistries, seeing if there are any changes in his EKG, monitoring his blood pressure."

"Is he on any medications?"

"A beta-blocker called Inderal," she said brusquely, as if it were none of his business. "All right? Anything else?"

"No, that's fine. Thank you."

For a long time, Charlie stared at his father. In sleep he seemed to have shed the cares of the world, his mouth slightly open, his breathing regular.

A few minutes later, Alfred Stone woke up, looked around disorientedly, and smiled when he saw Charlie. "Is that you, Charlie? How was the party?" he asked. He reached over to the night table and retrieved his glasses, then slowly eased them on. "There," he said. "Thanks for coming."

"Feeling any better?" Stone asked gently.

"A little. Mostly just weak now."

"It's a scary thing to go through." Stone looked at his

father penetratingly, wondering what sort of terrible stress could bring on a heart attack all of a sudden.

"The party . . . ?" Alfred Stone began.

"Uneventful."

"Winthrop," the elder Stone said, smiling wanly. "That old generous bastard."

Generous! Stone thought. *If you knew* . . . But he said only: "He sends his regards." There was now no question in his mind that Alfred Stone knew far more about this Lenin document than he was saying.

"Can you ask the Hovanians to take care of Peary? They've done it before. They like him."

"Everyone likes him. Anything I can get you—books, magazines, anything like that?"

"Oh, I'm fine. One of the nurses, that big English one, gave me *People* magazine. Have you ever seen it? What a fascinating magazine."

"I read it every week in line at the supermarket."

"Listen, Charlie," Alfred Stone said, and halted.

"Yes?"

"Well, I hope you didn't ask Winthrop about—about that matter you mentioned to me."

Stone didn't know how to reply. He had rarely had to lie to his father. The most important thing now was not to upset him. "I didn't ask him," he said at last.

"You know, you really took me by surprise. I suppose you could tell."

Stone nodded.

"I had heard of it. You know, they asked me about it at the hearings."

Stone, reluctant to press him, nodded again.

"That trip to Russia I took. The one that got me in all that trouble. I've always told you I was on official business, a fact-finding mission, a visit to our embassy in Moscow."

"There was another reason?"

"A favor to Winthrop. Winthrop couldn't get a visa to Russia."

"A favor?" Stone asked. The word sounded ominous as he spoke it.

"He was so good to me, Winthrop. Out of hundreds of historians in the country, he selected me to serve in the White House. I could hardly refuse."

"What did he want you to do?"

"He wanted me to meet with a woman. A real beauty."

"The woman you were photographed meeting with in the Moscow metro. And what did Lehman want you to do, exactly?"

"Very little. Just meet with her, on the sly, and give her a document he had concealed in a framed photograph of himself. What I mean is, he said it was a photograph, but I'm sure there was something concealed in the frame—why else would he bother? I assumed he wanted to smuggle a message to this woman, and he was unwilling to use the diplomatic pouch, which would mean relying on an American intelligence agent as a conduit. I didn't think I'd be followed to the rendezvous."

"Do you think she was a Soviet agent of some sort?"

His father frowned. "No, she wasn't."

"How do you know?"

Alfred Stone stared for a long time at the television screen, which was dark. "At first I thought she was a sweetheart of Lehman's. I thought he was helping her to get out of the country."

"But now—?"

He shrugged. "You know, Stalin died on March 5, 1953. Maybe a week before that, Winthrop asked me to go. Three days after Stalin's death, I arrived in Moscow."

"You think the document was connected in some way with Stalin's death?"

"In some way, yes. I'm convinced of it," Alfred Stone said, almost whispering. "But still—I didn't want Winthrop to be linked to it."

"You took the Fifth to protect Lehman."

"He said he'd do what he could to get me the lightest possible sentence."

"But you took the fall for him."

Alfred Stone looked around the room helplessly. "I

couldn't betray his trust." The beeps from the cardiac monitor were coming more quickly now.

Stone felt as if he would burst, wanting to shout, Do you know how he betrayed *you*?

"I often wish I'd married again," Alfred Stone said. "Margaret died so young. When *you* were so young."

Charlie examined the beige-tiled floor for a few moments, not knowing how to reply, hearing the beeps slow down; and in several minutes, his father had fallen asleep.

For ten minutes, he sat there, thinking, trying to understand why his father had accepted Lehman's betrayal, wondering how much of the truth Alfred Stone knew.

There was a noise at the door: a doctor examining the vital-signs sheet on the door. He was a pudgy, balding young man in a rumpled shirt and tie, carrying a clipboard.

"Are you Mr. Stone's son?"

"Yes."

"I'm Dr. Kass. Can I ask you a couple of questions?"

"Sure."

"Do you have any history of heart disease in your family? Do you know how your father's parents died?"

"I think his father died after a stroke."

"Is he taking any medications?"

"Not that I know of."

"Has he been under any stress lately?"

He's been under stress for forty years, Stone wanted to reply. "Yes, I think he has."

The physician strode briskly over to the bed, touched Alfred Stone's shoulder, and said, "Sorry to wake you, Professor. How are you feeling?"

"Sleepy, if you really want to know," Alfred Stone said.

"Let me just take a listen to the old ticker," Dr. Kass said, drawing back the blanket and placing a stethoscope on Alfred Stone's chest. After a minute, he said, "Sounds okay. Sounds okay."

"Probably sounds better than it feels," Alfred Stone said. He looked over to where Charlie was sitting and gave a wry smile. "As soon as you go to sleep, they wake you up. They have an instinct for it."

A few minutes later, he was fast asleep again. Charlie watched the traffic go by silently, twelve flights below. Quietly, he put his arms into the sleeves of his coat, preparing to leave, but changed his mind. He sat for a long while.

His father's eyes fluttered open. "You're still here, Charlie?"

"Yeah," Charlie said. "I am."

11

Moscow. Lefortovo Prison

All of the lurid and sexy passages had been torn out of the library's books by the inmates, even the stodgiest nineteenth-century love scenes. The prisoners were starved for sex; it was all they thought or talked about, and sometimes at night they would have what they called "séances," when one inmate would read these passages aloud to his cellmates. Or else one of them would recall, embellishing the details as he went along, a racy sexual encounter he had once had. Once, in one cell, they had even put up a photograph of Angela Davis to masturbate by.

In the KGB's Lefortovo Prison, where the porridge reminded you of burnt mucus, you thought about sex a good deal. Yet, if one were particularly inclined to read— and the conditions gave one a lot of time to do so—the library was excellent, and an inmate could get as many as five books a week, everything from Faulkner to Dickens to Lermontov to Gogol.

Stefan Yakovich Kramer, a twenty-six-year-old ambulance worker, had been in Lefortovo Prison, in central Moscow, for almost four months. He had not been tried yet, but he had been charged with violation of Article 70 of the Criminal Code—anti-Soviet agitation. That meant he had assembled with a crowd of other Jews in front of the OVIR office, which controlled emigration, to protest that they and their relatives and friends weren't being allowed out of the country.

Sure, there was a lot of talk about the new Russia under Gorbachev. And, indeed, more people were emigrating than in many years. But for every ten who applied to leave, maybe one was allowed to go.

Jews, ethnic Germans, and a few other minorities were officially permitted to leave the country. Yes. The Soviet government had announced to the world that everybody who wanted out was gone. And yet the imprisonment of innocent people continued.

Yes, there was talk about the new Russia, the "glasnost," and all that. But to Stefan, it was all bald lies.

Stefan, his brother, Avram, and his father, Yakov, had each applied three times, and three times, for the most ludicrous reasons, they had been turned down. Yakov had served in the Red Army during World War II, and now the authorities were maintaining that he knew state secrets, which hadn't even been true forty years ago. And the gates had slammed shut. And when Stefan and a few dozen of his friends and acquaintances had attempted a pathetic, scraggly demonstration, the secret police had shooed them away. And arrested only him, Stefan Yakovich Kramer.

What made things even worse was that his father had spent time in the gulag, the Stalinist concentration camps, for little more than being a Jew unlucky enough to have been taken prisoner of war by the Nazis. Although Yakov Kramer had managed, by dint of hard work and some clever politicking, to land a job as an editor at a prestigious publishing house, Progress Publishers, that was all in jeopardy now. Even after applying three times to leave the country, he was fortunate enough to be allowed to keep his job—most people were fired from their jobs the instant they applied to emigrate—but now he had been told that if he applied again he would lose the job, in a country without unemployment benefits.

There were people who were content, even happy, in the Soviet Union, but the Kramers were not among them.

Stefan sat on his cot, leaning against the cracked paint of the cement wall, and read aloud to his cellmate, Anatoly Ivanovich Fyodorov. Fyodorov was a rough sort, a tall, gangly, ill-educated guy who enjoyed talking. Stefan liked him. He had managed to pry from Fyodorov his life story. Fyodorov had been a soldier in Afghanistan who'd been disillusioned by the experience, he said, then a machinist in an automobile shop who had been caught for petty black-marketeering—moonlighting as a car mechanic. Fyodorov was his third cellmate in three months; the first two seemed to have been "stoolies," provocateurs, put in to try to wrest information out of him and incriminate him further. But Fyodorov was different; for weeks, he had little but the most elemental interest in the nature of Stefan's "crime," and, if anything, he incriminated himself. Obviously the prison authorities did what they could to provoke the political prisoners, and after a while, if their efforts failed, they gave up. Fyodorov was a little crude, but he was genial, and he loved to hear Stefan read poetry.

Stefan read aloud:

"Wretched and abundant,
Oppressed and powerful,
Weak and mighty,
Mother Russia!"

He looked up at the ceiling, around the room at the washbasin and the lavatory pan, and eventually over to Fyodorov, who was smiling.

"Who wrote that?" Fyodorov asked.

"Nekrasov. *Who Is Happy in Russia?*"

"Ah, that's brilliant. Read it again."

Stefan did, and when he was done, Fyodorov said, "The answer, my friend, is no one."

"Anatoly Ivanovich, I don't think either one of us is a good judge of happiness."

A few weeks later, Fyodorov was almost killed in a prison brawl during the evening meal. He was saved by Stefan.

Fyodorov had provoked some petty smuggler, who

somehow had gotten himself a knife. The guards were talking among themselves, clear across the room. Stefan suddenly glimpsed the flash of steel and slammed his body against the attacker's, throwing him off-balance, giving Fyodorov just enough time to get to his feet and subdue the smuggler.

"Thanks," Fyodorov grunted. "I owe you."

Once a day, the prisoners were allowed to exercise, walking or running on the prison's fenced-in roof under the supervision of the guards. Fyodorov normally used the exercise sessions as an opportunity to tell Stefan the things he would be afraid to say aloud in the cell—afraid because the guards were known to listen at the judas holes in the doors.

"Is your brother as naïve as you?" Fyodorov asked, somewhat out of breath from the running.

Stefan easily kept up a pace alongside. "Naïve? My brother's clean. He's smart; he doesn't get involved in politics. What do you mean, naïve?"

"A tree that falls and isn't heard falling hasn't fallen," Fyodorov said. "You can complain and complain until you turn blue, but if no one hears your complaint, it's as if it hasn't been uttered. If you want to be allowed out of the country, you have to make your complaint heard."

"We tried that already," Stefan said. "You suggest we do it again—gather together in a public place and stick placards up in the air and get thrown back into prison, is that it?" The rage that he had kept bottled up erupted momentarily. "God damn it all, I was thrown in this stinking place for assembling peacefully and asking for my rights under the Soviet constitution."

"Ah, fuck that. You're a bunch of trees that haven't fallen, you understand? The only thing the Soviet government understands is violence. Everyone knows that. You want to be let out, be a troublemaker. What you need to do is to appeal to world public opinion."

"A letter to the editor of *The New York Times*, is that what you mean?" Stefan asked bitterly.

"Come on. The Kremlin is terrified of a breakdown of public order. Don't you understand that?"

They were silent for a moment as they passed a guard, and then resumed the conversation. "You know nothing about bombs, do you?" Fyodorov asked.

"Bombs?"

"I owe you, man."

"I don't want to know anything about bombs."

"Look. You never know what you might want to know someday."

As they began another lap around the roof, Stefan started to protest, but something held him back, and he listened.

Over the next few weeks, Fyodorov taught Stefan all he knew about the making of bombs, about blasting caps and chemical pencils, dynamite and plastic. Each afternoon exercise period on the prison roof became a tutorial session. Fyodorov lectured, then interrogated, conducting his lessons in a Socratic manner. Fyodorov had done this sort of thing in Afghanistan, he explained.

It was teacher and student, master and apprentice, the car mechanic lecturing the young intellectual ambulance driver. They grew closer. "You've saved my life," Fyodorov once told him, in a rare, fleeting moment of emotion. "They could have put me in with any fucking stoolie. The old guy with the crippled hand. Any of those guys. Instead, they put me in with a literate, intelligent man. Me, a lousy black-market car jockey who got caught, with someone like you. I think they expected us to kill each other."

"It's nice to have a captive audience," Stefan said simply. He could not help liking the guy, someone his father would have dismissed as *nyekulturnii*, an uncultured boor.

It was not easy to describe the working of unseen mechanical objects, but Fyodorov did his best to describe the shape and appearance of the weapons of terrorism that he had learned to use in Kabul. Naturally mechanical, Fyodorov had figured out how to use the things on his own, he said, and although he had no use for them himself, he would teach anyone who wanted to know. Not many in Russia wanted to know. A few years ago, he said, a bunch of Estonians wanted to set off a bomb in the metro, and he managed to turn up some dynamite and some blasting caps from a source in Odessa—who in turn had gotten the stuff from East Germany and Poland and Czechoslovakia—and then he taught the Estonians how to use it. The underground trade in explosives in the Soviet Union was tiny and impossible to penetrate if you weren't well trusted, but Fyodorov had friends going back a long way.

"Probably you'll never come across something this sophisticated," Fyodorov told him in one of their last sessions on the prison roof. "I haven't seen a trembler switch in years, but they exist, and if you can find one you've got a fine switch for a car bomb."

"Trembler switch?"

"Or a vibration switch. Motion or vibration can close the switch, completing a circuit, setting off the bomb. It's a fairly simple apparatus, and not very big. A cylinder not much more than an inch and a half in diameter, about four inches long. There's a small copper ball inside a small cup. Around the edges of the cup, but not touching, are vertical copper rods that close to form a cage. Motion causes the ball to roll, bridging the gap between the cup and the cage, closing the switch. Can you envision it?"

"Yes," Stefan said. "For a car bomb, right?"

"Exactly. When you turn the car's motor on, it vibrates, and that motion can set the bomb off. Simple but ingenious. The best things are simple. There are other, more complicated things. Accelerometers and transducers that convert mechanical energy into electric energy. But I like the simple things."

Fyodorov told him about even more sophisticated things. "Hypersensitive fuses," he announced. "Oh, there's all kinds of stuff. A couple of years ago, the American CIA sabotaged a Middle Eastern terrorist group by giving them explosives with fuses that go off prematurely when they're jostled a bit. You see, there are lots and lots of tricks. The technology is fascinating."

* * *

A month later—just days before each of them was to be tried—they were released, suddenly and unexpectedly. Each was called out of the cell, brought before a commander, and given the good news. The two of them returned to their cell and waited for the guards to come and escort them out of the prison, and Fyodorov looked at Stefan Yakovich for a long time. "Hey, comrade," he said. "You got me through these four months. Your stories, your jokes. The Nekrasov and the Gogol. You got me through. And you saved my fucking life. I owe you."

12

New York

Saul Ansbach's private club was located in an old gray building on West 46th Street. A brass plaque on its white-painted door read PHOENIX CLUB. Inside the door, a broad staircase led up to a cloakroom, where dark herringbone topcoats hung beneath a long rack of fedoras: this was the kind of place where members wore hats, while the rest of the world walked around bare-headed. It was, of course, all-male: precisely the sort of place Charlotte found offensive.

They were New York's Brahmins who, some decades ago, had reluctantly admitted to their ranks gentlemen who, though distinguished partners in the right law firms and presidents of good, quiet banks and corporations, were not old-line New York. Saul had been asked to join when he was a partner in the prestigious law firm of Sheffield & Simpson, during a hiatus from his Agency career. No doubt the Phoenix Club's members enjoyed having among them a man so powerful in American intelligence.

Ansbach had taken Stone to lunch here every few months or so since the first time in New Haven, when he was trying to recruit Stone for Parnassus; they still met here from time to time, whenever Saul wanted to have a long conversation.

"I'm sorry about your father," Ansbach said. "He'll get through it with flying colors, though. He's a strong man."

"I hope you're right," Stone said. He had just taken a cab in from LaGuardia, and he felt peculiar about leaving his father alone in the hospital.

Ansbach put on his reading spectacles, Benjamin Franklin half-glasses, and held the photocopy up about twelve inches away from his eyes. Stone watched him examine the documents. Ansbach's forehead was creased with tension.

"You're right," he said at length. "This 'M-3' does refer to a U.S. mole in Moscow. But it's the first I've ever heard of it."

Stone nodded. A steward cleared away the remains of Ansbach's prime rib and Stone's hamburger. "Mr. Ansbach, would you like coffee?" he asked.

Saul nodded. "We both would." He continued, waving his hands in airy circles as if to push his thoughts along: "You think your father gave this Lenin Testament to a woman in Moscow on behalf of Winthrop."

"He handed over a document. It may have been the Lenin Testament."

"So Winthrop used your father to convey something, presumably not merely a framed photograph, to this woman, who then conveyed it to an American mole."

"A theory. But you're the boss; what do you think?" Stone wondered fleetingly why Ansbach was sweating even more copiously than usual. The room was not especially warm.

"That must be it," Ansbach said. He took off his half-glasses and put on his black-framed ones. "Jesus. We had a mole in Moscow I've never been informed of. Could that be what this whole thing is all about now? Charlie—the man the FBI interrogated—this Alden Cushing—you recognize the name?"

The steward returned, set down two bone-china cups, and poured coffee in silence.

"Lehman's business partner from years ago," Stone said. "He might be someone to talk to, if he's still around. Saul, what's the matter? I've never seen you like this."

"Cushing's dead." He took a small sip of coffee. His hands were trembling ever so slightly, and he spilled a few drops of coffee on the heavy white linen tablecloth. The drops expanded to large tan circles.

"Well, scratch that idea."

"No, Charlie. You don't understand. It was on the AP newswire this morning."

"This *morning*? My God!"

Stone shoved his coffee away. "The coincidence isn't . . ." He faltered, and began again: "He was at that dinner with Stalin in 1952. Could it be a coincidence that he just died?"

"But what do this mole and the Lenin Testament have to do with each other?" Ansbach said impatiently. "And what the hell does this all have to do with what's going on in Moscow?"

"Let's take one thing at a time," Stone said. "Like the remark Stalin made, to the effect that the esteemed Lenin is made of wax."

"What are you getting at?" Ansbach examined his fingernails.

"Just this," Stone said, and, changing his mind, he drew the coffee cup toward himself and took a swallow. "I spent a few minutes on the phone before I left Boston. Doing a little research. You know, it's entirely *possible* that Lenin's body is wax. Apparently the state of the art has gotten so good that a talented restorative artist—not just anyone, I'm saying, but someone really good—can create a replica of a human face so incredible that you couldn't tell, standing a few feet away, that it's not the real thing."

Ansbach drained his coffee cup and signaled the steward for another. "You're going to connect this to the HEDGEHOG report, I hope."

Stone continued: "Then there's the story of Evita." He closed his eyes to aid his memory. "In 1952 she died, when she was in her early thirties. Cancer. Juan called in an embalming specialist, who knew all the most sophisticated techniques. This fellow had developed a method that used an arterial injection of paraffin and formalin, which prevented dehydration." He recited: "Alcohol, glycerine, formalin, and thymol. Then he'd immerse a body in a solution of—of nitrocellulose dissolved in trichloroethylene and acetate, to leave a thin plasticlike film on the body."

"My God, Charlie. This from memory? You've got a mind like a goddamned Steinway concert grand, I'd forgotten. Okay, what's the connection?"

"Juan Perón wanted his beloved Evita to be on permanent display, the way Lenin is in Moscow. He was adamant about this, and even when Evita was on her deathbed they wouldn't allow her to take any drugs that might counteract the embalming chemicals, make embalming impossible."

Ansbach glanced at Stone sharply. "Chemicals?"

"Quite a number of drugs can act on the tissues in such a way as to block the infusion of the embalming solutions. They break down the body's capillary system so that when embalming is attempted it doesn't work. There's no osmotic pressure, the embalming fluid doesn't filter adequately, and the electrolytic balance is thrown off. So the embalming is incomplete and won't last."

"These drugs—do they include, for example, poisons?"

"Exactly," Stone said. "Arsenic, strychnine, any number of poisons can block the process. Other stuff, too. It's often not easy to embalm a man who's been poisoned."

"Jesus," Ansbach said. "That explains . . ."

"There are stories—just rumors, you know, but fairly widespread—that Lenin was poisoned. That Stalin had him done away with. I remember reading something about that in Trotsky's memoirs. I mean, nothing more than unsubstantiated blather. But still."

Ansbach nodded. "I've been hearing that rumor around Langley for decades."

"Do you know of a book called *Face of a Victim*? It

was published in the fifties by a Russian woman named Elizabeth Lermolo.''

"No.''

"In it, I remember this woman said that, while in an NKVD prison, she met an old man who was Lenin's personal chef in his last years. On the morning Lenin died, the old guy brought in breakfast, and Lenin signaled that he had something to say—he couldn't speak, but he slipped the guy a note saying he'd been poisoned.''

"The *founder* of the Soviet Union . . .'' Ansbach said quietly. "If it's true—then you're right. My God. The consequences would be enormous. The embalming of Lenin couldn't possibly have lasted, because he—the very founder of the Soviet state—was poisoned.'' He was silent while the waiter refilled his cup. "That's the last thing Gorbachev needs made public.'' Something was odd, almost automatic, about the way Saul was speaking, as if his mind was elsewhere.

"Saul, I'm not telling you anything you don't know,'' Stone said. "What's going on?''

Ansbach exhaled noisily. "Just . . . Just lay off, Charlie. Lay off it.''

"What are you saying?''

"Look, you know as well as I do that this isn't something purely historical.''

"Obviously. But it still doesn't explain how this mole M-3 is connected. What are you trying to tell me, Saul?''

"Nothing, Charlie. Just an instinct. A smell. This whole thing has the rotten smell of an intelligence operation gone bad, and I think you're just lifting up a corner of the rug. I shudder to think what you'll find if you keep lifting.''

"You're beginning to sound paranoid, Saul.''

"As my friend Henry Kissinger once said, Just because you're paranoid doesn't mean they're not really out to get you.''

"He wasn't the first to say it, Saul.''

"Look. You know damned well that the Agency has ways of expressing its displeasure. They—we—don't go in much for legal niceties. They can do more than terminate your contract."

Stone shook his head slowly, contemplatively. "I'm not really concerned about that," he said, his voice steely. "I think you know how important this is to me. It's a question of my father's reputation. His life."

"You're not going to drop this, Charlie, are you?"

"Not until I learn the truth about what happened to my father."

"Your father was *framed*, damn it! End of story. The *why* isn't important anymore."

"I notice you haven't given me any explicit orders. You're scared about this, and I can't blame you."

Ansbach gave him a long, stony glare. "Christ. What do you want, Charlie?"

"There's an old woman, living today, who actually was a private secretary to Lenin. Emigrated in the twenties, lives under an alias. I came across her name in one of the data banks."

"I know. I heard about her from Bill Donovan, in my OSS days. So?"

"I want to know her whereabouts. I think it's a good place to start."

Ansbach gave another sigh. "I don't like this at all," he said, and pushed back his chair.

Several hours later, Stone returned to his West Side apartment with photocopies of the dossier he'd taken from Lehman's archives. He removed his coat and hung it in the hall closet, beside the mountain-climbing equipment he so rarely had a chance to use these days.

He knelt down and ran a hand across the smooth marble floor, feeling for a slight ridge, which he located after a few seconds. Grasping the ridge, which even on close inspection looked like nothing more than a slight defect in the grout between two tiles, he pushed at it. One tile slid open, revealing a small safe. He dialed it open and placed the original dossier in it, alongside a small wad of cash, some papers, and the Smith & Wesson revolver he had used maybe once or twice, only for target practice at

a range in Lexington, Massachusetts, years ago. He'd
bought his father an identical one.

He closed the safe and slid the tile over it. Then, as
he circled the room, saw the flashing ruby light on his
answering machine, a winking red eye.

He hit the playback button. One was from a woman
he had met at a party and hoped he'd never hear from
again. One from his father, calling to thank him for coming
by and to say he was feeling better.

And the next two were from Saul Ansbach.

Saul sounded increasingly desperate. His words were
at times drowned out by the roar of traffic; clearly he'd
made the calls from a street phone. Ordinarily, Saul would
have used a secure line.

*"Charlie, it's Saul. I'm at the law firm. Call me as soon
as you get in."*

Beep.

Ansbach was still "of counsel" at Sheffield & Simpson,
and occasionally he and Charlie would meet there, when
Saul was attending a firm meeting and wanted to see an
analysis Stone had done.

*"It's Saul. You—Listen, you're on to something. I want
you to meet me at the law firm. Not at the office. I'll be
there from seven to around eight. And listen—don't call me
at the Foundation. I don't trust the phones there. This is
serious fucking business, Charlie."* There was a long, long
pause, during which an ambulance siren could be heard.
*"How much time do I get on this fucking machine? Charlie,
listen. I got some stuff for you. Had it flown in by courier—
pulled some strings."* Another long pause; the roar of a
truck. *"Does this machine cut you off? Charlie, shit. Get
over here."*

Stone raced for the door.

Sheffield & Simpson occupied the twelfth, fourteenth,
and fifteenth floors—there was no thirteenth—of a stately
old twenty-floor building near Wall Street, a building with
a grace and simplicity that the newer structures lacked.

Stone arrived a little after eight. The evening rush
hour was just about over; a few stragglers in topcoats and

carrying briefcases emerged from the ancient elevators. He'd always liked this old building—it whispered stability and solidity and longevity. The elevator was paneled in cherry wood, with lamps in sconces mounted on the walls.

He pressed the button for the fourteenth floor and leaned back against the elevator walls, admiring the well-oiled smoothness of the old machine. The elevator's doors opened at the fourteenth floor a few seconds later. There were a few lights still on; although most of the secretaries were gone, several of the associates were working. Stone silently thanked the deities that he hadn't become a lawyer.

And then he remembered that Saul would probably want to meet him upstairs, on the fifteenth floor, which at night was mostly empty; it was taken up by rooms of filing cabinets, old law books and reporters, discarded equipment. Half the floor was unrented. But there were a few conference rooms there, too. Whenever Ansbach wanted to meet in privacy, he chose one of the empty conference rooms upstairs.

Stone took the elevator up one flight, to the dimly lit fifteenth floor. Fluorescent light flickered from alternating ceiling panels; there was no one in sight. No sign yet of Ansbach. He passed a plate-glass window and noticed the view of New York twinkling below. The two conference rooms were halfway down the hall, on the right. Both doors were closed. Stone turned the knob of the first door and pulled it open.

"Saul Ansbach," he called out heartily.

And whispered: "Saul?"

What he saw made him freeze in terror.

Saul Ansbach, the big beefy man, sat reclining in a cushioned chair beside a conference table, staring straight ahead through his heavy black-framed glasses. His head lolled peculiarly. The eyeglass lenses were partially obscured by rivulets of blood that ran down from a neat, perfectly circular hole in his forehead, just above his brow. His hands were curled into loose fists, as if he'd been about to rise from his seat to challenge an intruder. Before he'd been shot dead.

Stone was unable to emit a sound. He opened his

mouth, his mind whirling with terror. He took a step forward, then a step back, before he heard the creaking of a
floorboard, the ever-so-faint groan of the wooden floor
beneath the wall-to-wall carpeting, beneath someone's
tread, a few feet away in the hall.

13

He took a few silent steps backward.

It was there again, the scrunch of a footfall in the
corridor. Someone was unquestionably there, standing,
shifting his weight.

The sound was coming from off to his left, outside
the room.

The blood that covered Saul Ansbach's face was visibly wet, sticky. He had just been killed, within the last
thirty minutes at most.

The killer was out there.

Stone turned his head slowly and saw the figure of a
man, poorly illuminated in the flickering hall light. He
stood perhaps ten or fifteen feet away, a squat, compact
man wearing a black leather jacket with wide lapels. Small
eyes, a bull neck. Jet-black hair combed straight back.
Something bulky concealed in the jacket's pocket, probably a gun. The man was looking directly at Stone, with
a calm expression of dull incuriosity.

And he saw what Stone knew, what Stone had seen.

Stone's heart hammered, his body surging with adrenaline. With an enormous lurch, he bounded down the
hallway.

The man was running now, great loping strides.

Careening down the hall, around the corner, Stone
whipped past the elevator, unable to see anything but the
stairway door twenty yards away.

The man was gaining on him, accelerating his pace
with amazing agility, a great burst of speed.

Jesus oh Jesus oh Jesus. Stone had never moved so fast. Please God get me out of here oh God. He flew across the space, grabbing at the door handle. If the door is locked—

The door was unlocked.

Thank you.

The man in the leather jacket was mere feet away. Stone lunged into the stairwell without looking, momentarily almost losing his balance as he clattered down the stairs. The man was behind him, his footsteps thundering on the metal-and-concrete steps. Stone could *feel* the man behind him, could feel the rush of cold air.

There was an agonized yelp of pain as the man stumbled. Stone could hear, as his legs pumped down, down, the impact of the man's leg against the steel.

Must get out of this stairwell, out of the direct line of fire. Why wasn't the man shooting? Now, for sure, he would, but Stone couldn't look back, wouldn't know when it came, when the bullet came singing toward the back of his head.

Out of the stairwell. Another door: Stone grabbed at the knob and felt the surge of relief when it *opened*. It couldn't be locked, Stone knew that; he would have to run. How many flights had he descended? Three? Four? The floor was dark, a deserted office, shut down for the night.

And nowhere to go.

The man had regained his balance; Stone had a few seconds. He could hear the footsteps sounding.

Desperately, he looked around for a way out.

He lunged at the elevator button, jamming his thumb against the down button, which lit up. Somewhere the elevator machinery hummed into life.

Oh, God, there was no time!

Stone ran toward the stairwell door, crazily searching for a lock of some kind, and when he found none, he wrapped his hands around the knob and *pulled* toward himself with all of his considerable mountain-climber's strength, pulling the door shut, and then the squat man with the jet-black hair was there, throwing himself against the door, tugging at the knob with more force than Stone could counter, and then—

The elevator, with a high-pitched *bing,* had arrived, its doors yawning lazily open, its interior light blazing into the dark lobby, its cherry-wood paneling bright and welcoming. Stone had no choice. He tore himself from the doorknob, lunging in an awkward sideways motion toward the elevator at the instant that the stairwell door swung open, and he was *inside* the elevator, and the man was in the lobby, extending an automatic gun and—

The explosion was enormous. The bullet crashed into the closing doors as the man jammed his free hand in between them, the elevator doors closing agonizingly *slowly* around the man's extended powerful fingers, which grasped the inside of the door to trigger the automatic opening mechanism—

But there was none. The ancient elevator had no modern safety precautions, and its doors were closed inexorably. The man yanked his hand back with a roar of pain, and the elevator sank slowly. For the first time in endless minutes, Stone took a giant gulp of breath.

He had escaped.

The elevator would outmove his pursuer, would descend much faster than the man could run, and it was the only one. In a haze he watched the numbers light up as it moved, with steadily increasing speed, down the building, down toward the main floor and freedom—

And then the elevator jolted to a stop.

Please God *no,* Stone shouted inwardly. The elevator was between floors, its power source no doubt, somehow, shut off.

He was trapped.

"God *damn* it," he said aloud, looking around at the gleaming wood of the interior. "Fucking stupid move." His voice shook with fear. He was a prisoner in this elevator cage. He lashed out wildly and struck the buttons for each floor. Nothing. The elevator did not move. He formed his hands into two claws and inserted them into the microscopic space between the double doors. There was *give,* he was forcing them apart. Behind the doors he could make out the discolored grayish concrete: he was definitely between floors. But the doors would open no farther than an inch or two.

He was trapped.

Suddenly he knew what the man would do. Of course. You could call the elevator up, or down, express, by throwing one switch, located somewhere in the building. Even the old elevators like this one could be moved from the first floor to the top, or the top floor to the first, without stopping in between.

He was a prisoner.

What was taking the man so long? Do it, just do it, get it over with, Stone chanted to himself. Get it over with. Jesus God, this is it. Whoever had murdered Saul Ansbach would certainly not hesitate to do the same to a witness.

He looked around the car. He could hear the blood rush past his ears, the sound of the ocean captured in a seashell, the sound of terror. He was sealed in this gleaming wooden box, paneled and elegant, an electric coffin.

—With an escape hatch on the ceiling. There it was. Of course; all elevators had them, were *required* to have them. A panel on the white-painted metal ceiling, a large rectangle fastened with protruding thumb screws. He reached his arms upward, as far as they would go, but the ceiling was too high; he could not quite reach it.

Think! Climbing the crack on a mountain's face, you had to make do with the elements, with whatever was there. What was here? Wooden paneling: a toehold. And—oh, thank God—a brass fixture, the sconce that held the lamp. He grabbed it; it held firm. He pulled at it with all his strength, lifting himself up, grabbing a hold on the panel's indentation, and with his left hand—yes—he twirled the thumbscrews, one, and then another, and then, in one sudden motion, he slammed against the hatch. With a metallic groan, years of corrosion and disuse at last gave way, and the panel was open.

And he was looking up at absolute darkness.

The elevator shaft.

He pulled himself up until he could reach into the hole, grasping the sides. His palms sliced against something sharp, and he could feel the skin torn open. The stars of pain shot through his left arm.

With his other hand, more carefully now, he grabbed, and thrust his head and shoulders into the dark opening. He had leverage; he pulled himself up, his hands slapping against greasy metal.

He knelt atop the elevator cabin and inhaled the dank, oil-smelling air. His eyes were straining to become accustomed to the pitch-darkness of the elevator shaft, but it wasn't absolute pitch-darkness. Somewhere way up there was a meager source of bluish light, maybe a skylight, and his surroundings came into sudden, horrible focus.

The vertical tunnel was perhaps eight feet by eight feet by—well, it was impossible to say how tall it was. His legs struck something: the coiled steel hoist cable on top of the car, which stretched vertically the length of the shaft, as far as Stone could see.

Terrified, Stone inspected further. On three sides the shaft was encased in pale glazed bricks; the other face was concrete. Two of the walls were crisscrossed with horizontal steel girders.

He could make out the rails on which the elevator rode, the vertical steel beams that seemed suspended in the shaft, two feet away from the walls. Were they electrified? If he grasped them, would he . . . ?

"Now what the fuck?" Stone said. Get back into the elevator, his instincts told him. You can get killed here.

And I *will* get killed in there, another inner voice responded.

Gingerly he reached out to the steel rail, his fingers coming closer and closer and then wispily brushing against it and—nothing. No. Thank God, it was not electrified. With one hand, and then the other, he gripped the rail.

There was only one way to go: up.

He slid his shoes, leather dress shoes not meant for climbing, against the elevator car's ceiling, until they hit the brick wall, angling the toe of his shoe into the cracks between the bricks. And slipped. The bricks were coated with some sort of grease, the deposit of decades of use. He could not get a toehold.

Layback, damn it. Just like you'd do climbing up a crack. Layback. Grab the rail and pull as hard as possible, and the simple pressure of your feet pushing against the brick will give you some traction.

Yes.

He pulled and pushed, pulled and pushed, and now he was moving up, slowly and awkwardly at first, then with increasing assurance, and then he allowed himself a glimpse above. A few more feet. He could tell he was close to the next floor: there was a vein of horizontal steel, the thing the elevator normally rested against when it came to a stop. He looked down. A mistake; the drop, even after only a minute of climbing, was dizzying. Sickening. You don't look down. Never look down; look up. He laybacked up, up, and then, from somewhere, he heard a click and then a hum. The elevator was starting up. His stomach lurched.

If it moved up, if he didn't release his hold, he would be crushed.

No.

Maniacally, he pulled himself up, then kicked at the double doors that opened into the shaft. Nothing. He flailed one arm outward, grabbing at the place where the doors met. *It would not open.* The elevator car hummed smoothly upward, ten feet away maybe, and then Stone saw the roller guides, these protruding round things connected to the double doors, the things the inner door hits, triggering the outer door. He kicked at it, *hard*—and the outer door opened. With one foot on the ledge, Stone leaped forward, and just as he did so, the top of the elevator car cracked against his shin, but he was *safe*, out of the shaft, sprawled on the floor.

His hands were bleeding, his legs scraped and bruised. He struggled to his feet and loped to the stairwell door, saw from a painted number in the stairwell that he was on the sixth-floor landing, and took the steps down three and four at a time.

The lobby was deserted, lit only by lamps from the street. His body heaving with pain and exhaustion, Stone ran toward the revolving door and out into the street.

14

Moscow

When Stefan Kramer returned to the free world—if, he mused, Moscow could really be considered "free"—he found that the world had gotten even more terrible during the four months he had been in Lefortovo Prison.

The food stores were even emptier, street crime was on the increase, people complained more bitterly than usual. He rented a room in a communal apartment with five people he barely knew, so that when he wanted a good meal he would visit his father's apartment, where Sonya, his father's lover—there was no other word for it; they weren't married—would always prepare a fine dinner of chicken and potatoes and a good hot *solyanka* soup.

Stefan didn't quite know what to make of Sonya. She was in her early sixties, with a kind face that appeared to have once been beautiful. Stefan thought of her as his mother; his real mother had died when he was a child.

There was something about Sonya—a dignity, a gravity, a gentleness—that set her apart from all the world-weary Russian women of her generation. She demanded nothing of life; she seemed to draw her oxygen only from helping others. Sometimes her timidity broke Stefan's heart.

Yet at times she seemed aloof, utterly private, impossibly remote. Then she would be distracted, her attention elsewhere, and she'd glance suddenly, sharply, at Stefan, as if she had no idea who he was, what she was doing here.

At dinner one night, barely a week after Stefan's release from Lefortovo, Sonya set down a plate of soup and placed her hand over Stefan's.

"Your brother has been arrested," she said, giving a sad glance at Yakov, who sat in pensive silence.

"*Avram?* What for?" Stefan could hardly believe it. Avram, the quiet, diligent, law-abiding researcher at the Polio Institute did not have it in him to do anything that might get him arrested.

For a moment, it looked as if his father's ruined face would contort into a cry of anguish.

"They say he wrote a letter to the Kremlin protesting their refusal to let us emigrate," Yakov replied. "They say he wrote a viciously anti-Soviet letter."

"What? That's insane. That makes no sense."

"I know," his father said sadly.

"It's a lie," Sonya put in quietly. "They must have set him up. It has to be a setup to keep you from emigrating."

"Where is he?" Stefan asked.

Sonya looked at Yakov, who suddenly bowed his head and held a crumpled napkin to his eyes, which brimmed with tears. He was unable to speak.

"He's in a *psikhushka*," Sonya said, putting her arms around Yakov's shoulders. A *psikhushka*—a Soviet psychiatric hospital-prison, the terrible place from which few ever emerged with their minds intact. "They just put him in yesterday."

"I thought they weren't putting political prisoners in those places," Stefan said.

"Well, they are," his father said.

"We've got to do something!" Stefan shouted suddenly.

"There's nothing we can do," Yakov said, looking up at his son.

Sonya shook her head dolefully, wanting to say more, but keeping her silence.

One day, a few weeks later, Stefan was shopping for food for his father and Sonya when, standing in an endless mineral-water line at Yeliseyevsky's, the food shop on Tverskaya Street that since the Revolution has been known officially as Gastronom Number 1, he spotted Fyodorov, looking ridiculously out of place.

"Hey, what the fuck are you doing here?" Stefan asked, clapping a hand on the mechanic's shoulder.

"Waiting for you, comrade," Fyodorov responded. "Where else would a nice cultured member of the intelligentsia buy his sturgeon? Actually, I saw you going in here last week, and it wasn't hard to figure out when you had your day off." He looked around, subtly, as if deciding what to buy next, and then said very quietly, "I've been asking around about you, and I heard about your brother."

Everyone always knew when someone was thrown into a *psikhushka*, and people never knew how to react. Should one be ashamed that a relative was a victim of the state's oppression? Stefan was touched that his old cellmate still cared enough to keep up with his family's misfortunes.

"Yeah," Stefan said simply.

Fyodorov said more quietly still, "Those fuckers don't stop, do they? I'm sorry to hear about it."

"Yeah, well . . ."

"Listen, comrade: I owe you."

"Oh, bullshit."

"You have a car?"

"No. Why?"

"Can you get one?"

"I suppose so—my dad's."

"Meet me tonight. I want to give you a token of my esteem."

The place Fyodorov had arranged to meet Stefan Yakovich Kramer was a deserted garage in the far south of Moscow that smelled of motor oil and gasoline. It was owned, Fyodorov explained, by a friend of his; Fyodorov used it to work on cars. Four months in jail hadn't diminished Fyodorov's enthusiasm for moonlighting.

Fyodorov emerged from under a bashed-up Zhiguli that was up on a lift. He was covered with grease.

"I didn't think you'd show up. A nice cultured boy like you."

"Come on," Stefan objected.

"I told you I owe you. Well, I called in some favors.

What I have for you is worth thousands and thousands of rubles on the black market, but that would be only if you could get it on the black market, which you can't. Since I don't believe in hiding your light under a bushel, let me tell you: it cost me a lot of nights under this goddamned lift."

He went to the back of the garage and returned with a tattered cardboard box. At first glance, it appeared to Stefan to be filled with junk—bits of wire and metal. On closer examination, he saw what it was—all of those things he had learned about on the prison roof. Somehow he had imagined them looking different. The box was filled with blocks of plastic explosives, cartridges of dynamite, chemical pencils, a couple of remote transmitters, and blasting caps.

"*Christ!*" Stefan exclaimed into the stillness.

"Enough for two car bombs and maybe three ordinary bombs. You're not going to be able to level the Central Committee building or anything, but you'll get an awful lot of attention, believe me. Now, go chop down some trees." He was beaming with pride. "Use it in good health. Think of it as a repayment."

Stefan didn't know how to reply. This was terrifying, unbelievable. The thought of his brother's arrest enraged him. But now—faced with the hardware of terrorism, the blocks of plastique, the coils of wire—Stefan was rendered speechless, paralyzed by indecision.

"I . . . I can't," he said.

"A token of my appreciation," Fyodorov said.

"But I can't. I mean it—I—"

"You're scared."

Stefan replied slowly: "Yes. I am."

"They won't release your brother. They never do. And if by some freaky chance they do, you won't recognize him, my friend."

Stefan nodded and looked around the greasy room. He was terrified someone might discover him here; he wanted to take off; yet he couldn't bring himself to abandon such a valuable, and possibly useful, gift.

"I'm here, friend. You know how to get in touch with me. And you will, my friend. You will."

15

New York

The pain exploded into a million shards, a million needles, a million stars. Stone pulled the alcohol-soaked gauze pad away from the long gash on his right cheek, then switched off the medicine-cabinet light. It was garishly bright. He had been hurt more badly than he'd realized: his face and hands were cut in a dozen places, and there was a painful contusion at the back of his head.

He would be all right, though. Even now the pain was beginning to subside. He walked slowly into his bedroom, collapsed on the bed, and examined the outside of the envelope Saul Ansbach had sent him.

The envelope. It had been slid underneath his apartment door, waiting for him when he returned, a voice from the grave.

A few minutes earlier, bleeding and out of breath, he had telephoned the New York Police Department and reported Saul's murder, then hung up before the call could be traced. It made no sense to get involved at this point.

Saul, his old friend. Murdered. Stone bit his lower lip.

The man who had chosen the shadowy world of intelligence over the safe and bland and tranquil and orderly world of corporate law.

Whoever murdered Saul must have . . . must have not wanted him investigating. . . . What were his words on the machine? *This is serious fucking business, Charlie.* And: *I don't trust the phones. . . .* Who was he afraid of? It didn't make sense for the CIA to kill their own, especially one so important in the organization. Did it?

How long, Stone wondered, before I'm linked as well? How long before it's not safe for me here?

He slid a finger under the flap of the manila envelope and tore it open. He pulled out a black-and-white, eight-by-ten glossy photograph.

Two people, a man and a woman, were sitting on a bench, conferring gravely. Around them people rushed by, blurred. Russians: Stone recognized the hats, the shoes, the clothing. The woman, too, was a Russian, a beautiful woman with delicate features, her glossy black hair in a loose chignon. Speaking to her, in earnest conversation, was someone Stone recognized well; it looked like a picture of himself. It was Alfred Stone, meeting with a Russian woman.

Could this be Sonya Kunetskaya?

Charlie turned the photo over and saw that it was stamped PROPERTY FEDERAL BUREAU OF INVESTIGATION CENTRAL FILE 002-324.

There was one more item in the envelope, a small note that bore the letterhead of Sheffield & Simpson. The scrawled, almost illegible handwriting was Saul's, evidently dashed off in great haste. Words and phrases were underlined, sometimes double-underlined.

Charlie—

You still haven't shown up, so I'm sending this by courier. Hope to God you get it.

Enclosed photo = SK. From FBI.

Bill Armitage at State and some other friends I trust say M-3 op was attempted CIA deep penetration '53 U.S.S.R.! Thinks it's rogue.

M-3 still in place!

Lenin's secretary—A. Zinoyeva—lives in East Neck, N.J. Deep cover = Irene Potter. 784 Wainwright Road.

Hold on to photo—info is power. You may need bargaining chip.

Careful, my friend.

—S.

His head thudding dully, Stone understood the message. The photo he held in his hand, the one the FBI had taken in Moscow and used as evidence against Alfred Stone, Saul had obtained from some friend at the FBI. *Not* from the CIA.

The old woman who had once been Lenin's secretary was living under a deep-cover alias, Irene Potter, provided for her by the U.S. government. Which meant she had once been useful for intelligence purposes of some kind. Otherwise, she wouldn't need a cover.

But the terrifying thing was the information Saul had got from his "friends": a *rogue* operation in 1953, involving an American mole—but unknown to responsible elements of American intelligence? A mole who was still in place in Moscow—and who would therefore be undoubtedly very, very highly placed indeed.

Was *that* the conspiracy at which the HEDGEHOG report hinted?

Nineteen fifty-three. The year was significant. It was the year of Joseph Stalin's death, a time of great turbulence in the Kremlin.

Had Alfred Stone been imprisoned to conceal an attempt to place an American agent deep into the Soviet government?

And—four decades later—had Saul Ansbach been murdered to protect the same secret? Why?

They kill their own.

I'm one of their own.

The thoughts were coming too swiftly now, their meaning too awful. Who else knew about this Lenin Testament, which—somehow, unexplainably—was connected with this rogue operation?

I do, Stone thought.

I and my father.

The notion was inconceivable.

I'm not safe here any longer. And I have to make sure my father is safe.

Boston

"What happened to you, Charlie?"

Alfred Stone was sitting up in bed, looking considerably healthier. They had disconnected him from the cardiac monitor. It was early the next morning, and Stone—who had not contacted the Parnassus office—had done his best to bandage the cuts on his face and hands.

"A foolish accident."

"You didn't go out climbing yesterday, did you?"

"That's right."

"New Hampshire."

"Right."

The large British nurse swept into the room, heedless of the conversation. "I'm just going to check your pump," she said. "Good morning, Mr. Stone."

"A pleasure to see you," Charlie said insincerely.

She finished a minute later and departed without a word.

"Did you know Rock Hudson was homosexual?" the elder Stone said. The tic had returned to his left eye; it winced as regularly as clockwork. He was nervous.

"Of course. Where'd you get that startling piece of old news?" What was *really* on his mind? Did he know what had happened? Had he heard what had happened to Saul Ansbach?

"*People* magazine. I had no idea." He smiled wanly; Stone now was certain his father was deeply anxious. "In any case, I think they're going to let me go home tomorrow."

"You're going to be well enough?"

"They seem to think so. I still feel weak, but I'm better. You didn't have a climbing accident, did you, really?"

"Really." But he wasn't fooling his father, he felt sure.

"Would you mind terribly spending tomorrow night

at the house? In case I need anything, you know." Casual, too casual. What did he *know*?

"I'd be glad to."

Stone was lost momentarily in thought. He remembered the rounded lines of the old Frigidaire that was still in his father's kitchen. The memory was vague now, remote.

I am a boy. Was it four? Five? Just a child, playing in the kitchen, already climbing everything. I'd been climbing on a dusty set of water pipes in the corner of the kitchen. Mother's not cleaning the house the way she used to. All she does now is sit at her typewriter pounding out letters. Later, when I'm older, she explains that they were letters to congressmen, civic groups, editors of newspapers, arguing Father's innocence.

Playing on the pipes, I reach up and hug a hot-water pipe—so unbelievably hot, I scream. My forearm is badly burned. Mother rushes in, terrified, hollering, a typing eraser parked behind her ear. She picks me up, crying and angry all at once. She finds the first-aid kit, bandages the burn.

And then Father comes home and sees the bandages, and he erupts like a long-dormant volcano.

I run, terrified, and cower in the crawl space under the stairs, listening. Father is beside himself with rage, pushing Mother against the Frigidaire, chanting, "What kind of mother are you? You're the only mother he has! You're the only mother he has!"

And Mother, who knows better than I why he is so crazed with anger, says through her sobs, "I didn't ask you to go to prison! I didn't make you go to prison! Be angry at him, don't be angry at me!"

Be angry at him.

He was never angry at Winthrop Lehman.

Why not?

Alfred Stone was now polishing his eyeglasses with a corner of the bedsheet. His eyes seemed luminous and penetrating. It was as if he could X-ray his son's mind and discern the thoughts within.

"Thanks, Charlie," he said distractedly. "Oh, what time is it? It's time for my show."

"Your *show*?"

"Television," Alfred Stone announced. He pushed a switch on the remote-control box beside his bed and seemed glad to have such a toy at his fingertips. "I've begun to watch the soap operas, God save us all."

Inscribed in granite on the exterior of the Boston Public Library is a slogan that takes up the length of a city block. THE COMMONWEALTH REQUIRES THE EDUCATION OF THE PEOPLE, it shouts to Copley Square, AS THE SAFEGUARD OF ORDER AND LIBERTY.

A fat lot of good education did Saul Ansbach, Stone thought grimly as he walked into the periodical reading room and found a stack of *Boston Globe*s going back two months. He began methodically to go through the newspapers, looking particularly for the obituaries.

A vagrant sat down in an easy chair a few feet away, emitting a foul odor. Stone skimmed the dog-eared newspapers all the more quickly for it.

By now, surely, the Parnassus office would know that Saul was dead. The place would be in chaos—and since Stone had been spotted, it was obviously unsafe for him there. Whoever was behind Saul's murder would be watching Stone carefully.

Which meant he would not be able to move easily— if it came to that—under his own passport. He needed another, and it seemed somehow safer to obtain it outside of New York City.

After half an hour, he found what he was looking for: a death notice for a thirty-two-year-old man who had lived in Melrose, a town north of Boston. Anywhere from late twenties to early forties would have done well; thirty-two was perfect. The man's name was Robert Gill; he had been a state worker who had been killed in an automobile accident six days earlier. Not, Stone was relieved to see, driving while intoxicated. That would have made things more difficult.

Robert Gill's address and phone number were listed

in the library's badly torn phone directory for the northern suburbs. Fortunately, there was only one Robert Gill in Melrose.

In the next few hours, Stone drove, in his rented Chevrolet, from public agency to public agency. He followed a procedure that had once been explained to him by a friend, a fastidiously dressed, high-priced private detective named Peter Sawyer.

With the information provided in the obituary—Gill's date of birth, parents' names, and so on—Stone obtained, for three dollars, a copy of Gill's birth certificate from the Commonwealth of Massachusetts Bureau of Vital Records and Statistics. Terrifically easy. Then an interminable wait at the Registry of Motor Vehicles for a copy of Robert Gill's driver's license, which he claimed he'd lost, and after an hour and a half Stone had a driver's license with his own photograph on it.

Simple.

Next he went to the Cambridge Post Office in Central Square and filled out an application for a post-office box in his own name and that of Robert Gill.

"That'll be six to eight weeks," the postal clerk, a beefy, gray-haired man, said as he looked over Stone's application, checking off various boxes. The clerk's eye fell upon a paper clip at the top of the form, and he glanced around to be sure he wasn't being seen removing the two twenty-dollar bills that Stone had attached. "I think there's a few that might have opened up recently," he said, coughingly self-consciously. "Let me check."

Stone next stopped at a passport-photo shop in downtown Boston, in Government Center, and had two color passport shots made while he waited. Armed with the driver's license and the birth certificate, he took the photographs to the passport office in the John F. Kennedy Federal Building across the street, where he filed for a replacement passport. His last one, he reported, had somehow gone missing in a recent move. You know how these things happen. Could you maybe expedite things? he asked: he was planning a trip abroad in a week.

Yes, he was told, that was possible. The passport would come in about a week or so.

Stone hoped he'd never have to use it.

As he got on the plane from Boston to Newark International Airport, he realized he had set himself on a course that had changed his life irrevocably. Now, on a hunt for the old woman who might reveal a decades-old secret—a secret that might explain Alfred Stone's disgrace, Saul Ansbach's murder, and perhaps even more—he knew that, whoever these elements were within the Agency, they'd never let him out of their grip.

Knowledge is power, Saul had told him.

Yes, but, as a member of Parnassus, surely Stone already *had* power—the knowledge he stored in his head of some of the CIA's most closely held intelligence on the Soviet Union. Was that power enough? The answer came with a sickening certainty: No.

For all the secrets he knew, there was nothing he could use to blackmail the Agency. He couldn't threaten to reveal anything; the Agency would merely shrug. He didn't know anything about their sources: they had carefully protected the origins of their intelligence even from the Parnassus elite.

I'm on my own, Stone thought, fastening his seat belt and gazing out the window at the runway.

When he landed in New Jersey, he immediately called his own line at the Parnassus Foundation. Sherry answered.

"Charlie!" She sounded surprised to hear his voice. "Where are you?"

Stone ignored her question. "Did Saul come in today, Sherry?"

She hesitated, then replied through a muffled sob, "Charlie, Saul's dead."

"Dead?"

"He was killed last night, Charlie," she managed to say, her British accent forgotten. "An accident. Langley is sending in someone to replace him, but we're all just torn apart. I can't—can't—believe it."

"You're quite sure it was an accident, Sherry?"

"What are you talking about? They told us. I mean, they—"

They told us. The cover-up had begun. Stone hung up abruptly, inserted another quarter, and called Lenny Wexler's number. The Foundation's telephones were secure, Stone knew, but this unprotected incoming line was risky without a scrambler. Yet he had no choice now.

Lenny himself answered. He sounded curiously distant. "Where've you been, Charlie?" he said. "Did you hear?"

"Lenny, I *saw*. Saul was shot to death."

"No, he wasn't," Wexler replied cautiously. "He got into a car accident. Charlie, I know you're upset—"

"*Damn* it, Lenny. What kind of bullshit is this? Who are you cooperating with? Where the hell is your loyalty?"

Now Lenny spoke quickly, softly. "Charlie, stay the fuck away from here. They'll get you next. Stay away from here, and me, and—"

And the line went dead. Lenny had been cut off.

The taste of fear was metallic in Stone's mouth.

16

Moscow

The day after his late-night garage meeting with Fyodorov, Stefan learned from his father that they would be allowed to visit Avram, Stefan's older brother, at the Serbsky Institute of Forensic Psychiatry, in which he was imprisoned. Rarely are *psikhushka* patients permitted to see anyone from the outside world, but Stefan and his father did not question this unusual good luck.

Instead, they were, both of them, filled with a corrosive anger at the capriciousness of Soviet justice, which could place Avram, a healthy and happy man, into a mental hospital. The world believed that this sort of thing didn't happen anymore in Moscow, in these days of glasnost and Gorbachev, but apparently they still could.

"Please," Sonya said, standing at the doorway, watching Yakov and Stefan leave. "I want to see Avram."

But Yakov insisted that she stay behind—that she not be too closely associated with the Kramer family—and he refused to relent.

So she bit her lower lip and nodded, and watched these two men she loved so fiercely make their way down the dank stairwell. She wanted to call after them, yet she caught herself just in time, and she listened as the echo from their footsteps grew softer and then disappeared.

They drove for a few minutes in silence, Stefan poking at a place in the old Volga's door where the padding had spilled out from a tear in a seam. "I hope they shave off Avram's stupid beard," Stefan joked weakly. "It's always looked awful." Avram, older by twelve years, was a tall, handsome, strapping man, but Stefan had always teased him about his beard, which made him look like a Talmudic scholar.

Stefan looked over at his father, who was not laughing. Yakov's sensitive eyes were filled with pain, accentuated by the horrible scarred flesh that surrounded them.

It had happened in the gulag. A handsome and vivacious boy, Yakov had joined the army during World War II, or the Great Patriotic War, as it was officially known; and, with millions of his peers, he had fought with great ardor to defend his homeland against the Nazis. He had been captured by the Germans and spent two years as a prisoner of war, until he was liberated by American troops and immediately returned to the Soviet Union—not to a joyous reception but to a labor camp. Stalin did not trust the Soviet POWs. He believed they had been brainwashed by the Nazis or by American intelligence and convinced to return to Russia as spies. So he imprisoned the lot of them.

Vikhorevka Prison Camp, near Irkutsk, was a hell-hole, and Kramer had grown steadily more disillusioned with the system that could have done such a thing to him. Some of his friends had been broken by their years in the camps, but not Kramer; he had established a friendship with some others there, an Estonian and a Lithuanian who shared his hatred for the Kremlin. Still, the two Balts kept their mouths shut, while Yakov began to speak out. Some of the other prisoners—thugs whose fury at being jailed made them hate people like Yakov, who dared to speak out—began to resent him. Their reaction was twisted but not uncommon.

One day, a couple of his fellow prisoners, granted the soft chore of cleaning duty, stole a jar of potent muriatic acid. And, in the middle of the night, they tossed it into Kramer's face.

Luckily, it had missed his eyes, but it brutally disfigured the right side of his face so badly that he would always resemble a monster more than a human being. There was no one in the camp trained in medicine, so he was treated with rags and alcohol, and his pain, which was unspeakable, grew worse. In time, the horrid red ropes of his facial skin blanched to a more tolerable white.

Even after he and the other prisoners were released by Khrushchev in 1956, Yakov Kramer was consigned to live with a hideous reminder of his stay in the gulag.

Many people found it impossible to look him in the face. He managed to get a job as a technical writer, and eventually was hired at Progress Publishers, where he indexed books. Kramer was given a cubicle far removed from the other workers, because his boss anticipated that the others would prefer not to have to look at him. His boss was right.

Stefan's father was a man of tremendous, though banked, anger. Now he sat at the wheel of the car in dark fury.

"We'll get him out, Papa," Stefan said, although neither one of them believed it.

The doctor in charge, a prim middle-aged woman named Dr. Zinaida Osipovna Bogdanova, wore a white coat and regarded the visitors with contempt. Clearly, she felt she was far too busy to have to speak to relatives of crazy people.

"Your son is schizophrenic," she was saying. Yakov and Stefan, knowing how futile it was to argue, watched her face with silent hostility. "Officially his diagnosis is criminal paranoid schizophrenia, and the course of treatment may be very long."

Stefan could not stop himself from remarking, "I wasn't aware that 'criminal paranoid schizophrenia' was a psychiatric diagnosis. Are you sure you aren't confusing your medicine with your politics?"

The doctor ignored him and continued haughtily, "You have five minutes with him. No more. Don't get him worked up."

As she turned to leave, Stefan asked, "Is he on any medication?"

She responded as if Stefan, too, were crazy. "Of course."

"What kind?"

She paused before saying, "Sedatives."

A few minutes later, she escorted Avram out, then left the family alone in the visiting room.

Stefan and his father did not believe their eyes.

Avram was a wholly different person, stooped in his hospital gown, gaunt, and he looked at his father and brother as if he didn't recognize them. Mucus dripped from his nose, saliva from his mouth. His tongue rolled and darted; his lips smacked and sucked.

"Oh, my *God*!" Yakov breathed.

Stefan could only stare, aghast.

"Avram," Yakov said, coming up to him slowly. "It's me, your father."

Avram looked at his father, his face betraying no recognition, his tongue rolling.

"Oh, God," Yakov said, embracing his son. "Oh, God. What have they done to you?" He held him for a long time, then let him go. Stefan embraced his brother tightly. All the time, Avram's face remained impassive, his eyes heavy-lidded, his mouth smacking insanely.

"Talk to me," Stefan said. "Can you talk to me?"

But Avram could not.

"Oh, God," Stefan whispered. "I've heard of this sort of thing! One of the emergency doctors I work with told me these hospitals give patients terrible drugs." He knew it had to be the antipsychotic drug haloperidol, which, administered in large doses, could cause Avram's grotesque, degenerative condition. The doctor had said it was called "tardive dyskinesia."

"Can he—can he be cured?" his father asked.

"I don't think so. It's—oh, Christ, it's—irreversible," he said, his voice breaking. Both Yakov and Stefan, watching this drugged hulk, could not stop the tears that sprang to their eyes.

Yakov embraced Avram again, and now the father was openly crying. "You never did anything. You were so —so careful, so innocent. How could they do this to you?"

Avram only stared and gaped. Somewhere deep down something registered, a tiny flash of anger beneath all the drugs, and now even his eyes brimmed with tears.

"We have to get him out of here," Yakov said very quietly, very firmly, to Stefan.

Suddenly the doctor was beside them, her voice loud and firm. "I'm afraid time's up."

Very late that night, in a deserted garage in the far south of Moscow, two men spoke by the light of a kerosene lamp.

"I've decided to take you up on your offer," Stefan told his old cellmate. "I hope it's still available."

17

East Neck, New Jersey

The old woman who had once been the personal secretary to Vladimir Ilyich Lenin lived in a tiny but immaculate ranch-style house with a perfectly manicured hedge in front and a lawn that resembled Astro-Turf. East Neck, New Jersey, was all even, broad streets lined with neat little square houses of tan stone and precise squares of lawn, which residents doubtless found homey. Stone found it depressing.

An odd place for such a person to live. Russian émigrés of recent vintage mostly coalesced in large cities, congregating in their own bustling, colorful Little Russias or Little Odessas. After a generation or two, once assimilated, they tended to live in cities and new suburbs, where the population turns over with some frequency. Not in tidy, middle-American spots like this, where all the neighbors have known one another for decades. Clearly, Anna Zinoyeva had chosen to distance herself from her compatriots.

Stone had arrived the night before and spent the evening in a motel where the beds had Magic Fingers massage vibrators built into the box springs. Early the next morning, he took a cab and got out several blocks from Zinoyeva's street. He walked slowly toward the house, watching carefully. Nothing. After what had happened to Ansbach, he'd take no chances.

Checking the street once more, he felt satisfied. In a quick motion he climbed the low porch and rang the bell.

Anna Zinoyeva, a diminutive woman whose wispy white hair barely covered her scalp, answered the door. She used a metal walker. Behind her, easily visible from the doorway, was a tiny sitting room furnished with a few straight-back upholstered chairs and a brown-tweed sofa. Even from here, everything about the room seemed to have been frozen in the late 1950s.

Her eyes squinted, giving her a slightly Asiatic appearance. Stone thought of her old boss, Lenin, whose eyes were also somewhat Asian.

"Irene Potter?" Stone asked, using her deep-cover name.

"Yes?"

"Anna Zinoyeva," Stone said calmly.

The old woman shook her head. "You are mistaken,"

she said in broken English. "Please go away from here."

"I'm not here to harm you," Stone said as gently as he could. "I need to talk with you." He handed her a letter he had typed earlier in the day, on Central Intelligence Agency stationery he had once gotten from Saul. It requested, in bland bureaucratic language, a routine update of her file, a perfectly normal, straightforward questioning. The letter, signed by a fictitious "Assistant Records Chief," requested her to speak to one Charles Stone.

Surely it had been years, even decades, since anyone from the American intelligence community had bothered to talk to her; her guard would be down.

She held the letter a few inches from her eyes, gray with cataracts, scrutinizing the text, the signature. It was obvious that she was almost blind. In a few moments, she looked up.

"What do you want from me?"

"Just a few minutes of your time," Stone said cheerily. "Didn't you receive a call?"

"No," she said warily. She shook her head again. "Go away from here." She made a feeble attempt to raise her walker, to ward off this unwelcome intruder.

Stone pushed his way into the house. The woman cried out: "Go! Please!"

"It's all right," Stone said gently. "It won't take more than a few minutes."

"No," Anna Zinoyeva said. "They promised me . . . They promised me no one would ever talk to me again! They said I would be left alone!"

"This won't take long. A mere formality."

She seemed to hesitate. "What do you want from me?" the old woman repeated unhappily, stepping aside to let Stone in.

In the end, it was Stone's gentle manner that allayed her suspicions. Sitting on the plastic-slipcovered sofa, she smoothed her faded housedress with gnarled yet somehow delicate hands, and told her story, haltingly at first, then as fluently as her poor English would allow.

She had come to work for Lenin when she was just nineteen—her father had been a friend of Vladimir Bonch-

Bruyevich, one of Lenin's closest friends—and she had never been more than a secretary in its strictest definition. She typed copies of Lenin's voluminous and seemingly endless correspondence and did other paperwork in Lenin's office in the Kremlin, from 1918 on, when the headquarters of the Soviet government was moved from Petrograd to Moscow. In 1923 she moved from Lenin's Kremlin office to Gorky, where Lenin was eventually to die.

Several years after Lenin's death, she asked permission to emigrate to the United States, and since it was still the 1920s and it was still possible to emigrate—and since she had served her country so honorably—she was given an exit visa. As one of the youngest secretaries on Lenin's staff, she had rarely been entrusted with anything of great importance or secrecy, she said. This was not to say that she didn't hear or see things. She did.

After she had been talking for half an hour or so, the suspicious squint in the eyes was replaced by a gaze that was in turn gentle and defiant.

"Twenty-three years I hear nothing from the great American intelligence," she said mischievously. She shook her head at the hopeless crudeness of her benefactors. "Nothing. Now you are so very interested in me."

"As I said, it's routine. We're filling in the blank spaces in your file."

For an instant, it looked as if she didn't understand, until she said, "And we must not have blank spaces," and smiled playfully. Fleetingly, the wizened face was transformed into that of a coquette of seventeen.

"It won't take much more time."

"I don't have much time left," she said equably, without a trace of self-pity. "Soon you will be able to stop sending me your enormous checks and draining treasury."

"It's not much," Stone agreed. The Agency was notoriously cheap with defectors.

"In Russia, they would give me very big pension because of my work for Ilyich," she scolded, frowning in mock-disgust. "Sometimes I wonder why I left."

Stone gave a nod of rueful sympathy, and then began: "If you can help—"

"Listen," she said, and leaned her head close to his, as if confiding a great secret. "I am old. More than sixty years ago, I come to this country. If the great American intelligence still did not get from me all what little I know, it can't be important." She lifted her head and cocked it to one side, then smiled. "Do not waste your time."

"Even if it concerns the Lenin Testament?"

The old woman was suddenly alert, and it took her several seconds to regain her poise. Then she smiled slyly. "Are you here to talk over old history with me? There are books you can read. Everyone knows about the Lenin Testament."

"The one I mean is another Lenin Testament."

"Is there another?" she asked, feigning boredom and shrugging. She clutched an empty teacup on the table beside her as if preparing to sip, then set it back down on the saucer with a clatter.

"I think you know."

"I think I do not," she replied steadily.

Stone smiled and decided to call an end to the fencing. "It came up in the course of a routine check through the files," he said.

He waited for her to respond, and when she didn't, he asked casually, "They did poison him, didn't they?"

For a long time, she did not reply. When she finally said something, it was almost inaudible. The refrigerator in the kitchen next door switched on with a hum and a gurgle.

"I think yes," she said. Her brio had given way to solemnity.

"What makes you think it?"

"Because—because he wrote letter about this, and he gave it for me to type. He tells me to make two copies. One for Krupskaya, his wife. The other . . ." She broke off and looked down at the floor.

"But the other copy—who was the other for?"

She waved her hands hopelessly in small circles. "I don't know."

"You know," Stone said.

There was a beat of silence, and he continued: "Your

contract with us requires you to be cooperative. It's entirely within my power to cut off all financial support. . . ."

She replied hurriedly, her words spilling out now in a torrent: "Oh, it's so long ago. It's not important. A foreigner . . . Lenin was afraid his house was filled with . . . intrigue. Oh, I think he was right. Everyone, every gardener and cook and chauffeur, was OGPU. The secret police."

She was speaking faster now, and Stone didn't understand fully what she meant to say. "Why?" he said. "Why did he give a copy to a foreigner?"

"He was afraid of Stalin—of what he might do to Krupskaya. He wanted make sure one copy is brought out of country."

"Who was the foreigner?"

She shook her head.

"You know, don't you?" Stone said tranquilly.

Her hesitation was unbearable. "Tall, handsome American. Businessman. An American he sees several times before his death. Is not important."

"Winthrop Lehman."

A pause, and then: "He saw Lenin many times," she said ruminatively, squinting her eyes. "Lehman."

"Did he see Lenin at Gorky?"

"Yes. Winthrop Lehman."

"What did the letter say? It had to do with the poisoning, didn't it?"

"No, not quite," she said. Now she spoke very slowly again. "He writes a—a draft—before he went to Gorky. Already ill. Says many bad things about Soviet state. Said it was a terrible mistake, it is becoming a police state. He said he . . . like Dr. Frankenstein, is creating a terrible, terrible monster."

Stone waited for more, but there was no more.

"That's a complete condemnation of the Soviet Union by its founder," Stone said quietly. The words sounded obvious and foolish. "Lehman has it."

"Once he demand to return to Moscow. We tried stop him, but he insisting. 'Hurry!' he was shouting to the chauffeur. When he got to Moscow, he went to his office in the Kremlin."

"Did you go with him?"

"No. I hear later. He look in his desk and find a secret drawer was opened. He is looking for a document. He is furious, is shouting at everyone. Never find it. But he . . . How do you say? He—*re-create* from memory."

"Dictated it to you," Stone said. "That's the one you made two copies of."

"Yes."

"Do you have a copy?"

"No, of course not. I think lost now."

"What about Krupskaya's copy?"

"They must take it from her."

"And Lehman's copy?"

"I don't know." The adjacent kitchen gave off the aroma of chicken soup, heavy with garlic.

Stone inhaled the comfortable yet forlorn smell of the house and looked around the room. How did she know they had poisoned Lenin? he wondered.

"Who did it?" he asked.

"Please don't dig it up," she pleaded. "Please don't dig up the past. Let people believe Ilyich died peacefully."

"They did an autopsy, didn't they? I seem to remember—"

"Please." She made a tiny gesture with her hands that signaled acquiescence. "Yes, they did. The day after he die, ten doctors examine the body. Open him up and look at organs and find nothing wrong. They open his skull." She frowned, pursed her lips in distaste, and continued: "Brain is . . ." She grimaced, flashed a set of cheap dentures that were stained bright yellow. "Solid. Cal-calcified." As she spoke the word, she gestured with her forefinger. "Metal instruments are ringing when they strike brain."

"Arteriosclerosis. They didn't look for poison?"

Stone had switched to Russian; the old woman would no doubt find it much more comfortable. Indeed, she looked up with relief.

"No, but why would they?" she said.

"They had no reason to believe he'd been poisoned."

"Do you know that Lenin's personal doctor, Dr. Guetier, refused to sign the autopsy report? He refused! He knew Lenin had been poisoned. This is a matter of the historical record!"

Stone stared.

She nodded slowly, significantly. "I think he knew."

"But *who*? Who poisoned him?"

"One of the servants, I think. They were all working for the OGPU. Stalin wanted Lenin out of way so he could take over the country. Why are you asking me this again? Why do you ask again?"

"Again?"

"You asked me all about this in 1953."

"Nineteen fifty-three?" A bus roared by on the interstate two blocks away. "Who asked you about this in 1953?" Stone asked.

Anna Zinoyeva regarded him for a long moment with her gray-clouded eyes as if she didn't believe him. Then she got up, slowly, supporting herself with one hand on the aluminum walker, the other on the arm of the couch. "I used to read the newspapers," she said defiantly. "I was always very good with faces. Ilyich always complimented me for this." She made her way to a walnut-veneered sideboard and opened the cabinet, removing a heavy green-leather-bound scrapbook, which she set on top of the sideboard's highly burnished surface. "Come," she said.

Stone walked over to the sideboard. She was turning the pasteboard pages slowly, as if they were made of lead, until she found the page she wanted. "Here," she said, her face almost touching the page.

She indicated a page on which was mounted an unevenly cut, brownish clipping from a Russian-émigré newspaper published in New York, the *Novoye Russkoye Slovo*. Only the year—1965—was visible; the month and day appeared to have been lost to a sloppy job of scissoring.

"I recognize the face, too," Stone said, trying to conceal his shock. The photograph was of William Armitage, a career State Department employee who the article announced was being named an under secretary. Armitage, Stone knew, was now the Deputy Secretary of State: a powerful and highly placed man in the administration.

Bill Armitage, whom Saul Ansbach had spoken with, perhaps only hours before his death.

"This is the man who talked to you?"

"Yes, him. This Armitage."

Stone nodded. A renegade organization, Saul had believed. How high up did this thing reach? "What did he want to know from you? Why was he interested—in 1953— in something that happened in 1924?"

The old woman scowled as if Stone had missed her point entirely, her expression asking how simpleminded could he be. "He was interested in what had *just* happened. The threats."

"Threats?"

She raised her voice. "The *threats*! Yes, the threats." Her eyes shone with fear.

"Who threatened you? Not our agents, I hope."

"The Russians." Tears had come to her eyes. "You know all this already! Don't . . ."

"Why did they threaten you?" Stone asked softly.

"They . . ." She shook her head again, a slow motion that shifted the course of the tears running down her cheeks. "They were looking for Lenin's Testament, and they were sure I had it. They tore my house apart, told me they would kill me. I told them I didn't have it. . . ."

"Who were they?"

"Chekists. Beria's men." She sounded as if she were speaking to a simple child. The forerunners to the KGB. Of course. "I was so *frightened*. They used the word *ikonoborchestvo*."

"Iconoclasm," Stone translated. The smashing of an icon.

"Yes. They said, 'You and your bloody Lenin will be the first to go. Your bloody icon.' "

Stone nodded. Yes, anti-Leninists: an old and virulent underground strain in the Soviet Union. "And this American, this Armitage—what did he want, exactly?"

"He wanted to know what they told me. I told him that they just wanted some document from me that I didn't have."

"You didn't tell him everything," Stone said without accusation, understanding.

"For a long time, he didn't believe me. Then he told me I must never say anything to anybody about what happened, about these Chekists. That very bad things might happen to me if I said anything. This is why I'm surprised you are asking me again about this."

"He wanted to protect a secret," said Stone.

"He wanted silence," she agreed. "He wanted me not to say a word about these Russians. You're nodding. You must understand."

"But the Russians could have gotten this document from Winthrop Lehman, couldn't they?"

The old woman's mouth trembled open slightly as her eyes unseeingly searched Stone's face. "No," she said. "I heard . . ."

"What?"

"I was told . . . they didn't need to, because Stalin had a . . . a control over him. Or maybe they couldn't, because they had some kind of—arrangement with him. I don't know." Her attention seemed to be fading. The woman was tired; her face had grown ashen.

"*Arrangement?*"

"Stalin—Stalin was so evil. He found a way to control this man, this Lehman."

Cowering against the Frigidaire, my mother, her tears turning her eye makeup into blue streams, is shouting: "I didn't make you go to prison! Be angry at him, don't be angry at me!"

Yes.

If Stalin was controlling Lehman . . . , Stone thought, astonished. Could it be? The adviser to Roosevelt and Truman, the man who had sent Alfred Stone to prison—was this the secret Lehman went to such lengths to conceal? Was it conceivable that Lehman had been in the employ of the Soviet government? "What kind of control?" he asked.

"I don't know. I don't *know*! I have no great secrets. I was only a secretary. Surely you must understand far more than me."

"Yes," Stone admitted, tasting the fear again.

There was a shout from some children playing down the block, then the sudden acceleration of a car that badly needed a new muffler, and then quiet, in which Stone could hear his heart thudding.

He thought: I don't think these Americans wanted anyone to know that they—whoever *they* are or were—were trying to overthrow the Soviet government.

He looked around at the gloomy little room, then at the old woman, whose deep-set eyes—eyes that had once gazed upon a man of history—had clouded with age and now were heavy with weariness. He thought: And now they're trying once again. The car with the bad muffler started up another time, raced by, and then there was nothing but silence.

18

Maryland

Very early in the morning, the limousines and sedans arrived at the secluded Maryland estate one after another, at precise five-minute intervals. At twenty minutes before seven, the last car, a gray Cadillac limousine, proceeded down the private, tree-lined roadway, through the scrolled iron gates that opened automatically.

It stopped a few hundred feet short of the main house, a sprawling Victorian mansion, and then maneuvered slowly into the wooden structure that appeared, from the outside, to be a large shed. When the limousine was inside and the doors had closed behind it, the steel platform that was the floor immediately hummed to life, dropping slowly and evenly. Within a minute, the floor had lowered seventy-five feet, into the pitch-dark chasm beneath the ground. Then the limousine pulled straight ahead to the oblong alcove whose walls were constructed of concrete finished in some sort of clear resin, joining the four other cars parked there, pulling up neatly alongside a black Saab turbo.

Fletcher Lansing, the last to arrive, got slowly out of the car with a nimbleness that belied his age. He was one of the great figures of the foreign-policy establishment, a close adviser to John Kennedy, one of what a journalist had once called "the best and the brightest." Lansing, his creased mouth firmly set beneath his prominent, thin nose, passed through an arch into the conference room, where the others were already seated, sipping coffee.

"Good morning, sir." This came from the Director of Central Intelligence, Ted Templeton. Like William Casey before him, Templeton was a veteran of the OSS, but, unlike Casey, he was career CIA, a large, rangy man with a thick head of gray hair, large ears, pouches under his eyes. He owed his job, the directorship, to Lansing, who had lobbied for him over more than one supper with the President in the White House residential quarters.

But Lansing, whose face was grim, gave only a curt nod to Templeton, and then to the others at the round black-marble-topped table. There was Ronald Sanders, the Deputy Director of Central Intelligence: forty-six, a former Notre Dame football quarterback, and a career CIA man as well. To his right was Evan Wainwright Reynolds, considered the chief architect of the National Security Agency and, though long retired, one of its founders, a vigorous, slender man in his early seventies who rarely spoke.

And to his left, finally, was the youngest man present, Roger Bayliss of the National Security Council. Bayliss, in his late thirties, wore a charcoal-gray Italian sharkskin suit. His career—his very position in the White House— had been maneuvered by the other men in this room. He owed everything to them. As the youngest, he was the secretary, and he took notes on a yellow legal pad, writing with a Montblanc ballpoint pen. Bayliss would have much preferred to use his Compaq laptop, but no outside electronic equipment was permitted in this ultrasecret enclave.

Bayliss watched pensively. He jiggled his right knee up and down, a nervous tic that afflicted him at times of great tension. He inspected a chipped thumbnail. It was time for one of his several extravagances of vanity, a manicure. He thought fleetingly of the woman with whom he'd spent last night, a blonde named Caryn. She was a congressional staffer, of course, and she'd been a firebrand in bed, and Bayliss was still a bit sore. She was naturally impressed that he was on the National Security Council—most women were—but if she had any *idea* of what was about to happen in Moscow, and of Bayliss's role in it all . . .

He glanced around at the room as Fletcher Lansing examined his notes. Everyone waited apprehensively for him to begin.

What bad news could there possibly be?

The extreme security precautions—this subterranean, electronically secure conference room beneath a private estate whose existence was unknown even to the most senior members of the American intelligence community—were deemed by the five men a necessity. They were known (the term had been coined by Fletcher Lansing, whose affection for Latinisms was legendary) as the Sanctum Sanctorum, an ultrasecret group of past and present intelligence officials that met infrequently—perhaps once in two or three years—to make decisions that, they were convinced, would soon alter the world's fate.

Bayliss's knee kept jiggling, up and down, up and down, with the rapidity of a hummingbird's wings. He studied Fletcher Lansing, the old spymaster who had created the Sanctum, with surreptitious intensity.

What was wrong?

Bayliss, an only child who had grown up watching his parents closely, unnervingly, prided himself on his unusual perceptiveness. He had come to realize that there was often some kind of benign pathology in those who were drawn to intelligence work. Part of the lure, of course, was nothing more than insider-itis, that old Washington disease that makes a person ravenous with a desire to be inside the nucleus of power. Once you get to the office early in the morning, and you're the first one to pore over the overnight cable traffic, you're hooked, you're infected.

But Lansing, Harvard and Harvard Law School (Law Review, of course), Supreme Court clerk, Secretary of the Navy, then one of the founders of the CIA—had forsaken the overt insider world of diplomacy and politics and statesmanship for the secret world, and that was because of another chromosome in his character genome, Bayliss believed.

Men like Lansing—and usually they *were* men—relished the secret exercise of power, out of the daylight, away from public scrutiny. Where else but in the world of intelligence could you plot against an opponent you had never met? They were the *éminences grises*, power-players with an abnormal attraction to secrecy, who never got credit because they never wanted any. And Bayliss, who was not without a measure of self-knowledge, recognized this same streak in himself.

Lansing belonged to a whole generation of aristocratic leaders, like Dean Acheson or Winthrop Lehman or Henry Stimson or Henry Cabot Lodge, whose time had passed. The crafty old pterodactyl, an illustrious servitor of presidents who were not as well born as he, considered himself, by now, one of the wise men, in an age when American foreign policy was like a fine old Bentley being driven ruinously, with a new, inexperienced president taking the wheel every few years, destroying the clutch while he learned to drive. A clutch could be replaced; world peace was far more fragile.

Yes. Bayliss knew that the Sanctum's operation was, in a sense, the last spasm of an old order never to be witnessed again, and he was proud to be part of it.

For the time had come. Never before in the history of the Soviet Union had such an opportunity presented itself. It would never come again.

The intelligence out of Moscow was clear: Gorbachev was about to be ousted. Talk of a coup was everywhere.

Fletcher Lansing had put it well at the Sanctum's last meeting, a mere two weeks ago. "The world we created is no more," he had said. "Nothing looks the same. Everyone seems to think that the Russians have overnight turned into teddy bears. But even if a snake sheds its skin, it's still a snake." Lansing was no crazy right-winger, Bayliss knew, but he was a veteran of the Cold War. He'd been present at the creation of the postwar order, and he knew how easily America, childlike and optimistic in many ways, could have its head turned by changes that were only ephemeral. "So, while we Americans are dazzled and mesmerized by the changes in Moscow, we all forget the long view. Fail to realize that Gorbachev can't last, and that when he's gone it will be too late." Seven decades of hardline Soviet elements will be just waiting in the wings to reclaim what they believe is rightly theirs. They'll not give up their power without a fight.

The Soviet empire was on the verge of collapse, spinning out of control. Its republics were seceding; its economy was crumbling. Now that the Berlin Wall had toppled, Moscow had lost its satellites forever.

The question was, when?

Because everyone knew what would happen when it did. When the shit hit the fan, as Ted Templeton so colorfully put it. The intelligence from the Kremlin was clear: Gorbachev's days were numbered. It was only a matter of time before he was out.

And then, a new, undoubtedly neo-Stalinist leadership would wrest control, put the lid on all of Gorbachev's feeble attempts at reform. Throughout the Soviet empire, there would be a crackdown that would make Tiananmen Square in the spring of 1989 seem like a playground. The leadership—which would need a way to unify the Soviet peoples—would require an enemy once again. An outside threat.

Their old archenemy: the West.

And what was the White House doing? Standing by idly, passively. America, the headless horseman.

Decades of superpower struggle, countless billions of dollars, thousands of lives, had been squandered on containing Communism, and now the White House stood by, blindly fatuous, shuffling their feet, not knowing what to do. We were, as usual, backing the wrong horse.

The Sanctum had the only solution, the only thing that would bring the world, once and for all, the peace it so desperately thirsted for.

And it would happen in a matter of weeks.

For they were about to catapult an American agent-in-place—a "mole," as the British novelist John Le Carré had termed it—to the top of the Kremlin. The leadership of the Soviet Union. For years, such a thing had been a subject of fanciful speculation in the government and out, a pipe dream, the stuff of spy thrillers, but now it was indeed about to happen. Only now, in fact, *could* it happen.

And only the men in this room knew it.

The existence of this mole was utterly secret to the American government, to the intelligence community at large, even to the White House: a secret to everyone but the few men in this chamber.

For, Bayliss knew, thus it had to be. The Sanctum group had first met in the early 1950s, convened by Lansing and Reynolds, to run the mole, M-3. The task required inviolable secrecy, and Lansing and his colleagues—who were, of course, in a position to know—realized that the intelligence and foreign-policy establishments were no longer reliable.

With the rise of the Soviet mole Harold "Kim" Philby virtually to the top of the British spy network, and the increasingly frequent leaks since that time, followed by the Senate investigations of the CIA during the seventies—and so on and so on—the group's secrecy became imperative. They could trust no one. Presidents and secretaries of state came and went, and none of them had ever been informed of the Sanctum's—or M-3's—existence.

At last, after decades of planning, the time was at hand. So what, Bayliss wondered with growing alarm, was the hitch?

Fletcher Lansing cleared his throat and began with some preliminaries. Whatever the bad news was, Lansing was holding off. Bayliss, who had developed the fine art of listening while thinking of something else entirely, began to think of the mind-boggling operation that was now about to change the world.

He knew that, over the years, the United States had cultivated several deep-penetration agents in Moscow, generally Soviet citizens sympathetic to the American side. One of the earliest, in the 1950s, had been code-named "Major B." There had been others, from Colonel Oleg Penkovsky of the GRU, to Lieutenant Colonel Pyotr Popov of Soviet military intelligence, to the weapons expert A. G. Tolkachev at the Moscow Aeronautical Institute. Each was discovered by the Soviets, each arrested.

Yes, there were others still in place, but each of these was small-fry compared with the asset the Sanctum group had run all these years.

To preserve and promote M-3, the Bay of Pigs operation had been scrubbed—and not even John Kennedy was told why. Likewise, data that American intelligence had on Nikita Khrushchev's unstable power base, right down to the hour he'd be thrown out of the Politburo, were information that not even Lyndon Johnson had had.

There were jokes in Washington, of course, that America couldn't wish for a "mole" that could do any more than Mikhail Gorbachev already had. But what these pundits didn't know was that Gorbachev had made M-3's rise to power virtually inevitable. Only amid such turmoil in the Kremlin would M-3 be able to seize power.

Bayliss felt he knew the importance of M-3 almost better than anyone in the Sanctum.

After all, he had been chosen as the Sanctum's contact with M-3's intermediaries. This contact had begun only a few weeks earlier, when the channel had been activated after decades of dormancy. The postcard that was slipped into his car by Aleksandr Malarek, the Soviet Embassy's first secretary, contained a microdot, an entire document reduced to the size of a typewriter's period.

Malarek was known to be KGB, but none of his KGB colleagues knew of his work in behalf of M-3. For M-3 would have nothing to do with KGB channels.

Bayliss remembered the last meeting of the Sanctum, when Lansing and Templeton had told him he was to co-ordinate arrangements with Malarek.

"You're aware of how careful you must be," Lansing admonished.

"Certainly, sir." Can they see me swallowing? Can they see how terrified I am?

"If you're somehow connected to this—if you're caught—you'll undoubtedly be put on trial for treason."

"Yes, sir."

"On the other hand," Lansing continued, *"if we are, all of us, successful . . ."* His voice trailed off as he looked around the table at the rest of the Sanctum group. *"If we succeed, you'll have been instrumental in changing history forever."*

Yes, Bayliss had thought. Forever.

Lansing, finished with his introductory remarks, now spoke in a voice that trembled with anger.

"The situation," he rasped, "is unforgivable." He struck the black marble table with a tight, liver-spotted fist, looked around at the bunkerlike walls of the chamber, and then continued. "We have had our moles before. But nothing compared with M-3."

Now the Deputy Director of Central Intelligence, Ronald Sanders, interrupted softly. "Little damage has been done. Nothing irrevocable."

"Blood has been shed!" Lansing shouted, his voice cracking. Bayliss had never seen him so angry, never seen him shed his façade of patrician reserve. "The blood of innocent men. The blood of men who have served this country loyally."

"Only that which was necessary," CIA Director Ted Templeton objected. Their voices were curiously dead in the soundproof, surveillance-proof chamber. "Saul Ansbach all but did himself in, raising alarms. We couldn't know how much he knew. I hated to allow it—Saul was once a friend of mine."

"But the others!"

"All of the sanctions have been carried out with scrupulous care. That was our agreement with Malarek's people." Templeton sighed noisily. "Nothing traceable."

Sanders, who had been nervously shifting in his chair, put in, a touch defensively: "Only one section of the Agency was involved in looking into this HEDGEHOG business. Parnassus. But Ted put a halt to it." He unconsciously addressed his remarks to the grand old men, Lansing and Reynolds.

Templeton nodded. "It's a good thing we were able to blow that chauffeur's cover. Jesus, I didn't know he was—"

"Gentlemen," Lansing interjected, "we are in a profession where blood is shed all the time to protect the blood of the greater masses. But I am disturbed by the extent of this, by the elimination of innocent men. Frankly, it violates everything I've ever stood for. But, morality apart, these sanctions strike me as highly dangerous. If *any* of them were ever traced, by KGB, by any other interested party—"

"Impossible," Templeton said. "The Sekretariat are highly trained. Extremely sophisticated. As long as we keep hands off, they'll do the job invisibly."

"But will they *finish* the job?" Evan Reynolds's remark was little more than a whisper, but instantly everyone at the table turned his way. He had voiced, if crudely, exactly what was on the mind of every man in the room.

There was a beat of silence before Bayliss mustered the courage to speak up. "Can we be absolutely sure this is the right person?"

"Roger," Templeton said with a dismissive shake of the head, "my people have voiceprints that match precisely the voice on the tape taken from Lehman's basement telephone. That, plus the tap on his phone, confirms that he's the one who's been stirring matters up. There's no question."

"But I thought you were assured Parnassus was—" Reynolds objected.

"All but one," Templeton said. "This one has kept prodding, for personal reasons that we couldn't have foreseen."

"I should think the subject must be dealt with delicately," Lansing said.

"Why?" Reynolds asked sharply. "If he has possession of the document, of the—the file, he may compromise the entire operation. Decades of cultivation. My life's work, for God's sake. We have no choice. But if he has copies concealed, then what?"

Templeton explained his plan, and when he was done, he could see the shock on the faces of the men around the table. There was a long silence, broken only by the most senior man at the table.

"Jesus God," Lansing breathed. "Jesus God, help us."

Washington is a city of foundations. Any number of organizations, from the most venal lobbying organizations to the most selfless nonprofit consumer groups, like to call themselves "foundations," because the name is at once neutral and dignified.

The American Flag Foundation, located on K Street in central Northwest Washington, occupies one floor of a modern complex that also houses law offices and the lobbying outposts of several Midwestern corporations. From its exterior, the building looks like every other office building in that part of town, an impression confirmed by the drab entrance and inefficient elevators.

But, were a visitor mistakenly to get off at the sixth floor, he would be amazed by the opulence before him. He would see a single secretary sitting at a large mahogany desk in an anteroom furnished with Persian rugs, marble tables, highly burnished paneling on the walls. He would notice, too, that the secretary's telephone rarely seems to ring.

Most who pay it any attention mistakenly believe the American Flag Foundation to be some kind of conservative think-tank. In reality, it is an organization of retired officers of several American intelligence organizations, chiefly the CIA, the NSA, and the Defense Intelligence Agency (DIA). These officers maintain close links to the agencies from which they are retired, and in fact many continue on their payrolls. But the links, and even the means of payment, are so byzantine that not even the most dogged congressional investigator would be able to establish for certain that the Foundation is in any way linked to American intelligence.

Which is the way the intelligence community wants it. By a presidential executive order, the CIA is forbidden to conduct espionage operations domestically, and indeed, since the Church Committee investigations of the mid-1970s, the CIA has in fact been scrupulous about this. It is a commonplace within certain elements of this and other intelligence agencies, however, that such proscriptions are foolish vestiges of noble democratic sentiment. Intelligence cannot function when it is handicapped by such rules, by having to depend upon domestic forces such as the FBI, or any other law-enforcement agency that does not operate abroad.

And so, long before the days of Colonel Oliver North and the National Security Council's secret dealings with Israel, Iran, and Nicaragua, the American Flag Foundation was set up to serve as a domestic-intelligence arm of the various agencies, a coordinating base for covert operations.

The phone rang, startling the secretary/receptionist, who was reading the Style section of *The Washington Post*. She answered it, then depressed a key on her intercom switchboard.

"General Knowlton," she said, "it's the Director of Central Intelligence."

Several minutes later, the phone rang in a small farmhouse outside of Alexandria, Virginia. The house was located on a rural road, miles from any other building; its electrified fence was concealed in high thickets of bushes and trees. The roof of the house was dotted with gray, conical microwave antennas.

"McManus," said the man who answered the phone. He was Major Leslie McManus, a retired officer of armed-forces intelligence. He listened for a minute, jotted down a few notes on a white pad. "Done."

19

Boston

After a tedious nine-hour drive during which he stopped only once, Stone was back in Boston.

Alfred Stone was in his hospital room, fully dressed, sitting up in a chair. The bed was made.

"You," he said, startled, when Charlie entered. "I called you in New York, even at—at your place of work. Where the hell have you been?"

"Sorry."

"I was just about to call a taxi. This morning they decided to let me check out. Would you mind taking me home?" He glanced around the hospital room with distaste. "I've had enough of this place."

It was just after nine o'clock at night.

Several hours earlier, a neatly dressed middle-aged couple had mounted the stairs of a small, squarish tan house and rung the doorbell. They waited a minute, two minutes; it seemed an eternity, but they knew the woman was home. Everything had been prepared meticulously; that was simply how their employers did things. The couple knew for certain that the old woman was asleep in her small, pathetically furnished bedroom upstairs. It would take her some time to answer the door.

The couple appeared to be husband and wife. The husband was in his early forties, balding, somewhat pudgy, but obviously quite strong. What little hair he had was dark, flecked with gray, and cropped close. He wore a camel's-hair overcoat over a blue pin-striped suit, a blue shirt, and a paisley tie. The woman who seemed to be his wife was a year or two younger, compact and poised; she was a rather plain woman who groomed herself fastidiously. She wore a touch too much eye shadow above her large brown eyes, and her straight brown hair was cut in neat, straight bangs. She wore a prim-looking floral-patterned dress with a Peter Pan collar.

There was a faint noise from behind the door, and the couple exchanged a brief glance.

The two spoke flawless English with a Midwestern twang. They made their rather modest living from the graphic-design firm they jointly owned and ran; they had very few customers. The woman, in fact, had actually been trained as a designer at the State Institute of Art in Leningrad for a few months, after she had completed her training in Moscow.

The door opened, and the small elderly woman peered out. "Yes?" she inquired.

She was even frailer than the couple had expected.

"Irene?" the younger woman asked, smiling gently, her eyes wide.

"Yes?" Suspicious now, the old woman tightened her small fingers around the grip of the aluminum walker.

"Irene, I'm Helen Stevens, and this is Bob. We're volunteers with County Social and Family Services." The dark-haired woman smiled again, almost apologetically, and added, "Ruth Bower gave us your name." Ruth Bower, the couple had been instructed, was the name of a neighbor of the old woman's who came by from time to time to help out around the house.

The old woman's cloudy, puzzled eyes relaxed now. "Oh, come in."

The younger woman chattered as she and her husband entered. "I don't know if Ruth mentioned that the agency sends us to help people do little things—shop, move boxes, whatever you need." She closed the door behind them.

The woman whose name was Anna Zinoyeva made her way slowly to the plastic-covered brown-tweed sofa in the small front room. "Oh, thank you very much," she said.

"Irene, listen," the man said, speaking for the first time, taking a seat next to the couch in a plastic-covered chair. "Did you meet with someone earlier today? It's very, very important that we know." He watched her expression, watching for a telltale flicker of fear, admission.

"Nobody," Anna Zinoyeva said, biting her lip.

Yes. She had spoken to somebody.

"What did he want from you?" the wife asked.

"I never saw anyone," the old woman protested, terrified now. "Please. No. I never saw—"

The young woman continued now, switching to Russian, using the old woman's real name.

"*No*," Anna Zinoyeva gasped. Again! They had come for her again! For a moment, she did not believe her ears. They knew her name, a name that, until this morning, had not been spoken in decades.

"Please leave me alone," she said, whimpering. Her body shook violently. She could not contain her terror. "What do you want to know from me? Please, what do you want to know?"

"All we want to know," the man said in a gentle, singsong voice, "is what the man asked you."

The old woman finally talked.

The young woman turned the old woman's body over, pulling the housedress up as far as the thigh, and made a deep incision with a knife. Moments earlier, they had broken her fragile neck, but the arterial blood still spurted upward, then slowed to a steady red flow. She waited until the flow had stopped, which did not take long.

"Ready," she said.

Her husband had donned surgical gloves. He removed a round glass vial and a long swab from the case he had brought.

"Is that dangerous?" she asked, indicating the liquid he was plunging, repeatedly, into the incision.

"I wouldn't touch it," he said. "*Clostridium welchii*. It's terrible stuff, but it does the job."

The organism hastened natural decomposition. When the body was discovered, it would appear that the old lady had died weeks ago: perhaps slipped and fell, hit her head. Such things can happen to old people who live alone.

If the couple had had the time, they could have waited around to watch it work. In a matter of days, there would be nothing left of the body except the skeleton and a few tendons and a pile of mush, nothing left to identify. Nothing at all except a heap of bubbling tissue.

The man removed the swab from the wound and stood up. "There," he said.

Stone drove up the blacktopped driveway of his father's house, glancing warily from side to side with such subtlety that his father, sitting beside him in the front seat, did not seem to notice. But no one was here, it seemed. He got out and carried his suitcase and his father's small overnight bag up to the front door. Alfred Stone walked gingerly alongside.

Charlie switched off the house alarm with one key, then opened the front door with two others. The house was dark, the heavy furniture gleaming and lemon-smelling, the Persian rugs vacuumed, their fringes perfectly straight.

"Well," Alfred Stone announced. "I trust there are sheets on your bed upstairs."

"Can you get up the stairs all right?" Charlie asked.

"I'm a lot stronger than I look."

"Let me carry your suitcase to your room; then I'll go next door and get the dog. You'll probably want to go to bed early."

He took both bags up the stairs, and a few minutes later he heard his father's voice calling.

"Charlie?"

Stone set down the bag in his father's room and walked quickly to the top of the stairs. "Yes?"

He looked down and saw his father holding in one hand Saul Ansbach's envelope, which Stone had left in the pocket of his overcoat. In his father's other hand was the eight-by-ten glossy photograph.

Charlie could feel his pulse quicken.

"I was hanging up your coat," Alfred Stone said. "This fell out." His eyes were wide, and the blood, quite literally, had drained from his face. "How did you get this? *Why?*"

A few miles to the south, in the seedy part of Boston known as the Combat Zone, the several-block-wide area that is home to pornographic movie houses, sexual-aid shops, prostitution, and drugs, a man in a black leather jacket was sitting in a darkened movie theater watching a bosomy blonde fellate an especially well-endowed black man. It was early evening, and the theater was uncrowded: perhaps twenty viewers, who sat as far apart from one another as possible. A few old men masturbated openly.

"*Dobriy vecher.*"

Another man now sat beside the man in the leather jacket. This one was bearded and wore a dark-blue windbreaker.

"*Dobriy vecher, tovarishch,*" the man in the leather jacket replied. Good evening, comrade.

The two Russian émigrés sat in silence for a moment, until both were satisfied they were unnoticed. The man in the leather jacket left the theater, followed a few minutes later by the other man.

"It's the woman you met with, isn't it?" Charlie asked. "Sonya Kunetskaya."

His father looked shaken. "Yes."

"Is she alive?"

Alfred Stone shrugged as if he didn't care, but his eyes indicated otherwise.

"What do you *really* know about her?" Stone asked impassionedly. "Could she have been a link to someone, an agent, in Russia that Lehman was controlling?"

"Why are you asking me these things, Charlie?"

"We shouldn't talk now. I'm sorry. You're tired; you should go to sleep. It can wait a few days."

"No, Charlie. I think we should talk now. I want to know what you've been finding out."

"Please, let's talk another time."

"Now, Charlie," Alfred Stone demanded.

Gently, Stone told his father some of what he had

learned, from Saul's allegations to the tale told by the old woman in New Jersey. He softened the story, leaving out Saul's murder; it would not do to shock his father now.

Alfred Stone listened, his mouth slightly agape. "Keep going," he said. "There are things I have to tell *you*, too."

A white van proceeded up Washington Street, out of the Combat Zone, toward Cambridge. The two men sat inside, the bearded man at the wheel. In the backseat was another, a large man with unfashionably long sideburns who had come up from Baltimore.

The van was a 1985 Dodge, specially adapted by an expert craftsman in Pennsylvania who had served a ten-year jail term for participating in an armed robbery. He had thought he was adapting the van for ordinary criminals, but he knew enough to be discreet: his livelihood, as well as his life, depended upon it. He had constructed a veritable tank. Steel plates had been welded to the inside, with a pull-down steel visor to protect the driver from gunfire, with slits at eye level. There were holes for gun ports. The van could withstand virtually any gunfire. It would take nothing short of a bazooka to interfere with its progress.

The van was equipped with several .44-caliber magnum handguns and a number of Thompson submachine guns. But the two men did not expect to use any firepower at all on this mission. The assignment would be, as the Americans said, a piece of cake.

The man at the wheel was a part-time taxi driver, as so many Russian émigrés seemed to be. He had lived in Boston for three years, having been selected for the ultrasecret organization six months before he left Moscow. He lived alone in an impoverished Boston suburb and kept to himself, just another anonymous émigré in a city full of them. In reality, he, like the man in the leather jacket, whom he did not know, had been sent to this country and supported handsomely because they were men of unusual talents, men who could follow orders perfectly and kill efficiently if required.

They drove up Massachusetts Avenue, through Harvard Square, and then found the street off Brattle.

"*Ne plokho*," the man in the leather jacket said admiringly of the large residential houses on Hilliard Street. Not bad at all.

"But how would I know about things like covert operations?" Alfred Stone protested later, after Charlie had retrieved Peary, and father and son were sitting at the kitchen table. "I was never involved in such things." He moved the salt and pepper shakers around the Formica kitchen table, making ellipses around a glass of water and a brown plastic pharmacist's pill bottle, as if they were all chess pieces.

"You were Lehman's assistant. You were the assistant to Truman's national-security adviser."

"Oh, God. We were involved in things like Inchon, the troubles with MacArthur, and the Chinese Communists. The recapture of Seoul. That kind of thing."

"You never heard anything about an attempt to pull off a coup in Moscow?"

"A coup?" Alfred Stone laughed. "John Foster Dulles's fondest wish. The enemy you know is better than the one you don't. Hamlet, I think: 'Rather bear those ills we have than fly to others that we know not of.' "

"You heard nothing about a coup? Nothing? Not gossip, not passing references in documents?"

"I'm not saying it wasn't attempted." He twisted open the pill bottle and shook an Inderal into his palm. Then he put it in his mouth and washed it down with a long draught of tap water.

"Yes, I know," Charlie said. "We—the U.S., I mean—tried a couple of times to have Stalin knocked off. Tried to work on getting rid of Khrushchev after the Cuban Missile Crisis. Sure."

"Charlie," his father said exasperatedly, "if you're claiming that Winthrop Lehman, a fixture in the White House since the Roosevelt administration, was secretly involved in a coup against Stalin, I must say I wouldn't be surprised in the least. I don't even see anything wrong with it—Stalin was a dangerous tyrant; everyone knew that."

"Exactly," Charlie said. "What's wrong with a plot to unseat one of the twentieth century's two greatest dictators?"

"Right."

"If that's all it was. But that can't be the full story."

"Why not?"

"Because there'd be no need to cover up such an operation. There'd be no reason to. For one thing, most of the principals would be dead."

"So what are you suggesting?"

"I'm suggesting that something is alive today, something so serious and so secret that people's lives can be extinguished simply for knowing a tiny piece of the puzzle." He stared straight ahead for a moment, wondering how much to tell his father. "Now I need to know something from you. You've said you went to Moscow because Lehman asked you to go. But what else is there? Why did you *really* go? There's more to it, isn't there?"

Alfred Stone sat silently at the kitchen table, his fingers moving oddly back and forth on the Formica as if by their own volition. He did not speak.

"Why did you ruin your life for Winthrop Lehman?"

His father gave an odd smile.

"We all have our secrets, Charlie. I want you to do me a favor. You're investigating all this for me. I can't tell you what that means to me." His eyes shone with something Charlie took to be gratitude. "But now I want you to stop."

"I can't."

"The game isn't worth the candle."

"It's not a game."

"No, damn it. It's not a game. But why do you persist? Why are you doing this?"

"Initially, because I was assigned to. I was asked to find out about the Lenin Testament. I can't really tell you why."

"Well, there's someone you can talk to, if you insist on pursuing this. One of my former students might be able to help you. If anyone would know, he would—and if you needed an ally, he'd be there for you. He's on the National Security Council—he's got roughly the same job I had."

"Thanks."

"Former students, even those who've grasped their way to the top the way he has, tend to enjoy doing favors for their old mentors. Massages their egos." He folded his fingers into a tent, interlaced them, then bent them backward until a few of the knuckles cracked. Suddenly he said, "Charlie, let's go to Maine this weekend. I don't think it will be too much for me, and I could use a chance to convalesce somewhere pleasant."

"Maine?" His father meant the lodge in southern Maine they used to take for a month every summer, during most of the years of his boyhood. The place—"lodge" was almost too grand a word for the rambling old farmhouse—had been one of Charlie's favorite places. He remembered the smell of burning wood that permeated all the blankets in the house. The two of them would have long, lazy chats. They'd go out fishing, or duck-hunting. In the afternoons, Charlie would take the outboard motorboat and circle the lake, bombing over the water, while his father snoozed in a hammock. Sometimes Charlie would go out climbing, solo, on the nearby range. During the year, his father tended to be uncommunicative; at the lodge, he unwound.

"I'd love to," Charlie said. "You have something to tell me."

"Yes."

"About all this?"

"Right."

"Don't hold back—"

"I won't. Just give me a few days. I've held out for years; I can hold out another few days."

"A hint, then."

"Just that it involves me and you. The past. I'll tell you everything. Charlie, you know about the fox and the hounds, right?"

"Another metaphor?"

"Haven't I told you that one before? The hounds run for their lunch, but the fox runs for his life. Right now you're a hound. Don't become a fox. Will you do that for me?"

"I can't, Dad."

"You can. Don't be a fox. You've got information now; you can threaten to use it, if need be. For *me,* Charlie. Give it up for me, all right? You'll see why."

Charlie was silent for five seconds, ten, twenty. He sighed. "I hate to do it," he said slowly. "But I will."

"Thank you. Now, I do need your help. Help me find that damned dog." He walked to the kitchen door that gave onto the yard and opened it. Craning his neck, he called to Peary. "He likes staying outside at night. It's curious. Most dogs prefer it inside."

The two men, father and son, stood at the back door. "What I was doing," Charlie said at length, "I did for you."

Peary came up to the back door, his collar jingling musically.

"I know," Alfred Stone said as he massaged the dog's ears. "It—don't make me—" He fought back tears, bowing his head, obviously ashamed. After a minute, he could speak again. "I appreciate it."

At one-fifteen, the Russian in the leather jacket, who had been walking down Hilliard Street at ten-minute intervals, saw that all the lights in Alfred Stone's house had been extinguished.

"*Speshi,*" he told his comrade, returning to the armored van. "*Pora.*" Hurry; it's time.

The bearded one went to the back of the van and located a shoulder bag that contained, among other tools, a pair of heavy-gauge wire-cutters, heavy black leather gloves, and a glass-cutter. They made their way around to the back of the house with the determined stride of two Cambridge residents returning home from a dinner party.

The power box was exactly where they were told it would be, at the side of the house. The bearded man, wearing the rubber gloves, loosened three bolts and was then able to pull out the power cable, thereby shutting off the electricity in the house. With the wire-cutters he severed the telephone cable.

At the same time, his comrade had tried the kitchen window and found it locked. He affixed a suction cup to the glass and, with the glass-cutter, scored a large circle. Then he rapped it quickly but quietly, which loosened the circle; the suction cup kept the glass from shattering on the kitchen floor. He reached his hand in, unlocked the window from the inside, and slid it open.

Within three minutes, the two men were, almost noiselessly, inside the house.

Stone slept uneasily. He had uncovered too much simply to give it up; there were too many unanswered questions.

He lay in bed, staring up at the ceiling, tracing with his eyes the web of cracks he had watched for so many nights as a child. Suddenly he heard a soft, muffled thump. Downstairs? Someone passing by outside the house? At night one's ears were easily deceived. A shutter closing?

Then, inside, Peary started barking, which was strange, because he almost never barked at night.

Stone turned in bed to glance at his digital clock. For a moment he thought it wasn't there; then he realized that it was on the table, but it was dark. Could he have accidentally unplugged it? He sat up, and reached over to switch on the lamp. Dead. The power must have gone off.

There was a phone in the hallway. He walked out of his bedroom to the old beige phone, to call the power company. A line was obviously down somewhere. Sometimes a car would hit a pole, knocking down a power line. He picked up the phone. No dial tone.

Then there was a high-pitched yelp, a sound that wasn't quite human, and Stone knew it was the dog.

Someone *was* down there.

He turned slowly toward his bedroom to get a pair of shoes, to go downstairs and investigate, and—

There was someone in the hallway, a large bearded man, and he was coming at him. And something about the man looked terrifyingly familiar. . . .

Stone whirled fully around to face the intruder. "*What the fuck*—" he shouted. Stone leaped at him, grabbed his arm, forced it upward at an angle. The interloper slammed his fist into Stone's abdomen; Stone, who was taller, threw him to the floor, relying on the element of surprise. But the man was more powerful, and he lunged forward, cracking a fist into Stone's face as he propelled himself forward. Stone reeled backward, suddenly seeing, as he hit the wall, that the man had a gun, in a holster concealed beneath his windbreaker. Stone threw himself at the attacker again. He was on home turf, protecting himself and his father inside their home, and the adrenaline surge he felt was enormous. With the flat of his hand he cracked into the man's chin, forcing it upward. Then he shoved him hard, hard enough to throw him into a long mirror that hung in the hallway. It shattered, the shards of glass cascading noisily to the floor. Stone reached again, and now he felt a sharp jab from behind. Something had pierced his skin.

There was another man behind him now; he was outnumbered. As he turned, he saw what had jabbed into his flesh, his backside: a hypodermic needle.

A shout came from the end of the hallway. His father had opened his bedroom door and was hoarsely calling out in terror.

"Get back," Stone shouted. "Stay back!" He turned to the first man, and as he threw his fist he felt dizzy, uncoordinated, and his fist loosened as he lost his balance. He seemed to be falling headlong, falling incredibly far, and then everything went dark.

A bell. A steadily penetrating bell was the first thing he would remember hearing. The sound was unbearably sharp. His head was hurt; it felt swollen. There was something coarse and abrasive rubbing his cheek. Carpeting. Stone was lying on the floor of his father's study, his head on the Oriental rug. Everything was incredibly bright— daylight.

The ringing was the doorbell, which was buzzing angrily. He tried to lift himself from the floor, but he was dizzy, nauseated, sick. It was painful, but he had to stop the noise.

He grasped the edge of his father's oak desk as a brace, and pulled himself up slowly.

He stared in horror, incredulity. He felt his blood freeze, his heart explode.

It was his father.

It couldn't be, it couldn't be. It had to be some horrible delusion. I'm asleep still, Stone told himself, I'm dreaming something unspeakable, this isn't real.

The blood was everywhere—on the desk, on the blotter, dark, sticky, congealed puddles of human blood. Blood covering his father's pajamas, like a spill of crimson dye. The deep gashes crisscrossed the body, bloody lines, cuts, stab marks, extending upward from his chest, his heart, to his throat, which gaped open.

"No, no, no," Stone moaned. "Oh, Jesus Christ, no, my God, no." He stood, paralyzed with horror.

His father had been stabbed to death. His body was sprawled in the desk chair, his defaced head tilted all the way back. He was covered with deep, violent stab wounds, the mangled victim of a psychotic attacker.

Protruding from one of the wounds in his father's side, Stone now saw, was a long, black-handled knife. A Sabatier knife, one of those from his father's set in the kitchen, one of the ones Stone had sharpened so recently.

He stumbled crazily toward the body of his father, a low, keening cry escaping his throat. He would bring him to life, he would resuscitate him. It was possible. Surely he wasn't so far gone. It was possible. He would save his life, he would fix him. *"Oh, Jesus Christ!"* he screamed. He gasped, clawing at the body.

The doorbell had stopped, and then something hurtled against the door. He heard a tremendously loud crash.

There was no time to see what the noise was. He had to save his father's life. He would save him.

Somewhere in the house were voices, men's voices, people shouting. He could hear someone calling his name, but he would not answer now. No time. There was no time.

He put his hands on his father's torn cheeks, held up the lifeless head, screaming with vocal cords that no longer could make a sound. No, no, he tried to say, leave me alone.

He caught a glimpse of blue through the drapes. Police. They wanted to come in, but there was no time.

No time, Stone tried to shout out at them. I have to save his life.

"Open up," a loud voice said.

They had not come to help, some part of Stone's brain told him. Leave. They are not here to save your father. Leave.

He would have to escape. For his father's sake, he would have to escape.

20

Moscow

Finally, it was the visit to the Serbsky Institute that turned Stefan Kramer and his father into terrorists.

The mental deterioration of his brother, Avram Kramer, was, however, only the last straw. Sometimes Stefan believed that his family had been singled out by fate for a miserable existence. Driving home that night from Serbsky, Stefan's father told him the full tale of his own private nightmare, his own imprisonment, for the first time.

He'd been captured by the Germans while fighting in the Great Patriotic War. In another country, in another time, he would have become a war hero; in Russia he was a traitor for having been so valorous and so foolhardy as to be captured.

In the camp he saw horrors that hardened him for the rest of his life.

One of his campmates, who'd been arrested for unspecified "anti-Soviet agitation," refused to sign a confession, and so the authorities had inflicted on him one of the most famous cruelties. They had removed his pants and undershorts and seated him on the floor, while two sergeants sat on his legs, and the interrogator had placed the toe of his boot atop the poor man's penis and testicles and had begun to press, slowly.

The man confessed within five seconds, just before he would have passed out.

Another prisoner had been wounded as seriously when an iron ramrod had been heated red-hot and placed against his anus, and had he not shouted out his guilt they would have plunged it in as far as it would go; even so, his anal membrane hemorrhaged and bled for days.

But Yakov Kramer had been spared—until the two zeks, political prisoners, had splashed acid in his face.

Yet not until later did his loathing for the Soviet system harden. It was the day when he'd first learned, some weeks after the fact, that Stalin had died. All the prisoners had been roused, as usual, at four o'clock, trundled off to the mess hall for "black cabbage soup," which was made of nettles and was utterly unpalatable, and then sent off to the clay pit, where they dug clay to be made into bricks. On this shift they had more or less been left alone: the supervising guard stood idly by some distance away.

As he dug, Kramer looked at his fellow inmates. Their shaven heads were gray, and their miserable darting eyes had sunk into their heads, surrounded by a brownish discoloration. They looked like walking cadavers, and Kramer knew that he was so ugly no one could even bear to look at him.

Kramer struck up a conversation with a man who had recently come in from Moscow. What was it like there now? Yakov wanted to know. Was it worse, even, than before the war?

And the Muscovite had told him a story that had made the rounds in Moscow. It seemed that a Moscow district Party conference had taken place, at the end of which the secretary of the Party had called for a tribute to the late great man, Comrade Stalin, and of course everyone had stood and applauded. They beamed and stretched out their hands in the Russian manner and clapped loudly. And the ovation went on, and on. Five minutes, then ten minutes had gone by, and the members of the audience were so weakened they feared they would drop. Yet they could not stop clapping. The KGB was in attendance, and they were watching the audience carefully for signs of slackening enthusiasm. The audience continued to clap, weak and in pain, desperately. Finally, a local factory manager, who was standing at the front of the room with the Party leaders, took it upon himself to sit down, and with tremendous relief the rest of the room followed. And that night the factory manager was arrested. Well, this story was so widely told in Moscow, the man said, that it had to be true.

Kramer, listening aghast, threw his shovel deep into the earth and waited for a moment while the guard passed. "Stalin's dead," he muttered, "but his wardens live."

That day, he vowed that, if ever he got out of there alive, he would never forget what had been done to him and to his brethren who had died in the prisons and the camps, and he would see to it that Russia never forgot, either. . . .

In 1956, when Nikita Khrushchev gave his famous "secret speech" to the Twentieth Party Congress denouncing Stalin, millions of zeks were suddenly released, Yakov among them. He later became friendly with a small group of zeks who had also survived what he'd been through. They helped one another adjust to life outside the camps, watching one another grow and raise children and still sustain within themselves a deep hatred for the system that had done to them what it had done.

The others seemed to get more and more embittered. They talked, increasingly, of terrorism—of stirring things up, venting their hostility, blowing something up.

One day in the early 1960s, a member of his group—Kramer wanted no part of it—decided to set off a bomb. Through a friend at the scientific-instruments factory where he worked, the man was able to get the components for a crude TNT bomb, and left it in a valise on Gorky Street. The bomb was even more powerful than they'd expected, and several innocent bystanders were badly hurt. He had slipped a letter to an American wire-service reporter, who published the barely literate broadside against the Soviet government.

This had happened decades ago. The amazing thing was that the man had never gotten caught.

"But sometimes," Yakov said, concluding his story, "things can go right."

"Yes," his son replied. His eyes seemed vacant. "Sometimes they can."

That night, Stefan decided to become a terrorist, and, late into the evening, father and son devised a campaign of terror designed to free Avram.

Stefan came over to his father's apartment and sat at the kitchen table. Sonya was out for the evening, visiting a friend, which was fortunate: Yakov insisted that she not be involved.

"Nothing else will free Avram," Stefan said. He was tall and lanky and wore a sweatshirt whose frayed sleeves were too short. He pulled at them nervously.

"But we can't *demand* Avram's release," his father objected. "The authorities will know immediately who's behind the terror. They'll connect it right away to us—"

"No. That's the beauty of my plan. We'll demand the release of *all* political prisoners held in the Serbsky Institute. There are dozens of them—no one will suspect us."

"Yes," Yakov said, thinking aloud. "And we make the appeal *private*—a letter directly addressed to Gorbachev only. Yes. Release these people, and the violence stops. If you don't, we threaten to go public with our demands. And the Kremlin will have to give in to protect themselves—it's a matter of pure self-interest."

"But why should the letter be private?"

"So the Kremlin can agree to our demands without losing face. Without appearing to be weak. Without fearing they'd be encouraging other acts of terrorism."

"I see," Stefan said, pulling again at his sleeves.

"But do you know anything about making bombs?"

After a moment's pause, Stefan replied, "Yes. I do.

I mean, not a tremendous amount—but I learned a bit in prison—"

Yakov gave a short, bitter laugh. "Your time there wasn't altogether wasted. But without the equipment—"

"I can get it."

Yakov shook his head.

"The question is," Stefan said, "where do we do it?"

"We've got to attract maximum attention," his father said. "Our government is skilled at covering things up, making them disappear, denying they ever happened. It's got to be in public. A symbolic target."

"Such as?"

"Such as Red Square, or the metro, or Central Telegraph," he replied. "Such as one particular Kremlin leader with a particularly odious reputation."

"*Borisov*," Stefan suddenly exclaimed.

Borisov, the Central Committee's head of the Administrative Agencies Department, was known as one of the most notorious apparatchiks in the immense Soviet *nomenklatura*, the privileged class. More than anyone else in the Soviet power structure, he had urged the widespread use of psychiatric hospitals to quell dissent. And now, after most of the psychiatric prisoners had been released, Borisov was agitating to restore this insidious form of punishment. People believed he was as close to a fiend as anyone alive, now that Stalin was dead.

"Borisov," his father agreed. "*Takoi khui!*" he added. The prick.

"We'll find out where he lives," Stefan said. "That shouldn't be hard to do."

"Stefan," Yakov said, involuntarily placing a hand up to the striated mass of scar tissue that disfigured his nose, his lips, and part of his eye. "What are we doing? I'm too old for this."

Stefan compressed his lips. He suddenly went cold; he felt gooseflesh on the back of his neck. "It's my job," he said. "I'll do it."

Suddenly the door to the apartment opened, startling the two men.

It was Sonya. "Oh, I'm sorry," she said. "I'm interrupting you two."

"No, my dear," Kramer said gently. "We were just finishing up."

21

The militiaman in the narrow booth at 26 Kutuzov Prospekt was instructed to report any suspicious loiterers—he was, after all, protecting a building that housed members of the Central Committee—but rarely if ever did he have to pick up the phone. He sat in his booth, checking the identity of the drivers of cars entering the lot, nodding brusquely, and doing very little else. It wasn't a very interesting job; in the winters it was cold, and he would wear two pairs of military-issue gloves.

The guard didn't much like to read, but the loneliness of the post provided little other escape. So he read the newspapers—*Pravda* and *Izvestiya* and *Evening Moscow* and so on—and nodded officiously at the cars that passed the booth. In the middle of the night, not too many cars passed into the lot.

At three o'clock, he was relieved by the guard on the second night shift. The two guards chatted for ten minutes or so, scarcely watching the parking lot. Which was virtually silent, anyway.

But at that moment, a man entered the parking lot.

Dressed in the gray-quilted work coat of a laborer, Stefan Kramer walked by with the bored, lagging stride of a worker who would much rather be home asleep.

If the guards happened to see him slipping in, they would undoubtedly question him. Stefan would say that one of the damned elevators was broken, and he'd been rudely summoned from bed by the building's superintendent. There was some sort of problem, either with the hoist cables or the sling or the landing-zone detector—the guy didn't know what the hell he was talking about. Hadn't the guards gotten phoned orders from the superintendent to admit him? And the guards, whose primary instincts were to preserve their own jobs, would admit the guy who knew so much about elevators rather than suffer the wrath of a Central Committee pansy who had to, God forbid, *walk* down three flights of stairs.

But no one stopped Stefan.

The black Volga was at the far end of the large parking lot, just as he expected it to be. A few days earlier, Stefan had once again contacted his old cellmate from Lefortovo, Fyodorov, and asked him to find someone who knew something about the residents of this particular Central Committee apartment building. Fyodorov managed to turn up a car mechanic who'd done some work here, and who knew where Sergei Borisov parked his car.

Good; the car was out of sight of the sentry booth. No one could see him.

He set to work immediately, sliding himself underneath the car. The asphalt pavement was cold.

As he worked, his breath rose in clouds around him.

He'd molded the white plastic explosive, which Fyodorov had provided, into two sausages, then put them into plastic bags. Connected to each of these sausages was a blasting cap connected in turn to an electrically operated detonator, and both of these detonators were connected to a radio receiver—a pocket pager of the sort that Western physicians use on call. The pager's speaker, which normally emits the beeping noise, had been removed and replaced with an electrical relay. When the unit received a signal from the transmitter—which would transmit up to several kilometers away—the relay would close a switch, completing a circuit, and the car would blow up.

Stefan placed one of the sausages under the gas tank and another at the front of the car, checked to make sure there were no wires showing; the first part of the job was done.

He inched his way, on his back, under Borisov's car, then under another car, until he could get up without being seen from either the building or the guard booth. Leaving was a problem: better not to risk being questioned. So he spent what remained of the night in a janitor's closet underneath a stairwell, as his old cellmate had suggested.

By dint of careful study, Stefan had learned quite a bit about Borisov's habits. Fyodorov was most helpful in this. Stefan was able to learn when Borisov's driver arrived; when Borisov customarily emerged from his apartment; which of the many black Volgas in the parking lot at 26 Kutuzov Prospekt was Borisov's; and when the guard changed at the parking-lot booth.

At six-thirty in the morning, when the night staff left and the day staff arrived, Stefan emerged with a small group of floor guards.

For the next hour, he waited in his father's old car, just down the block, from which he could see all the comings and goings at 26 Kutuzov Prospekt. At exactly seven-thirty, Borisov's chauffeur arrived.

Stefan began to have second thoughts.

The chauffeur, a young, plain-looking Russian, looked like the sort of guy who had a wife and maybe a kid or two at home. Stefan disliked seeing him die; the chauffeur was no monster. But he'd have to go with Borisov; there was nothing to be done.

Stefan had accepted the very difficult idea of taking innocent human life.

At seven-forty, Borisov came out of the building with the chauffeur, five minutes later than Fyodorov had predicted. Stefan recognized him instantly from his photographs. He was a pudgy, self-contented man in an expensive suit that might have fitted him five or six years ago. He had evidently put on weight since.

The chauffeur escorted Borisov to the Volga and then knelt down to inspect the underside of the car, in a gesture that appeared nothing more than habit. It was virtually unthinkable that a car belonging to a member of the Central Committee would be tampered with in any way. Such things rarely if ever happened in Russia.

Finding nothing, the chauffeur got into the driver's seat.

Stefan watched the Volga pull out of the lot in front

of a silver Mercedes-Benz, watched the chauffeur nod at the guard in the booth and pull into the traffic on Kutuzov Prospekt. Stefan followed a good distance behind: no reason to arouse suspicion, since he knew the route Borisov always took.

The thought of the act he was about to commit—the enormity of it—sickened Stefan, but he also knew that, if they didn't go through with it this time, he risked the discovery of the bomb, and the failure of their entire mission.

Borisov's car traveled down Kutuzov Prospekt, turned onto the adjoining Kalinin Prospekt, a major thoroughfare, then stopped at a traffic light. Borisov appeared to be concentrating on a sheaf of papers.

Quickly Stefan screwed the seven-inch-long antenna into the transmitter and put his forefinger on the button.

He closed his eyes for an instant and could see the face of his brother before him. He whispered, "For you, Avram," and pressed the button.

The sound was deafening, even hundreds of feet away. The Volga exploded into a ball of dark-orange fire as the car split in two and pieces of it sprayed the street, still afire. An enormous column of smoke rose; pedestrians gaped in amazement. The job was done.

One of the pieces of the explosion landed on the sidewalk very near Andrew Langen, a second secretary in the U.S. Embassy in Moscow, who was in truth employed by the Soviet Russian Division of the Directorate of Operations of the Central Intelligence Agency. Langen knew very little about explosives, but he had recently attended an Agency seminar on terrorism, and he was quick-thinking enough to pick up this peculiar bit of detritus and take it to work with him. In the process, he gave himself quite a painful burn on his left hand.

The Borisov bombing rated front-page treatment around the world, from London's lurid *News of the World* and assorted other British tabloids to *Le Monde* of Paris and *Bild Zeitung* of Hamburg. The *New York Post* ran a full-page headline: "Red Boss Slain." On the front page of *The Wall Street Journal,* under the heading "What's News," the news appeared with typical *Journal* restraint: "A prominent Soviet official, Sergei I. Borisov, was killed in Moscow when a bomb planted in his automobile was detonated on one of the city's main boulevards. No group claimed responsibility." *The New York Times* featured an analysis on its Op-Ed page by a Soviet expert at Columbia University's Harriman Institute who dilated on domestic opposition to the Kremlin. Ted Koppel devoted an episode of "Nightline" to the assassination. Tass, the Soviet news service that had become so much more open in recent years, did not mention it.

22

The President of the Soviet Union, Mikhail S. Gorbachev, does not have an official residence—no White House or Buckingham Palace. He maintains a residence in Moscow, a dacha near Moscow, and a dacha by the Black Sea. Unlike his predecessors, who most often lived in the building at 26 Kutuzov Prospekt, Mikhail Gorbachev preferred to stay at a dacha just west of the city, on Rublyovskoye Shosse.

Gorbachev had summoned his guests late at night, after midnight. Normally, he did not keep nocturnal hours; he was usually in bed by eleven.

And rarely, if ever, did Gorbachev hold meetings in his dacha. His three guests trembled with anticipation, knowing that the matter was of the utmost urgency.

The three Zil limousines pulled past the do-not-enter sign in front of the dacha, where each was stopped by a pair of armed guards, who inspected the passengers and then waved them by. As they disembarked, the three men were inspected by another set of guards, who searched them for concealed weapons.

The three—the KGB's Andrei Pavlichenko; Anatoly Lukyanov, who was one of Gorbachev's most trusted aides; and Aleksandr Yakovlev, Gorbachev's closest ally on the Politburo—entered the dacha quietly. They passed through the front sitting room, which was decorated by Raisa Gorbacheva in rich English fabrics, to the President's study.

Gorbachev was sitting behind his desk, his bald pate illuminated by a round circle of light from a desk lamp. He was dressed casually, in gray slacks and a blue pullover sweater. The man radiated confidence and strength, but he also looked tired. The smudges of gray under his eyes were darker than usual.

"Please, come in," Gorbachev said. "Sit." He indicated several chairs.

When they were seated, he began. He seemed to be under considerable strain. "I'm sorry to disturb you—take you away from your wives or your mistresses." He gave a brief smile. "But you are men I know I can trust. And I need your advice."

Each of his visitors nodded.

"We are faced with a problem of great consequence. This is the second act of terrorism in Moscow in two weeks," Gorbachev continued, knowing that his visitors had heard the news about Borisov. "Of the members of the Politburo, you are the only ones I trust fully. I need your help." He turned to his newly appointed KGB chief. "Andrei Dmitrovich. Sergei Borisov was your friend."

Pavlichenko flushed with anger, biting his lower lip. He bowed his head, then looked up. "That's right."

Aleksandr Yakovlev, a balding man whose tinted glasses set off a pudgy nose, interjected: "Is it possible that these acts are being perpetrated by mere dissidents? Is it *possible*?"

"Yes," said Lukyanov. "These terrorists have somehow managed to gain access to equipment made in the West, perhaps Europe, perhaps America. They must be working with anti-Soviet elements—"

"No." The KGB chairman interrupted, almost timidly at first.

"What makes you say that?" Gorbachev asked.

Pavlichenko bit his lower lip again, and then spoke, as if combating a powerful resolve not to say a word. "I mentioned at the Politburo meeting that the explosive used in one of the bombs was Composition C-4, which is made in the United States."

"Yes," Lukyanov said impatiently, "but what—"

"I didn't say everything." He let out a long, measured breath, rubbed the flat of his palm against his jaw. "I've got my people hard at work on this. And they've come up with some results even I didn't want to hear. The stuff isn't just any C-4. It's a particular, unique formulation." He looked around the room, then squarely at Gorbachev, and shrugged. "Made only for the Central Intelligence Agency."

The shock did not register immediately on Gorbachev's face, and when it did, the barest flicker of fear showed in his eyes. He spoke steadily. "What are you suggesting?"

"Look, the Americans would be crazy to do anything to undermine you, right? But that assumes the conventional logic of power politics," the KGB chairman said gravely.

"I don't follow," Yakovlev said.

"Tensions between Moscow and Washington are at an all-time low," Pavlichenko said. "Since the war, anyway. So who in Washington in their right minds would want us out of power?"

Gorbachev shrugged. "A lot of people would like to see me pushing papers back in Stavropol."

"No doubt," Pavlichenko said. "But they're not in Washington."

"There, too, I'd imagine," Gorbachev said.

"The military-industrial complex," suggested Lukyanov, whose understanding of America was not terribly sophisticated.

"All right," Pavlichenko said. "We can assume anything. No doubt there are reactionary forces everywhere, who would benefit from the old, vintage Cold War. Such as the entire Communist Party *apparat*. Members of the

Politburo, who are about to lose their jobs. Yes. No doubt."

"But—?" Gorbachev said.

"I'm suggesting that the terrorism may well be co-ordinated directly by American intelligence. And I am suggesting that the Americans may—*may*—be working with forces within the Soviet Union. Perhaps within our ranks. I am saying that there may be forces within our country that are trying to unseat us."

PART TWO

THE PURSUIT

Emperors are necessarily wretched men, since only their assassination can convince the public that the conspiracies against their lives are real.

—Domitian

23

Moscow

If it's not easy being an American woman in Moscow, Charlotte Harper had decided, it's just about impossible being a married American woman separated from your husband. Moscow, as everyone knew, was hardly bustling with eligible males.

On arriving in Moscow a year and a half ago, she had kept to herself, avoiding any romantic entanglements, protected by the simple lack of opportunities. She was determined to consider her separation from Charlie merely temporary—they'd work things out, he'd learn to respect her need to work, and all that psychobabble stuff.

But it did not take long for her to grow terribly lonely. Two months ago, she had briefly become romantically involved—if "romantically" was the right word—with the press attaché at the U.S. Embassy, a middle-aged man named Frank Paradiso, who was no doubt a CIA official.

She was torn about it, knowing in her heart that fear and loneliness were the wrong reasons to become attached to someone, that her marriage was far more important than any dalliance. When she had first met Frank, at a press briefing at the embassy, she had been attracted by his energy and his sarcastic humor. He seemed intelligent and sensitive, and he came without cargo: he was divorced. He had asked her out to lunch first, at the National Hotel, and then to dinner at the Praga, and one thing had led to another. It had lasted fully a month. Since then she'd spent her nights alone—often lonely, but at the same time feeling a bit better about herself than she had with Paradiso.

Though on depressed days she thought she might have passed her peak, Charlotte knew that she was attractive, or, as she preferred to think of it, telegenic. Her blond hair and radiant smile projected well against a backdrop of the Kremlin. But, of course, the *reporting* was what was important, or so she told herself.

She had the reputation for being the best-connected American journalist in Moscow, one unpleasant result of which was that some of her colleagues looked upon her with envy. The prevailing notion was that TV reporters were useless here anyway—all they really had time to do, in the two or three minutes they had on the nightly newscast, was to read off an item that had appeared in *Pravda*, show a clip of an interview with some Soviet apparatchik, and do a stand-up in front of the Kremlin or Saint Basil's Cathedral.

All those ink-stained wretches from the world of print journalism—*The Washington Post, The New York Times, The Wall Street Journal*—fancied themselves serious observers of the Soviet scene. Everyone else, they were sure, was just window-dressing. The wire-service reporters were little more than court stenographers, they felt, and the worst of the bunch were the TV reporters, who got all the fame and recognition and didn't know shit about Russia. Didn't even speak Russian. And to some extent the snobs were right; but Charlotte was an exception.

In a few years, she had become one of the stars of the evening news. Her editor seemed to think she could shoot up the ranks, maybe even make weekend anchor, within a year or two. As they put it, the big thing at the networks these days was "glamorizing" the Moscow beat.

But she'd had it with Moscow. Had it with the gray skies and the huge puddles of grimy slush, the fierce crowds, the pushing and shoving in the metro, the empty stores. Paradoxically, as much as she'd grown to despise this forlorn city, she was fed up, too, with the isolation that being a correspondent here forced upon you.

After a year and a half—despite her fascination with the language, the history, the culture—she was aching for home. She wanted, maybe, to get assigned to the State Department, to get back on the fast track. To return home. And she wanted to repair what she had with Charlie Stone, regain that old happiness, have a family.

She was sick of Moscow. And yet, every once in a while, something exciting happened and she was glad she was there.

Only a few days ago, a high Soviet official had been assassinated when a bomb in his car went off on Kalinin Prospekt. It was an extraordinary story: the first time in her memory that such an act of terrorism had taken place in public in the Soviet Union. But virtually nothing was known about it.

If anyone could ferret out anything about the story, Charlotte knew, she could.

She arrived at the ABC office, spent a few minutes chatting idly with Vera, the sweet, tiny Russian woman who cleaned, did various errands, and made tea, and Ivan, the middle-aged, bearded man who looked like a peasant of old and who read through the Soviet press for her. Both of them, no doubt, had to report on her to the KGB, but they were kindly, benevolent people nonetheless, who simply liked to do their jobs well.

Both of them had opinions about who might have assassinated Borisov—the Estonians, Vera believed; plain old dissidents, Ivan maintained. But there was nothing in the newspapers, and not even a mention of it on the Soviet evening news program "Vremya," which Vera had video-taped for Charlotte, as she always did.

Every once in a while, Charlotte got ideas from just sitting around talking with Ivan and Vera. They liked her; she spoke to them in Russian. And she liked them. But they knew no more than anyone else in Russia did about this, not a damn thing.

A telex had come in from the head of the network news division in New York, who wanted to come to Moscow and wanted her to arrange a meeting with . . . Gorbachev. Of course. The big guys in the network always thought they could just issue orders like that to their employees in Moscow. She shook her head and smiled.

Then she went through the coils of paper that had spewed forth during the night from the teletype, glancing through news dispatches from around the world, where of course the Borisov story figured prominently.

She settled back in her desk chair and thought. Somehow she had to crack the story. A few minutes later, she made a brief, cryptic phone call, then went out to her car.

In an hour, she was sitting in the dining room of a new cooperative restaurant that served hearty Georgian food, speaking with the editor of a prominent Soviet journal. He was a good, reliable source; often he "leaked" things to her, information he had picked up from friends in the new Congress of People's Deputies. For his part, he trusted her discretion, knowing she would take care to disguise where she'd received her information and would treat whatever he gave her with sensitivity.

"No," the editor said, shaking his head, his mouth full of chicken tabaka. "We hear nothing of this." He preferred speaking in English, and he spoke it well. "But you're aware that the man who was assassinated—this Borisov—was known to be a good friend of the chairman of the KGB."

"I've heard it," Charlotte said.

The editor shrugged and gave her a significant glance. "What does that tell you?"

"I don't know," she said, preferring to hear his interpretation. "You tell me."

He shrugged again. "It tells me that there may be some very serious power struggle within our own government. Gorbachev depends upon Pavlichenko, the man he appointed to KGB. He needs Pavlichenko's support, right?"

"Right. The guy needs the KGB to keep him in power—so he can carry out his reforms."

"Yes. Well, then, maybe there are some people—is it not possible?—who are not sympathetic with Gorbachev's people."

"Obviously, but—people who'd resort to *terrorism*? You mean people within the government?"

The editor shrugged again.

After lunch, she went over to the old U.S. Embassy building on Tschaikovsky Street, where she had a quick cup of coffee with her friend Josh Litten of *The New York Times*, then stopped by her mailbox in the press section upstairs. There were the usual assortment of magazines, a couple of personal letters, a statement from her New York bank. Nothing much.

She returned to the office and glanced at the news coming over the teletype from the Associated Press wire service. Nothing.

Then she looked again.

It was the name "Stone" that caught her attention. She looked again. The first words that assembled themselves were "slaying" and "Alfred Stone" and then, aghast, she leaned over the coiled teletype printout and read in disbelief.

Alfred Stone, the Harvard historian jailed in the 1950s for allegedly spying for the Soviet Union, had been found murdered.

She all but stopped breathing.

Alfred Stone. That dear, sweet man. No.

And, the story continued, the murderer was believed to be the man's own son, Charles Stone.

Charlie. It wasn't possible.

Reeling, she tore off the length of printout, staggered backward into her office, and collapsed onto the couch. She felt as if she were about to faint.

An hour later, she was still rereading the story, still in shock.

Charlie Stone.

He was innocent. He had to be.

That document he had stolen from Lehman's archives—could this all have to do with that? Something about a code, a number. Something about Lehman and Alfred Stone and . . . what was it, now? He had mentioned this woman in Moscow with whom Alfred Stone had met—Sonya? Yes. Sonya Kunetskaya. Charlie had wanted her to track Sonya down. Somehow he thought Sonya would lead them to the truth about what had happened to Alfred Stone. But that had all been years and years ago.

Hadn't it?

Surely this was no coincidence.

Charlie could not have murdered his father. It was absolutely unthinkable.

He needed her help now. There was no time to lose.

24

Saugus, Massachusetts

The motel bed was littered with Styrofoam cartons, plastic soft-drink bottles, empty Quarter Pounder boxes. Stone awoke, rolled over, and heard the crunch of Styrofoam.

He looked around the motel room, glimpsed the empty vodka bottles, remembered at once where he was.

Saugus. He was in a motel in Saugus, eight miles or so north of Boston.

He was a wreck. His eyes were bleary; he hadn't shaved for five days, since his father's murder. He had left the motel room only to get food and drink.

How had he gotten here? It amazed him that he had found the strength to get to this godforsaken motel on the main drag in Saugus, a tawdry succession of strip joints, cheap steak places, and several bad Chinese restaurants.

He had suffered some sort of breakdown, he was quite sure, yet he had been marginally able to function, as if in suspended animation.

He had, after all, escaped.

He flashed back to awakening on the floor of his father's study, discovering his father brutally murdered. Something had snapped in him. He remembered holding his father's bloodied head, staring at it, *willing* the eyes to open.

And then there had been a crash at the door, and three policemen had burst in, and, as crazed as he was, he knew what they were there for: to arrest him. He had heard them say it, and some powerful part of his brain had told him not to stand there any longer, but to run. He had vaulted through the back door, through yard after yard. He had run out in the middle of Garden Street, narrowly avoiding being hit, and waved down a cab, and told the driver to just *drive*. Made no fucking difference where, he had said. *Just drive!* I just want to get out of the city. The driver had pulled over and demanded to see his money; Stone had waved his wallet at him. Stone had gotten lucky: the driver had actually driven him to Saugus, where he instructed him to stop at this cheap motel, then got out, throwing far too much money at the driver for his trouble.

For days thereafter, while he waited for the shock to ebb, he existed on pizzas and Chinese food delivered to his room, vodka and Scotch and beer and McDonald's burgers he picked up on the rare ventures he allowed himself. So disreputable was the motel's usual clientele that the owner said nothing. Some guy on a bender, he told his wife one afternoon, when she was unable to get into Stone's room to clean. They knew the oddball as Smith, but that was hardly unusual: half of their guests were named Smith.

Now, this morning, the shock had finally worn off, leaving only grief, anger, and puzzlement. He remembered, after his mother had died, he had been overwhelmed with deep, unfathomable sadness, the sort of sadness only a young boy can feel, a belief that the world might as well end. And then something had happened: his sadness had metamorphosed into anger, a hard fist of rage—at his father, at his friends, his schoolmates. For a while, he was a holy terror, but it had gotten him through the worst of the pain. And now the unspeakable terror of seeing his father *murdered* had mutated into a vast reserve of fury.

It would get him through again.

For the first time in five days, he knew he was strong and capable enough to leave the motel. He had put a few things together. Whoever had killed his father had also killed Saul Ansbach—and who else?

But why hadn't they killed him, too? Surely they could have. The fact that they hadn't done so made it clear this was a grotesque setup. The logic, however, eluded him.

Perhaps Saul really had been right. Maybe this all had something to do with a rogue operation. What if someone, or some group of people, with tremendous resources believed he was on the trail of secrets of great importance—and now they wanted the secrets to stay buried?

But who could know what the truth was? James Angleton, the legendary CIA chief of counterintelligence, had once borrowed a phrase from T. S. Eliot to describe the business of espionage and counterintelligence as a "wilderness of mirrors." That it was: the truth was often concealed behind a reflection of a reflection of a reflection. . . .

A few things he knew for certain: that he was being watched, that he had somehow to establish his innocence, and that he could no longer trust anybody. He could not work within the system, because the system, down to the local police force, had been infiltrated.

Parnassus, too, had been compromised; Lenny Wexler had made that clear. Stone could no longer trust anyone there.

Yet he had to return to Boston.

He needed to get to his safe-deposit box at the bank, to get his money, his passport, and the false passport, which by now had to be waiting for him at the post office.

And the dossier. He had to get the dossier he'd left in his father's house, the dossier and the photographs, if they were still there. If they hadn't been taken.

He had to return to the scene of the nightmare.

There was only one way out, and that was to discover who was involved in this thing, this rogue operation or whatever it was. Find them and confront them, threaten to reveal their existence.

Only with such incontrovertible data would Stone be able to defend himself, protect himself. No longer was it a question of clearing his father's name. Now it was a matter of survival.

Charlie Stone, however, could not return to Cambridge. He would have to return as someone else.

He got up from the bed and walked over to the mirror.

He stared at himself for the first time in days, and was shocked. He looked twenty or thirty years older. Partly it was the growth of beard, partly the large bluish circles under his red eyes.

For an instant, Stone was quite sure he could smell smoke, sulfuric and acrid. The smell of gunshot.

He was no longer in a motel room. No. He was sitting in a marsh, on the shores of the small lake in Maine where he and his father used to go duck-hunting, twenty miles north of the lodge. His hands, his feet were numb from the cold.

He'd been sitting in the cramped blind for hours, that camouflage structure of wire and leaves that looks, to a duck, like shrubbery. Next to him was his father, hearty and fit, whispering to him. The two of them had been sitting there so long they had begun to feel like part of the forest, the dark of the early morning and the quiet making them oddly reflective.

Charlie was eleven, and this was his first time hunting. He didn't want to kill the ducks, pretty creatures. He didn't want to do it.

Sitting there, Charlie got colder and colder. It always happened that way: you sweated mightily while you set up, feeling ridiculously overdressed, and then, suddenly, having burned up so much energy, you'd shiver with the cold, sitting. Sitting and waiting.

"Listen, Charlie," Alfred Stone now said, gently. "Don't even think of them as living beings. They're targets. All right? They're part of nature. Just like the chicken your mother makes. That's all."

Shivering, Charlie shook his head and did not reply. He watched the decoys bobbing at the lake's edge, a few feet away. Watched the steam rise from the thermos of hot coffee. Watched the sun rise in streaks of orange and red.

"Crouch down," Alfred Stone said, so quietly. "There. Look."

And then—the glorious, unforgettable sight of the birds suddenly appearing over the treetops, their wings flapping furiously, four or five of them. As Alfred Stone gave the duck call to signal them in, Charlie steeled his resolve. His hand was so cold he hesitated to touch the shotgun's trigger guard.

Then he saw the birds freeze, setting their wings, locking rigid, and zooming in from downwind, like miniature 747s coming in for a landing.

"Come on, now, Charlie," his father whispered.

Charlie stiffened his shoulders and clicked off the safety, just as he'd been taught to do, and then, just as the birds flared their wings to land, he did it. He fired.

The first shot missed.

But the second: a dream shot. The feathers flew. The bird dropped like a bag of pennies, and it was over. A matter of seconds.

Charlie looked up, beaming, and caught the pride in his father's eyes.

Now, looking at himself in the smudged motel mirror, thinking of the guns and the death, Charlie thought of Alfred Stone, dead, his eyes staring, and he shuddered.

It was time to re-enter the world. Stone opened the motel-room door, momentarily stunned by the bracing fresh air. It was morning, surprisingly bright and warm, a perfect October day. At the discount drugstore across Route 1, he found what he wanted: shaving cream, some disposable razors, some shampoo, a tube of tanning lotion. At the cash register he saw a stack of *Boston Globe*s.

His picture was on the front page.

PORTRAIT OF A KILLER, the headline read. There it was, a photograph, taken from his CIA file, its coat-and-tie respectability clashing with the luridness of the headline. No one was in line; Stone picked up the newspaper and scanned the story. The whole article had been faked up, supplied by someone intent on portraying him as dangerous and crazed, a brilliant and unbalanced employee of the Central Intelligence Agency who had suddenly and without reason lost his grip on sanity. The reporter had seized upon the information supplied both by the Boston police and unnamed "government sources" and created out of it a persuasive mosaic that was the stuff of tabloids.

A large quantity of heroin and PCP, "angel dust," had been found in Stone's bedroom at the house, the article said, which indicated to police that the son might well have been in a violent altered state. There was a reference to the grotesque murder of Saul Ansbach, and an allegation that Stone might be a suspect in that case as well. There were baffled remarks from several of Stone's former colleagues at Georgetown and M.I.T., then a recitation of Alfred Stone's tortured past, which gave the story an even more peculiar twist.

"Can I help you?"

The clerk was a teenage girl, chewing bubble gum.

Stone looked at the shampoo and the shaving supplies. "Just—just the paper, the tanning stuff, and the shampoo, please," he said. "I'll put this other stuff back." He had an idea: better not to shave. "And where do you have hair products?"

Half a mile away, at a Salvation Army store, he found a grotesque yellowish-brown woolen overcoat that was too long, tattered pants, a pair of old leather boots that almost fit, and a few other bedraggled changes of clothing. A black-and-orange display in a toy-and-novelty store down the block gave him an idea. It was mid-October, almost Halloween. He bought some spirit gum and a bag of black stage-makeup hair.

When he got back to the motel, he settled his bill, then returned to the room. He shampooed his hair and applied the black hair dye, which, according to the instructions, would disappear after six washings. Half an hour later, he toweled his hair dry and saw, to his satisfaction, that his hair was now several shades darker than his usual brown. Then he doused his hair with a quantity of Vitalis. It looked as if he had not washed it in months. Slowly and carefully he daubed the instant-tanning lotion on his face, neck, and hands, and worked it in carefully. Within a few hours, his skin had taken on the deep color of someone who has spent a great deal of time in the sun.

He applied the spirit gum to his beard and carefully worked on the costume hair. After ten minutes of steady labor, he inspected the results in the mirror. His beard was a long, wispy, dreadful-looking thing. But the overall result was dramatic.

With his filthy, ragged clothes, his beard, and his stringy hair—added to his sunburned, dissolute face—he looked like a vagrant, a mendicant Rasputin. A close inspection would give him away. But from ten feet he looked like an entirely different person, the sort of person that most people don't look at very closely at all.

25

Silver Spring, Maryland

The man from the Soviet Embassy and his friend from the White House met for breakfast at a small diner in Silver Spring. They both agreed that, though it was impossible realistically for them to meet in absolute secrecy, it was nevertheless a good idea to attract as little attention as possible. Anyone who observed them—and in this place it was unlikely anyone would—would think they were social acquaintances of the sort Washington seems to breed.

The diner was an old-fashioned place with Formica tables and booths with jukeboxes. A large sign in front said simply EAT, a throwback touch that had attracted Bayliss's attention on his morning drive to work one day several weeks earlier.

Each of them ordered coffee, which was served in sturdy white ceramic mugs, and Malarek had two eggs over easy, a rasher of bacon, and wheat toast. Bayliss was impressed with Malarek's familiarity with American greasy-spoon menus.

The tension was palpable. "It was goddamned foolproof," Bayliss told his Soviet friend. "Everything, down to the arrest, the charges brought against him. Damn it! So what the hell happened?"

"Apparently our people administered an insufficient dose of the chemical. Stone awoke too early. They wanted to be cautious about administering the dosage. I can't entirely fault them for it." His English, Bayliss noticed, was just about perfect, his accent minimal. "But had *your* people arrived sooner than they did—"

"It was far too complex, too elaborate," Bayliss said, shaking his head.

"The plan was a good one, I have no doubt of that," Malarek answered, with what struck Bayliss as defensiveness. "I'm sure you realize the advantages of this approach: as soon as the interrogation was completed, he'd have been found to have killed himself in prison, deeply contrite over his wasted life, and so forth and so on."

Bayliss looked up sharply. He had lost his appetite now. He bowed his head, then covered his eyes with one hand. "I'd never have imagined," he said in a low voice, "that I'd ever be involved in sanctioning a murder."

"We're doing the right thing," Malarek told him soothingly.

Bayliss rubbed his eyes. "This is difficult for me." He raised his head and resumed thickly: "All right. Nothing is lost. The local police forces are using the NCIC, the National Crime Information Computer, out of the fugitive bureau at FBI headquarters here in Washington. The Massachusetts State Police fugitive squad have unmarked cars throughout the state; security on public transit has been notified. The guy's name's been posted everywhere. He's not going to be able to go anywhere. We've got court orders, fugitive-flight warrants, search warrants, you name it. They've gone through his phone bills, address books, his Rolodex—the works. Every place he turns will be covered. He's bound to realize that he's got no choice but to turn himself in. And then we've got him."

"If you know where he is," Malarek pointed out, spreading butter on a slice of wheat toast. "Otherwise . . ." His voice trailed off, and he shrugged.

"He's wanted not only for murder but for a rather serious, though unspecified, violation of U.S. treason laws. After all, he *is* an employee of the CIA. He's a wanted man. I wouldn't worry about it."

Malarek shrugged again, his expression unreadable.

"But there has to be a way to talk the guy down," Bayliss insisted. "Lure him in, keep him alive. *Alive* he'd be more useful to us, help plug the leaks."

"I think this plan will prove quite adequate," Malarek said, knowing that it would not do at all, that more, much more, would have to be done.

26

Saugus, Massachusetts

Stone found a pay phone a few blocks away from the motel. It was open to the elements, and with the traffic noise it was hard to hear.

Who could he call?

He wondered whether he could rely on his old friend from his Boston days, Chip Rosen, now a metropolitan reporter for the *Boston Globe*. Perhaps.

Then he remembered Peter Sawyer, the private detective in Boston who'd taught him how to pick locks. He had lived upstairs from the apartment Charlotte and Stone had shared when Stone was teaching at M.I.T. They'd gotten to be good friends, and although they barely kept in touch, Stone trusted Sawyer implicitly.

He dialed Sawyer's number, got an answering machine, and was leaving a brief message without giving a name, knowing that Sawyer would recognize the voice, when all of a sudden Sawyer himself picked up the phone.

"Christ, where the fuck are you?"

"Peter, you know I can't—"

"The phone. Right. Listen, man, are you in some kind of mess."

"I didn't do it. You know that."

"Come on! Of course I know it. Jesus, what a fucking disaster! As soon as I heard about it, I asked around. It's got to be a setup."

"Peter, I need your help."

"What's all that noise in the background? Where're you calling from, the middle of the Mass. Turnpike?"

"I've been framed, Peter. I need help."

"You're telling me. They're all over the place, looking for you."

"Who?"

"Who? Who do you think? The cops, probably Uncle, the Feebees, too."

"Uncle?"

"Uncle Sam. The FBI. It's a big thing. Whoever did this wants your ass. Don't even think about turning yourself in, Charlie. Listen. In about a minute, I want you to terminate this call."

"Trace?"

"Right. Keep calling back; no call should last longer than two minutes. All right? And don't bother calling the cops."

"But you've got friends, don't you? You were a cop once."

"Forget it. They've been asking me questions— they're talking to anyone who knows you."

"What do you know about it?"

"I know the whole thing's a frame, and a brilliant one. Believe me, I asked my share of questions when I heard it was you, buddy."

"I was drugged."

"So I hear."

"The *Globe* said they found heroin in my bedroom and in my apartment."

"I'm sure they did. Whoever murdered your father planted the shit, too. Had to be. Hang up, Charlie."

Stone found another pay phone across the street. He

noticed as he walked that people were going out of their way to avoid him. The disguise was working.

He dialed Sawyer's number again, and this time Sawyer answered on the first ring.

"You believe me, Peter, don't you?" Stone said quietly. "I mean, you don't even have any doubt, right?"

"Your prints are on the knife, you won't be surprised to know."

"*Jesus!* Of course they are. I sharpened the whole set, Peter. I used them a number of times." A middle-aged woman walked toward him as if she wanted to use the phone, then turned away in disgust.

"My point exactly. But the thing is, some of the prints were smudged, and not by human skin oil. By something like rubber gloves. Not something *like,* but precisely that. Disposable rubber gloves, the kind that have talcum powder on the inside and the outside. So there's also traces of talc on the knife."

"How the hell do you know all this?"

"I got a friend of mine on the job to get me a copy of the police report. Before they locked it up."

"Let me call you back."

Five minutes later, Stone found a phone inside a newsstand, and as he picked it up the vendor began to yell at him: "Get out of here unless you're going to buy something."

Silently, Stone left. After a long walk, he found another phone, several blocks away.

"So what do I do?"

"I don't know what to tell you. Hide out for a bit, until the search blows over. After a while, you know, they'll give up. Business goes on as usual, police resources are limited. Get yourself a lawyer, maybe. I don't know what the fuck you should do."

"I don't have anywhere to go."

"I wish I could hide you here. But this is one of the first places they'd look. They'll be looking at your friends' houses, anyplace you might be likely to go in Boston— and especially New York. Plainclothesmen, unannounced visits, the works. I've already had a couple of visits. Don't come near me, Charlie. I hate to say it. Promise me you'll stay out of town."

"I'll see."

"*Jesus!*" Sawyer exploded. "Are you out of your fucking *mind*? Your name is being read off at police roll calls at all stations. They've got flyers in all the patrol cars. And your father's house—forget about it."

"Why?"

"That's the *numero uno* place they'll be watching. You go back to Boston, it's suicide."

"I can't talk anymore. Listen, Peter, I appreciate it. Everything. I mean it."

"Forget about it, Charlie."

"I'll call you later on. Peter, I need your help. Badly."

"I'm sorry—"

"What do you mean, sorry?"

"There's rumors."

"About me."

"I don't want to lose my license. That's what I'm hearing. I wish I could help you, Charlie, but I can't. Stay away from me. For you and for me."

Stone hung up the phone and hailed a taxi. None would stop; none would even slow down for the vagrant with the long beard and the greasy hair. Finally, he set off for Boston on foot.

27

Cambridge

A little over four hours later, Stone was standing in front of the granite steps of the Cambridge Post Office, Central Square branch. Along the way he had acquired a shopping cart, which he had stolen from in front of a supermarket, and in it some trash bags filled with garbage.

He had the advantage of surprise. His adversaries,

whether they were police or intelligence or a private group of fanatics, could not reasonably expect him to return to Boston. No one but a crazy person would do it. But how closely could they really be watching, how far-reaching was their surveillance? They could be anywhere, or nowhere.

In front of the post office three cars were idling: a police car, an old Dodge, a fairly new Chrysler. Stone stood behind his shopping cart, watching them. All three of the drivers were waiting. After a few minutes, the Dodge left. The driver of the Chrysler seemed to be consulting a map.

It was a risk, but everything was a risk now. Yet it was unlikely that the police car was staking out the post office—no one knew he had rented a box. There was only a key, and Stone had it in his pocket.

Two other vagrants were sitting on the post-office steps, and both of them watched him silently as he rolled his cart by. Now what? You didn't just abandon the cart if it contained all your earthly possessions.

Stone began pulling the cart up the stairs, a step at a time, then rolled it through the doors. Nothing happened; no one followed. Completely safe.

His post-office box was off to the left, against the far wall. Would it seem strange for a shopping-bag man to have a post-office box? But no one was watching.

In the box was a supermarket circular and a yellow slip of paper that informed him that Mr. Robert Gill had a registered and certified envelope. To get it he would have to go to the registry window.

He walked across the post-office lobby to the line, in the slow gait he had perfected on the long walk from Saugus. The woman in front of him, who looked as if she might be some city bureaucrat on her lunch hour, stared at him.

The *Boston Globe*. His picture had been printed for several days running, in the *Globe* and certainly in the *Herald,* the tabloid for the common man. Did she recognize him? Stone studied the floor. She turned around and glared at the slow-moving clerk. People never actually expected to *see* a killer themselves. Charles Manson could be standing in the express line at the supermarket and no one would give him a second thought unless he had more than twelve items in his cart.

Finally, it was his turn. Silently, he shoved the yellow slip at the clerk.

The clerk gazed at him with unveiled amusement. "You have any identification?"

Identification!

Ah, the driver's license! He remembered that he had Robert Gill's driver's license in his wallet; he removed it and pushed it across the metal counter through the window.

The clerk stared at it and then at Stone. "This isn't you." Indeed, the picture bore almost no resemblance to him.

Stone looked up at the clerk plaintively. "I grew a beard," he said in a low growl.

The clerk looked again, then shrugged. Two minutes later, Stone had Robert Gill's brand-new passport.

He got the cart down the stairs more easily than he had gotten it up, and wheeled it down Mass. Ave. Next stop: the bank. But the police station was two blocks away, and there were too many police cruisers in the area. Any one of them might contain an especially sharp-eyed cop. Stone took a left and wheeled the cart down a steep hill.

Within fifteen minutes, he was in Harvard Square, in front of the Adams Trust Bank. His father had a safe-deposit box here, on which Charlie was the "cotenant," as the bank called it: he had filled out a signature card and had a key to it. Cotenants have "right of survivorship"—everything in his father's box now belonged to him.

He always kept the key in his wallet. The box held cash, and Stone needed it.

But the bank was dangerous. A vagrant was sure to arouse suspicion, especially in a bank that catered to Cambridge's richest citizens.

As he approached the bank's entrance with his shopping cart, he noticed a policeman watching him. "Hey," the policeman called out. "What are you doing?"

Stone looked down and kept going.

"I'm talking to you. Get the hell out of here. You can't be here."

There was nothing to do, short of revealing himself, so Stone wheeled the cart around without saying a word.

Half an hour later, he left the cart in an alley and approached the bank from another direction. The cop was gone. He pushed the revolving door and went in.

On the streets he was invisible; in commercial establishments he was the center of attention. Several tellers looked up as he entered. He walked over to the counter where he had rented the box. A dark-haired, well-scrubbed young man approached.

"Please leave at once," the man said.

"I want to get into a safe-deposit box," Stone said quickly.

The man looked at him uncomfortably for a moment. "Your name?"

"Look," Stone said. "I really do have a box here. I realize what I look like. I've been through some hard times." He spoke quickly, running his sentences together so that they would make more sense in the aggregate than they did separately. "I've been deinstitutionalized, but I'm okay now."

"I'm sorry," the man said, without sorrow.

Stone pulled out his key ring and removed the two safe-deposit-box keys, placing them on the counter. "Can we sit down?"

"Certainly," the man said, relenting a bit. He led them over to a desk and sat down behind it. "I must say, I was a little taken aback. Most of our customers—"

"You don't have to explain," Stone said gently. "I'll get cleaned up just as soon as I get my money."

"You know how this procedure works," the man said. He was obviously still suspicious.

"Of course. I sign an access slip. You compare my

signature with the copy of it you've got on a card in your file."

"Right. What's your name?"

"Charles Stone."

The man hesitated. *Did he recognize the name?* "Just a minute, Mr. Stone."

Was there a button on the floor behind the desk, just as there was at the tellers' counter?

The bank officer got up from the desk. "Let me get your records, Mr. Stone," he said, and walked toward the rear of the tellers' counter.

A minute later, the bank officer returned with the two signature cards. Clearly not recognizing the names on the card, he let Stone into the vault.

His father's safe-deposit box was a shock. Jumbled in with the bills of sale and stock certificates and municipal bearer bonds and deeds was a small white envelope. And underneath that was cash. An enormous quantity of cash: well over a hundred thousand dollars in twenties and one hundreds, a pile of bank notes several inches high. He could scarcely believe his eyes.

He asked for a white canvas money bag, which the astonished bank officer got for him quickly. A minute later, he was out on the street, the bag of money concealed under his frayed coat.

He had made his way slowly out of Harvard Square, taking the smaller side streets. Around five o'clock, he found a small diner in Inman Square, parked the cart in an alley, and went in for a cheap dinner. As he ate the gray meat loaf and mashed potatoes and sipped hot coffee, he opened the envelope.

Inside was a letter, typed on his father's old Underwood at least ten years ago. The paper had begun to yellow.

Dear Charlie,

I'm writing this just in case anything happens to me. If nothing does, you won't get this anyway.

The money here is, as you may have surmised, money that Winthrop Lehman has paid me steadily over the years since 1953, in amounts from ten thousand a year to twice that. Some of it I've spent, but a lot of it's here. He gave this, he said, to help me with whatever expenses I should ever have. I guess he understood the meaning of my favorite line from Pasternak—you know it: "You are eternity's hostage, a captive of time." Aren't we all?

Someday I'll tell you the whole story about Lehman. About Moscow, about the Staroobriadtsy. There is much to explain, and someday I hope to be able to explain everything to you.

Stone sat, reading and rereading the note, until the waitress asked if he wanted a refill. That line from Pasternak—obviously it referred to Alfred Stone's terrible public immolation.

Staroobriadtsy. The Russian term for the "Old Believers." Stone knew the Old Believers were a seventeenth-century Russian faction of Orthodox faithful who had rejected the sudden, wholesale changes in the Church. There were bloody battles, and then they went underground. But who were the Staroobriadtsy today?

What was his father trying to tell him?

Night had fallen by the time Stone arrived at Hilliard Street. A blue-and-white police cruiser was parked in front of his father's house, two policemen inside, drinking coffee from Dunkin' Donuts cups. Stone passed by with his cart, careful not to look at them.

He could not enter the house from the front; that was obvious. They had put routine surveillance here, which meant that anyone entering would be scrutinized. But the police clearly could not keep this up forever; they were not that well equipped. And cops, being human, have to take a piss sometime, get a cup of coffee. He could outwait them. Still, he couldn't risk loitering in the neighborhood, either.

He drew a deep breath of the cold October air.

An image of his father, bloodied and mutilated, suddenly appeared in his mind. He was instantly filled with anger once again, and something new: a desire for vengeance.

He wheeled the cart around to the end of the block and, shivering from the cold, abandoned it. He remembered a pay phone nearby and dialed the Cambridge police.

"There's a robbery in progress," Stone shouted in a North Cambridge accent. "Guy was shot."

The officer on duty answered quickly, "Where?"

"Here. Store 24 in Harvard Square. I'm the night manager. Jesus!" He hung up.

By the time Stone walked around to the rear of the house, the patrol car that had been parked in front was gone. His calculation had been right on the mark: a serious crime reported in the immediate area would be handled by several of the nearest cruisers. But how long would the ruse keep them away?

A telephone trunk cable entered the house at the side. Stone, balancing the sack of money, ran quickly to it. He did not have a knife, but he pulled up a stake from the small garden and used its sharp end, laboriously, to sever the telephone cable.

Then he ran, in a low crouch, over to the porch and pulled himself up to peer into the kitchen window. Through the kitchen he could see the front door just beyond it.

It *was* alarmed. A suitcase-sized piece of apparatus had been placed near the door, attached to a length of wire that plugged directly into the wall telephone jack. That had now been disabled, with the telephone wires cut. A similar device, he saw, had been placed just below the window at which he knelt.

He yanked the window up; it was locked. Raising his elbow, he jabbed it sharply against the pane, which shattered on contact. Suddenly he was inside his father's house again.

It was eerily dark, and he knew he could not turn on any lights. Shapes were unfamiliar, menacing. He could smell the odor of antiseptic; someone had cleaned the place. He listened a minute. Not a sound, no one breathing, nothing. He had to move quickly. He walked silently through the kitchen, then through the dining room into the living room, which was partially lit by the streetlight below. He could not risk being seen from the street. Any shadows, any shapes would be noticed. He hoped the alarm would sound only by means of the phone lines. If not . . . But he didn't want to think about that.

Any moment now, they would realize that the call from Store 24 was a hoax, and the police would return.

The house had been thoroughly torn apart. Everything had been stripped from the walls, every drawer opened. They had searched the entire place.

He loped up the stairs to his bedroom, where he had left the envelope containing the photographs and the copy of the dossier from Lehman's archives.

Nothing.

It was gone. Somehow *they* had found it and removed it. One of his last hopes, and it was gone.

The gun.

He ran to his father's bedroom. The Smith & Wesson 9mm automatic he'd bought for his father was still there on the closet shelf, hidden in an empty paper box. Next to it was a full fourteen-round magazine. He slipped it into his coat pocket, along with the clip. He could not afford to stay here any longer.

One minute later, he leaped out of the kitchen window and hit the soft earth just as the police cruiser pulled up, its headlights blinding him.

28

He cursed aloud and ducked down behind the high wooden fence that separated his father's yard from the adjoining one, then ran as fast as he could. There were footstcps behind him.

He ran unthinkingly, his adrenaline surging. A shout came: "Halt! Police!" One of them fired a gun, a warning shot, which exploded against the slat of a wooden fence. Stone threw himself to the ground, clutching the canvas bag of money, and then crawled along the narrow concrete alleyway between two buildings on Brattle Street.

A siren shrilled nearby.

A few hundred feet away was the back of a row of commercial buildings: a liquor store, a video-rental place, a cheap clothing shop. He remembered having once noticed a walkway between the liquor store and the video place, actually a crawl space between two brick buildings put up twenty years apart.

His pursuers were at least a hundred feet behind him. In a few seconds, they would round the corner and see where he was headed. With an extra burst of speed, he threw himself into the crawl space, cracking his skull against the brick. His body flooded with agonizing, unspeakable pain. But he had to keep going. He squeezed himself between the buildings, his feet moving through the accumulation of trash, and he was on the other side.

A car!

It was his only hope. A young black woman was sitting in her dented Honda, which was idling in front of the liquor store. Waiting for a friend or a husband, probably. Stone lunged for the passenger door and pulled it open. The woman screamed.

"Drive!" Stone ordered her. He reached over and clapped his hand over her mouth, stifling the scream. Any minute, the police would be here.

The woman thrashed around, her eyes wide.

Stone pulled the unloaded gun out of his pocket and pointed it at her. Damn it! he thought; why didn't I take the time to load it?

"I don't want to hurt you," Stone said rapidly, "but I will if I have to. Drive me over to Brookline. You'll be all right."

The woman, terrified, swung into traffic.

A few minutes later, she had driven the car across the Boston University Bridge, to Commonwealth Avenue.

"*Now what?*" she whispered. Tears were streaming down her face.

"A left here."

"Don't kill me. Please."

"Pull over here."

Stone reached into his pocket and pulled out a twenty-dollar bill, which was crumpled and stained. "I know this doesn't make up for the terror, but take it. I'm sorry." He threw it onto the car seat and jumped out.

The apartment building was one street over. Just inside the glass doors was a large panel of buttons. He found the one he wanted and pressed the buzzer.

"Who is it?" the voice squawked tinnily through the speaker.

"Charlie Stone. Let me in."

The inside door buzzed a few seconds later; Stone pushed it open and vaulted up the stairs two and three at a time.

"Jesus, what happened to you?" Chip Rosen said as he opened the door. He was a large man about Stone's age. "My God. Jesus, Charlie."

Rosen's wife, Karen, a small brunette, stood behind him, her hand covering her mouth. Stone had met her once and knew only that she was a lawyer at a big firm downtown.

"Come in, Charlie."

"You've heard," Stone said as he came into the apartment.

"Of course we've heard. Everyone's heard," Karen said.

"I need your help."

"Of course, Charlie," Chip said. "You've got blood on the back of your head."

"Thank God you two were home," Stone said, exhaling slowly. For the first time, he was aware of how rapidly his heart was beating. He set down the canvas bag and slipped the coat off. "I really need some help."

"You've got it," Chip said. "First thing, though, you

look like you need a good hot shower, then a good stiff drink."

Stone sighed with relief. "I can't tell you what a nightmare the last few days have been."

"Take care of that nasty cut on the back of your head. There's some Betadine in the medicine cabinet. You take a shower; I'll bring you a set of clothes. Then we can talk."

In the bathroom, Stone removed the clothes he'd purchased at the Salvation Army store in Saugus, then found a bottle of rubbing alcohol and some cotton balls and began to remove the false beard. He shaved with a can of Barbasol that was on top of the toilet and one of Rosen's Bic disposable razors, lathering the foam, shaving slowly and luxuriously. He wanted—*needed*—to relax, but even now he couldn't completely let his guard down.

He needed allies, friends, a safe harbor. He needed a place to hide while he figured out what to do. Maybe Rosen could use some of his contacts within the newspaper community to help get the story out. And maybe Karen could provide a legal way out of this nightmare.

He could hear Chip and Karen speaking in low voices in the kitchen. This was a tremendous imposition, he knew; he would repay them somehow.

He ran the shower, making it as hot as he could stand, and then got in. It felt wonderful. He washed his hair and the rest of his body, and stood there under the cascade, meditating to clear his head. He was in enormous danger, and this reprieve would not last. He had to have a plan.

He heard a clipped ring from somewhere in the apartment and wondered what it was, then recognized the sound. Chip or Karen was picking up the phone to make a call. He strained to hear what was being said, but the noise of the shower made eavesdropping impossible.

The door to the bathroom opened briefly, and Stone, his reflexes still taut, jolted to attention. It was only Chip, laying out some clothes on the back of a chair.

"Thanks, Chip," Stone said.

"No problem. Take your time."

When he had dressed in Chip's suit, which was slightly

too small but felt good nevertheless, he dabbed some Betadine on the gash at the back of his head and bandaged it.

Then he came out of the bathroom and saw that Chip and Karen had poured three martinis. Stone took his and sank into a comfortable chair. He would sleep easily tonight.

"I'm sorry about your father," Karen said. "It's horrible."

Stone nodded.

Karen looked grave. "Charlie, aren't you in some kind of intelligence work? I know it's none of my business, but is this related to that?"

Stone shrugged.

"Then what do you think is going on?" Chip asked.

"I have no idea," Stone said, unable to trust them with what little he knew of the truth.

"What do you plan to do next?" Karen asked. Neither one of them was looking at him. Was it possible they, too, didn't trust him? Was it possible they thought he was lying?

"That's partly up to you," Stone said. "If I can stay just a few days—"

"We'd be glad to have you," Chip said. "There's a guest room we never use."

"I—I don't know how to thank you. I need to regain my bearings, make some calls."

"I can find you a lawyer if you want," Karen said.

"I appreciate it. But first I need to contact certain people. Chip, I need you to tell me something. All those *Globe* articles on me. Who gave the paper that information? The Boston police?"

"It wasn't all police," Chip said. "I asked the reporter who did the series, Ted Jankowitz, and he told me it was the FBI. Listen, aren't you hungry? Let me get you something."

Karen got up and went toward the kitchen.

"Who was it?" Stone asked. "What did this FBI guy say?"

"He was saying all this stuff about your being involved

in some violation of government treason law or something. I'm sure it's not true."

"Of course it's not true, Chip."

"That's what I told Jankowitz."

Stone got up from the chair and put down his martini glass. He went to the window that looked out onto the street.

"What is it?" Chip asked.

"That car out there. It wasn't there before."

"What are you talking about? Take it easy, Charlie."

But a car was there, directly in front of the building, a squarish new American-made car of the type favored by law-enforcement agencies for undercover surveillance. No one was in it; it was parked in a No Parking zone, with its flashers on.

Footsteps now echoed on the stairs outside. Someone had definitely entered the building.

"*What the fuck have you done?*" Stone shouted. "You called while I was in the shower. I *heard* it!"

Chip's voice was muted and steely. "I'm sorry. You've got to understand."

"*You bastard.*" Stone grabbed his canvas bag, his old clothes, checked wildly for the passports, the gun.

"You've got to understand," Chip repeated. "We had no choice. Anyone who harbors a murder suspect or aids in any way can be charged with being an accessory. We had to cooperate." He was speaking quietly, quickly. "Look, Charlie, just sit down. Give yourself up. Whatever the truth is, it'll come out. Give yourself up. You can't go anywhere. No one's going to shelter you."

The footsteps were now coming from the landing one flight below.

There was only one exit to the apartment, and it led directly into the path of the people coming up the stairs. Stone, holding the canvas bag, flung open the door and saw what he had noticed on the way in: a fire door off the landing that led to a back staircase. Once, leaving a party at Chip's somewhat inebriated, he had accidentally taken that staircase, which led outside, to the back of the building.

His pursuers were yards away, within view, coming up the main stairs. Two of them, both dressed in suits. "That's him!" one shouted, and both began running toward Stone.

He had maybe twenty yards on them. He raced down the stairs, taking them three and four at a time until he found himself on the street, the men close behind. He ran without direction, as fast as his legs would carry him, an enormous fear powering him. Behind him, he could hear shouts, the footsteps louder as they came nearer.

He plunged into the traffic of Commonwealth Avenue, heard the squeal of brakes, horns blasting, as the cars swerved around him and their drivers cursed.

Stone had no idea how close the men were—feet? yards? He did not dare look back.

In the center strip of Commonwealth Avenue run the trains of the Green Line subway, the cars aboveground before their descent below Kenmore Square into central Boston. He saw one coming, headed toward the city. It had just stopped, and now, proceeding at full speed, the train blocked his path. There was no way around it. His pursuers were just behind; if he turned around, they would have him.

It was adrenaline, coupled with tremendous fear, that propelled him *toward* the train rather than away from it. He leaped at it.

His feet landed on the jutting ledge of one of the car's doors. He grabbed one of the protruding handles. He was on the moving car, his grip tight, every muscle in his body strained to the utmost to keep him flat against the train. Inside, passengers were shouting. He could not keep holding.

The Green Line stops frequently, an annoyance to its regular riders, but fortunate for Stone now. Less than a quarter-mile down the track, the train came to a halt, its hydraulic brakes whining. He jumped back to allow the doors to open, and then he propelled himself inside the crowded train.

He had lost the men in suits. They had not been able to outrun the train, although they had tried, and he could just see them back in the distance. He reached into his pocket and produced a handful of change, which he threw into the coin box to mollify the driver, and sank into a seat, heaving great sighs. His heart was hammering.

The car was abuzz, the passengers staring at him and talking loudly, many of them backing away. In Chip Rosen's good suit, he didn't exactly look like a common criminal, but it was clear he wasn't your average commuter, either.

Of course they had gotten to Chip. *They* had gotten to all his friends, as Sawyer said they would, threatening each with substantial criminal prosecution if he or she harbored Stone.

So who was left to help?

Stone looked out the car's window and saw, his heart sinking, that there was another train right behind him. *God damn it,* he almost said aloud. You wait and wait for a Green Line car, and then they come, all bunched up, two and three trains within two minutes.

The men were in the train immediately behind him.

The trains were underground now, in the dark tunnel beneath Kenmore Square. Stone had once memorized the stops, an idle exercise to occupy time when the train was stalled for an annoyingly long stretch between stations. He ran through them: one, two, three . . . five stops. At each one there was great danger. These men might well be equipped with radios, talking with others throughout the city. At any stop someone might come aboard, someone carefully briefed on his appearance.

He held his breath, tried his best to melt in with the crowd, yet knowing that it was useless if anyone was waiting for him. *Auditorium, Copley, Arlington* . . . He reeled off the stops in his head, trying to keep panic from overtaking him.

Auditorium seemed clear, Stone saw with great relief, and so was the next stop. At Arlington Station he got out, shoving passengers aside, then hurled himself at the revolving-door exit and ran up the stairs to Arlington Street.

There, just up ahead on the left, was the Ritz-Carlton. He slowed his pace in order not to arouse suspicion and entered the lobby of the hotel. On the right side of the lobby was the hotel's bar, which was sparsely populated tonight—after the businessmen's happy hour but before the postdinner crowd came in. At the bar he spotted a woman, sitting alone. She was in her forties, well dressed, smoking a cigarette as she drank some sort of highball. A divorcée, a widow, or just a single woman, Stone calculated, but she would not be sitting alone at the bar if she didn't want company. She could always order drinks from room service if she wanted to drink alone.

Stone sat on the stool next to her and flashed a quick, pleasant smile. "How're you doing?"

"I've been better," the woman said. Her face was made up with too much powder, an orangish mask that cracked around the eyes and lips. Her mascara was a deep blue. "I've been worse." She took a drag on her cigarette and flecked the ash as she exhaled. Her carefully plucked pencil-thin eyebrows arched into high inverted commas.

They wouldn't be searching for a couple. Just as he was about to turn on his charm, he glimpsed something in his peripheral vision.

A man was at the entrance to the bar, looking around swiftly. At the side of his suit jacket was a slight, almost imperceptible bulge: the holster of a gun.

"Excuse me a minute, all right?" Stone slid slowly off the barstool and edged backward, keeping his face out of sight.

With a sudden burst of speed, he lurched toward the swinging doors that gave onto the hotel's kitchen.

Stone saw instantly that he was cornered; there wasn't a single concealed place in the kitchen, and the only other exit led, he could see, into the restaurant.

There had to be a service entrance, the door that led out onto the loading dock, where the crates of fruits and vegetables were brought in. The door! He had to make it to the door.

A waiter crossed his path, holding aloft a tray of drinks. "What the hell are you doing here?" the waiter demanded.

Stone lunged for the door, knocking the waiter aside, the glasses shattering on the tiled floor behind him, and in an instant he was outside. A large green truck, labeled ROYAL INSTITUTIONAL FOOD SERVICE in white block letters, was idling at the loading dock. Stone jumped off the concrete platform, flung open the truck's rear doors, and closed them, falling backward, painfully, onto large square cartons. The engine rumbled as the truck pulled away from the dock.

29

Moscow

The chairman of the KGB, Andrei Pavlichenko, walked tensely along the long corridor, down an expanse of Oriental carpeting, past sets of double doors. He was on the fifth floor of the building that houses the Central Committee, on Staraya Square, three blocks from the Kremlin, headed toward Mikhail Gorbachev's hideaway office.

The call from the President had come an hour earlier. Pavlichenko was at home, in his apartment on Kutuzov Prospekt, where he had lived alone since the death of his wife four years earlier. He avoided going home whenever possible, trying not to leave himself pockets of free time into which his loneliness could seep.

When he arrived at the antechamber outside the President's office, he nodded at the male secretaries, then continued through another antechamber, until he had reached Gorbachev's small office.

Gorbachev's two other offices, in the Kremlin and on the other side of the Central Committee building, were largely ceremonial, designated for receiving foreign visitors. The President did his real work, held his most important meetings here, in a small, spartan room dominated by a large, immaculate mahogany desk. On the walls of the room hung portraits of Lenin and Marx, exactly the same prints that are found in virtually every Soviet official's office. In the center of the desk was a gray telephone with push buttons connected to twenty lines.

Well, this is it, Pavlichenko thought gloomily. The Politburo is clamoring for my head, and Gorbachev won't be able to resist making me the fall guy.

He was admitted immediately, and was pleased to see that no one else was present. Just the President, who looked less tired than he had that night in his dacha, but still worn. He was dressed in a dove-gray suit, which Pavlichenko knew had been made in London by the Savile Row firm Gieves and Hawkes. Pavlichenko, too, favored Savile Row suits; he was glad that, at last, Western attire was politically correct. Gorbachev also wore a top-of-the-line gold Rolex; Pavlichenko wore a somewhat less expensive Rolex. Gorbachev, Pavlichenko knew, sent his shirts and underwear out to the elite laundry near the Hotel Ukraine that serviced the Kremlin; Pavlichenko—who knew that imitation really wasn't a bad form of flattery at all—also had his laundry done there.

They sat around a mahogany coffee table, Gorbachev on a leather couch, Pavlichenko in an adjoining armchair.

"Well, Andrei Dmitrovich," the President intoned, coming directly to the point as always, "what have you learned?" No fat in his conversations; no small talk. Gorbachev, who certainly could be charming, held his charm in check when there was work to be done.

Pavlichenko answered without hesitation. "I think these bombings are just the beginning."

Gorbachev replied with poise. "Meaning?"

"I mean, a coup."

"Yes," Gorbachev began irritably, "we've already discussed—"

"I'm afraid," Pavlichenko interrupted almost inaudibly, "that the evidence is beginning to point that way. All my people, all my number-crunchers and eggheads, seem to think that's what's going on." He ran a hand over his face, feeling stubble; he hadn't had time to shave.

"So," Gorbachev said. His shoulders seemed to sag visibly, although his expression remained neutral.

Pavlichenko knew well that there is nothing the Soviet Politburo fears more than a coup d'état.

This is almost certainly because the Soviet Union was established by a coup d'état on November 7, 1917, a small but lightning-fast attack on the democratic provisional government. The Politburo, therefore, recognizes that such a threat exists at all times.

Gorbachev had reason to be fearful.

The Soviet Union was in turmoil, with nationalist uprisings—public demonstrations!—throughout the remaining Soviet republics, which, one after another, were calling openly for independence from Moscow. Even the Russian Republic was pulling away from the Kremlin. Only the Ukraine would never be permitted independence from Moscow. Never, that is, short of war. And the Soviet bloc was crumbling. The Berlin Wall had been dismantled, and with it went East Germany and Poland and Hungary and Czechoslovakia and Bulgaria. . . . The Soviet Communist Party had lost its decades-long grip on power; the old-line leadership was steadily being replaced. The Soviet empire was, in the space of a few short years, almost gone, and Gorbachev was to blame.

Pavlichenko could almost see Gorbachev's mental calculations. The President could count on perhaps three or four solid votes in the Politburo. At any time, there was the possibility of a coup, of his enemies on the Politburo's ousting him as they had done Khrushchev in 1964. There was clamoring in the Supreme Soviet and the Congress of People's Deputies for Gorbachev's removal. Boris Yeltsin, as head of the Russian Republic, clearly wanted Gorbachev out, and Yeltsin had enormous support.

"There may be forces," the KGB chairman said after Gorbachev had been silent for almost a full minute, "conspirators who no doubt have access to tremendous resources. At least, this is what my people are postulating."

"Here in Moscow?" Gorbachev said, almost scoffing.

"Perhaps. Yet, as I've said before, there may be links to the West. I'm vague, because, frankly, we don't know."

"Meaning?"

Pavlichenko only shrugged.

"How high?"

"You mean, in the West?"

"I mean here."

"Sir?"

"How highly placed? Do you think these . . . forces . . . are controlled from the Politburo level?"

"I think it's likely," Pavlichenko replied.

Gorbachev's response was surprising under the circumstances. "I don't want anything to interfere with the November summit," he said, suddenly louder. He shook his head. "I don't want anything to prevent it." He got to his feet, signifying that the meeting was over. "If there's a link to the West, whether it's the White House or Langley or *anyone*, I must know. Is that clear? I want nothing to disrupt the summit, but I am not prepared to have the world view us as cowards."

"Yes, sir." Pavlichenko was inwardly relieved that Gorbachev was not out for his blood, although that could still come anytime.

"It's one of us, isn't it?" Gorbachev sighed.

"Look, I don't have to tell you—you've got a list of enemies as long as—"

"Such as?"

Pavlichenko shrugged.

"Sherbanov?" Gorbachev asked. Vladimir V. Sherbanov, the defense minister, was an alternate member of the Politburo, which meant he didn't vote. It was remarkable: the head of the Soviet military, for the first time in decades, wasn't a voting member of the Soviet leadership! Gorbachev had maneuvered this arrangement, knowing how the Red Army opposed his slashing the military budget.

"That's . . ." Pavlichenko furrowed his brow. "That's completely impossible. He's a pain in the ass, but he's also one of the most loyal people around. He's completely reliable."

Gorbachev was silent for a long time before he spoke. "No one is anymore."

30

MOSCOW

Charlotte Harper had been harassed by the Soviet authorities several times before during her tenure in Moscow, but never had she been arrested.

With the President coming to Moscow to meet with Gorbachev, she'd thought it might be interesting to do a story on an extreme-right-wing neofascist organization that had recently begun to meet in Moscow. They wore black shirts and swastikas and were calling for pogroms against all non-Russian nationalities. It was truly sensational stuff—explosive, really, since the Soviet authorities wanted to distract attention from such groups, which had begun to spring up in Moscow with disconcerting frequency.

She made a few calls, and several people seemed to be willing to talk on camera. So she and her cameraman, Randy, dashed to the office car, a red Volvo, and drove out to an apartment in the newly developed section of southwestern Moscow.

When she arrived, she saw that she wasn't alone: there were several Moscow policemen, the *militsiya*, standing outside the apartment building, waiting. They were burly and red-faced and looked like taller versions of Nikita Khrushchev.

As soon as the police saw the American television reporter and her cameramen unload their equipment from the station wagon, one of them came up to her and said, in Russian, "No camera. No interview."

Charlotte's Russian was fluent. "We're not breaking any laws."

"I'll break your camera."

"Just try." It wasn't wise to provoke a Russian cop, but this had slipped out. "Randy, let's go ahead."

The cop followed them to the entrance of the building, where he and another one blocked their way. "Forbidden," the second cop said.

"Switch on the camera, Randy," Charlotte said in English, quickly and quietly. "At least we'll get something."

Randy turned it on. The footage of the *militsiyoneri* blocking their access would, by itself, tell part of the story of how sensitive the Soviets were, even with glasnost— well, no, *especially* with glasnost—to such issues.

At that moment, the cop, realizing what was going on, stuck his hand out and flattened it against the camera lens.

"Hey, watch it!" Randy said. "That's an expensive piece of equipment, you bastard."

The *militsiyoneri* were surrounding them now, and one of them shoved Randy harder.

"All right!" Charlotte shouted in Russian, fuming. "All right, we'll turn it off." In a lower voice, she added, "Goddamn you."

The *militsiya* arrested Charlotte and Randy, threw them unceremoniously into a paddy wagon, and brought them to a tiny local police station, which was empty. The two Americans were locked in a bare room.

Randy looked at Charlotte and said, "Oh, great. Now what the hell are we going to do?"

"Don't worry about it," she said.

Within an hour, another policeman, who appeared to be a senior officer, entered the room.

Even before he had a chance to speak, Charlotte said in Russian, "You realize we didn't break any laws. I happen to have very close ties with the American Embassy"— this much was true—"and I think you should know that if you don't release us at once you will single-handedly be precipitating an international incident." She softened her demand with her warmest smile. You had to manage these things adeptly; it wouldn't do to challenge the ego of a

Soviet cop. "With the summit so near, would you want to risk that?" she asked sweetly.

She looked up and saw that there was another man standing in the doorway, listening: a gray-haired military man, in full uniform. He had, she saw, sad gray eyes.

He held out his hand to shake Charlotte's. "My name is Colonel Vlasik," he said. "Nikita Vlasik." He spoke in excellent English.

Charlotte paused and then took his hand. "Charlotte Harper."

"I know who you are, Miss Harper. I watch your broadcasts from time to time."

"I'm flattered." Probably he watched pirated videotapes of the stories she sent over the satellite. That meant he must be fairly influential within the military hierarchy.

He made a gesture with his hand, and the policeman left.

"You make a very good argument," he said. "But that line of thinking rarely works on our policemen. They don't think of political consequences. They think of, pardon my expression, covering their asses."

Charlotte laughed. Where did *this* guy come from? she wondered.

He continued, "We need people like you on our side."

"Thanks, but I've already got a side." The colonel meant well, and so she responded gently.

"You remind me of my daughter," the colonel said.

"Oh, really?" Russian men, Charlotte was once again reminded, were incorrigible—sexist, chauvinistic, laughably old-fashioned, and infuriating.

"Both of you have—how do you call it?—spunk." He laughed. "If you are going to break our laws, Miss Harper, let me give you a few pointers on how to do it without getting into trouble. My men have much to do. Maybe you can save us all the trouble of arresting you next time."

"Maybe you can tell your men not to bother a reporter when she's doing her job."

He flashed a winning smile. "I can't argue. But let me give you a little advice."

"All right," she said dubiously.

"Get to know our Criminal Code. If anything happens to you, just—what is your expression?—give them hell. Don't let your interrogators make you talk. Article 46 of the Soviet Criminal Code says you don't have to answer questions. Article 142 says you never have to sign any documents. Any interrogator who hears you mention these will shit in his pants. Please forgive my language."

Charlotte smiled. "You're forgiven."

She returned to the office and began to do some routine catch-up work, rooting through *Pravda* and *Izvestiya* and *Literaturnaya Gazeta* and some of the other unspeakably dull Soviet publications. Then, glancing mindlessly through the AP newswire printouts, she glimpsed a small item about the Alfred Stone affair: Charles Stone was still at large, being sought in connection with the murder.

Days had gone by, and she had done nothing to find Sonya Kunetskaya, who Charlie believed was a key to the mystery he was trying to solve. He needed her help.

The first place to look, of course, was the phone book. Not such an easy proposition: telephone books are enormously scarce in Russia. The last one was published in 1973, and the Ministry of Communications had only put out fifty thousand copies for a city of eight million people.

The 1973 book did list an S. Kunetskaya, and she dialed the number.

The listing was out of date. The phone was answered by a gruff-voiced man who insisted he had never heard of this Kunetskaya.

It was certainly possible that the man was lying, but even if he weren't, she had reached a dead end. There was nothing to do but *go* there, to the address listed in the book, and see for herself.

The address was on Krasnopresnenskaya Street, an area known, despite the Soviet Union's "classless-society" claims, as a working-class neighborhood. The building was run-down and shabby.

The man who answered the bell was coldly hostile: he had no interest in talking to an American journalist.

"I don't know of any Kunetskaya," he barked at her. "Go away."

Finally, after Charlotte had rung the bells of all of the man's neighbors, she found what she'd been seeking.

"Of course I remember Sonya Kunetskaya," said a plain-looking *babushka* abruptly. "Why do you want to know? She moved years ago."

"Do you have her address?"

The woman fixed Charlotte with a suspicious glare. "Who are you?"

"I'm an old friend of hers," Charlotte said. "From America. I haven't seen her in years, and you know how hard it is to get phone numbers."

The *babushka* shrugged. "I'll see."

A few minutes later, the *babushka* returned with a small, grimy address book. "Here it is," the old woman said. "I knew I had it somewhere."

31

Washington

The accommodations Stone found upon arriving in Washington were dismal but anonymous. From the Yellow Pages he'd selected a rooming house in Adams-Morgan. It was a seventy-five-year-old house badly in need of a paint job, with twelve rooms on three disheveled floors. Stone's room, on the third floor, contained an infinitesimal kitchenette, a dreadfully soft bed covered with what looked and smelled like a horse blanket, and not much else. He paid, in advance and in cash, for two nights. The proprietor, an elderly woman who wore an ill-fitting green double-knit polyester pantsuit, was annoyed at the short stay, and said so—she preferred guests who stayed at least two weeks—but she took his money anyway.

Hours earlier, back in Boston, the food-service truck had left the Ritz and immediately proceeded to its next stop, a luxury hotel in another part of town. Of course it would have done little good for Stone to try to hide in the truck, so he presented himself to the driver, who, when he recovered from his shock, appeared to believe Stone's story that he was evading the irate husband of a woman with whom he had had a rendezvous at the Ritz. The driver was actually amused by the tale, and kindly offered to drop Stone off anywhere on the truck's route. He also offered Stone a seat in the front of the cab, which proved a good deal more comfortable than the boxes in the back.

The driver let Stone off at a truck stop on the outskirts of Boston, where he hitched a ride in a truck that was delivering discount women's clothing as far south as Philadelphia. In the early part of the morning, shortly after four o'clock, Stone found himself in a truck stop near Philadelphia, and, after a full breakfast and several cups of coffee, located a truck that was going directly to Washington.

By the middle of the afternoon, he had gotten himself organized enough to do the things necessary for survival. He could no longer risk carrying around such a great number of bills; he went to a bank and converted some of it into larger denominations. With some of the cash, he bought traveler's checks, using Robert Gill's passport. The rest he planned to hide later. He visited several clothing stores, bought a few changes of clothes, casual as well as business wear, and a small leather traveling case with a concealed pocket in the lining. There he placed his passport and driver's license in the name of Robert Gill. Briefly, he returned to the rooming house and worked for a few hours with razor blade and glue, carefully inserting his real passport and the rest of the cash in the binding of two hardcover books, inside the liners of his shoes, and beneath the lining of his leather case.

He found a pay phone and called Directory Assistance for the Washington area. Unsurprisingly, Deputy Secretary of State William Armitage's number was unlisted.

Stone knew that he could not talk to Armitage at State, even if he could get in to see him; much better to reach him at home. And a surprise call could reveal a tremendous amount.

Armitage had interrogated Anna Zinoyeva in 1953; was he one of *them*? His immediate, uncensored reaction to Stone's unexpected appearance might well reveal whether he was a vital link in this conspiracy.

Obviously Armitage was a risk, but Stone had little choice now.

He called the State Department and asked the operator for the office of Deputy Secretary of State William Armitage. A female receptionist in Armitage's office answered.

"This is Ken Owens from *The Washington Post*," Stone told the secretary. "Listen, I talked to one of Mr. Armitage's assistants yesterday, and I've lost his name."

"One of his assistants?"

"Yeah. A guy."

"There's a couple of people it might be," the secretary said. "A fellow? Was it Paul Rigazio?"

"Right. That was it. Thanks."

"Would you like to speak with him?"

"Later on. I needed to get his name. Thanks. Oh, and do you have his extension?" The secretary gave him Paul Rigazio's telephone extension, and Stone hung up.

He next called the State Department's personnel office. "This is Paul Rigazio in Bill Armitage's office. Extension 7410. Bill left a message for me to call him at home, and he didn't leave me his new number."

"All right," said the woman who answered the phone. "One moment." She returned to the line half a minute later. "I don't see any *new* number here, sir."

"Which one do you have?" The woman read it back; Stone thanked her and hung up.

One more call to make, to be safe. He would need Armitage's home address if there was no answer; if need be, he could surprise the Secretary, thereby eliminating the chance for Armitage to call anyone else.

The telephone business office is notoriously a wary

place, stingy with information, fiercely protective of the privacy of its subscribers. Lower down the hierarchy, however, things get looser. He called the telephone company's repair office, gave his name as William Armitage, and announced with vexation that his home phone was having problems. "Look, I'm at work now so I don't have time to talk," he told the man who took his call. "There's some kind of rapid beeping noise on my line."

"What's the number, sir?"

Stone gave it. "Do I get billed for this repair?" he asked with annoyance.

"Not at all, sir. We'll have someone check the line right away."

"Listen, while I've got you here—I didn't get my last bill."

"You should probably contact the business office—"

"Listen, I moved recently and I sent in a change-of-address form to you folks a while back. Now, which address do you have on your screen there?"

"Seventy-nine Upper Hawthorne."

"You got the right one," Stone said, sounding genuinely puzzled. "Who knows. Thanks."

Five days earlier, two powerfully built men in their early forties had paid a visit to the telephone security department of Chesapeake & Potomac Telephone in central Washington, D.C. The men, who claimed to be from the Federal Bureau of Investigation and carried identification cards to confirm it, were expected; the security agent in charge had received a call that morning from someone who had said he was a special agent at the FBI and two of his men would be coming by for some routine court-ordered monitoring.

The two men presented the necessary document: a court order signed by a federal judge. Although their identification was false, and the morning's caller was not from the FBI but from an organization that called itself the American Flag Foundation, the court order was the real thing. The judge who had authorized the wiretaps was a longtime friend of the Director of Central Intelligence and a firm believer in the necessity of the occasional domestic covert operation.

The two men were ushered into a small room, given headsets, and shown how to work a console on which they could hear all conversations on a certain seven telephone lines in the Washington area.

"Mr. Armitage?"

The voice that answered was that of an older man, whose clipped tones and rounded vowels indicated someone of good breeding, as well as a man used to having his orders followed.

"Who's calling?"

"Matt Kelley. I'm an associate of Winthrop Lehman's."

"I see." Armitage's patrician tone had suddenly changed; now he was more cautious. "Is that how you got my number?"

"That's right. Winthrop wanted me to get in touch with you."

Everything depended upon Armitage's response. Would there be that telltale pause, some evidence that he was surprised, proof that he was no longer in contact with Lehman? If *not*, Stone would hang up at once, safe in assuming that Armitage was poison—one of *them*.

"He did?" Armitage said. "What on earth for?"

Stone's brain was spinning, doing hundreds of calculations. Armitage *sounded* sincere.

"He didn't tell you to expect my call?"

"I haven't talked to Winthrop in twelve or thirteen years."

"It has to do with the death of Alfred Stone. Do you know the name?"

"Hell, yes. I knew the man, or at least met him. Grisly thing, what happened. What do you want from me?"

Armitage *had* to be on the level.

"I need to talk to you."

"You're being very mysterious."

"I'm afraid I have to be."

"Call me at the office tomorrow afternoon. I'm kind of raked, but I'll try to squeeze in—"

"No. Not at the State Department."

"Who *are* you?"

"It's too sensitive to discuss there. Can we meet somewhere else? At your home, perhaps."

"I've got some people coming over for dinner, Mr.— what did you say your name was?"

"Kelley."

"Kelley. Let me get back to you in a couple of minutes, and I'll try to work something out."

"I'll call you back."

"Any reason you can't give me your number?" Armitage asked, his voice rising in suspicion.

"No," Stone said at once. "None at all." He looked at the pay phone and read off the number.

"I'll get back to you in ten minutes."

Stone fished a scrap of paper from his pocket, scrawled on it "out of order," and tucked it into the phone's coin slot. He stood by the phone until a young black woman came by to use it, noticed the sign, and walked off.

The call came five minutes later. The voice wasn't Armitage's.

"Mr. Kelley? This is Morton Bloom. I'm Bill Armitage's assistant. Bill asked me to call you while he talks to some of his dinner guests and tries to reschedule."

"Why couldn't he call me himself? I thought I made that clear—I don't want to involve anyone else."

"I'm sorry, sir. I guess he thought it wouldn't make a difference. I'm his aide-de-camp, sort of a chief factotum, bodyguard, that sort of thing."

"I see."

"The point is, he does want to meet with you, and he appreciates your desire to keep sort of a low profile."

"I'm glad he does. How soon can he see me?"

"Are you free tonight?"

"Certainly."

"Tonight, then. Where are you?"

"In Washington."

"Bill feels pretty strongly that it's best not to meet at his house. He said you'd understand."

"Yes," Stone acknowledged.

"He wants you to meet him at an out-of-the-way place we can watch, to make sure you weren't tailed."

"I understand. Where does he suggest?"

"Do you know Arlington at all?"

"No."

"There's a shopping mall right near the Metro stop where there's a coffee shop. Mr. Armitage can be there at, say, nine o'clock, if that's convenient."

Bloom described the precise booth in the coffee shop where he, Armitage, and Stone would meet. "If we're a few minutes late, don't panic," Bloom added. "It's my job to be careful, and I like to do my job well. You understand."

When he hung up, he tried Armitage's number, received a busy signal, and then called State Department Personnel. Was there a Morton Bloom employed in the State Department? There was, he was told: in Armitage's office.

Relieved, Stone hung up.

Several hours later, carrying his Smith & Wesson in the pocket of his jacket, he left the Arlington Metro station and walked to the mall. He found the coffee shop, the Panorama, easily. It was a small place, well lighted; Stone saw through the front plate-glass window that there were about eight customers. He was reassured. If this was a setup, it was a lousy place. Too public.

Ten minutes before nine. No one was sitting in the booth, which was marked with a table tent marked "reserved." The sign looked foolish: a reserved table in an uncrowded coffee shop. Probably Armitage or Bloom had called and asked them to do that. But why would someone as dignified as Armitage want to meet in such a tacky place?

He crossed the street and watched the entrance, standing in the doorway of a travel agency.

Ten minutes went by. It was nine o'clock, and still no one was there. They expected him to arrive first, but he would surprise them.

Soon he looked at his watch again; it was exactly nine-fifteen, and still no sign of them. Something seemed off about the whole business.

He left the travel-agency doorway and walked down the street toward the Metro, and then he heard the explosion.

He jumped, terrified. It was a deep, booming noise, accompanied by the sound of shattering glass, and it came from the end of the coffee shop. The small building was now afire. Stone saw the flames shooting out of the windows and heard a fire alarm clamoring. He began to run.

32

Moscow

The Prospekt Mira metro station is adorned with some of the most beautiful architecture in perhaps the world's most beautiful subway system. The floors are granite tile; the corridors are colonnaded with rococo arches and illuminated by elegant chandeliers. The corridor into which the escalator deposits throngs of pedestrians is lined with marble benches. During rush hour—which, in Moscow, is hours long—the benches are crowded with weary travelers, *babushka*s with string bags, henna-haired women with squirming children, irritable factory workers resting briefcases full of tangerines on their laps.

A tall, lanky man in an ill-fitting suit had been sitting on a bench for five minutes, attracting no attention. He looked insignificant, distracted. To a casual observer he would have seemed to be an office worker in one of Moscow's thousands of vestigial state offices. He looked like the kind of man you always ended up sitting next to in the metro.

No one would remember seeing Stefan Kramer, and no one would recall that he opened the cheap, scuffed briefcase on the ground before him, reached a hand in among the sheaves of papers, and did something. Of course, no one could observe that he had squeezed the chemical pencil, just as the train arrived and hundreds of people rushed on and off the train.

Then, just as he was about to insert himself into the heaving crowd in the subway car, having left his briefcase in the station beside a crowd of Red Army soldiers, he turned around.

The soldiers—a platoon, most likely—were slowly, cumbersomely assembling, and Stefan knew from experience that they would be there, obeying their commander's order not to move, for five minutes more or so.

Jesus, Stefan thought. No one was supposed to be standing around on the platform.

The soldiers would die.

Stefan's head was spinning. They were soldiers of the very government that had destroyed his brother's mind, yet they were very likely decent, innocent young men, even younger than himself.

He glanced quickly at these soldiers, seventeen- and eighteen-year-old boys, gangly and ruddy-cheeked, who knew nothing of politics and gulags and torture, and thought only of the great honor of serving the state.

Stefan could not kill them.

He drew back from the crowded subway car just as it pulled away from the platform. Then he retrieved his briefcase, which stood abandoned near the soldiers, strolled with it to the end of the platform, and found a deserted area.

His heart was pounding; the thing could go off at any second.

He placed the briefcase against the marble wall, a long distance away from anyone, and opened his newspaper as if reading. No one seemed to be paying him any attention.

When another train came again, he got on it, nervous but at the same time relieved, and listened for the explosion.

A few days earlier, his father had typed a letter on an electric typewriter in the offices of Progress Publishers. The typewriter had no distinguishing features; the letter was typed on blank paper; and it had been sent to the office of President Gorbachev in care of one of Gorbachev's assistants, whose name Yakov had selected from a photograph on the front page of *Izvestiya*.

In the letter, Yakov had demanded, simply and clearly, the release without delay of all the inmates of the Serbsky Institute being held for political reasons. If there was no response within one week, Yakov had written, the terror would continue.

With the American President coming to Moscow, this threat would undoubtedly be quite real to the Politburo.

Yakov and Stefan knew that the assassination of the Central Committee member Sergei Borisov had received worldwide attention. The Kremlin would not want another such incident, and the price that the Kramers were demanding was, after all, quite small.

They met, father and son, once more at the oilcloth-covered kitchen table. Sonya had gone out again. Stefan often thought about her, wondering why his father was so adamant that she not be told. Surely she would disapprove of so dangerous an action. But was there something else, some other reason Yakov wanted to protect his lover?

"I don't want innocent people killed if we can avoid it," Yakov had said. His face registered a deep sadness.

Stefan nodded his head in agreement. "The thought of it makes me sick. I still can't think about Borisov. As horrible a man as he was, I can't do such things."

"All right," Yakov said. "If you select the metro, make sure you are careful not to hurt innocent people."

"I will."

"The bomb—how powerful will this one be?"

"A wad of plastic explosive of this size will create a very large explosion."

"And what's this?" Yakov asked, holding up a section

of brass tube five inches long that resembled a pen but had a screw-and-nut assembly at one end. "Is it dangerous?" He set it down gently.

"No," Stefan laughed, "not by itself. It's a mechanical firing device. Very simple, actually."

After a moment, Yakov looked up from the bomb components. "For Avram," he said.

The device did its work in a few minutes, by which time Stefan was long gone.

The platform was suddenly illuminated by a blinding, bluish light; then, a fraction of a second later, it was rocked by an immense explosion, thunderous and earsplitting. No one was nearby, and so no one was badly hurt, but people who had just entered the platform began screaming in terror as rubble from the detonation showered hundreds of feet away.

The explosion was the subject of rumors that spread throughout Moscow at lightning speed: another attack by the terrorists. People gossiping at their offices the next day had any number of theories; none of them might have suspected that the perpetrators were a few very ordinary men, acting out of love for a brother and son.

Had Andrew Langen not happened to be walking down Kalinin Prospekt when Sergei Borisov's car blew up, the CIA would have had no idea that the explosion had involved KGB technology. Had the CIA not learned that, it wouldn't have instructed Langen as a matter of highest priority to follow all similar acts of terrorism very closely.

So it was that, as soon as word of the metro incident got around—and it got around quickly—Langen was at pains to obtain evidence of the quality he had quite fortuitously found just a few weeks earlier. As soon as the bomb went off, killing no one but injuring more than twenty bystanders, the area was sealed by the combined forces of the Soviet militia and the KGB. There seemed no way to procure shrapnel from the explosion this time.

Until, as it happened, the old Russian *muzhik* who

did repair and maintenance work in the courtyard of the
U.S. Embassy chanced to mention to Langen that, yes, he
had heard all about the terrible thing that happened in the
metro: he had a friend, a custodial worker in the employ
of the *militsiya*, who was called in to clean, repair, and
restore the site.

The *muzhik* was cleared by the KGB—all Soviet na-
tionals who worked in the embassy were—but he was no
Chekist, and for a healthy bribe he agreed to see what he
could do. The next morning he produced a chocolate box
full of oddments taken from the damaged portion of the
Prospekt Mira corridor. He had wrapped each fragment
of detritus for Langen in tissue paper and fondled them
as if they were moon rocks. Which, in a sense, they were.

33

Arlington, Virginia

Stone ran up the street toward the Arlington Metro entrance, then stopped when he spotted a gas station whose
parking lot held a half-dozen or so cars.

The station was closed and dark. He took out his Swiss
Army knife and, with the screwdriver blade, pried open
the front-vent window of a rusty yellow 1970 Volkswagen
Beetle. When he reached his hand in, he managed to crank
down the larger side window and open the door. Inside,
he slid the front seat back and twisted himself around so
he could peer under the dashboard. It took a minute for
his eyes to adjust to the dark, the only light a streetlamp
down the block.

He located the ignition switch on the dashboard,
reached behind to the tangle of four wires that came out
of it, and yanked them out of the switch. One of them,
the red wire, touched the metal of the dashboard and gave

off a spark of electricity. It was the "hot" lead. He bent it away from the others.

Ah, he thought. Being a "gearhead," a car buff, had to come in handy someday.

Now he had to find the right sequence of two connections. He raised himself up off the floor of the car and sat. With the largest blade he stripped the remaining three wires, and then connected the green wire to the hot wire. Nothing happened.

"Shit." Since he'd found the Beetle in a gas-station lot, it was entirely possible that the car was defunct. Next he tried the blue wire, and the starter motor cranked, a short cough, before it died. Victory, phase one. Then he touched the white wire to the connection, and the starter motor cranked again, but again the car wouldn't start.

The wiring was wrong. He disconnected the green wire, connected the blue to the red, and let out a whoop as the radio came on, along with the speedometer lights.

"Got it," he said as he touched the white wire briefly to the connection and the car roared to life.

An hour later, he had arrived in Falls Church; after asking street directions of a cabbie cruising for a fare, he found Armitage's house.

Estate, more properly: it was an immense colonial structure of red brick on hundreds of acres of wooded land. All the lights in the house were out, which was not surprising, since it was almost midnight. Stone parked the VW on the street, within view of the house, and kept the car running while he thought.

His escape had been close; the terrifying events of the past hour had left him still shaking, literally.

Was Armitage one of *them,* as he'd begun to think of his faceless pursuers? Or, quite the reverse, were these people trying to keep him *away* from Armitage, having somehow obtained access to Armitage's telephone lines? Anything was possible. There was only one way to find out.

He had the advantage of surprise. If Armitage was one of the conspirators, he would expect that Stone had been killed in the explosion. He would not expect him at his front door. And yet . . .

Suspicion had saved him a few hours ago. Was he being suspicious, careful enough now?

The Armitage home was set on a slight knoll, and therefore it was possible to see three sides of the house from the road. The place looked completely clear.

He shut off the ignition and walked carefully to the front door. He rang the doorbell.

A minute later, he rang again. Two minutes after that, the door opened.

It was Armitage; Stone recognized him from his news photos. He was wearing a crimson silk dressing gown that had been hastily thrown over white silk pajamas, and he had clearly been awakened. Even in such a state, he looked dignified, his white hair set off starkly by his deep suntan.

Armitage did not appear to recognize him; his expression was one of annoyance and distrust.

"What the hell is this?"

"I didn't see you at our little rendezvous," Stone said darkly.

"Who are you? Do you know what time it is?"

"We spoke earlier this evening. I'm Lehman's assistant, Matt Kelley."

"I told you not to come here!"

"Now I see why," Stone replied.

The white-haired man squinted in puzzlement. "I canceled my goddamn dinner plans and then I called that number you gave me," he sputtered. "It was a goddamn pay phone! Some passerby answered it. I waited to hear from you, and nothing. You're lucky I only canceled on my brother. What do you think this is? I resent your—"

A woman's voice called from the interior of the house: "Who is it, Bill?"

"Nothing," Armitage replied. "I'll get rid of him. Go back to sleep, honey."

Was this man telling the truth? "I tried your line," Stone said slowly, watching him carefully, "and it was busy, so I—"

"Busy? I sat by the phone for ten minutes, waiting."

"Morton Bloom called me—" Stone began.

"Morton Bloom! That's impossible. He isn't even in the country. He's been assigned to Geneva. He hasn't been in Washington for seven months!"

Stone felt his pulse quicken. "I wanted to know about an old woman named Anna Zinoyeva," he said levelly. "A secretary to Lenin. A frightened little woman you paid a threatening visit to in 1953."

"I don't know what the hell you're talking about," Armitage said, stepping back to close the door. "Now, I want you out of here—"

"Please don't waste my time," Stone said. He had pulled out the Smith & Wesson and pointed it, which was something he had hoped wouldn't be necessary.

"Put that goddamned thing away! My wife is already calling the police." Armitage was frightened, and he was lying.

"I only want to talk with you for a little while," Stone said calmly. "That's all. We talk, and everything will be fine."

"Who the hell are you?" the statesman rasped, terrified.

Armitage listened to Stone with undisguised astonishment. They had been sitting in the large, book-lined library of Armitage's house for a quarter of an hour while Stone talked, Armitage interrupting only to pose questions and clarify points.

Stone kept the gun at his side, ready to pick it up if needed, but Armitage now seemed willing to cooperate, especially when he learned that Stone was an employee of Parnassus—and an employee and a friend of Armitage's friend Saul Ansbach.

"Saul called me, you know," Armitage said when Stone had finished. "He mentioned your name. And he was quite agitated. He mentioned this report from the asset in Moscow and his suspicions that American renegades might be involved." He shook his head. "Frankly, I dismissed his suspicions as alarmist."

Stone, listening, looked around at the floor-to-ceiling

walnut shelves, the framed and signed photographs of Armitage with Lyndon Johnson, John Foster Dulles, Jimmy Carter, Ronald Reagan. Armitage's rise to the penultimate position in the State Department had not been a matter of party loyalties; his friends were both Republicans and Democrats. He evidently had quite a few influential friends.

"And when I heard about Saul, and then read about your father—absolutely ghastly—"

"Yes," Stone said hastily, cutting Armitage off, not wanting to relive the pain of his father's death. "And Saul was right, wasn't he?"

"Right about what?" Armitage asked with undisguised hostility.

"There is some kind of organization deep within the government that has been trying to overturn the Kremlin for decades—outside of Langley, outside of the CIA or the DIA or the White House. And it's going on right now."

"Oh, that's nonsense."

"Nonsense? Saul Ansbach *died,* damn it! He was murdered to cover this up." Stone continued in a whisper: "You're one of them, aren't you?"

"*No!*" Armitage shouted with surprising vehemence.

"Then you know—you know much more than you're saying."

Armitage's eyes roamed the room frantically. He clasped his hands tensely, then got up, retied the silk belt around his dressing gown, and walked to his desk drawer.

Stone released the safety on the gun. "Don't surprise me with anything," he said.

Armitage's eyes widened briefly; then he shook his head, smiling uncertainly. "I wasn't planning to. I want to get my pipe. Anyway, I have every reason to be uncertain about *you,* storming into my house at midnight with your crazy tales."

"You're right," Stone said, still pointing the gun.

Armitage shrugged again and pulled from the desk drawer a pipe and a tobacco pouch.

"Sorry."

"Quite all right," Armitage said as he filled the pipe's

bowl and tamped it down. "I suppose I'd do the same thing if I were in your position. Assume you can't trust anyone, catch them by surprise as you did me." When he had the pipe going, he returned to his chair.

"If you're not one of these people, then answer me this," Stone said. "Let's go back to 1953. You knew Beria's people had strong-armed this woman, Anna Zinoyeva, looking for a document—the Lenin Testament—which would throw Russia into such turmoil that, in the confusion, a coup could take place."

Armitage nodded.

"And you were sent to make sure she kept her silence," Stone resumed. "Contain things. See if she had this document and make sure it only fell into the right hands."

"That's right."

"Then who sent you to see her?"

Armitage now shook his head slowly. "My reputation—" he began.

Stone lifted the gun again. "I want to tell you something," he said with a terrible intensity. "My father was murdered. I have been set up for the crime of murdering my own father. And I'm prepared to do anything now to survive. If that includes committing murder myself, please understand that I wouldn't hesitate for a second."

Tears welled up in Armitage's eyes. When he spoke, it was after a silence that seemed endless. "Winthrop."

"*Lehman?* But why was Lehman—"

"Oh, God." He put down his pipe and then began to speak. "During . . . You see, during the war I was lucky enough to secure a position with army intelligence. I got involved in the War Department's investigation of military intelligence during Pearl Harbor. My boss was none other than the chief of staff of the army, General George C. Marshall. So I was in the right place in the right time." He waved his hand tremulously around the room, indicating the antiques, the rugs, the books. "Obviously my family's wealth and connections didn't hurt. After the war, I moved to State, and at some social affair or other, I don't remember when exactly, I met the famous Winthrop Lehman, the President's national-security assistant. We got to be friends, Winthrop and I. The sort of friends endemic to Washington, I mean—more a partnership of mutual respect for achievement, coupled with a 'You scratch my back, I'll scratch yours' sort of thing."

"How were you able to scratch his back?"

"I wondered the same thing at the time, since Lehman knew most of official Washington. But it turned out that he needed a good, reliable contact at State—a fifth columnist, as it were—in the Bureau of Intelligence and Research."

"To do what?"

"Keep watch. Keep things in line. Little of any substance."

"Be specific."

Armitage sighed. "He was concerned about the hemorrhaging of classified information in those days. With McCarthy on the rampage, secrets were being spilled everywhere. That's the irony. McCarthy, ostensibly the great enemy of communism, was helping the communists more than anyone else ever could. So Winthrop wanted me to keep watch for any revelation that had to do with a top-secret designation, M-3, which I was only told referred to a mole."

"And what did you get in return for helping Lehman?"

"In return, Mr. Stone, I got something very valuable. Those were difficult days for the State Department. Tail gunner Joe McCarthy, that bastard, called us 'the striped-pants boys,' and he was gunning for quite a few of us. Lehman saw to it that I was left alone. But one day a good piece of intelligence came our way, the result of a black-bag job, the sort of thing that was a lot more common then than now. One of our contract agents managed to gain access to the Soviet diplomatic pouch. In those days, it actually was a large leather pouch, filled with coded documents and memoranda and letters and whatnot. Among the many rather useful things we microfilmed was a cream-colored envelope addressed to my friend Winthrop Lehman on blank stationery. No letterhead, no signature, and the message was so banal it was obviously encoded."

"From whom?"

"We got the answer from the paper. It was private-stock paper used exclusively by the MGB, as the KGB was then called."

"And?"

"And then I knew I had something rather important, that my friend Winthrop was in secret contact with the Soviet secret police. And so I was involved, though not by choice, you see. Once I knew that, and Lehman knew I knew, I was part of his game."

"But why were you involved? Why *you*?"

"They needed me. They needed the rather considerable resources of the State Department. Lehman was coordinating a scheme to fund a coup by Lavrentii Beria. And I used my connections within the State Department to channel money that Winthrop Lehman provided, three-quarters of a million dollars, to the Swiss bank account that Beria had set up for himself."

"*Lehman!* Lehman personally funded the coup attempt?"

Armitage nodded pensively. "I believed in the cause, too."

"Putting that crazy man Beria into power?"

"No. Destabilizing the Soviet government. Now, of course, I realize that instability in the Kremlin is the most dangerous thing of all."

"What was the name of Beria's assistant, this 'M-3' I mentioned?"

"I never knew it. Believe me, I was kept in the dark. I never knew who else was involved."

"But there are ways to find out. You must have files, records of this operation. Some way to *prove*, establish beyond doubt, what was being done."

"None."

"But records on Lehman?" Stone suggested. "There must be records you can get access to."

The Secretary looked shaken as he replied. "When I heard about Saul, I got scared. I thought I might be next, and I went about collecting what I could, in order to have some kind of protection. *But they're missing!* The FBI files on Lehman are missing—and so are State Department consular records in Suitland, Maryland, decimal files at the National Archives. *Everything on Lehman is gone!*"

"There must be records of who removed them."

"Nothing. They're stolen, all of them."

"Stolen? Well, what solid, irrefutable proof *do* you have?"

"Proof? Absolutely none."

Stone was pensive a moment. "Even without it . . . Perhaps, with your reputation, your connections, you can speak the right word to the right people."

"And say what? Without any sort of proof whatsoever? I'd be a laughingstock. No one would believe me. You don't understand—a lot of people are frightened. Files are being combed. Something is going on *today*, some kind of power struggle."

"Yes," Stone said. How much *did* this man know? "You mean a power struggle in American intelligence? Be specific."

"I can't. It's just—intuition. The way a very good internal-medicine specialist just *knows* when something is wrong with the body. After all these years in government, I *know*. There's talk. Talk in the corridors, whispered things, casual asides."

"Who's involved in it?"

"Renegades, perhaps. Ollie North types. I don't know. I'm sorry; I can't be more substantive than that."

"I need specifics—someone who knows for certain and is willing to go public." He thought: My father knew someone on the NSC, a former student of his. I could contact him. And there was that FBI agent who interviewed Cushing—Warren Pogue, wasn't that his name?

"Do you understand," Stone said, "that the CIA itself has been penetrated? That it's rotten?" "Rotten"—that was the term Saul had used. "That what's about to happen in Moscow may well be worse than a return of Stalinism? It may be the beginning of a world war."

"*What?*" Armitage whispered.

"How can you afford," Stone asked, "*not* to do anything?"

At six o'clock in the morning, after a fitful four hours of sleep, Deputy Secretary of State William Armitage awoke, put on a pot of coffee, and then made a telephone call to his aide Paul Rigazio. He directed Rigazio to conduct a thorough search of all records on State Department premises that contained any reference to Winthrop Lehman and a certain decades-old conspiracy.

As was his custom, in the morning he worked at home, doing paperwork and making calls. At nine o'clock, his wife, Catherine, kissed him goodbye and left the house for her unpaid volunteer job at the Audubon Society in Washington, at which she worked in fund-raising from ten until one in the afternoon.

At nine-twenty, the doorbell rang, and Armitage went to answer it.

He smiled in recognition. It was one of the State Department's messenger boys. He wasn't expecting any delivery, but sometimes they failed to notify him.

"Morning, Larry," he said.

At four-thirty that afternoon, Catherine Armitage returned to their Falls Church home.

In the closet off the bedroom she found her husband, completely nude, hanging by a length of electrical cord that had been wrapped in a soft cotton dishrag, apparently to ensure that the wire did not cut into his neck. The cord hung from a fixture on the closet's ceiling. On the floor beside the stool that her husband had evidently been standing on when it slipped was a pornographic magazine, open to its centerfold.

The death was ascribed, by the county coroner, to something called "autoerotic asphyxia," an unintentional hanging that results from a bizarre practice whereby the victim masturbates and intensifies the orgasm by cutting off the supply of oxygen to the brain, almost—but not quite—hanging himself. It is a deviant practice far more common among teenagers than distinguished elder statesmen.

In keeping with the discretion that many families of social standing require at such times, the cause of Secretary Armitage's death was kept strictly quiet. The public announcement mentioned a heart condition. Only the immediate family knew better.

34

Moscow

Far more secretive than the KGB, and far less well known, is the Glavnoye Razvedyvatelnoye Upravleniye, the Chief Intelligence Directorate of the General Staff of the Soviet Union, or the GRU. This agency, which is entirely independent of—and has a long history of fierce rivalry with—the KGB, is located in a nine-story glass tower outside Moscow known as the Aquarium. It is surrounded on three sides by the Khodinka military airfield, and on the other side by a building simply labeled INSTITUTE OF COSMIC BIOLOGY; the entire compound is protected by electrified barbed wire and patrol dogs.

Early in the morning, a young man was entering the office of his superior, the first deputy chief of the GRU. His face was epicene, with high arching eyebrows, a small nose, large ears, and freckles everywhere. Yet in his eyes were traces of a spirit prematurely aged, a cynicism too deep for his thirty-some years. He had served in Afghanistan, where he had directed the blowing up of bridges and certain buildings in Kabul.

He wore the uniform of the GRU's Third Department, or Spetsnaz. The Spetsnaz are the GRU's elite espionage-and-terrorist brigade, trained to infiltrate behind enemy lines in wartime, to locate and destroy nuclear facilities, lines of communication, and other strategic targets, and to assassinate enemy leaders. They also provide support, training, and equipment for numerous terrorist groups. In general, the Spetsnaz troops are the Soviet Union's most skilled saboteurs.

This young man was the Spetsnaz's leading specialist in explosive and incendiary devices. He saluted as his superior nodded hello from behind a large desk, in back of which was an expanse of floor-to-ceiling window.

The older man, a colonel general, was a white-haired man who carried himself with the aristocratic bearing of an old White Russian, his uniform a fruit salad of medals.

No sooner had the explosives expert seated himself than the older man slid a small square note across the highly burnished surface.

The Spetsnaz man took it and felt the blood rush to his head.

There was only one word: "Sekretariat."

The younger man had been secretly recruited to the Sekretariat two years before, after his impressive tour of duty in Afghanistan.

He nodded.

Then he watched the colonel general bend down and dial a knob in front of his desk: a safe. When it was open, his superior withdrew a manila folder and then slid that across the desk.

"Your most important assignment," the chief murmured.

The explosives expert picked up the folder, opened it, and saw that it contained blueprints. He glanced at them, and then paled.

"No," he gasped.

"This is a historic moment," the colonel general said. "For all of us. I am pleased you will be a part of it."

35

Washington

At shortly after ten o'clock in the morning, Roger Bayliss entered the lobby of one of Washington's finest old hotels, the Hope-Stanford and strode across the sumptuous Oriental carpet, past marble Corinthian columns and eighteenth-century silk tapestries, to the registration desk. He spoke briefly to the clerk, then walked over to the elevator bank.

He looked around the lobby impatiently, visibly the sort of man who did not like to be kept waiting, and when the first elevator came, he took it to the fifth floor. There he turned left until he found room 547. Taped to the door was an envelope with his name on it. Wrinkling his brow in annoyance, he turned and returned to the elevators, where he pressed the "down" button.

Watching him from the stairwell at the end of the corridor was Charlie Stone.

Everything was going well so far, Stone reflected. He was alone: *Good; perhaps I'm being overly suspicious.*

An hour and a half earlier, Stone had called Bayliss. Roger Bayliss had been one of Alfred Stone's prize students, and even though the NSC official hardly knew the son of his old graduate-school mentor, Alfred Stone had obviously trusted him. Trusted him enough to have asked for his help.

"Of course I heard what happened to you," Bayliss had exclaimed over the phone. "Jesus Christ. And your father . . ." There was a long silence for a moment, as if Bayliss had had difficulty gaining control of his emotions, and then he continued. "Charlie, I've heard quite a bit

about your situation. More than you'd probably believe.
I think it's important we talk."

"Good. As soon as possible."

"Look, Charlie. Don't take this the wrong way, but
I don't want to be seen with you. You understand, being
on the NSC, I can hardly risk—"

"All right," Stone cut him off. "I'll call you soon with
a place to meet."

Of course, Stone had figured it out already. Conventional logic dictated that they meet in a public place; public
places, the theory went, are the safest harbor. But Stone
was a fugitive from the law. For him, nowhere was safe.
And Bayliss—Bayliss was a question mark. Who knew if
he could really be trusted?

At quarter of ten, Stone had called Bayliss back and
told him to come to the Hope-Stanford and ask for his
room number at the registration desk.

The front-desk clerk had been, with a little financial
suasion, quite compliant. As requested, he gave Bayliss a
room number—of an unoccupied room. After watching
Bayliss walk toward the elevators, and waiting a minute
to make sure no one had followed him, the clerk called
up to the room of the man he knew as Mr. Taylor and left
a message that Bayliss had arrived in the hotel unac-
companied.

The clerk, a recent college graduate who was trying
to make it as an actor, enjoyed the intrigue of it all: Mr.
Taylor had explained only that he was a mergers-and-
acquisitions attorney in town to conduct some sensitive
negotiations in absolute secrecy. One couldn't be too careful, Taylor had said. Greed, the attorney had explained
to the clerk while invisibly slipping him a fifty-dollar bill,
knows no bounds.

The envelope Bayliss had taken from the door of room
547 had contained another room number, 320, two floors
below, along with Stone's apologies for the inconvenience.
A necessary inconvenience, Stone had decided: it gave him
more time to observe Bayliss, make sure he was neither
followed nor accompanied.

Naturally, Bayliss had taken the elevator, not the stairs, down two flights; most hotel guests tend to avoid the stairs. Stone made it to 320 more than thirty seconds before Bayliss did.

As soon as he entered the suite, Stone saw the red message light on the phone glowing. He picked it up, got the message, and hung up, relieved. A double check: Bayliss didn't have anyone waiting for him in the lobby.

The coast was clear.

Relax.

He glanced around the room, taking in the surroundings, glad to be enjoying this brief luxury after the rooming house, the desperate running of the last few days. It was pleasant to be in a place with antique oak furnishings, mahogany walls, plush monogrammed towels.

There was a knock, and Stone opened the door, tense once again.

"Hello, Roger."

"Charlie," Bayliss said, extending two hands and grasping Stone's hand in both of his. "Good to meet you, and I'm so sorry it's in such awful circumstances. I was surprised to see that note in there telling me to go to 320." He laughed briefly. "Very thorough of you. Don't worry; I probably outdid you. I made damn sure no one saw me coming here. Last thing I need."

"Come on in."

Stone led Bayliss to a cluster of overstuffed chairs, feeling the cold, hard revolver he had placed under his waistband at the small of his back. A gun would protect him, Stone knew, but in many ways he would be even safer not revealing he had one. He watched Bayliss, taking in the NSC official's expensive, perhaps bespoke, charcoal-gray suit and highly polished shoes.

"You're not a murderer," Bayliss said, exhaling, settling into an armchair. "I know it. The question is, what can I do to help you?"

Stone took the chair opposite his. "Let's start this way: what did you mean when you said you'd heard more about my situation than I'd believe?"

Bayliss nodded, then exhaled slowly. "I may be violating the National Security Act by telling you this," he began. "I *know* I'm violating a lot of other secrets. I think you know your father's death wasn't the result of a random act of violence."

Stone nodded.

"There's something going on. A convulsion. Something very big."

Something going on: Armitage's words. "What do you mean exactly, Roger?"

"This is difficult for me, Charlie. I don't know where to start." He paused a long time. "You're one of the stars of Parnassus. So you've heard, of course, of the Big Mole theory?"

What the hell was he talking about? Stone replied slowly, "It's been wholly discredited, Roger."

Bayliss was, Stone knew, referring to the theory that for the last several decades an agent—a Soviet agent—has slowly and methodically worked his way up the CIA's hierarchy, performing well but not too well, making friends but not too many. Probably, the theory went, married to an American woman, with American children, an all-American kind of PTA–and–Kiwanis Club dad, who has been siphoning the most classified American intelligence back to Moscow. It was the great suspicion of the late James Jesus Angleton, the longtime CIA counterintelligence chief, who nearly tore the Central Intelligence Agency apart in the 1970s in his crusade to find the mole, until Angleton was fired by William Colby in 1974.

Bayliss shrugged.

"The confection of a paranoid genius," Stone said.

Bayliss leaned forward, speaking with great intensity. "To all outward appearances, the ravings of a man who'd been in the sick world of counterintelligence so long his mind bent. When in reality the most inviolable stronghold of American intelligence is rotten to the core."

Stone felt as if his stomach had turned suddenly to ice. "You're saying it's for real," he whispered, shaking his head. "What the hell does it have to do with my father?"

"Listen, Charlie—I told you before I shouldn't be

telling you any of this, and I meant it. I need your word on this."

"You have it."

"If you so much as breathe a word, I'll deny it. We believe your father may have been killed to protect this asset's identity—"

"By *Russians*?" Stone shot back.

"Not so simple. *Certain* Russians. People who are intent on seeing that the identity of this mole remain absolutely secret."

"But my father couldn't possibly have known anything," Stone whispered.

"Your father knew some things he wasn't supposed to. Things that were clearly dangerous to these people."

"Oh, come *on*," Stone snapped, getting to his feet. He began pacing around the room, trying to think, trying to make sense of everything he'd learned in the last several days, things that no longer seemed to make any sense at all. "Why you? Why do *you* happen to know so much about this?"

"Why?" Bayliss said, turning in his chair to face Stone. "I don't know. Maybe because I happened to be at a certain party one night. Maybe because I happen to know a certain Russian diplomat."

"I don't understand." Stone sat on the edge of a writing table, suddenly too tired to stand.

"That I can't go into. But I need you to think for me. *Think*, Charlie. They weren't just after your father. They were after you as well. What do you know? What did you find out that might have anything to do with your father's 1953 trip to Moscow? For that matter, *anything*, no matter how inconsequential it might seem to you."

Stone shook his head, his lips tight, as he tried to think.

Bayliss now spoke with a gentleness that surprised Stone. "Your father would have wanted you to help me," he said. "Alfred Stone loved his country deeply. Served in the White House, suffered smears on his loyalty, and *loved* this country, goddamn it. And I think he would have wanted his son to do everything in his power to help. Our national security may be jeopardized. Hundreds may die, Charlie. Perhaps thousands. I don't exaggerate when I tell you that peace between the superpowers may well be at stake."

Stone got up from the writing desk and walked toward the far corner of the room, folding his arms contemplatively. It made sense, everything Bayliss said; it *fit*.

"If I could go into more detail, Charlie, I would. It's not just the U.S. that's threatened. It's Moscow as well. There must be something, some shred of information you garnered, perhaps some document, some phone call," Bayliss insisted. "Anything."

Stone simply sighed, furrowing his brow. He shook his head.

"I need you to come in, talk to some of our people. Tell them what you know, everything. It's *vital*, Charlie."

"I'm afraid I can't do that, Roger," Stone said, watching Bayliss from across the room. "I need your help, your protection. But you *yourself* don't know who's involved in this and who isn't. You could be betrayed the way I've been betrayed. I'm sorry."

"You're not safe out here, on the run, hiding."

"I've survived so far. With your help, I won't have to hide much longer."

"It would be a good idea for you to come in. Let our people take care of you. Protect you."

"I'm sorry."

"For your own good, Charlie. I'm going to have to insist on it."

Stone gave a quick, derisory laugh. "*Insist* on it?" he repeated.

"It's too dangerous for you, knowing whatever you know, exposed like this. You've got to come with me."

Stone massaged the bridge of his nose, closing his eyes wearily. "I don't know who to trust anymore."

"You can trust me, Charlie. You know that. Your father knew that."

"I'll contact you in a few days, Roger," Stone said.

"Don't leave this room, Charlie," Bayliss said, a peculiar edge to his voice. "You don't have a lot of choice in the matter, really." He got to his feet and moved slowly to the door; he seemed to block it. "We're going to take you in."

"I didn't agree to that," Stone said levelly, maneuvering toward where Bayliss was standing, toward the door.

"I don't think you understand," Bayliss said coldly. "You're endangering things you have no *idea* about. Our goddamned national security. I was hoping we wouldn't have to resort to compulsion. You're not walking out that door. Let's do this quietly, Stone."

"Why are you treading so softly, Roger? You could have stormed this hotel, had me surrounded."

"I'd much rather have had you come along voluntarily. And besides—" Bayliss reached his left hand around under his suit jacket.

Stone instinctively reached for his gun, then saw what Bayliss had produced: a small square metal object. Stone smiled, his composure unruffled. "A transmitter."

"Our entire conversation," Bayliss said, "has been broadcast on a hundred and forty megaherz. Our people are right outside the door, waiting for my signal.

"You're an impressive, clever man, but an amateur, Stone." All pretense at civility had vanished. "Give it up. You're in way over your head. I'm sorry you preferred not to cooperate." He spoke mournfully now. "I wish it hadn't come to this."

From behind the hotel-room door came a whisper-quiet scrape of metal against metal, and then the door swung open. The three men from the American Flag Foundation entered, their pistols drawn.

"Jesus," one of them began.

The room was empty. Utterly silent, except for a low, almost inaudible groaning.

They'd waited for Bayliss's signal to enter, but then the signal unaccountably went dead. Perhaps Bayliss had shut it off. Ten minutes later, the men had taken it upon themselves to move in.

They split up professionally, one of the men heading

toward the closed bathroom door. The sounds seemed to be coming from inside. He sidled up to the doorjamb and flung the door open with a sudden motion.

There, in the bathtub, bound with strips of toweling, was Roger Bayliss, unconscious or semiconscious, gagged with a monogrammed washcloth. He was restrained by the long snakelike cord of the hand-held shower looped around his neck.

Stone could hear the sounds of traffic from the street below. He stood now on the broad granite ledge, which was protected by a parapet, outside the hotel's fourth floor. For a few seconds—there was no time to spare—he inspected the window of a hotel room that appeared to be empty. Then he figured out how to force the window, and he was inside. Within two minutes, he got to the hotel's parking garage and was home free.

Escaping Bayliss had not been especially difficult. He had disabled the transmitter, knocked Bayliss unconscious, then tied him up; Stone was far stronger. But he could not leave the hotel room by the door, behind which were Bayliss's backups. There was no choice: he had to leave through the window. Since it was the third floor, he would have to climb—up, which was easier and safer than down.

There was an instant's apprehension, and then he felt a calm wash over him, the same wonderful calm he felt when he began a particularly tricky climb. This was nothing, a ledge that had to be three feet wide, and a parapet. A snap.

He spotted a section of the edifice where the ornamentation—the gargoyles and gingerbread, stained dark with automobile exhaust—seemed sturdy enough. And then he hoisted himself up to the floor above, gripping onto the granite protrusions.

A little over an hour later, Stone pulled his stolen yellow VW into a parking space at Washington's National Airport, his head still reeling. He glanced apprehensively in the rearview mirror, satisfied that he looked presentable. He did not appear to be a man on the run for his life, with the exception of his abraded hands.

Now, carrying his small valise, he heard the final boarding call for a Pan Am flight to Chicago echoing in the terminal building. If he hurried, he could just make this one; no sense in waiting. He strode urgently, eyes watchful, trying to make sense of the lies Bayliss had told. A convulsion in the American government to cover up a highly placed mole in the CIA. Was Bayliss telling the truth, even a small part of it? *Something is going on*, Armitage had told him.

Could it be true?

Quickly Stone removed a small bag from his carry-on bag and placed it in a locker. It contained only his gun, and, as much as he disliked being without it, there was no way to get it through the metal detectors. There were ways to get some guns through, Stone knew, but not this one. He could always pick one up if he needed it.

And, he reflected as he put down the cash for a ticket under an assumed name, he would probably need one soon.

36

Moscow

Charlotte Harper eased herself into an almost unbearably hot bath. The steam gave off the pungent smell of eucalyptus, from mineral bath-salts that were supposed to replicate the hot springs at European spas, relieve muscular tensions, reduce fatigue. At least the stuff cleared her head.

There were times when living alone was simply great, and this was one of them. A bath at two o'clock in the morning wasn't possible when you were living with someone, at least not with music playing on the stereo, as it was now: a soothing Bach oboe sonata.

She'd worked late because she had to keep pace with

the hours in the U.S., which was eight hours earlier. She was exhausted from doing the tedious and largely pointless stories that the network wanted about how Moscow was preparing for the summit. Especially when the real story was the wave of terrorism that had struck Moscow.

A bomb had gone off that day in the Moscow subway. That by itself would have been an important story, since terrorism occurred rarely in Moscow. Coming so soon after the Borisov asassination, however, it was even more significant.

But did it really indicate opposition to Gorbachev within the Soviet leadership? The first one, the Borisov assassination, yes, possibly. But a bomb in the metro? It just didn't fit. Soaking, she began slowly to relax, and her mind floated free, until it seized upon an idea.

She got up, dried herself off, and wrapped herself in a thick purple terry-cloth robe.

Twenty minutes later, she was unlocking the door to the ABC office, which was in the adjoining entryway in the same building.

It was half past two in the morning, and the office was dark and vacant. Good: she needed to think in solitude. She switched on the lights, glanced at the ever-chattering teletype, and sat down at her desk. The fluorescent lights buzzed. She thought, chair tipped back, as she examined the ceiling. Momentarily, she wondered, as she usually did in this position, where they planted the electronic bugs. Everyone knew that correspondents' offices and homes were bugged. She remembered hearing a story about one of *The New York Times* reporters, years ago, sitting in his office alone on New Year's Eve and remarking aloud that he wondered what the KGB did on such a night. Then the guy's phone had rung, and he had picked it up and heard only the sound of a champagne cork popping.

She got up, walked over to the small reference library, and found a file she'd compiled for herself before leaving for Moscow.

In a few minutes, she found what she was looking for. In her "terrorism/U.S.S.R." file, she found a brief entry about the death of a man who had occupied the very same position as Sergei Borisov had, only decades earlier. He was named Mironov, and he'd perished in a suspicious airplane crash during the Khrushchev years. He'd been appointed by Khrushchev, and had been hated by certain important enemies of Khrushchev within the KGB.

So maybe the editor was right. Maybe there *was* intrigue within the Kremlin.

Then she found another item, about a wave of terrorist incidents in Moscow in 1977. On January 8, 1977, an explosion went off in the Moscow subway, killing seven people and wounding forty-four. The Soviet authorities charged and eventually executed three Armenian dissidents in the case, although there wasn't any evidence linking them to the crime. A number of commentators that year believed that the whole thing was a setup, that the regime was just trying to discredit the dissident movement. Could *that* be what was going on now? Especially with the eruptions in virtually every republic of the Soviet Union?

Who would know?

There *was* someone who might know. She had a source—a valuable informant she protected carefully, because he worked for the KGB. A technician who secretly loathed his employers, he called himself only "Sergei."

It wouldn't be easy, but she could contact him. It would take a few days to reach him, probably. But maybe he'd know, or else he'd have a useful theory, or he'd know where to look.

In the meantime, though, she faced the dilemma of how to report what little she knew. How did you cover such a thing? Not one Soviet official was willing to be interviewed on camera about it; it was clear that they hadn't decided what their public-relations strategy would be. There were rumors—there were *always* rumors—that the thing wouldn't have happened had the new head of the KGB, Andrei Pavlichenko, not been suffering from heart trouble. She made a mental note to try to find one of Pavlichenko's doctors and check on his prognosis.

*   *   *

Later that morning, she, her cameraman, Randy, and her producer, a young woman named Gail Howe, drove in the company Volvo to Charlotte's favorite stand-up site, on an embankment of the Moscow River directly across from the Kremlin.

The air was cold, and there were a few flurries of snow that whipped across her face and stuck to her coat. She rehearsed her lines a few times, marking the words she wanted to emphasize with a pencil, and then the camera was rolling.

"For the first time, the official Soviet news agency, Tass, has *acknowledged* the acts of terrorism that have alarmed so much of Moscow," she said. "By condemning the subway incident as 'the work of a band of hooligans and lunatics,' the Soviet authorities have sought to play down the importance of the bomb. This country fears most of all a breakdown of order, and with the summit fast approaching, these fears are higher than ever. One official here told me, 'We in the Soviet Union are not free of violent crime, although I must say we are not plagued by the terrorism and the assassinations and the murders that beset the countries of the West.' Only time will tell." She paused for dramatic effect, and added, "This is Charlotte Harper, ABC News, Moscow."

Right, she thought as the Volvo pulled away from the Moscow River. Another meaningless piece.

Just give me time, she told herself defiantly.

Early the next evening, she called the telephone number the *babushka* had given her. She'd tried it dozens of times over the last few days, with no luck, and she wondered if it were the right one.

Then a woman's voice answered.

"Sonya Kunetskaya, please?" Charlotte's Russian was fluent, but she could not disguise her foreign accent. Yet she had to be careful not to scare the woman off.

A long pause. "Yes, this is she."

"I have a message for you from a friend."

"A friend?" The woman was alarmed. "What friend?"

"I can't say over the phone."

"Who is this?"

"The message is urgent," Charlotte said. It was vital to be cryptic. "I just want to drop it by. But if you're busy . . ."

"I—I'm not— Who *are* you?"

"Please," Charlotte said. "It won't take any time."

Another long pause, and then: "All right, I suppose." Hesitantly, she gave Charlotte directions to her home.

Sonya Kunetskaya's apartment was all the way across town, as it turned out, at the far north, almost at the last metro stop. Charlotte was nervous about taking her car, which, with its foreign-correspondent license plates, was a magnet for KGB tails.

The metro was jammed. She got off at the stop closest to the Exhibition of Economic Achievement, a large obelisk that swooped up to a point—the sharpest phallus in the world, Charlotte thought. Near it was Ostankino, where a vast czarist estate had once been located, now the site of the Gostelradio, the State Television and Radio headquarters. The area around the metro was sparsely settled.

The woman lived a few blocks away, in an immense red brick building with endless numbered entrances, a dismal semimodern complex. The door to the entryway swung shut behind Charlotte with a clatter that made her jump, and the lobby, if that was the word for it, was shabby: concrete covered in peeling dark-blue paint, which smelled strongly of urine. A mangy gray cat scurried by, and Charlotte saw to her horror that it had no eyes, just empty sockets. She stifled a small scream, and checked Sonya's apartment number.

The door to number 26 was covered with cheap padded Leatherette, punctuated by metal studs. The woman who opened the door was diminutive, in her early sixties. Her brown hair was peppered with gray, cut in a modified pageboy with bangs. She wore a faded floral-print housedress and steel-rimmed glasses. "Come in, please," she said. "I am Sonya Kunetskaya." And she extended a bony hand.

"Charlotte Harper."

She led the way down a dark corridor into a sitting room furnished in heavy wooden pieces and sofas covered with a faded pattern. A man who looked about Sonya's age was sitting in one of the easy chairs. His white hair was combed straight back.

He was the most horrific-looking man Charlotte had ever seen. It took all of her willpower to meet the man's eye. His face was a mass of discolored scar tissue.

"This is my friend Yakov," Sonya Kunetskaya said. Yakov sat in the chair with a self-possession that seemed to indicate he was no visitor.

"You said you had an urgent message for me," the woman prompted.

"Well, perhaps I overstated," Charlotte said. She remembered that Charlie had said Sonya Kunetskaya had met with Alfred Stone in Moscow, that she was connected in some way with Winthrop Lehman. What was her connection to Lehman? "I bring you regards from Winthrop Lehman."

For a long time, there was silence.

"Who are you?" Sonya asked.

"I'm a reporter for ABC News. I was told to look you up."

There was a long, uncomfortable silence. "Is this something you wanted to talk to me about in private?" Sonya asked. "Did Lehman tell you to call me?" There was an edge of desperation about the woman. She looked almost stricken, and her friend—or was it her husband?—looked uncomfortable. What was going on? Charlotte wondered.

"Yes, that's right." I'm stabbing in the dark, Charlotte thought. Why is this woman so nervous? "Have you known him long?"

"I met him in 1962," the Russian woman said, seeming puzzled, but more at ease recounting a story she had obviously told many times. "I was an editor for Progress Publishers then."

"But how did you get to meet someone as famous as Winthrop Lehman?"

"I was at a party at Boris Pasternak's dacha at Peredelkino. I was Pasternak's editor on a volume of poetry he was translating, and he invited me to a dinner party. Winthrop Lehman was also there."

"Nineteen sixty-two? Pasternak must have been an old man."

"Oh, yes. He must have been in his seventies." She nodded vigorously.

"And what was Lehman doing in Moscow?"

Sonya hesitated momentarily, as if deciding precisely what to say. "I don't know for certain. He visits occasionally."

But Charlotte was stuck on something now and wouldn't give it up. "You were Pasternak's editor in 1962, is that right?" she asked.

"Yes, that's right," Sonya said. "Boris Pasternak. All of you Americans know *Doctor Zhivago,* but have you read his poems?"

The question lingered in the air, awkwardly.

"Yes, I have," Charlotte replied, "and they're beautiful. I'm quite impressed that you worked with Pasternak."

"He's considered a great poet in our country," Sonya said.

"Pasternak wasn't alive in 1962. I'm afraid you picked the wrong date. He died in 1960."

"So long ago," Sonya said quietly. "I cannot remember, I'm sorry."

And Charlotte knew for certain that the woman was lying.

37

Chicago

Stone arrived at Chicago's O'Hare Airport in mid-afternoon, tense and exhausted.

The file in Lehman's archives had led him to Armitage. Pogue's name was in that file, too.

Once again he tried directory assistance, but Warren Pogue's number was unlisted. He called the FBI in Washington, but Pogue had left instructions that he was not to be disturbed in retirement. They refused to give out his address or phone number.

There had to be a solution.

He stopped at an airport coffee shop, bought a cup of coffee and a plastic-tasting ham sandwich, which he chewed slowly, considering. He needed some very specialized help, and he knew precisely where he could get it: a name that had been at the back of his mind from the minute he realized he had to go to Chicago. A woman he'd known since college—a friend of Charlotte's, actually—who was an attorney. More specifically, an assistant state's attorney in Chicago, which meant she probably worked closely with the Chicago police. Maybe—probably—she could get an unlisted phone number.

Paula Singer had been Charlotte's roommate during freshman year, and she had kept in touch with Charlie and Charlotte over the years. Once, five or so years ago, she had stayed with them for a few weeks in their New York apartment, desperately unhappy over the breakup of a longtime romance, needing solace and companionship.

If she'd be willing to help now, she'd be invaluable. Maybe he could find temporary refuge, for a night.

Her name was not in his Rolodex or address book;

she could not be known as a friend. He might be safe with her, at least overnight.

Stone looked around the coffee shop, instinctively suspicious by now. He desperately needed Paula Singer's assistance, but the one thing he must not do was to be followed to her.

Tracking her down was, thank God, easy; she was listed in the phone directory. Her apartment was on Barry Street, on the North Side of Chicago, an area with an especially high density of youngish professionals. She was not home, of course, by the time Stone arrived at her house in the late afternoon. He would have to wait. He lingered in a coffee shop until the waitress made it clear he was no longer welcome.

As it turned out, Paula did not arrive at her house until almost nine o'clock, wearing a finely tailored burgundy business suit, a black tweed overcoat, and a pair of Reebok running shoes. In college she had worn an unvarying outfit of denim jacket, corduroy skirt, and leggings; now she was all crisp, upwardly mobile professionalism.

Balancing her briefcase and a stack of mail, Paula inserted her key in the front-door lock, oblivious of Stone, a few feet away in the shadows.

"Paula," Stone said quietly.

She jumped, dropping her briefcase. "*Jesus*, who is it?"

"Charlie Stone."

She looked in Stone's direction and finally caught sight of him. "Oh, my God. My God. It *is* you." Her tone was not one of pleasure. She was terrified. "Please, *don't*."

He realized with dismay what she meant. "I know what you've heard. Paula, it's a lie. You know me. You have to help me." He tried to keep the desperation out of his voice, but there it was. "Help me, Paula."

Reluctantly, she pushed the door open and motioned him in.

"You eat yet?"

"No," Stone said.

"Let me see what I've got in the fridge." Paula's initial terror had given way to a wary geniality; Stone, apparently, had persuaded her. She'd offered to let him stay with her. "I don't really do cooking, you know?"

Her kitchen was a tiny, narrow galley with a window counter through which you could serve food; to eat, you sat on tall stools at a bar on the other side. It reminded Stone of the arrangement Mary Richards had had on the "Mary Tyler Moore Show." He stood beside her, trying not to get in her way as she stared dolefully into the refrigerator, finding nothing, and at last locating one frozen dinner, a Le Menu chicken-parmigiana entrée, in the freezer. "Look, nothing fancy here. Hope you don't mind if we split this," she said, popping it into the microwave oven. Beneath her hearty poise, she seemed flustered. "You want booze or something? Sorry, but I don't have any wine around. Scotch or nothing."

"Scotch is fine. Paula, I need you to get an unlisted phone number and an address for me, first thing in the morning. I know you've got the resources to do it."

She poured out the drinks. "Look," she said falteringly. "I don't know how to say this. I heard about what happened. About the stabbing and all that. The papers have been calling you a fugitive. Everyone talks about it."

Stone noticed that she was standing some distance away. "You don't believe it, I hope."

"I don't know what to think. If you tell me not to, I won't. I mean, you want me to get a number, okay. But I want some facts. Like, what are you doing? And why *here*? I know you're here to hide out. I figured that out."

"Only for a night or two," Stone said. "Just until I reach this person who can help me. I don't want to get you in any kind of trouble. Believe me. But you're not known to anyone as a friend of mine—"

"Thanks."

"That's not what I mean. You know that."

"I know. But who are you running from? What the hell really happened, Charlie?"

* * *

The microwave beeped, and she removed the plastic tray. When she pulled back the plastic film, a cloud of steam rose from the chicken. She cut the portion neatly in half, put one piece on a plate for him, and began to eat out of the tray. They alternated bites of chicken with sips of Scotch. She sat very close, and her legs touched his.

He would not tell her about his connection to Parnassus, to the CIA; she believed he was employed by the State Department, in New York, doing analysis of the Soviet Union, and he didn't correct her now.

His story was sanitized, but even so it shocked her. Something in her was moved. She spoke quietly now, her voice almost trembling, rising and falling with anger. "Jesus," she said. She had stopped eating, and she turned to face him. "If this is all true—this is a goddamned nightmare."

Stone looked down at his Scotch glass, nodding.

"I'll get the info for you, Stone. I got a guy. One of the cops I worked with, doing witness prep on a really high-profile DWI—a drunk-driving case, you know?—he's a good guy. Got a crush on me, I think."

"Great."

"Married with *eight* kids. Not so great. So he's got a friend who's a billing clerk at the phone company, if you really want to know. That's how even the cops do it, bypassing all the paperwork crap, the court-ordered shit."

Stone smiled, slowly allowing himself to unwind. Good old brassy Paula. Charlotte's college roommate, Paula was smart, unyielding, caustic, often abrasive. In college, she'd seemed absolutely sexless; *that* had changed, but she was as plainspoken, as alarmingly frank, as ever. Twenty years ago, she'd been overweight, with pudgy cheeks, brown eyes, long brown hair. Now she was much more slender, her hair short and soft around her face: an attractive, magnetic woman.

"You like it, Paula? Your job?"

"Yeah, Stone, I *like* making about one-tenth what all my friends in private practice make," she retorted. Her voice softened. "Yeah, I like it. I like it a lot."

"Too much work, probably."

"Sure. Shit, yeah. Mind-boggling caseload. Barely enough time to interview the witnesses, you know? There's hundreds of ASAs—assistant state's attorneys—and all we're really supposed to care about is numbers. Convictions. Biggest bang for the buck. You got a shithead you *know* is guilty and your testimony is weak, forget it. Bargain it down."

Stone smiled, shaking his head as he listened. He appreciated what she was doing, trying to take his mind off his own trouble.

"Plus, the place I work in. Like a concentration camp. Really. The big, scary Criminal Courts Building at Twenty-sixth and California, metal detectors, graffiti all over the place, weirdos, and—get this—guards with *rifles* pointing down at you from towers."

"Nice. But you're doing what you want, more or less, right? Doing some good. I mean, you're not defending corporations who dump toxic wastes."

Paula gave an exasperated sigh. "Yeah. Sometimes. You know me, I'm always fighting battles. I took on this one case last year, against the advice of just about everyone in the office. My boss told me to lay off. *State of Illinois* v. *Patricio*, a rape case. A local judge accused of raping a thirteen-year-old neighbor girl, and, goddamn it, he did it, Charlie. I *know* it. But the goddamned judge had dozens of bigwigs, all these prominent people, ready to testify in his behalf, including some big-deal judges. Major players, even a bishop. My boss said plea-bargain it down to a lesser included offense, to minor assault. Avoid a trial we couldn't win. He didn't think our testimony was strong enough; the jury wouldn't buy it. So I really called in my markers on this one, you know? I said, Look, I've been here for you, I've done fucking everything you wanted. Now give me this."

"And?"

"And I lost."

"I'm sorry."

"Yeah, me, too." She hoisted the Scotch bottle and

refilled their glasses. "So, hey, how's Charlotte? She seems to be doing pretty well for herself. You can't put the news on without seeing her face."

"Yeah, she is."

"Are you two—I don't know how to say this, but when I last talked to Charlotte, like a year or so ago—"

"We're separated, Paula. We're still married. I think."

"I'm glad to hear it," she said, although she didn't sound it. "Who'd have thought she'd do so well? You know what I mean." She shook her head slowly. "Jesus."

"It's true, she's really doing great." There was something double-edged about her compliments—was there still some old rivalry between Paula and Charlotte?

As the Scotch hit Stone's empty stomach, he began to find her sexy, and he suspected that she felt the same thing about him. Maybe she had always been attracted to him.

"You know," she said, sipping her Scotch deeply, "when you two were in bed, in college, I used to hear everything."

She looked at him provocatively. Their faces were only inches apart. There wasn't any question now what she was thinking. He moved his lips closer, and she did the same. Their lips met tentatively and then came closer still. After a moment, she pulled her mouth away and ran her left hand through his hair. "I always liked your curls," she said softly.

"I'm starting to lose them, I think," he said hoarsely. "Listen, Paula." His nostrils took in her perfume, something cinnamony and musky. She slipped off her suit jacket. Under her silk blouse he could see her breasts, which were large. Her nipples jutted out against the fabric. He wanted desperately to remove her clothes, to see her naked, and he was embarrassed by his desire.

"Paula, this is wrong."

"Do you think Charlotte's not seeing people?" Paula whispered, her breath hot against his ear. Her hand moved lightly over his erect penis. For a moment Stone almost lost his balance on the stool.

Stone didn't say anything, but, confused and guilty, he returned her kiss, his tongue piercing her mouth, exploring the softness.

"Hey, listen, Charlie, I'm glad you showed up," she whispered, and they both got up to move to the other room.

When they got to the couch, she unbuckled his belt and slipped her right hand, still cold from holding the Scotch glass, into his Jockey shorts and onto his buttocks, then moved it around to the front. He held his breath, and he could hear her breathing heavily. He unbuttoned her blouse, and marveled at her erect nipples, large brown disks. He bent to put his mouth on them, feeling both very wrong and very right, pleasures he hadn't felt in a long time.

Washington

The first secretary of the Soviet Embassy in Washington, D.C., Aleksandr Malarek, arrived at his office unusually early the next morning. He helped himself to a glass of tea from the seventeenth-century silver samovar he kept in a corner of his spacious office and sat down at his desk to review the overnight cable traffic from Moscow.

As *rezident*, or the highest-ranking KGB official in the United States, he oversaw the entire range of KGB operations in the U.S., which were now, in the days of glasnost, directed mostly at the acquisition of high technology. He was assisted by the four other *rezident*s, in New York and San Francisco.

But his time in the last weeks had been spent entirely on something his KGB compatriots must never know about.

Malarek did not consider himself a traitor. He was a faithful servant of the Soviet state: he loved his country, and no longer did he question whether he was being disloyal. No, he believed firmly that he was helping to save his great country.

But he was increasingly displeased with the Americans, his colleagues—the Sanctum. In their attempts to locate one particular man, the Americans were being far too lax.

As *rezident*, Malarek was able to draw upon the KGB's network of illegals and sleepers dispersed throughout the United States. The illegals, or agents living under false identities, were controlled by the KGB's Department Eight, Directorate S, which is responsible for planning assassinations and sabotage. Trained for years outside of Moscow, these men (and a few women) were given forged passports and documents and slipped into the U.S. Here they supported themselves quietly in unremarkable jobs and met as infrequently as possible with their controls in the *rezidentura*. They were expensive assets, to be used with extreme delicacy. Often they carried out assignments in the Middle East, under the cover of businessmen.

And a number of them worked not for the KGB but for the Sekretariat. Which meant that, given the present urgency, these particular illegals had had to carry out "wet affairs"—murders.

It is generally believed that the intelligence agencies of the Soviet Union and the United States no longer engage in the taking of human life. In fact, such actions are avoided whenever possible, since they run the risk of exposure, perhaps causing grave political damage.

But wet affairs do continue, on both the Soviet and the American sides, although rarely directed at each other. Whenever possible, the work is done by proxies—the Cuban Security Service (DGI) or American criminals. The Sekretariat, however—because its existence was so carefully concealed from both Washington and Moscow, as well as the KGB—could not entrust these jobs to anyone but their own.

At half past eight, there was a knock on the door. It was Malarek's assistant, the Line PR, in charge of political intelligence. He was Semyon L. Sergeyev, a small, balding man with a graying mustache. He was a few years younger than Malarek, although he looked older and perennially anxious. He, too, was Sekretariat.

Sergeyev's face was grave. "The situation with Armitage has been taken care of," Sergeyev said as he entered and took a seat.

"Cleanly?"

Sergeyev explained, and Malarek smiled at the cleverness.

Malarek took some pride in the elegance of the operation. A code clerk in the State Department's security-classified-file section, compromised by several years of bribes discreetly channeled by Malarek's office, had informed Sergeyev that Deputy Secretary Armitage had requisitioned a particular X-classified file. Malarek had immediately dispatched one of his assets, working as a courier at the State Department, to do the job. It had been done with the efficiency Malarek expected.

Malarek was silent for a long time, pensively smoothing the lapels of his American-made Harris-tweed suit. "What precisely was in the files William Armitage requested?" he said at length.

"A dossier on a retired agent of the Federal Bureau of Investigation named Warren Pogue."

Malarek raised his eyebrows. He recognized the name; he was quite familiar with a number of files connected with this matter. "Ah. Is it possible our man intends to contact him?"

"Sanctum thinks it's unlikely but possible. By later in the day, they'll have a team of watchers."

"Watching isn't enough. If this man is contacted by Stone in any way, he obviously has to be killed. Even if contact has already been made. But *cleanly*. There must be no connection with us."

Sergeyev had been nodding steadily. "Yes, sir. There is a way."

"And Stone," Malarek began, distracted, but he did not have to continue. Sergeyev knew perfectly well that decades of scrupulous planning on the part of a few very powerful men in the capitals of the two superpowers must not be undone by a single desperate man, whose location remained unknown.

38

Moscow

Stefan Kramer was about to set off their last bomb.

Little remained of the explosives that his old cellmate had given him, enough perhaps for one TNT bomb and one plastique.

He had the night off from work—as an ambulance driver, he usually worked nights—and now he and Yakov sat in his bedroom in the shambling communal apartment in which he lived, assembling the most basic sort of bomb: a few cartridges of dynamite attached to a blasting cap and a chemical pencil. In fact, he did all the work, and Yakov, sitting alongside him on the too-soft bed, kept him company.

The room was musty; the single bed in the center of the frayed blue rug was covered with a spread that had once been cranberry-red and was now a quilt of bald patches. The walls were a depressing hospital tan.

"Stefan," Yakov said, "we're making a mistake."

"Why?"

"With every bomb, the chances of our being caught increase enormously. The *militsiya* must be looking for us now, everywhere."

"As long as I'm careful—"

"No. We've tried. There's no response from the authorities. Nothing. Not a word. Avram is still a prisoner."

"Be patient. Things take time," Stefan told his father.

Yakov shrugged. "You should move out of this apartment. Try to find someplace nicer. We have room, you know. You can move back in with us. . . ."

"The Politburo moves slowly," Stefan continued. "We must give them a decent interval to quarrel among themselves. We can send them another letter. But I think we've got to avoid making our *motives* publicly known. Then our chances of getting Avram released will shrink to almost nothing. Keep it private, and the government can still save face."

"I just don't know," his father said.

"This is a package bomb," Stefan said, holding the contraption up.

But Yakov shook his head. "I have a very bad feeling about this," he said.

Late that afternoon, wearing a standard blue worker's uniform that one of his apartment-mates had left lying around unused, Stefan walked to Sverdlov Square, around to the side of the enormous Bolshoi Theater with its portico of eight columns.

There are many entrances at the side, and during the day none of them is guarded. He selected the one that seemed most likely to be the service entrance and went in. In his blue uniform and, over it, a quilted gray worker's coat, he looked like a deliveryman of the sort whose deliveries would interest no one. He carried a cardboard box filled with a stack of papers that might have been programs but were actually nothing more than discarded invoices he'd taken from a nearby trash heap.

"I'm looking for the dressing rooms," he grumpily told a passerby in the corridor. "You know where they are?"

The passerby pointed the way, and soon he found a hall that appeared to be where the performers' quarters were. Actually, any Bolshoi office would have done, but why not aim as high as possible? The hall was deserted, and he began to open the doors, one by one. If he surprised anyone, or anyone surprised him, he would say he had a box of stuff that he was supposed to give to any stage manager, and he'd pretend that he was lost. But the second door he tried was unlocked, and no one was inside. He put down the box and quickly searched the room, and his heart leaped when he found exactly what he wanted, and so quickly, too: a work pass left on a dressing table by one of the ballerinas. It was small and red and embossed with an official golden seal. Quickly he stuffed it into his pocket, picked up the box of forms, and re-entered the hallway. Two ballerinas in tutus and toe shoes passed by, giggling, but did not give him a glance. Part one of the operation was a success, which was not surprising. People in dressing rooms tend to be careless about their possessions.

That evening, he returned to the Bolshoi.

The bomb consisted of a chemical pencil inserted into a cartridge of dynamite. It would not be very powerful, but it would cause a tremendously large noise in the huge theater. It was small—seven-eighths of an inch by eight inches—so it fit neatly into the large, beautiful bouquet of flowers wrapped in cellophane.

Any sort of close inspection would reveal the apparatus underneath the flowers, but Stefan calculated that there would not be time for a close inspection. The Bolshoi pass would help with that: he would be seen as an employee of the company making a delivery to some important minister from, perhaps, the director of the theater.

At night, the Bolshoi Theater is lit up majestically; its portico glows with an almost amber light. In front of the portico's eight columns is a striking equestrian statue of Apollo at his chariot. Within is a splendid Baroque auditorium, sumptuously appointed in gilt and red plush, which seats an audience of almost three thousand.

The common Russian usually cannot obtain tickets for a performance unless he is willing to wait in line for endless hours on the chance that the few available tickets will not be sold out. For the most part, the audience comprises the more privileged Russians—members of the Central Committee, KGB, Supreme Soviet, and Congress of People's Deputies—foreign diplomats, and the like. Often the ornate boxes are occupied by people of Politburo rank and their families.

The night was cold and rainy. Stefan waited in his car until the crowd in front of the theater disappeared and all the latecomers had gone in. Then he got out of the car, still wearing his blue uniform, and carried the bouquet to the front entrance of the theater.

Now he handed the stolen red Bolshoi work pass to the fat woman who sat in a chair by the door. Luckily, these passes have no pictures on them; with their calligraphic script, they look more like tiny, shirt-pocket diplomas.

In the car, a few minutes earlier, Stefan had squeezed the chemical pencil—it would not do to be seen tinkering with it in public—so he calculated he had ten minutes before the bouquet exploded. He had allowed a minute for admission to the theater and two minutes to find a place to put the bouquet: ideally, a reserved private box that was empty, its regular patrons off somewhere on business. There were always several vacant boxes, even if there were rarely any available seats. And then one minute to exit safely from the theater, and it would detonate.

But the porcine-faced woman frowned. "Hold on a minute," she said suspiciously. "What are these flowers for?"

Stefan affected the sardonic tone of someone who has been at the bottom of the social hierarchy a long time. "For some big-ass minister or something. I don't know. He wants to give this to the prima ballerina after the show."

Like any good *babushku*, she was hung up on propriety. "Why don't you use the *chyorny khod*?" she demanded, using the old Russian term for "back entrance."

He glared at her. Already almost a minute had gone by. *Hurry up, you fat bitch!* he thought. *Or we'll both go up in smoke!*

"Look, I'm in a hurry," he told her. "The guy wants it yesterday, you understand?"

The *babushka* wagged a pudgy finger at him and got slowly to her feet to consult with another woman, who was sitting at an adjacent entrance.

His heart beat wildly now. He could imagine the acid inside the chemical pencil eating its way through the threadlike metal wire, a hairsbreadth away from detonating the explosion.

"All right, come on," the woman said reluctantly.

Stefan walked as quickly as he could into the grand

entrance to the theater and up two carpeted flights, around
to the first box he came to, and found it—locked!

Of course! He had neglected the most obvious possibility of all—that, if a box weren't being used tonight,
the management would keep it locked!—and now he held
in his arms a bomb that would go off momentarily.

Desperately, he ran down the hall and opened the
door to the neighboring box. It was full of people, a well-
dressed man and his heavily made-up wife and three well-
scrubbed children. He closed it, hoped he hadn't been
seen, although he thought the youngest child had turned
around and seen his face, and went on to the next box,
and the next.

The door to the fifth box he came to was open and—
thank God—empty. Probably its occupants had informed
the theater that they would be arriving quite late, and the
management had kept it open pending their arrival. He
got to his knees, shoved the bouquet inside, and closed it.
He ran down the nearest staircase, his heart now pounding
so hard he thought it would fail. Have to get out of here,
he thought, but I mustn't run. Running will alert anyone
and everyone that I'm the culprit. Must get to the exit and
walk past the old ladies. God help me, he prayed. He had
not prayed for decades. God help me.

There it was, the entrance to the theater, with the
two ladies sitting on their metal folding chairs, and just as
he nodded his head at them, he could hear a terrifyingly
loud explosion in the theater, followed by an instant of
silence and then a roar, a chorus of screams.

He couldn't help himself: he ran through the doors
and out. Behind him he could hear a woman's voice shouting after him, but he didn't stop until he was in his car
and had safely pulled away into the light evening traffic.

39

Chicago

Warren Pogue was a contented man. He'd always feared retirement—the idea of sitting around doing nothing had terrified him—but retirement had turned out to be quite pleasant. The FBI had been good to him, and his forty-four years in the Bureau had netted him a respectable pension.

His other friends sat around the house and watched TV and complained, but Warren Pogue kept busy. He was more active than he'd ever been in his life. His wife, Fran, had been even more terrified than he at the prospect of his retiring, but she enjoyed it now, too. He mowed the lawn and gardened and kept their small, immaculately manicured backyard on Mozart Street, in the extreme north section of Chicago known as Rogers Park. He played golf and had even taken up tennis.

And he flew. During World War II, he'd been in the air force, and he'd fallen in love with flying. That was it for forty years, and then, a few weeks after he'd retired from the Bureau, he got together with a few friends and bought a single-engine four-seat Piper Arrow.

So once a week, Saturday, he went flying. Today was Saturday, and he'd been up for an hour. Time to go. He talked to the air-traffic controller and requested clearance to land.

Pogue dipped the plane to twenty-five thousand feet and dialed in the flaps to thirty percent. The throttle back, he made a sharp left, another left, another left: a full circle, watching the hands on the altimeter steadily clicking counterclockwise as he decreased altitude and glided in to the final approach. Just before the wheels touched down, he pulled the nose up so the rear wheels landed first.

A clean landing, he thought with satisfaction. He steered the plane to the parking ground, lining the nose up carefully, the wings precisely in line with the ones on either side. He shut off the ignition, the fuel tanks, the battery switch, and got out. He anchored the plane to the hook embedded in the ground.

He thought about his only daughter, Lori, who was thirty-two and still not married. She'd be coming in tonight to stay for a few days. He wondered whether he'd let it slip and tell her she ought to settle down already and get herself a husband and a family.

Leaving the airport, he said goodbye to Jim, the mechanic, and got in his car. Half an hour later, he pulled up the driveway to his small home.

The driveway could use another blacktopping, he thought.

Pogue was a chain-smoker. His voice, deep and gravelly, reminded Stone of some character on the old "Perry Mason" show, although he couldn't remember which one.

The retired FBI agent looked to be in his late sixties. He was fat, with a potbelly that jutted like a shelf above the hoop of his black leather belt. His wife was a small woman with ash-blond hair who appeared long enough to say hello and then disappeared to an upstairs room to watch television. His place was tiny, a ranch-style house with perfectly rectangular hedges in front and a lawn that resembled Astro-Turf.

Paula had tracked down Pogue's address and phone number first thing in the morning—she had left her house long before Stone got up, probably because they both felt awkward about having made love.

Then Stone had called Pogue, telling him he was working with the director of the FBI on a book about some of the Bureau's greatest exploits—and Pogue was on the list. Stone counted on there not being enough time for Pogue to make phone calls—"I've got a plane to catch in about two hours," Stone said, "and this will hardly take any time." And, amazingly, Pogue had said yes.

"I agree," Pogue was saying, a broad smile creasing

his face, as he unwrapped the cellophane from a pack of Marlboros, pulled out a cigarette, and lit it. "The FBI under Hoover was a bunch of fucking heroes. Not like the candy-ass losers you see around today, you know what I mean?"

Stone nodded, smiling amiably. Ten or fifteen more minutes of this, Stone told himself. You can stand it. You're sitting here talking to the guy who went to Moscow to gather information on your own father, the guy whose trumped-up evidence sent Alfred Stone to the federal penitentiary, and you're chatting as if you were two lifelong buddies at an Elks reunion.

At last the opportunity came up. Stone remarked in passing that, well, didn't Pogue have something to do with the famous Alfred Stone case?

"*Something* to do with it?" Pogue shot back. "I single-handedly covered it."

"I'm impressed," Stone said, grinning. Bastard. "Didn't you catch the Stone guy in Moscow, meeting with a Russian spy?"

Pogue bowed his head modestly, and lifted it again, exhaling evenly as he did so. "All right." He looked around as if someone else were in the room, the prefatory gestures of a seasoned raconteur. "I've been involved in almost eight hundred cases. On this one, I remember every fucking detail. It's the one that got me promoted from peon right up the ranks. I was on the Soviet espionage squad. We were on to the commie spy network—Klaus Fuchs, the Rosenbergs, Alfred Stone, starting from the time we cracked some secret Soviet codes during the war. I was just out of my apprenticeship, wearing my white shirt and my snap-brim hat and all that. As soon as we got word that Lehman's assistant was going to Moscow, I got the orders to follow him. See if he met with the same lady his boss did, you know." He smiled, smoke escaping from his lips. Although Pogue was hardly giving away any secrets, his demeanor suggested he was breaking a number of security regulations. "You know who Winthrop Lehman is."

"Sure. But who's Fyodor Dunayev?"

Fyodor Dunayev's name had appeared on one of the

documents in Lehman's archives, interrogated by Pogue.

Pogue expelled a lungful of smoke violently, with a hacking cough.

Then he stared, and stared, his cigarette burning. Ten, twenty, thirty seconds. The gray ash of the cigarette grew steadily longer. "Who the fuck are you?"

"I told you. I'm—"

"Who the *fuck* are you?" the FBI man shouted. "You aren't writing any fucking history of the FBI."

"All right," Stone said calmly, sitting perfectly still. He had a gun; was it wise to pull it out now? Pogue might well be a dangerous adversary. "You're right. I'm not working on a history of the FBI, and I apologize for coming to you under a pretext."

"If you're a goddamned federal—"

"I'm not a federal anything. I'm Alfred Stone's son."

There was a grim set to Pogue's jaw. He crushed out his cigarette in the large star-shaped glass ashtray, then lit another.

"Don't try anything," he said menacingly.

"I'm not planning to. Believe me, I realize you were doing your job. I don't blame you."

"Get the fuck out of my house."

"You interrogated a guy named Fyodor Dunayev. I want to know who he was. Is he a Russian? An émigré? A defector?"

"*Get the fuck out of here,*" Pogue bellowed.

"Let him stay."

It was his wife. She stood clutching the banister on the carpeted staircase. She had been listening for quite some time, Stone now realized.

"Fran, get upstairs," Pogue said, pointing at her with the lit cigarette. "This is none of your business."

"No, Warren. You should talk to the man."

"Get the hell upstairs, Fran. This doesn't concern you."

His wife descended the stairs slowly, still clutching the banister as she went. "No, Warren," she repeated. "You've felt guilty about the Alfred Stone affair for years.

You know he shouldn't have been put in prison, and you didn't say anything. For years."

"Fran—" Pogue said, more softly.

"You knew you did the wrong thing in the fifties. You put an innocent man in jail. That's not what you stand for. You've felt terrible about it. Now, make up for it, Warren. The poor man's son is here, Warren. Tell him what he wants to know!"

"Leave us, Fran," Pogue said.

Pogue's wife made her way back up the stairs, just as slowly as she had come down.

And Warren Pogue, with a crestfallen expression, spoke without looking at Stone. "Fyodor Dunayev was a defector from Stalin's secret service who lives in Paris," he said. He spoke in a sort of monotone, as if the very process of remembering, reaching back into a buried vault of recollection, was painful. He exhaled, the smoke seeping out of his mouth and nostrils. "I suppose it doesn't make a goddamned difference what I tell you now."

An hour later, Stone walked through Rogers Park, numb from shock. He reached into his jacket pocket to reassure himself that the miniature cassette tape recorder was still there. The Nagra he had found in a Washington electronics-specialty shop was capable of recording conversations across a large room for up to six hours on a single cassette—and that machine had secretly recorded the testimony of William Armitage and Warren Pogue.

He would have to go to Paris.

There, Pogue had said, lived a Russian émigré who knew more than anyone else about the Beria coup. Ancient history that would reveal the present. He would have names of the people involved, either on the American side or the Russian side—people who were now, years later, about to throw the world into upheaval.

Fyodor Dunayev had served in Stalin's secret police, the forerunner of the KGB. He had been one of Beria's trusted agents, so much so that he had been sent on a mission in 1953 to terrorize an old woman in Chicago. Anna Zinoyeva. To try to obtain a document.

There were three of them, Pogue had said, among the fiercest of Beria's agents. One was Dunayev. Another had died in a purge immediately after Stalin's death. The third one, Osip Vyshinsky, was still believed to live in the Soviet Union. After Beria's execution, Dunayev had defected, knowing his days were numbered.

He *had* to see Dunayev.

A dense fog now blanketed the city; figures at a distance seemed shrouded and mysterious. As he walked past a movie theater and a delicatessen, he felt something. *Saw* something, more accurately—something in his peripheral vision, a figure that the fog made unrecognizable. Almost unrecognizable, but the cues remained, silhouettes, gaits. Suddenly he knew he was being followed again.

They had tracked him to Chicago.

No, dear God. It couldn't be.

No.

Stone stepped up his pace, and the man on the opposite side of the street, still not quite visible, walked faster, too. Stone turned a corner, and now the man crossed the street, following at a distance of just a hundred yards. There was something familiar about the man, something eerily familiar. A bulky man in a black leather jacket, a goatee. Stone had seen him before. He was quite sure of it.

Now Stone turned another corner, sharply, and immediately spotted an alley. He ducked in and flattened himself against the brick. The follower would catch up to him in seconds.

A discarded table leg on the ground caught Stone's attention, its metal glinting. Quickly he retrieved it with his good, right hand. It was the heavy iron leg of an old-fashioned kitchen table.

Now!

He swung the iron rod at the follower, catching him by surprise. The rod cracked into his shoulder, and then Stone immediately lunged at the man and pummeled him to the ground, and at that instant he suddenly knew where he had seen him.

In Cambridge.

This was the man who, along with accomplices, had killed his father. He was the murderer.

The man rose from the ground, a bit sluggish, and as he did so, he slipped a hand swiftly into his jacket pocket.

A tremendous rage suddenly gripped Stone, and with a force that was scarcely human, he slammed his body into his attacker's. But the man had recovered now, and Stone felt a fist crack into his face.

Stone tried at the last second to protect himself, but he was too late. Instantly, swinging his fists back, he could taste, smell, blood, and he moved with an insane fury, cracking the iron rod against the attacker's shoulders, then—though the man tried in vain to knock Stone off balance—against the top of his head, swinging with enormous force.

This is for my father! he thought, crazed, feeling a warmth ooze over his lips and chin.

The man was dead.

The attacker's body lay sprawled on the ground in the alley, hidden by the dumpster from the view of passersby. His face was bloodied.

Stone stared for a long moment in disbelief. He had killed a man.

He reached into the man's jacket and found the gun in the holster, a Llama M-87 with a full magazine, which he removed and shoved in his front pocket. The man's wallet was in his breast pocket. He flipped it open and saw the usual false identification papers, credit cards, and licenses under various names. Digging farther, Stone found a concealed compartment, which he forced open. In it was a small plastic telephone-company card, on which was embossed a calling-card number. A phone number the attacker had no doubt used to place telephone calls to a central office, whose area code was Washington, D.C.

With bloodied hands, Stone pocketed the plastic card, and then he began to run.

40

When Stone had left, Pogue removed a handkerchief from his front pocket and mopped his forehead.

Oh, Jesus, he thought. Oh, Jesus. What's this fellow stumbled onto?

He picked up the phone and called Jim at the airport, asking him to fuel the Piper all the way up, check on the weather conditions, make sure it was clear to land in Indiana. He had to move fast. He had to get to Indianapolis, Indiana, immediately.

He picked up the phone again and called Justice Bidwell's private number. Justice Harold Bidwell, the retired associate justice of the Supreme Court. Still one of the most powerful men in the country and, even five years after his retirement, still intimately connected to everyone in Washington who counted. Justice Hal Bidwell, whose nomination to the Supreme Court had been assured thirty-five years ago when a young, ambitious FBI agent named Warren Pogue had managed to dig up compromising material on all of Bidwell's rivals.

The phone rang, once, twice, three times.

Bidwell would know instantly what it was about. Pogue realized how unorthodox it was for him to call Bidwell directly, but the matter was urgent.

"Your Honor," Pogue said when Bidwell answered. "I must see you right away. I'll be arriving at Indianapolis in"—he checked his watch—"about two hours."

"What are you—"

"The channel," Pogue said tensely. "It's been corrupted! We—all of us—we're in danger!"

"I'll have my man pick you up," Bidwell replied, a slight quaver in his rich baritone.

* * *

The methodical preciseness of flying calmed Pogue. You had to go through a litany—A and then B and then C. The law said you had to consult a printed checklist, even if you knew the procedure by heart. It always relaxed him, and his heart was going so fast, he needed a little relaxation. Needed a clear head.

He looked the Piper Arrow over carefully, as he always did before he went up: looked in the engine cowling, the spark plugs, the fan belt. The oil level, the distributor caps. He checked the wings for any cracks, checked the pressure of the tires, the gas caps under both wings, even shook the tail. Everything was fine.

The battery and the auxiliary battery were both charged. Pogue got into the plane and fastened the seat belt. He tried the mechanical steering equipment, turned the wheels, tested the pedals, pushed on the steering wheel. He got in and revved it up to four thousand rpm, kept his foot on the brake, felt the plane rattle. The pressure gauges were fine. Tired of the shaking, he let the plane idle. One, two, three: there was a pleasing order to it. He switched from the fuel tank to the reserve tank, felt the engine falter for an instant, but that was normal. The wheel flaps were fine, too, and he kept them in neutral for takeoff.

Using the radio navigation equipment, he called the tower to ask for the barometer reading, and set the altimeter. Then he checked his flight plan, the Loran navigation aids, and dialed in his wavelength. And then he requested permission for taxiing to takeoff.

He dialed the pitch of the propeller to the maximum, pushed the throttle lever, revved up again, and with the throttle all the way forward removed his foot from the brake and felt the plane lurch ahead. The plane bounced down the runway and felt pleasantly light, running along at seventy-five miles an hour. He eased back on the nose, and the plane lifted off the ground.

He was on his way.

When the plane had reached three thousand feet, he throttled the engine back to three thousand rpm as he gradually climbed up to five thousand feet.

The secret was out. How, Pogue didn't know. But it was out. He wondered if his visitor knew what sort of danger he was uncovering.

But suddenly Pogue's thoughts were interrupted by a signal from his nose: a peculiar smell. The smell of over-heating, of oil burning. That made no sense; he'd checked everything out carefully. How could that be?

Probably just a jet trail, he thought, and he looked around through the Plexiglas window. No, no jet trail. He saw no smoke at all. He banked the plane up and down to look for a smoke trail. Yes: there was a blackish-blue vapor trail behind him.

The engine temperature had started to climb. Why? He'd kept a steady altitude for the last several minutes. He brought the plane down to a lower altitude, down to four thousand feet, and instantly saw the engine temper-ature begin to shoot up. He examined the oil gauge and noted with horror that the level had dropped from full to half.

Was there an oil leak? He tried to enrich the mixture, throttle the engine back, reduce the speed from 160 miles per hour to 125. Please, Lord, he thought, don't screw the pooch. Don't let me fuck up.

He had to get to Bidwell, had to get to Bidwell's files. He picked up his radio handset and called an operator, giving his QM number, the number of his telephone ac-count. Thank God you could make phone calls from this craft.

"Operator," came the woman's voice reassuringly over the radio.

"Operator, I need you to place a third-party call for me," Pogue began.

Harold Bidwell's estate, outside of Indianapolis, was generally considered the finest in the area, a handsome Georgian house set back a good distance from the main road. At precisely eleven o'clock in the morning, the front-door bell rang.

The uniformed butler opened the door and saw that the person who had rung the doorbell was a postman.

"Harold Bidwell?" the postman asked.

"This is his residence," the butler said. He was a balding, bespectacled, portly man in his fifties whose mustache was flecked with gray.

"Certified letter," said the postman.

"I can sign for that, thank you," the butler said. The mailman, a young man with dark hair, stepped into the foyer and handed the butler the envelope on a clipboard.

The butler took it, leaning over to write. "I don't see," he muttered, "where I'm supposed—"

But he did not finish the sentence.

He gagged on the wire that the postman had slipped around his neck and had swiftly tightened. The butler's tongue lolled out, his eyes bulged in an expression of sheerest terror, his face a beet red, his entire face contorted in a scream that would never come. His glasses clattered on the marble floor.

The postman closed the front door behind him and dropped the corpse on the floor as he entered the house.

Upstairs, Harold Bidwell was sitting in an armchair, where he had been sitting for a very long time in his silk dressing gown, terrified. It had been over half an hour since Warren Pogue had called, and he had been unable to stop trembling.

The channel was corrupted. How could it be?

Now the phone was ringing, and Bidwell reached over to get it, but then he heard a noise from the hallway, a *rustling* of some kind.

"Rico," Bidwell called out.

It was not Rico. It was a man with dark hair wearing navy-blue pants and a light-blue shirt—a U.S. mailman. What was he doing in the house?

"What the—" Bidwell began.

The mailman had a revolver and was pointing it at him. "Don't move," the intruder said. He had a foreign accent that Bidwell couldn't identify. "Please stay right where you are and you won't get hurt."

"What do you want?" Bidwell asked desperately.

"Take whatever you want. Just take it—please don't shoot me."

"I want you to take these pills," the mailman said, coming nearer. The hand that wasn't holding a gun was extended, two tablets in the flat of his palm.

"*No!*"

"Don't worry," the young man said. "These are just Demerol. Just a nice tranquilizer. I don't want to have to shoot you."

Bidwell was shaking his head violently. "Don't. Please. Don't."

The gun was now at his head. "Swallow these," the man said quietly. "I want you to be very calm. Open your mouth."

Bidwell did as he was told. The man placed the two tablets on his tongue. "It's poison," Bidwell managed to say as he swallowed. "Where's Rico?"

"It's not poison," the man said reassuringly. "I just want you to be very quiet. A pleasant narcotic. Now, please open your mouth. I want to make sure you've swallowed them." He inserted several fingers into Bidwell's mouth, moved them around, and was satisfied. "These will take effect quite soon. Now I want you to open your safe. While you're still alert."

"I don't have a safe," Bidwell protested.

"Come with me, please," the intruder said, his gun still at Bidwell's temple. Bidwell got to his feet. The man slowly walked the judge over to the one of the built-in bookcases behind the desk and pulled at a row of books, which came open in one segment, exposing the dial of a safe. "Please don't lie to me. I also know what's inside, and if need be I can open it myself. Please. Save me the bother."

Bidwell spun the dial, his fingers trembling. His first attempt failed; the safe remained locked.

"Don't make another mistake," the young man cautioned. "I'm perfectly aware that if three attempts fail the safe's lock is electronically frozen for an hour. Please, get it right."

Bidwell spun the dial once again, this time opening it.

"Thank you," the man said. He reached into the small safe, past the jewelry, and extracted a large, bulging manila envelope. "The gold and diamonds I leave to your heirs," he said. "This is all I want."

Bidwell now knew. "*You!*" His lips formed the words slowly now. "You're . . . one . . ." A thought occurred to him suddenly, and he narrowed his eyes. "My *heirs*?"

"I think it's time for a bath, Judge Bidwell."

Bidwell could only shake his head slowly, his eyes wide with terror.

The young man escorted the judge out of the room and into the hall, the gun always at the old man's temple. The bathroom was directly ahead.

Bidwell suddenly reached out a hand and pressed the oak door frame of the bedroom as they passed.

The young man smiled and did nothing. "I've disabled the burglar alarm," he said. "That won't work."

They had reached the bathroom, which seemed terribly bright to Bidwell now, its overhead light shining glaringly on the white-and-black tiles. The young man guided Bidwell over to the toilet seat and sat him down on the closed lid. Bidwell's eyes began to droop.

Then the man in the mailman's uniform went over to the marble bathtub with its gold-plated fixtures and turned on both taps to full force. The water gushed out, splashing into the tub, filling it quickly.

Bidwell's eyes were now almost closed. "What do you want with me?" he moaned, his voice almost inaudible under the roar of the water. "I've kept the secret. I've never said a word. You're all madmen. I never said a word."

The bath was now half full, and the young man began removing Bidwell's clothes, starting with his silk dressing gown, unknotting the tie. In a short time, Bidwell was naked.

"Into the tub," the young man said.

Bidwell slowly, slowly climbed into the tub. He whimpered softly. "The water's *cold*!" he rasped.

"Now lie down."

Bidwell lay down in the tub. His eyes were devoid of expression.

The young man rolled up his sleeves, took a large natural sponge from the bathroom vanity, and placed it over the old man's face, depressing until Bidwell's head was fully submerged, and the last bubbles of breath stopped.

"It's so easy to fall asleep in the bath," he said aloud.

As the phone rang, its reassuring tone crackling over the speaker, Pogue frantically increased the pitch on the propeller, downshifting to increase power at fewer engine revolutions. No luck. The plane was overheating.

Now the engine was slowing, and now, with a silence that terrified him, it stopped. Absolute, horrible silence. The plane began to sink. He tried the starter, but it would not fire up.

The phone was ringing. Jesus, Mary, and Joseph. Pick it up, you son of a bitch. *Pick it up.*

He began to talk aloud, to the unhearing handset. "Please, God," he repeated several times. His limbs were frozen in fear. "Please, God."

The phone continued to ring blandly. *Where was Bidwell?*

There was a wooded area below him. He thanked God for that; he could be over a city instead, and that would be that. The plane began to glide. Below him he saw a highway, where he could attempt an emergency landing.

In about sixty seconds, he would be on the ground, and he prayed to God that the landing worked.

He let the handset drop to the floor.

The operator's voice came over the box: "Sir, I'm sorry. Your party doesn't seem to be answering."

His thoughts raced. What had happened? He had been thorough in his preflight check. It was impossible.

There was the highway, perhaps two hundred feet below. It would happen. He was safe.

He did not count on a crosswind.

He gasped, and then let out a long, shrill scream of terror.

The wind, without warning, carried the plane to the right, directly into the path of a bridge over the highway, into the concrete abutment, where it exploded into a ball of fire.

In the instant before he was killed, he suddenly understood *why*, why this had to happen now.

41

Chicago

The fog had gotten so dense that Stone could not see even twenty feet ahead. His body weak, his limbs trembling from fear, he ran without once stopping. He could not blot out the horrifying image of his attacker's body, sprawled in the alley a few blocks from Warren Pogue's house.

He took a circuitous route to Paula's apartment to make sure he was not followed. But visibility was so poor that anyone who might have been trying to follow Stone would have lost him in a second anyway.

It was a Saturday, which meant that Paula only had to work a half-day. She was home when Stone arrived, and she immediately took in his torn clothes.

"Oh, Christ, Charlie. What the hell happened?"

Stone told her.

"Oh, my God. You goddamn killed a man."

"Everything came to the surface, Paula," Stone whispered. "My father—everything—"

"We gotta get you out of here, out of Chicago."

"*We?* No, Paula. I don't want you to get involved any further."

"I'm not involved."

"Bullshit, Paula!" Stone exploded. "I should never have put you in danger in the first place."

"Charlie—"

"I was extremely careful to make sure no one saw me arrive, yesterday or today. No one knows I'm here. No one can connect you to me. As long as we keep it that way, you're safe. Now, I'm going to get a plane out of here—I've got to get to a guy in Paris. He may be the only one who can help me. You know I'm grateful for everything you've done, and—"

"Stone," Paula said, her voice rising with anger. "You're not flying anywhere tonight," Paula said. "The airports are closed. Fogged in."

"Jesus Christ. I can't stay in the city! They're sure to find—"

"My parents live in Toronto. We can drive there and you can fly out. Shit, it's an okay drive. Anyway, from Canada it's probably safer, don't you think?"

Stone spoke slowly, thinking aloud. "It's common knowledge that the U.S. Immigration and Naturalization Service has some sort of computer to check on people leaving and entering. People have been nabbed on the spot, at gunpoint. But most people don't know that Canada's not on our computer. . . ."

"There you go." She gave a slight smile. "Anyway, don't forget, they're not after *me*."

"Paula," Stone said, "as long as you're seen with me, you're in real danger." He shook his head, then bit his lower lip. "I won't take that chance. I don't want anything to happen to you."

"Don't condescend to me, damn it," Paula snapped. "I'm fully capable of making my own decisions, you get it? You fucking show up on my doorstep, now you're stuck with me." She slipped an arm around his waist and continued, sweetly, "Anyway, Stone, I know how to take care of myself. I don't plan to die. I've got too big a caseload."

"Paula—"

"Tomorrow's Sunday. I can take a personal day on Monday, if I have to. If we leave now, we can be in Toronto by late tonight."

Stone grinned at her enthusiasm, in spite of himself. "Now, I need to take a look at a map."

"You got it."

"Hey, you know something, Singer? Underneath that façade of grim professionalism there's a real live human being."

"Thanks," Paula said sarcastically, poking him in one buttock with her fist. "Fuck you very much."

They drove in Paula's white Audi Fox along I-94 and then north on I-96 along the great expanse of Lake Michigan. Bruised and wounded from the fight in the alley, he found driving tiring and painful, so she drove, and soon he was fast asleep.

After a few hours, Paula woke him up.

"Where are we?" he mumbled.

"You asked me to wake you when we got into Michigan. You're a barrel of fun as a traveling companion. I'm almost falling asleep at the wheel here, and I can't put the radio on for fear of waking the wounded. We're just north of a place called—what the hell is it?—Millburg. State of Michigan."

"What time is it?"

"Four-thirty. Afternoon, not morning."

"Thanks."

"Why'd you want to get up now, anyway?"

Stone pulled a map from the map holder and examined it for a moment. "We need to make a detour."

"What for?"

"Let's stay on 96 for a while. Don't make the turnoff here."

"Why?"

"It's complicated."

"I'm a smart woman, Stone. I can deal with complicated situations."

Stone was silent, studying the map. "I'll explain later. I promise. Just keep going north. Fifty or sixty more miles. Okay?"

"This isn't the way to Toronto."

"I know."

"You're wide awake enough to talk?"

"Yeah. Just barely," Stone said.

She paused, then said: "Let's hear it. What's going on?"

"I'll let you know when I figure it out," was all Stone allowed himself to say.

A little over an hour later, they came to Haskell, a small town on the shores of Lake Michigan, just over the line that divides Van Buren County from Allegan County. On the outskirts of town was a small general store appended to an old-fashioned Good Gulf filling station.

"Pull over here, please," Stone said. "I need to get a few things."

Paula looked at him quickly, shrugged, and steered the car into the station.

A few minutes later, he returned to the car with a pack of Merit cigarettes, a box of Ohio Blue Tip strike-anywhere matches, and a roll of toilet paper. "I forget, do you smoke?" he asked, lighting a cigarette.

"No," she said, wrinkling her nose in disgust. "I didn't know *you* did."

"I used to, and I do now."

"Toilet paper?"

Stone smiled cryptically, went around to the trunk, and pulled out a small, cheap suitcase he had picked up in Chicago that morning, which contained a few items of clothing and a backpack. He took off one of his shoes and pulled a concealed wad of bills from its lining. Then he returned to the front seat and pointed to a spot on the map. "This is about five miles north of here," he said. "I'll meet you there in, let's say, two hours."

"What the hell is this, Charlie?"

"Stop off somewhere for dinner. Take your time. Read. I'll meet you in two hours."

"How are you going to get there? On foot?"

"Don't worry about it. I'll be there. Be patient if I'm a little late."

Haskell was a minuscule town on the shore of Lake Michigan whose livelihood seemed to come from fishing and related industries all having to do with the lake. There was hardly any "downtown," except a White Castle burger joint, a bar, a bank, and a couple of buildings that seemed to hold offices of various kinds. Directly down the hill from the main drag, Stone could see a timber jetty.

He stopped a passerby and asked about accommodations in the town. He was directed to a small, comfortable-looking clapboard inn called, unsurprisingly, the Haskell Inn. Stone introduced himself by his real name and shook the proprietor's hand. He registered as Charles Stone, using his credit card. Most of the rooms were vacant, the innkeeper said; he could have his choice.

Drawing on a cigarette, Stone said, "Whatever's comfortable. I'm a smoker, obviously, so if you've got a smoker's room or something . . ."

"Nothing like that," the innkeeper, a small balding man, said. "You've got your pick, just about. Just don't smoke in bed. That's our one hard-and-fast rule."

"Don't worry," Stone assured him. He looked around the inn, taking in the worn Oriental rugs and the cherry paneling. "The place looks great."

"Thanks," the innkeeper said, genuinely pleased. "You in town on business, Mr. Stone?" It was clear from the way he asked it that the possibility of such a thing was remote.

"No. Pleasure. Getaway, really. I've been going through some rough times these past few weeks."

"Here to escape," the balding man said, nodding.

"Basically. When I was a boy, my father and I used to go fishing around here. Is there a place in town that rents fishing boats?"

"There isn't a town on the lake that doesn't. Sure. Capp's."

"Well, if you don't mind, I'll just check in and maybe even go out for a spin tonight. See if I can get a boat."

Capp's Boat Rental was located in a small shack on a small wooden pier. The owner, a rough-hewn, large, red-faced man, seemed to be closing up for the day. Stone, toting the backpack, introduced himself, also by his real name, and told him what he wanted.

"Sure, we got fishing boats," the owner said. "Look, what do you want? We got everything from a sixteen-foot skiff to a one-hundred-eleven-foot boat. Fifty-three-foot Weejack, holds twelve guys. Thirty-six-foot Nauti-Buoy."

"Just something small, for myself. Motorized, of course."

"How about a Hawk?"

"How big is it?"

"Twenty-six-foot. Sport fisherman. Holds six; nice and comfortable for one. Just you?"

"Right. How much?"

"Fifty bucks a day." The price seemed to have been set on the spot. He added hastily, "Of course, we supply everything. Rod and reel, bait, even lures. I mean, you probably got your own equipment, but we supply it anyway."

"Sounds just fine. I'll take it out now. Is that all right?"

"*Tonight?* No way, José. You gotta be out of your mind. It's dark already."

"I know that." Stone explained about what a difficult past few weeks he'd had, how he desperately needed to go out for a spin, even if a brief one. A hundred dollars an hour wasn't so bad, now, was it?

Reluctantly, the owner took Stone down to the pier. The Hawk was old and not in the best repair, but it would do. Stone checked to make sure there was an inflatable life raft and life jacket, then examined the rusty metal tackle-box. "Everything's here," Stone observed.

"I don't like to rent at night," the owner said truculently.

"I thought we discussed that."

"I don't know you from Adam. These boats belong to friends of mine. I got a responsibility to make sure they don't get stolen."

"But they're all insured. They have to be."

"I want a deposit."

Stone pulled another hundred-dollar bill from his wallet. "Okay?"

"Okay."

"There's gas in the tank?"

"Three-quarters full, I think."

Stone unscrewed the gas cap to look inside.

"Hey," the owner said suddenly. "Careful with that butt, guy. Gas is flammable, you know."

"Sorry," Stone said, tossing the cigarette into the water. "Boy, you got enough gas in there to get to Canada and back," he joked. He slipped the rope off the steel post at the end of the jetty, got on board, and turned the ignition switch. It started right up. The boat rumbled beneath his feet. He removed his backpack and put on the orange life jacket.

"I'll be back in an hour or so," Stone yelled to the owner as he lit another cigarette.

He ran the boat at top speed, bouncing over swells on the lake's surface, and made several large circles, enjoying the powerful little boat's speed. In a few minutes, he was out of sight of shore. He steered the wheel to the right, moving parallel with the shoreline until he approached a dark patch of woods looming perhaps five hundred feet off, and then he shut off the engine.

The sudden quiet was almost palpable. He could hear the distant croak of a few bullfrogs. The water here was deep, Stone noted, and not stagnant, yet the shore was quite close. He could not be seen from any point on the shore.

He threw the life raft onto the water and watched it drift about, tethered to the boat by a thin rope. After grabbing the oars and setting them by the stern, near the floating life raft, he unzipped his canvas backpack and took out the roll of toilet paper and the matches. He unscrewed the gas cap and began unrolling the toilet paper into the tank, then jammed the rest of the roll into the tank's opening. It fit snugly. He took a cigarette from the pack and lodged it into the roll so that it stuck out like an accusing finger, tobacco end out.

Then he pulled the cigarette out and, with one of the matches, lit the cigarette, drawing on it until it glowed bright red in the darkness. He wedged it back into the toilet-paper roll with the burning end away from the gas tank.

Leaving the backpack on board, he climbed over the edge while holding the oars, lowered himself into the icy water, and got onto the raft. His wounded arm made him nearly scream out in pain. After a shaky start, during which he almost landed headfirst in the water, he managed to row the raft quickly, and quietly, away from the boat. Because he was favoring his left arm, this proved to be more difficult than he'd anticipated. A few minutes later, he felt the scrape of sand; he had reached shore.

He pulled himself up, shivering from the cold in his soaked jeans and sweatshirt, and pulled the stopper from the raft to let the air out. If his calculations were accurate, he had only about ten or fifteen minutes to walk, during which he would probably catch a bad cold. His left arm throbbed.

Suddenly there was a terrific explosion, a low *boom*, and a great flash of light. He glanced around quickly and saw that the Hawk was now a ball of flame, illuminating the surface of the lake in bright, festive orange.

He accelerated his pace, trudging through the woods with the oars and the deflating rubber raft all clutched beneath his right arm. Even running did not warm him; he could feel himself shivering, the discomfort of the cold battling with the throbbing of his left arm in the pain centers in his brain.

Two hundred feet ahead or so, he saw Paula's white Audi under a highway arc lamp, parked next to a picnic table. The dome light was on, and Paula was reading. He ran as fast as he could for the warmth of the car.

Weakly, Stone opened the door, startling Paula. She stared at him in disbelief.

"I need to put some stuff in the trunk," Stone said.

"What the hell—?"

I no longer exist, he thought. But he said nothing.

42

Langley, Virginia

From the window of the Director's seventh-floor office at CIA headquarters in Langley, all you could see was forest, miles of the rolling Virginia woods. A splendid view, Roger Bayliss thought. It was marred only by a small round plastic device resembling a hockey puck, affixed to many windows in the CIA, which emits an ultra-high-pitched sound to foil laser surveillance of room conversations.

Director Templeton sat at his large contemporary white-marble-topped desk. Roger Bayliss stood, pacing nervously back and forth before the window. In front of Templeton's desk was the Deputy Director of Central Intelligence, Ronald Sanders.

Next to him sat the senior agency psychiatrist, a sixty-two-year-old man named Marvin Kittelson. Kittelson, who knew everything about Charles Stone except why he was being pursued, was small and wiry with a deeply lined face. He had a gruff, coarse manner, which was somewhat muted in the Director's presence. A former navy lieutenant, he had received his psychiatric training at the University of California at Berkeley, and later made a name for himself at the Agency as head of the Technical Services Staff's behavioral-sciences division. His expertise was in personality assessment; during times of crisis, Templeton—and the President—had called upon Kittelson to provide assessments of various world leaders, from Gorbachev to Castro to Qaddafi. Within the Agency, Kittelson was widely considered a genius.

"Our initial strategy failed miserably," Templeton said. "It's obvious now, with hindsight, that we should have moved in on him sooner, rather than using him to lead us to others."

His three listeners nodded agreement, and Templeton continued. "Now the trail's gone cold." He addressed Bayliss directly. "Your strategy to abduct him was clearly misconceived."

Bayliss looked suitably chastened. "The man's far more agile, far more clever than we'd anticipated."

"Stone's a goddamned *wild card*," Templeton barked. "Some kind of fucking lunatic. Instead of turning himself in, giving it up, he's persisting." He shook his head and scowled. "I just don't understand it."

"Ted, don't forget how long Edwin Wilson eluded us," Sanders put in. Edwin P. Wilson was by now a legendary case in CIA annals: a renegade CIA agent, con man, and illegal arms dealer to Muammar Qaddafi, who had managed to escape a CIA manhunt for four years.

"But Stone's a goddamned *amateur!*" the Director said. "I don't care if he's the smartest analyst we have, he's just not trained as a field operative!"

"He's an amateur, yes," said Sanders, "and he's alone and outnumbered. But he's resourceful and as strong as a goddamned ox. And he's desperate."

Unlike Templeton and Sanders, the Agency psychiatrist knew nothing of Bayliss's attempt to entrap Stone, and he was savvy enough not to probe things that weren't his affair. He smiled neutrally.

"Our people are plugged into every domestic and just about every foreign airline's computers," the Director said, exasperated. "If his name appears on any airline anywhere in the Western world, we'll nab him in a second. And we've got his name on TECS." The Treasury Enforcement Communications System is the national computerized system for tracking all persons who pass through U.S. ports of entry and departure.

Templeton turned to Kittelson. "Marvin, let's hear from you. The man has managed to elude not just *our* field personnel but the Russians' as well. It just doesn't make any goddamned sense."

"It makes a good deal of sense, Mr. Director," Kittelson replied, pulling several sheets of notes from a manila file folder. "May I say, you folks, with your computers and your fancy software and your high-tech surveillance devices, you forget one thing."

Templeton's scowl lengthened. "Such as?"

"The human factor. I've gone through everything he's written, every analysis of Soviet politics he's ever done for Parnassus and before, and it's clear he has a chess-player's mind. It's brilliant stuff. Really shrewd."

"We know that," Sanders interjected. "But that hardly explains—"

"You have professionals following this man," Kittelson persisted with a shrug. "But, precisely because he's an amateur, he doesn't observe the laws that professionals do. He doesn't follow predictable behavior patterns. Unlike most amateurs, though, he persists, as you say, with a vehemence that's striking. You might say he's ruthless."

Bayliss nodded.

Kittelson continued: "I've put together a full profile on the man, and everything in his makeup, everything in his personal history, suggests that he's become extremely dangerous."

Ronald Sanders, the former Notre Dame quarterback, expressed his derision by sighing noisily. "Marvin," the Director cut in, but Kittelson kept speaking.

"What I'm suggesting is this. He's something of a loner with a strong drive for perfection, an abhorrence for self-pity. It's logical that his coping mechanism to defend against the traumas he's recently suffered was, in effect, to decompensate."

"Explain," Templeton said.

"I believe Stone's exhibiting a 'pathological grief reaction.' I see this quite often among our Clandestine Services personnel. It's an occupational hazard; it presents in those who tend to enter such lines of work."

"All right," the Director prompted.

"What you're really saying," Sanders remarked with a dismissive shake of his head, "is that this guy's a nasty piece of work."

"He's become highly unpredictable and therefore dangerous," Kittelson said with some irritation. "Rather than succumbing to grief, he calculates and exacts revenge.

He may have trouble distinguishing reality from fantasy, and so he masters his considerable resources to fight. Only by acting out his rage can he cope with his grief. Look, I'll tell you this. If I were to make up a textbook profile of the genesis of a human killing machine, I couldn't do any better."

One of the three telephones on Templeton's desk rang, and Templeton picked it up at once. He listened, grunted, and hung up.

"Well, Marv, you're right. Stone is out of control."

"What are you talking about?" Bayliss demanded.

"They just found one of our people dead in Chicago, in the Rogers Park area."

Bayliss whirled around, suddenly understanding. "The files Armitage tried to get!" So Stone actually *had* gone to visit this retired FBI agent.

"Roger," Templeton ordered, "contact Malarek. I want maximum force on this. Stone's obviously in the vicinity." He got up from his chair, looked at the two men, and then murmured: "I think the trail has finally gotten warm."

43

Toronto

Wrapped in a blanket, Stone fell asleep almost immediately. Paula put the heat up full blast, and gradually Stone's chills melted away. They took 196 north to Grand Rapids; there they got on 96 and took it across Michigan, skirting Lansing, and into Detroit, where Paula stopped briefly at a Ramada Inn for coffee. It was close to midnight when they arrived at the border crossing at Windsor, Ontario.

"Wake up, Charlie," Paula said. "Time to become Patrick Bartlett." She had borrowed some credit cards and a birth certificate from one of her neighbors, identification enough for the lax Canadian border guards. Stone knew it would be foolish to use his own, and he wanted to avoid showing his forged passport until it was absolutely necessary.

The passing was brief and perfunctory. The immigration agent glanced at Paula's and Stone's IDs and asked what the purpose of their visit was.

"We're visiting my mother," Paula explained. That was that, and they were over the border.

"Do you think they'd really have put your name on some kind of computer?" Paula asked when they were safely down 401.

"Yes," Stone said groggily. "By now I'm almost certain they're watching every border crossing."

Within a day, his "death" would undoubtedly be reported to the Haskell town police. The owner of Capp's Boat Rental would probably remember the man named Charles Stone, would remember most of all that he had told the fellow not to smoke around gasoline. The innkeeper would remember Stone, too. The accidental death would be quickly investigated, and just as quickly set down in the police logs. But would it be *believed* by his pursuers? Probably not forever. Stone would know soon enough, but for the time being he considered that he had some breathing space.

"Charlie," Paula said, an hour after they had crossed the border.

"Yes?"

"Listen, I wanted to tell you something. About our— making love and all that." She was visibly embarrassed, and she spoke slowly. "I know we shouldn't have done it, so don't think I've got the wrong idea, okay?"

Stone nodded.

A long moment passed; then Paula continued: "But I just wanted to tell you. I haven't made love with anyone in, like, a year."

Stone nodded again.

"This isn't easy for me to talk about, okay?"

"Take your time," Stone said gently.

There was another lull, and then: "You know how I

went after that rapist, that case I told you about? I mean, the guy was guilty as hell, and I guess anyone would be mad, especially a woman. But—Jesus, Charlie, I was attacked last year."

"What do you mean, attacked?"

"I mean, nothing happened. Thank God. But it was close. I was coming home from work really late one night, in that shitty neighborhood." She fell silent, and then continued. "The guy was scared off by a passerby, thank God."

"Paula—"

"You know, I took a martial-arts class after that, so I could defend myself, but that was the easy part. The hard part was, you know, dealing with sex."

"I understand—"

"No, listen. I just wanted to say . . ." She didn't finish the thought, but Stone understood, touched by this rare display of Paula's tenderness.

They arrived in Toronto when the sun was just beginning to rise, at around five o'clock Sunday morning. They had made very good time; Paula had stopped for coffee only twice.

Paula Singer's mother lived in a spacious old brick house in the Rosedale area of Toronto. She was asleep when they arrived, but she was expecting them, and had left a key for them under a mat.

"My bedroom is clear on the other side of the house from my mother's room," Paula whispered as they walked through the garage into the house. "We'll have privacy."

"To sleep," Stone said.

They fell asleep quickly in Paula's large and comfortable bed, and in the late morning they woke up and made love. Then each of them showered and came down to the kitchen, where Paula kissed her mother, Stone said hello, and they ravenously consumed the large breakfast that Eleanor Singer had prepared for them.

Stone took Paula's car into the center of the city to buy a new set of clothes in Eaton Centre. He returned a few hours later utterly transformed.

Paula gave a little shriek when she saw him. "What have you done to yourself? Your curls!"

"You don't like it?" Stone had gone to a barbershop and had his hair shorn so that he now had a buzz-cut. A pair of heavy black-framed eyeglasses made him look like someone else entirely. To complete the outfit, he wore a worker's uniform of dark-blue shirt and pants.

"You look like a janitor. Like a deinstitutionalized janitor, I mean."

"Anything but a guy on the lam. Although, I have to say, people do get the wrong impression—on the way over here, I passed a park where a bunch of skinhead punks were hanging out. One of them shouted out to me, 'Hey, skinheads live forever, man!' "

"You have another passport, I assume."

"Right."

"What about the picture? Does it match up?"

"That's not how passport agents work. They look for points of similarity, just as anyone would. They'll look at my face, then at the passport, and they'll realize that it's the same person, who happens to have gotten a haircut and a pair of glasses. People change glasses and haircuts all the time. They'll be looking to confirm it's the same person, and the facial resemblance is there. But if they're looking for Charlie Stone, they won't find me by name, and the description isn't going to help them, since I look like hundreds of thousands of other guys my age."

By late afternoon, Stone had made flight reservations to London on British Airways. He had rejected the notion of taking a more circuitous route to Paris—to Atlanta, say, and then to London—because he thought it best to avoid any American ports of entry or exit, where a description of him might be logged into the computers. From London, he could get to Paris by ferry, thereby leaving no paper trail.

Before departing for the airport, he took Paula aside and handed her the Llama semiautomatic pistol that he had taken off the man he had killed in Chicago. Paula gasped as if she had never seen a gun before, and shook her head violently. "No way, man. No way am I going to touch that thing. Jesus, I don't even know how to use one of them."

"Take it, Paula. It'll make me feel safer knowing you have it." She stared at him, and then, reluctantly, she nodded.

When they arrived at the airport, Stone stopped at a newsstand to buy some newspapers and magazines for the flight, and he was at once struck by a front-page story in a Toronto newspaper. It was an AP story filed from Moscow about yet another terrorist bombing in central Moscow, this one inside the Bolshoi Theater. Stone bought the paper and read it numbly, alarmed.

Was this the coup that the HEDGEHOG report had warned about? Would it be a series of bombings, masquerading as terrorism, and then—and then a violent assault?

He checked his watch, found a phone booth, and placed an operator-assisted long-distance call to Moscow.

To Charlotte.

There was the distant crackling and static roar, a sequence of mechanical noises, tones, and then a high-pitched, regular beep. The phone was ringing at Charlotte's apartment. It was after one o'clock in the morning, too late to call, but there might not be a chance later. He had to know what she had found, if indeed she'd looked. She'd understand.

After ten rings, there was a thick, slurred "hello": Charlotte's voice.

Stone felt his chest constrict. "It's me." His voice reverberated electronically, a metallic echo.

Mustn't say a name. Correspondents' phones are tapped in Moscow, Stone knew. No doubt of that.

A long pause. Charlotte's voice, husky from sleep, sexy, thrilling. "Oh, God. Where are you?"

"I'm—I'm safe. I need your help."

A long, long pause. An eternity.

Would she agree to do one more thing for him, knowing as she surely did what a desperate situation he was in? If anyone could do it, it was Charlotte—the best-connected reporter in Moscow. But how much could he say on the phone? How to communicate it safely? *Elliptically:* a conversation that to whoever else was listening would sound natural if puzzling, but to Charlotte would mean something.

"Listen," she began, but he interrupted. There was no time. He took a deep breath and plunged ahead, spewing a disjointed, oddly emphasized bluster of words. "Got a question for you. What would you recommend an *American* spend most time visiting: the Kremlin Armory, the Bolshoi Theater, or the beautiful Prospekt Mira metro station? Or all three? I know they're all architecturally fascinating; what do they have in common? They're all certainly *involving* enough, aren't they?"

Charlotte, in bed, stared at the dark bedroom wall, gripping the phone tightly. What was he trying to say? She wondered where he was; what he was doing. Didn't he know how dangerous it was for him to be talking to her on the phone this way? Didn't he realize that her phone was tapped, that he was endangering both of them? She'd have to terminate the call at once.

She felt the hot tears streaming down her cheeks, and, her heart racing, she replaced the phone in its cradle.

He listened for her reply, not knowing how she would respond, and then he felt a jolt when he realized she had hung up. Stone stood in the booth, looking around at the airport terminal, dazed. By turns hurt, angry, unbelieving.

He had tried, to no avail.

Damn her. Damn Charlotte.

Paula accompanied Charlie to the British Airways desk, where he took out his wallet and paid cash for the ticket. The only seats remaining were in first class; the money was not really an issue, but Stone would have much preferred the anonymity of economy class.

"Your passport, please," the ticketing agent, a redheaded girl in her mid-twenties, said.

Stone gave her the Robert Gill passport, which she inspected cursorily; then she looked up at him.

"Could you wait here a minute, please?" she asked.

Stone nodded and smiled pleasantly. He caught

Paula's frantic glance, and gave a small shrug, as if to say, I don't know what the hell's going on, either.

The ticketing agent was now joined by an older man in a British Airways blazer, who approached and asked matter-of-factly, "Mr. Gill, do you have any other identification on you?"

Stone's heart began to race. "Certainly," he said, making rapid, silent calculations. "Is there a problem?"

"Not at all, sir."

Stone handed him Robert Gill's driver's license.

The man stared at it for a moment, and then looked up. "Fine, sir. I'm sorry, but we're required to confirm the ID of anyone who pays cash. Airline policy."

"No problem," Stone said with false joviality. "I'd do the same thing in your place."

Charlie and Paula walked toward the departure gate. Stone saw the metal detectors, standard equipment in virtually every airport in the world by now, and was thankful he had decided to leave the gun behind. He embraced Paula, and he noticed there were tears in her eyes. "Hey, listen," he said. "I can't tell you how much I appreciate what you've done for me. I just want to make sure you're never, ever connected with me in any way. I want to make sure you're okay."

"How am I going to know *you're* okay?" she asked as she saw him to the gate.

"Don't try to get in touch with me, whatever you do. Don't talk to anyone about me; don't let anyone know you saw me. Promise me that."

"Okay. I promise. But will you get word to me somehow?"

"All right. I'll use an alias; you'll know it's me."

"What alias?"

"Haskell."

"Haskell?"

"After Haskell, Michigan. The place where a fellow named Charlie Stone had a boating accident and met his untimely demise."

44

Haskell, Michigan

The Tastee Do-Nut shop on Elm Street in Haskell, Michigan, is legendary for its glazed buttermilk doughnuts. Its coffee is less than legendary, but no one ever complained about it to the Tastee's owner, Millie Okun.

At a little after ten in the morning, precisely half of a buttermilk doughnut sat uneaten on a plate in front of Randall Jergensen, Haskell's chief of police and one of its two police officers. Chief Jergensen had already had three of them; besides, he was deeply involved in the Haskell *Mercury*'s lively report of the all-county basketball championship game last night.

Chief Jergensen was a large-framed, large-bellied man with a round face and a chin that barely demarcated his face from the ample folds of his neck. He was forty-seven, and he had been divorced for almost three years from his wife, Wendy. He thought about her every day and then immediately praised the Lord that he lived alone.

"Millie," he said from behind the *Mercury*, not looking up. "How 'bout a refill?"

"Coming right up, Randy," Millie Okun said, sweeping the glass coffeepot from the Bunn-O-Matic and lofting it over to Chief Jergensen's mug.

At that moment, Randy Jergensen's squawk box went off.

"Shit," he said, and eyed the fresh coffee longingly.

By the time he arrived at the station house, most of the story was already in place. His deputy, Will Kuntz, had gotten a call from Freddie Capp, reporting that one of his boats had blown up on the lake. With some fool in it. Freddie's report was confirmed by the Coast Guard. Sounded an awful lot like a damn-fool accident; Freddie remembered that the guy, who'd said he just wanted the boat for an hour, was a smoker. Probably he just went and blew himself up.

Goddamned tourist, up from Chicago. With a great sigh of annoyance, Chief Jergensen got in the cruiser and paid a call on Freddie Capp. Freddie had the guy's name, from the driver's-license data he'd copied down. Then Jergensen took a spin down the shore until he found the site of the accident, a great big mess of charred wood and metal floating on the surface of the water and poking up out of it. Fire just goddamn burned itself out before the fire trucks got there. The man, whose name was Charles Stone, had evidently ignited the gas tank. Deserved it, Jergensen thought, spitting into the water.

Shortly after noon, Jergensen had talked to Ruth and Henry Cowell at the Haskell Inn and gotten this Charles Stone's credit-card imprint. He had enough now to notify the next of kin. This was the part of his job he disliked most.

He picked up the phone to call New York, and then put it down, dreading the task.

Oh, yes. He hadn't completed standard operating procedure yet, he remembered with some relief, thankful that he could put off the call a little longer.

"Willy," he called out to his deputy. "Run this one up on the NCIC computer, will you?" He was referring to the National Crime Information Center's computerized listing of all persons with arrest warrants outstanding. Nothing ever came of it, at least this far from the crime centers, but you had to do it anyway.

Jergensen settled back to enjoy a grape soda and a crossword puzzle. He thought he had the three-letter word for "Oriental sash" figured out, when his deputy called something out.

"Huh?"

"Bingo, Randy. Jesus, the FBI's got a fugitive-flight warrant out on him. Whoa—*treason* laws! The guy was wanted by just about every federal agency."

"Well, we just found him, Will. In about twenty thousand pieces at the bottom of the lake. Obviously he was trying to escape to Canada. Probably afraid he'd get nabbed at the border. Instead, he blew himself right up to the sky." He snorted. "Send *that* over the wire."

Jergensen returned to the puzzle and remembered that the Oriental sash was "obi," and he wrote it down with a dull stub of a pencil.

PART THREE

THE EMPIRE
OF
THE DEAD

It is symbolic that the massed multitudes see their leaders atop the Lenin Mausoleum on November 7 and May 1 and special occasions. They stand on him. Inside the pyramidal tomb made of red-black, gleaming granite brought from Vinnitsa in the Ukraine lies the lifelike dead man.

—Louis Fischer, *The Life of Lenin* (1964)

45

The black Chaika zoomed down October 25th Street at top speed, black Volga escorts in front and behind, through Spassky Gate, and into the Kremlin.

Inside was the first deputy chief of the GRU and the leading munitions expert of the GRU's elite Spetsnaz troops. As they passed through Red Square, they could see the long line of people waiting to get into Lenin's tomb in the distance. At the Spassky Gate checkpoint the car paused only momentarily, then proceeded through an iron gate into the section of the Kremlin that is closed to tourists.

The Chaika pulled up alongside the Council of Ministers building, and the bodyguard got out of the front seat to hold the door open for the two men.

The aristocratic, white-haired colonel general and his young Spetsnaz explosives specialist were entering the seat of Soviet government. They passed several sets of blue-uniformed Kremlin Guards, who asked for their documents cursorily. The older man moved quickly, and the younger one just barely managed to keep up as they moved toward a green-painted elevator down a corridor that appeared to be used only for official business.

The elevator had a plain metal floor, and although it might have been constructed decades ago, the electronics were apparently up-to-date, and it descended smoothly. The name on the elevator was "Otis," an American elevator company.

It opened on another corridor, tiled in a mustard color. The GRU officer led the young man past several more sets of guards. The corridor gradually narrowed, and it was clear that they were below ground level. The only light came from buzzing fluorescent bulbs in the ceiling not far above their heads.

At last, when they had been walking for almost five minutes, during which neither man had spoken, they arrived at another entrance. In front of it stood a pair of uniformed guards, who demanded their documents once again and then saluted.

Now down a set of steps made of polished black stone, and into the chamber. It was dark and cool and smelled vaguely of chlorine, like a swimming pool. The older man at once located the light switch and turned the lights on.

The room was a large smooth rectangle, apparently used to store armaments. There were crates of rifles and ammunition and assorted equipment piled along the walls.

"Well, you've studied the blueprints," the older man said quietly. "You insisted upon seeing the structure at firsthand. Here it is." He did not have to add that the trip entailed some risk, but it would, most likely, seem simply a routine inspection by the GRU's chief of security.

The explosives expert looked around and did a quick estimation. "Ten meters," he said, "by ten meters, by five meters high," he announced.

"Correct."

"That's five hundred cubic meters." His confident voice echoed against the concrete walls. "From ground level, the structure is 12.25 meters high by 24.5 meters long. Add another five meters in height for this chamber and ten for the room above, which is also below ground level. That makes, ah, 27.25 meters high. Now, tell me, sir: what is this room customarily used for?"

"It's an arsenal."

"The building is made of granite, though, isn't it? Heavy stuff."

"Much of it is granite, yes. Some labradorite, some marble. This room, and most of the inside walls, are made of reinforced concrete."

The younger man spoke very quietly now, but even his whisper seemed loud as it reverberated in the chamber. "I imagine that . . . that our superior has considered the possibility of a nuclear device. A small one."

"He has ruled it out."

"Why?"

His superior smiled. "Any number of reasons. Nuclear materials are guarded so closely that to remove a bomb, even upon orders from the very top, would attract immediate and widespread attention. Secrecy is of paramount importance. Furthermore, we don't need the Red Army immediately jumping to the conclusion that the Americans did it, which might set off a global thermonuclear exchange."

The younger man nodded thoughtfully.

"Of course, there is another, more convincing reason why a nuclear device cannot be used. Keep in mind the level of our Soviet defense preparedness."

"I don't understand."

"Too much time in the laboratory, and not enough time keeping your ears open. The Defense Ministry, many years ago, placed in certain checkpoints in Red Square, in buildings and beneath the ground and even in vehicles that perpetually patrol Moscow, neutron detectors and gamma detectors. Expressly, you can imagine, in order to detect the presence of a nuclear device. To protect the Kremlin from a nuclear bomb being smuggled in. The Americans have a similar system to protect Washington. Nuclear weapons are out of the question. Certainly a nuclear device would be a mistake on the simple grounds that it's difficult to believe a terrorist in this country could gain access to one."

"Will all these guards be here on Revolution Day?"

"Of course. And more."

"Then I would rule out plastic explosives as well. They are a bad idea."

"Why?"

"Plastic explosives are quite powerful, but it would take a huge quantity to do the job. Hundreds of kilos. Crates of it. If there weren't a problem of guards, I would say plastic explosives would do quite well."

"Then what's the answer?"

The expert smiled. "An FAE bomb—a fuel-air-explosive."

"Explain."

"The FAE bomb is one of the most sophisticated explosives weapons in any arsenal. It was developed by the Americans only recently, at the end of the Vietnam War. It's enormously powerful; an FAE bomb is capable of leveling great buildings, even whole city blocks. And besides, for size it's incomparable. The whole apparatus can fit in a small bag. All you need is a tank of fuel, propane, some grenades, some blasting caps, a little bit of plastique, and a timing device. A couple of other things. I'd suggest a simple digital timer device."

"Why? It's quite easy to detonate bombs using radio transmitters, isn't it?"

"That's right. But these conditions are different. A remote signal for detonation, especially through walls as thick as these, must go over a radio UHF band. That means that, if anyone happens to be monitoring the radio bands—which cannot be ruled out, given the safety precautions our own people will be taking that day—there is a chance that the signal could be jammed. No, we don't even need to use a remote."

"All right, then. But how will it work? What will be timed, exactly?"

"The timer will be set to release a cloud of gas in the chamber here and, at the time you designate, the small plastic bombs will go off, detonating the highly combustible cloud of fuel mixed with oxygen."

"Will it be powerful enough?"

"*Powerful?* Sir, nobody within a *hundred meters* will survive."

"Listen very carefully: this must not fail. When you strike at a king, you must kill him."

46

Paris

Stone awoke very early in the morning, dazed from jet lag and the dislocation of waking up in a strange city. His head throbbed dully, and for a moment he did not remember where he was.

Sitting up, he allowed his eyes to focus and surveyed the hotel room, enjoying the quiet elegance, the velvet wallpaper of gray stripe, the bathroom whose walls and floor were of smooth green Venetian marble, and the view of the beautiful cathedral of Saint-Germain-des-Prés. For a dead man, he thought grimly, I've certainly got a decent hotel room.

He had arrived in Paris late in the afternoon the previous day. As soon as his plane had landed at Heathrow, he had taken a taxi into London, directly to the French Embassy, where he obtained a "rush" visa to travel to Paris immediately, explaining that there had been a sudden change in his business plans. Tense and exhausted, he had considered catching the next flight to Paris, but stuck with his original plan—the Sealink ferry from Dover to Calais, where he could disappear into the crowds of tourists.

He knew Paris with a passing familiarity, having visited twice, years ago. On those occasions, Paris had been an adversary of sorts, a thing to be conquered, explored, learned. Now it was a welcome refuge, a warren of potential sanctuaries. His first instinct had been to choose a tiny, anonymous hotel. Most such places are run by proprietors eager to make an extra franc, and therefore probably vulnerable to bribery. Stone needed a hotel whose management he could trust not to cooperate unquestioningly with the authorities, if and when it came to that. He needed a place with a small, discreet staff resistant to pay-offs, which would fiercely protect its records.

The hotel he had selected was a small, rather expensive place called L'Hôtel, on the narrow rue des Beaux-Arts. Its rooms were small, as are most Paris hotel rooms, but furnished in exquisite taste. Oscar Wilde had lived here (well, died actually), which was hardly a recommendation, as had Maurice Chevalier, which was. Number 46 was sumptuous, and flooded with sunlight in the afternoons.

He had registered under the name Jones and was relieved to find that the concierge did not ask for his passport. There was a time, years back, when hotels in Paris used to report the names and passport numbers of their guests to the police at the end of each day, but that was, fortunately, a thing of the past. Once or twice a year, the police may ask to inspect a hotel's guest-registration cards, but rarely if ever do hotels submit these cards to the police otherwise. Despite all the talk in France about precautions being taken to combat terrorism, the simple fact is that one can stay under an alias indefinitely and never be caught. If the "accident" on Lake Michigan was at all successful, he would be safe here for a few days. He hoped.

He had quickly fallen into a sleep that was so deep it felt almost drugged. Now he ordered a breakfast in the room, café au lait and a croissant, and began to collect his thoughts. Little time remained, and there were two people he had to find as soon as possible.

In the years after the Russian Revolution, Paris was deluged by refugees from the Soviet Union. They formed their own subculture in the city, their own restaurants and nightclubs and social organizations, much as a later generation of émigrés would in New York City. But as the émigrés died off, their neighborhoods vanished, leaving only the merest traces of Russian heritage.

One such trace is located in the Eighth Arrondissement, nestled among the high-rent jewelers and chocolate shops, just off the Champs-Elysées. There, on rue Daru, is the Cathédrale Saint-Alexandre Nevsky, a Byzantine church crowded with ancient icons, a gathering place for the few remaining "white Russians." Stone arrived there in the late morning and found the church empty, the only person in the building a young woman who sat at a small desk that held a display of postcards.

He had only a name, Fyodor Dunayev, but there was little doubt the man lived under an alias, well concealed and well protected. Anyone who had served in Stalin's secret service and then defected would live each day in mortal fear. But Stone realized there was a way to get to the retired agent.

He now knew two potentially useful facts about Dunayev. One—from Warren Pogue—was that Dunayev had been accompanied by a man named Vyshinsky. The other was a morsel of information that Anna Zinoyeva had remembered from the newspaper account of Dunayev's defection, a detail memorable because it was so curious. Dunayev had found shelter in Paris, decades ago, under the auspices of an émigré relief organization whose name Stone recognized from something he had once read. The organization was funded and supported by the Russian Orthodox Church in Paris. Stone had found it strange that an atheistic old Chekist would accept aid from a religious organization, but such were the paradoxes of the Russian people. Scratch a Communist and you'll find a fervent Russian Orthodox believer.

The young woman looked up. *"Oui?"*

"Parlez-vous anglais?"

"Yes." She smiled pleasantly.

Stone chatted for a few minutes about the church. He was an American tourist, he told the woman, of Russian background. The woman's face lit up: she, too, was of Russian heritage. She spoke English with a Russian accent—obviously her parents had been émigrés—and she got up from the desk to show Stone proudly around the church. They talked about Russia for a while, and about the woman's relatives, and finally Stone casually mentioned that, since he was in Paris, he thought he might look up an old man, a Russian, a friend of a friend. Could she help?

"What's his name?"

Stone hesitated momentarily, and then decided it was highly unlikely the name would mean anything to the woman. "Fyodor Dunayev."

The woman shook her head: she had never heard of him.

"Let me ask the Father," she said. "He knows most of the Russian émigrés. Or if he doesn't, he may know people who do."

Stone followed her out of the church and into the small building next door that served as a combination office and rectory. He waited tensely in the small, bare office. Would Dunayev still be alive? Living under his own name? Maybe he'd have disappeared into anonymity forever.

She returned a few minutes later. Now she looked at him differently, alarm registering in her face.

"If you will wait here," she said, "one of the people in the office may be able to help you."

Stone sensed danger. "Can this person get me his phone number?"

"No," the woman said anxiously. "But if you will wait—"

"No," Stone said. "Listen carefully. Your friend is right to be careful. You have no idea who I am. But let me assure you that Dunayev would be glad to hear from an old friend. I'll give you something to give to Dunayev—will you do that for me?"

"I suppose . . ." she said falteringly.

"All right." It was just as well; in writing he could pose convincingly as a Russian, whereas on the phone his accent would give him away at once. He asked the woman for a piece of paper and an envelope. Seated at a small, unused desk, he wrote out a brief note in Russian. "Urgent that I see you at once," he wrote. "I am sent by your friend Vyshinsky." It was a gamble, in some ways an enormous gamble, that Osip Vyshinsky was still alive. Perhaps out of curiosity alone—and reassured by seeing the name of an old colleague, which amounted to a species of recommendation—Dunayev would want to see the visitor.

He sealed the envelope and handed it to the woman. "Please tell your friend to hurry," he said.

Stone passed the next two hours at a Russian restaurant directly across the street. He had a small, late lunch of *pirozhki* and lingered over coffee, watching the church's entrance tensely. A few people came and went—tourists, it seemed. No one stayed long.

When he returned to the cathedral—certain from his observation that there wasn't a trap—the young woman still seemed wary. "We have reached him. He says he will be delighted to see you," she said. "Here is what he wants you to do."

Chicago

Paula Singer disliked eating lunch at her disheveled metal government-issue desk, but she also disliked going out and braving the jostling lunchtime crowds at the coffee shops and Greek take-out places that surrounded the court building. Either choice, as far as she was concerned, was grim, but no one ever said being an assistant state's attorney was going to be glamorous. So she sat at her desk, eating a ham-and-Swiss sandwich while browsing through the newspaper.

She'd been thinking nonstop about Charlie Stone since the moment he'd shocked her by showing up on her front porch. She wondered where he was, whether he was still in Paris, whether he had found the person he wanted to reach.

And whether there was anything she could do.

She turned to the sports pages of the *Chicago Tribune*, and then her eye was caught by a small obituary. Something snagged at her memory, and for an instant she paused before flipping the page to the box scores. Then she turned back, recognizing the name.

Warren Pogue. The FBI agent Charlie had talked to in Chicago, the man whose address and phone number Charlie had asked her to get.

Paula was suddenly oblivious of the office noise around her. She groaned softly as she read: "The victim, whom Indiana police identify as Chicago native Warren

Pogue, a retired agent of the Federal Bureau of Investigation, was apparently killed when his small plane lost velocity. . . ."

The date.

Warren Pogue had died the same day Charlie had talked with him.

Charlie had been right. People *were* being murdered.

Charlie would be next. She was sure of it. He was next, unless she did something to help.

For a few moments, she sat there, staring straight ahead, frantic, not knowing what to do. And then she remembered the name of the influential man Charlie said he had met with in Washington, William Armitage, and she knew she had to place a call. Charlie had insisted she stay out of it, but he was only trying to protect her.

She could protect *herself*, damn it.

Paula had to make a long-distance call. She knew that phone calls could be traced if you stayed on too long. But there were ways to make it impossible to trace a call, right? She got up and walked over to her boss's office, and found that he was out. Probably at lunch. Great; his phones were available.

One of his telephones was a secure terminal desk set with high voice/data security, a Motorola STU-III SecTel. He almost never used it; in fact, he had gotten weeks of grief for investing government money in the thing. Probably using an untappable line would make no difference, but every little precaution helped.

Using the Motorola, she called a friend in New York who was a partner at what she thought of as a big scary law firm: one of those people who made ten times what she made.

"Kevin," she said when her friend answered, "I need you to do me a favor."

Kevin was obliging, and, best of all, he asked no questions. By means of a conference call, he patched her through to Washington, to the office of Deputy Secretary of State William Armitage. If by *any* chance the call was traced, they would get no further than a number at an enormous law firm in New York. Good luck.

She drummed her fingers nervously on the metal surface of the desk, wondering whether she'd be able to speak with Armitage directly, wondering whether he'd believe what she had to say about the death of an old FBI man in Chicago.

Finally, a female voice came on the line and announced, "Office of the Deputy Secretary of State."

Paula gave her brief prepared spiel, ready to fence for a time with the secretary.

And then she went cold with terror.

"You haven't heard?" the secretary asked solicitously. "I'm sorry, but Mr. Armitage passed away several days ago."

She hung up the phone and sat at the desk, massaging her temples, sick with fear. Her eyes ached. She opened her purse and pulled out something that Charlie had given her.

It was a blood-smudged plastic card, the size and shape of a credit card. On it was embossed a telephone number, which you could use to charge a call if you were out on the road.

Charlie had taken it from the guy he'd killed, the guy who had attacked him in Chicago. It must be a simple matter, he'd said, to track this back to the source, to find a name to which to connect the man who was following him. Paula had grabbed it out of his hands and insisted she'd try.

Now, her mouth dry from apprehension, she picked up the phone and started to dial.

47

Moscow

The headquarters of the KGB's First Chief Directorate is located in Yasenevo, on the outskirts of Moscow, in a new, elegantly curved building whose resemblance to the CIA's headquarters is said to be no coincidence. In this building are the offices and laboratories of the Special Investigations Department, within which is the Soviet Union's finest forensics laboratory. Whenever a bomb goes off in Russia, the Middle East, or anywhere else of concern to the Soviet government, samples are sent here for analysis.

One of the senior forensic chemists was Sergei F. Abramov, a plump, balding man of forty-two with a perfectly round face, smooth skin, and dimpled pudgy hands. He was married to a librarian at a technical institute, and had two daughters.

Abramov was grumpy this morning. His curiosity had been aroused by a peculiar message he'd gotten from an American television reporter he had met with once in a while, always with the utmost secrecy. She knew him only as Sergei. Charlotte Harper seemed smart and on the level, and she'd wanted to know whether he could confirm a rumor she'd heard that the wave of bombings that had recently struck Moscow really had something to do with the United States.

It wasn't possible.

And why hadn't he been consulted on the examination of the bomb samples?

He walked into the lab, short-tempered and out of sorts, and hung his coat up on the hook on the wall.

The department secretary, Dusya, laughed raucously when he came in. He usually found her vaguely annoying, a dyed blonde whose dark roots always showed, with a double chin and too much blue eye makeup. Also, she always tried to flirt with him, which was repulsive.

"So now you're trying to grow a mustache!" she called out.

"All right, Dusya," Abramov said. "Do me a favor and requisition for me some samples. And the ones before that. You know."

"Fine," Dusya said, pouting. "So what's with the mustache? Are you going to tell me or not?"

* * *

The Kremlin Armory bomb was the easiest of all to check, since not much of it had combusted. He saw at once that it was Composition C-4, the whitish American-made stuff. He didn't even have to do anything more than a gross morphological exam, but just to make sure, he dissolved a portion of it and spun it down in a centrifuge. The residue results were clear: there was motor oil in it. It was definitely C-4.

He massaged his neck and thought momentarily about his kids, who had turned into giant pains in the ass. Well, the younger one, Maria, was doing well. It was the older one, Zinaida, who was giving him such trouble. She was a teenager already, beginning to look like a woman, and she was spending too much time with some thug four years older than she was, a long-haired guy of eighteen. He was sure they were sleeping together, but what could you do about that anymore? Zinaida skulked around the apartment, stayed out late, quarreled with anyone who crossed her path. Abramov shook his head and turned back to the matter at hand.

So it was C-4. Abramov knew C-4 like the back of his hand. C-4 contained the explosive hexahydro-1,3,5-trinitro-S-triazine, or RDX, the most powerful explosive in the world. And a lot of other gunk, like plasticizers and rubber binders. Every so often—more and more often, it seemed—he'd get a chunk of C-4 to analyze, using infrared spectrophotometry, on the Analect FX-6250 Fourier transform. Sometimes gas chromatography/mass spectrometry. You could tell a lot—whether it was British PE-4, which has a different binder from American C-4, or Czech NP-10, the black explosive material with a PETN base, or whether it was good old home-grown Soviet-made stuff.

He remembered running the battery of tests on a bunch of samples taken from a wave of bombings that had struck an anti-Qaddafi Libyan community in Manchester, England. He discovered that the plastic explosive used in the bombs—surely set by Qaddafi's people—was *American-made*! Which meant that some American elements were supporting Qaddafi, or at least selling it to him. This was a startling finding, and it led to an intensive KGB investigation.

The other samples were a little trickier.

He made a fresh pot of tea, poured himself a cup, and stirred in two spoons of sugar. Usually the tests he ran were dull as hell, revealing nothing. But these samples—he was intrigued.

The reporter was right, but there had to be more to it. This was fun—a little like a detective novel. Time like this, he loved his job. Buoyed by his discovery, he made a mental note to take Zinaida aside and tell her about the facts of life, but gently—God knows he didn't want to provoke the little firebrand.

He took a sip of tea, added another spoon of sugar, and sat down to look under the microscope. The Prospekt Mira bomb was plastique as well. No surprise.

So he did a purge-and-trap, a vapor absorption, gently heating the sample in a vacuum in a closed container. This drew the organic material into a tube of activated charcoal, a trap connected to a vacuum line. After the vapor was trapped, Abramov removed the explosive compounds from the charcoal with dichloromethane.

He put it under the microscope again, and then dissolved the solid in an organic solvent and cleaned it up to run some more tests.

There wasn't a lot of organic high explosive left. A tiny amount, really, probably measurable only in picograms. That meant he'd have to use the TEA, or thermal energy analyzer, an extremely sensitive gas-phase chemiluminescence device. It used a heated chamber at low pressure and a cryogenic trap to produce electronically excited nitrogen dioxide, which gives off precisely recorded wavelengths of light when it undergoes radioactive decay.

He worked slowly and painstakingly, and by the early afternoon he recognized the sample's molecular structure.

Now something was *really* peculiar.

He checked his figures twice, comparing them with the library of spectra. When he checked a third time, he knew what was so eerily familiar.

He'd tested this particular explosive hundreds of times before.

This was no mere American plastique.

The formulation was unmistakable. Every sample of plastic explosive that had been used in the recent Moscow bombs had been manufactured at a company in Kingsport, Tennessee, called the Holston Army Ammunition Plant. This was the only place anywhere in the United States that manufactured C-4.

But there was something more.

It matched exactly the unique formulation of a special batch of C-4 that was manufactured exclusively for the Central Intelligence Agency.

He was one hundred percent certain.

He took another sip of his third cup of tea and began to dictate a report.

48

Paris

Stone waited for Dunayev at a café called A la Bonne Franquette, on rue de la Roquette, near the Père-Lachaise Cemetery. Five, then ten minutes went by, and no sign of the émigré.

Stone checked his watch, irritated, and ordered a *pastis*. It tasted a little like Nyquil.

As he sat, he glanced around the bar for anyone who might resemble Dunayev. No one. A woman at the bar, clearly a prostitute, caught his glance and smiled. She was in her early sixties, with badly dyed long red hair and too much face powder, which did a poor job of concealing her wrinkles. Stone gave a neutral smile and turned away: thanks, but no thanks.

Twenty minutes had gone by, and still no Dunayev.

The instructions from the woman at the cathedral had been quite specific. She stressed that Stone be punctual. And now Dunayev was twenty-five minutes late.

Had something happened to him, too? Had they gotten to him—just like all the others? He looked warily around the café for anyone faintly out of place, any indication that Dunayev had set him up. There seemed to be none.

The prostitute smiled at him again, and walked over, her walk an exaggerated sway, a lascivious swiveling of the hips. "Do you have a light?" she asked in a deep, guttural smoker's voice. She spoke English; she obviously pegged him as an American.

"No, I'm sorry."

She smiled, her teeth badly discolored, shrugged, and got some matches from the bartender. A few minutes later, she approached again. "Are you waiting for anyone?" she asked, bringing her cigarette up to her mouth with a highly stylized flourish, her head tilted to one side. It was as if she had learned to smoke by studying old movies.

"Yes, I am."

The prostitute exhaled a lungful of cigarette smoke. "May I join you?"

"Sorry, no."

"Maybe I can help you find whoever you are looking for," she said, flashing a sepia-toned smile.

Stone nodded, understanding now.

"I think," the woman said, "we may have a mutual friend."

So that was it. Dunayev, obviously an extremely cautious old agent, wanted a go-between to insulate him.

"Please, come with me," she said. Stone rose from the table, left a few francs to cover the bill, and followed her out of the café.

"Mr. Dunayev apologizes for being so careful," she said as they walked along rue de la Roquette. "He says you may understand."

"It's perfectly understandable."

"He is very excited to see a friend of an old friend." She continued to chatter, guiding him along a small side street, then stopping at a boxy maroon-and-black car that Stone recognized as a DCV, the cheap, ubiquitous, not very safe vehicle that originally had only three wheels, before the French government mandated a change to four. "Please," she said, walking around to the driver's side. "I'll take you to him."

The door was unlocked. Stone got into the front seat next to her and knew at once that something was wrong. He froze in terror, then turned his head slowly and saw the glint of a pistol, pointed at him from the backseat.

He sat stiffly as the woman reached over and frisked him with a skill that seemed professional. Turning his head ever so slowly, the blood roaring in his ears, he saw more clearly the figure in the backseat. A man who must have been crouching there, waiting.

He had been set up—but why? Dunayev was a *defector*, a killer who had turned his back on the Soviet state not out of ideology but out of fear for his life. Was it possible he, too, was involved with the fanatics in the West who were running M-3?

"Please don't try anything," came the voice from behind. A Frenchman, his English heavily accented. The DCV had pulled away from the curb into traffic. "Look in the rearview mirror. Do you see the car behind us?"

Stone nodded slowly. The Citroën behind them seemed to be following closely. Dunayev was thorough; Stone would give him that.

"Do you plan to tell me where you're taking me?" Stone asked.

There was no reply.

They drove for several minutes in silence, the red-haired woman constantly glancing at the Citroën in the mirror. As she drove with one hand, she smoked with the other. Stone watched in silence, calculating, waiting for the right instant.

Now they were entering a neighborhood that seemed markedly rougher than the one they had just left. Many of the buildings were crumbling; those that were not seemed deserted. There was a hardware store whose windows were punctuated with bullet holes, a grocery store that was open but seemed to have no customers. Finally, they pulled into a driveway that gave onto a courtyard. The Citroën continued down the street.

"All right," the man said from the backseat. "Go."

Stone opened the car door and stepped out into the courtyard. Directly in front of him stood an older man in a short black leather coat, still muscular despite his age. He appeared to be in his seventies, with a long fringe of gray hair around a large bald spot. His pale face was dotted with wens. His right arm was extended, as if in greeting. But he was holding a pistol, trained at Stone's head. The gun was old, Stone saw at once, the sort of reliable companion that a retired spy would be reluctant to part with. Not the familiar, standard-issue Soviet Army 9mm Makarov. Probably a Tokarev automatic, which the Red Army hadn't issued in some thirty years.

Was this Dunayev?

Stone lifted his eyes from the pistol and smiled. "What sort of welcome is this?" he said in Russian.

"So you are sent by Vyshinsky," the man said at length.

Stone nodded.

The man spat on the ground, his gun still trained on Stone. "Then I would like to send Vyshinsky a return message," he said coldly, quietly. "Your head."

Oh, God. What had this ruse turned into? "Are you Dunayev?"

"I am Dunayev," the man replied. Stone could hear the steady, quiet scuff of feet on gravel behind him. The man and the woman who had brought him here. Slowly he was being surrounded. Dunayev spoke louder now. "If Vyshinsky, that goddamned son of a bitch, thinks he will be clever with me, try to find me, then he can rot in hell. I have been waiting for years for this."

With a sickening realization, Stone saw what had happened. He had used the name not of a friend, a compatriot, but of an avowed enemy. Vyshinsky, who had remained behind in Russia—of course. He would consider Dunayev a traitor.

"I want you to listen to me carefully," Stone said, his

heart hammering. He felt a rush of air as the two behind him moved closer. "You know I am not a Russian, Gospodin Dunayev."

Dunayev blinked, his gun steady.

"You recognize my accent, do you not?"

No reply.

"It's an American accent. You know that; you're quite experienced at dealing with Americans. You were posted to the United States in 1953, assigned to locate a document that Beria wanted."

Dunayev seemed to waver for an instant.

"You threatened a defenseless woman who had once been a personal secretary to Lenin. She gave me your name. Not Vyshinsky. I want you to understand that."

"Your explanation isn't sufficient."

"Vyshinsky was the name of the other person who went with you to visit this woman. I knew you wouldn't agree to see me unless I came with—with some bona fides. That was the best I could do. Obviously I miscalculated."

Dunayev nodded now, almost smiling. "You are American. I can hear that. Yes." He raised his voice again, suddenly. "Then *who are you*?"

Stone began to explain, carefully if not completely, leaving out no detail that would arouse the émigré's deep-seated suspicion. He told him about being a man on the run who had been framed, was wanted by certain renegade American authorities because of what he had found out. Stone had an instinctual understanding of Dunayev's character, and he used it with dexterity. Dunayev was not only a Russian who had known the terrors of a government out of control, but he was also a defector who had lived for years in Europe. Many Europeans who have lived through the years of World War II—the Resistance, the underground movements, the refugees—are naturally sympathetic to the plight of the fugitive who is fleeing the law.

When Stone had finished, Dunayev slowly lowered the gun. "*Dostatochno*," he told the others: Enough, it's okay. Stone turned and saw the red-haired prostitute and her friend walking casually to the car. He heard their car start, then pull out of the courtyard.

"Accept my apologies for this," Dunayev said.

Stone let his breath out slowly, relief seeping into his body. "I need your help now, very badly," he said. "I think you can provide the key to something that's going on right now in Washington and Moscow."

"*Now?* But I'm—"

"Years ago, you were sent by Lavrentii Beria to find something that he needed to pull off a coup—"

"*How do you—?*"

"You were protecting someone, isn't that right?" Stone shifted his feet on the ground, his brain spinning. "A contact between Beria and certain Americans, whose name remains a secret even today."

Dunayev's nod was so subtle it was barely noticeable.

"And one of the links in that chain was a woman named Sonya Kunetskaya," Stone said, as an explanation crossed his mind with great clarity.

Yes. The explanation of the present *did* lie in the past. It was the only way in; CIA data banks would do no good.

The chief of Stalin's secret police, Beria, surely trusted very few with the details of his plan, and he trusted no one more than the mole code-named M-3. Dunayev, who had been allowed to live, *had* to have been kept on the periphery. He knew not the most sensitive state secrets but . . .

"You know something about her. You *must*," Stone said.

The Russian smiled crookedly. "I was the contact man between Beria and Sonya Kunetskaya," he said. "You guess correctly."

Stone could barely contain his astonishment.

"I am rather proud of this," the retired Soviet agent continued. "Beria would not have assigned just anyone to carry his messages to the daughter of the American millionaire Winthrop Lehman."

49

The horrifying thing was, it made absolute sense.

Even half an hour later, Stone could barely concentrate. Stalin's "control" over Lehman—that was it.

Of course. So simple.

"This sort of thing happens from time to time," Dunayev explained, unaware of the effect the revelation was having on his listener. "Many times, you know, Americans or Europeans have gone to the Soviet Union to live, and then they fall in love with a Russian man or woman, and they have a child. Then, when the time comes to go, they suddenly find that the Soviet authorities will not grant the child an exit visa."

They were walking up the long path into Père-Lachaise Cemetery. For the dead, Père-Lachaise is *the* place to be in Paris: it holds the graves of Marcel Proust and Oscar Wilde and hundreds, thousands, of others. It is built vertically, its cramped paths winding their way up hills, crisscrossing with other paths, an overgrown mossy maze.

"A number of American men who could not find work during the Depression went to Russia," Dunayev said. "Some of them went for political reasons, because they preferred Communism, until they saw the real thing—the real monster—close at hand. Some of them genuinely went for the work. And then they had children, and they found that the children, who were Soviet citizens, were not welcome to leave. Oh, very often this happened. During the Second World War, several American news reporters assigned to Moscow fell in love with Russian women, and then their wives and young children were kept as prisoners. Hostages. Perhaps you know that the great American industrialist Armand Hammer spent ten years in Moscow, during the 1920s, and he and his brother both fathered children by Russian women. One child was allowed to leave; one was not."

"That explains Lehman's 'cooperation,' " Stone thought aloud. They stood now before the grave of Frédéric Chopin, a small white monument topped with a statue of a weeping girl. In her lap had been placed several red roses.

The émigré nodded.

"They had his daughter, and they wouldn't let her go," Stone said. "He must have used various people to communicate with her. Including my father."

Dunayev continued walking. He seemed not to comprehend what Stone had said.

"When you say you were the contact between Beria and Lehman's daughter, what do you mean, precisely?"

"Beria had learned somehow, from Stalin, that Lehman had a document of tremendous power. A document, or documents."

Stone nodded. How much did this ex-spy know of the Lenin Testament? *How* did he know?

"And he sent you to get it from Lehman?"

"From Lehman's daughter."

"Because Lehman could never have had direct contact with officials in the Soviet intelligence services," Stone concluded. "It would have destroyed his government career."

"Exactly. And Beria knew that."

"And he never saw his daughter after he left Moscow?"

"No. Once she was allowed to visit Paris, where she saw her father, although she was closely guarded."

"When was that?"

"In 1953, I think."

"So why didn't Lehman free her then?" Stone demanded. "If Sonya was in the West, surely he could have arranged for a kidnapping—"

"Oh, no," Dunayev said, and laughed. "The young woman wouldn't have wanted that at all. You see, her mother was still alive in Russia, and I'm sure she would have wanted to ensure her safety."

"A chain of hostages," Stone mused aloud. "What do you know about this document that Lehman had?"

"Nothing. Only that he had it."

"And did Beria ever get it?"

"No. He tried."

"How?"

"He offered to release Sonya in exchange for this document. It meant a great deal to him. It was extremely important, for some reason."

The cemetery was peaceful, quiet; Stone did not feel as if he were in Paris but, rather, in some pastoral, wooded area, the ruined graves like natural outcroppings of stone. Some of the wreaths had turned brown. Here and there was a mausoleum that had fallen into disrepair, its windows shattered, its interior defiled with beer bottles.

"Why didn't Lehman agree to the trade?" Stone asked finally.

"Oh, but he did agree. He wanted his own daughter back very badly."

"He did? But—"

"But Beria was shot before the deal could go through."

"Ah, yes," Stone said. "Yes. And did you deal with Beria directly? Or with one of his aides?"

"With Beria directly. He wanted absolute privacy."

"Have you heard the designation M-3 before?"

"M-3?" Dunayev repeated slowly.

"A mole in Beria's organization, and also someone he trusted implicitly."

They passed the grave of Simone Signoret and entered the columbarium. Each marble plaque was engraved with gold letters and decorated with artificial flowers. "I don't know of a mole," Dunayev said. "But, then, I wouldn't know, would I? If I knew, then Beria would have known, and then there would have been no mole." For the first time, the émigré laughed.

"But you know about Beria's attempt to seize power?"

"Of course. Everyone heard—after the fact. After he

was shot, we were all told." He now seemed to be leading the way somewhere, walking with purposiveness.

"You heard nothing of an attempt by private citizens in the West to help bring about the coup that Beria wanted?"

The émigré was already walking quickly, and Stone had to jog to keep up with the old man. Before them was a sleek black granite gravestone, highly polished, as reflective as a mirror. On its left side was an oval photograph, set into the granite.

Dunayev was silent, looking directly at the gravestone.

"You recognize this photograph, perhaps?" he asked.

Stone recognized it at once. The face was hardly older at all than the face in the photographs that Saul Ansbach had located for him, The spare gold inlaid lettering read:

Sonya
KUNETSKAYA
18 Janvier 1929–12 Avril 1955

"You see, Winthrop Lehman has been free now for many years," Dunayev said grimly. "His daughter is dead."

Washington

At the normally sedate headquarters of the American Flag Foundation on K Street in central Northwest Washington, there erupted a small commotion at around four in the afternoon, when one of the Foundation's computer specialists, twenty-eight-year-old Army Reserve Corporal Glen Fisher, heard a rapid beeping on one of his terminals. He swung his swivel chair over to take a look, and when he saw what it was, he let out a whoop. "Tarnow!" he said, beckoning one of his colleagues.

The popular belief that a phone call of less than a minute cannot be traced is no longer accurate. The computer terminal over which Glen Fisher was keeping watch was connected to a bit of electronic wizardry known as the "pen register," a trap-and-trace system that traces the originating numbers of telephone callers instantly. The Foundation's field personnel had placed several telephone intercepts on offices and residences throughout Washington. Whenever a call was received over these lines, the phone number of the caller appeared on the monitors in the Foundation's offices.

A few of the lines were given special attention, including that of the late Deputy Secretary of State William Armitage. Now a call had come in to the Armitage residence, from Chicago.

"Plug it in, Glen," Tarnow urged.

"Hey, what do you think I'm doing, man?" Fisher shot back, rapidly entering the ten-digit number into another terminal, which contained a data base of several thousand contacts all known to have had an association with the former CIA analyst gone rogue, Charles Stone.

The terminal grunted mechanically for several seconds, and then the name came up on the screen.

"All *right*," Fisher said, patting the monitor affectionately. "The general's going to be one happy guy."

Paris

Stone stared in shock.

"Can't be," he managed to mutter. "I don't . . ."

The old man was nodding sadly. "Does this help you?" he asked. "Or does this further complicate things?"

"No—" Stone began, and then froze.

His nerves, his instincts, his peripheral vision—the events of the last few weeks had tuned them to an exquisite sensitivity, and now he sensed something out of the ordinary, not the slow paces of the other cemetery visitors, but a sudden movement toward them.

"Get down," he ordered the old man.

Dunayev glanced in the direction Stone had been looking, and at that instant there was an explosion of gunfire. Stone dove forward, slamming Dunayev to the ground, just as a bullet cracked an old headstone only inches away. Stone felt his head spattered with fragments of stone. There wasn't time to calculate; the shadowy gunman was perhaps a hundred feet to the right, and there was nothing between them. The next shot could be to their heads.

Another report. Almost instantaneously a bullet cratered the earth above Sonya Kunetskaya's grave.

"This way!" Stone hissed. "Stay down!" He shoved the old man, whose face was bleeding, toward a tall, wide crypt.

Yes.

Safe cover—for the moment. No doubt the gunman could, from his vantage point, see them clearly. He would have to move, adjust the angle of firing. Dunayev now had his gun out and contorted his body awkwardly, trying to stay behind the white marble and yet establish a clear line of fire.

There he was, silhouetted, crouching into a firing position. The gunman could hit both of them now without obstacle. Stone glanced around—was there more than one of them? No—just the play of sun against the monuments, the shadows of the ancient graveyard.

"Back," Dunayev ordered, releasing the safety on his gun and aiming.

Then—another explosion! Stone flattened himself against the old man, forcing him out of the way—but this time the shot came from the *left*. There *was* another gunman, and he had struck down the first.

The two of them, Stone and Dunayev, sat absolutely still for a moment that seemed endless. Not a sound. The firing had stopped. What had begun so suddenly had now ended. Dunayev lowered his gun, his expression shocked.

Stone looked up, weak with tension. Dunayev looked up, too, trembling.

"What happened?" the old Chekist asked, hushed.

"I don't know," Stone said, truthfully. "We're alive. That's all I know."

The two men walked over to the crumpled body of the slain marksman. A distant commotion was growing steadily louder, the approaching voices of people no doubt alarmed by the gunfire.

"What are you *doing*?" Stone cried out.

Dunayev bent over and, with the agility of a lifelong spy, inserted a thumb into the dead man's mouth, bloodied and twisted in the agony of his death. With a quick motion he forced the mouth open and peered in.

"*It's true*," he gasped. Dunayev ran his hands over the man's torso. Nimbly, he tore at the man's jacket until he could see the skin at the underarm. Evidently he was looking for something, and found nothing.

"Let's get out of here," Stone said. He looked away from the bloody mess of the would-be assassin's face, sickened, reminded immediately of the nightmare in Cambridge. "*What's* true? Let's go; we can't be connected with this."

Dunayev rose and followed Stone down the knoll, toward the path that led out of the cemetery.

"Who shot him?" Stone asked. "Where'd the other one go?"

Dunayev, out of breath, seemed not to have heard him. At last he spoke, distracted.

"The dental work is Russian; I'd recognize it anywhere. But he's not KGB, or, for that matter, GRU."

"How the hell can you tell that?"

"Two ways." Dunayev grimaced. "One, the dental work is vastly superior to anything done by those butchers in the Lubyanka who call themselves dentists. It's Russian, but it's the inordinately expensive sort I always thought was reserved only for members of the Politburo."

"That hardly—"

"No, that's soft evidence. But there's something much firmer. Every KGB or GRU clandestine operative has, sewn beneath the top layer of his skin, one or two infinitesimal metallic ampules of poison, usually cyanide. Standard KGB procedure, to make certain a captured agent escapes interrogation—by means of his own death. They usually appear in any of three places, but this man had nothing. The man who tried to kill you—and I do think they were aiming at you—was a Soviet national not affiliated with any known intelligence agency."

They had reached the cemetery's exit, and Stone turned to the elderly spy. His voice was steely. "Damn it, that doesn't surprise me. Nowhere near as much as what happened a few minutes ago. What I want to know is, *who shot that man*? You saw it as well as I did, but you haven't said a word about it. Someone saved my life—*our lives. Who?*"

Before long, they were at Dunayev's flat. It was a dismal, bare place, sparsely furnished with shabby furniture. The front room had clearly been decorated by a bachelor with no regard to design; the walls were a gloomy sand color, and Russian volumes competed for space on bookshelves with odds and ends collected over a lifetime of transient living.

The Russian had poured himself a glass of Smirnoff vodka, still visibly shaken. For a long time, he rambled on about what had happened, meaningless blather that the old Russian needed to calm himself.

In time, Dunayev began to speak more calmly. "Most of the specifics I don't know," he said. "I know there is a network, run out of Moscow. People say this network for some reason protects certain defectors, certain émigrés. Perhaps our man was one of those."

Stone paused to consider what Dunayev was saying. A network of former Chekists? He was uneasy, suddenly, about his newfound comradeship with a former Chekist; if you sleep with dogs, the saying went, you get fleas. The fleas, Stone hoped, would wash off. This man knew things, and Stone had to use him. He had supplied Dunayev with several pieces of the puzzle; now he needed the old Chekist's memory.

Dunayev nervously reached for a pack of Gauloises and lit one. He inhaled deeply and, as he exhaled, began to talk. "A few days ago, an old man named Arkady Stefanov was killed in Novosibirsk, in the Soviet Union—struck down by a car. He, too, was retired NKVD. My friends tell me Stefanov was on his way to an interview with a correspondent for the *Manchester Guardian*, for, as it turns out, a soft feature piece on how life in Russia has changed."

Stone nodded. "He, too, was one of Beria's trusted assistants, am I right?"

"Yes," Dunayev said. "Stefanov, I know, got involved with Beria's attempted coup. He was in the shit up to his ears."

"How?"

"One of Beria's errand boys. He forced Beria's personal physician to write a false report testifying that Beria had suffered a heart attack. I guess Beria planned to be absent, so he could marshal his forces. Probably wanted the absence to be believable to his colleagues, so they wouldn't get any more suspicious than they already were."

"Damn it, Stefanov's dead now."

"As I told you." Dunayev laughed, flashing his gold teeth. "And forget about the good doctor—he was executed as soon as they found out he'd collaborated with Beria. Poor bastard."

"Stefanov must have known something about the identity of M-3," Stone said. He narrowed his eyes, thinking of something. "But why would he be eliminated now over a coup attempt that happened *decades* ago?" And then he remembered the HEDGEHOG report that had begun this whole thing, the report from the Agency's asset in Moscow hinting that a convulsion was about to take place in the Kremlin.

"Do you think," Stone continued, "that this so-called Lenin Testament in some way reveals the identity of the mole?"

"Yes. Yes, I've always thought so. Yes."

Stone nodded. "The timing," he said. "These things can't be coincidental."

"Timing?" Dunayev asked.

It's about to happen, Stone realized.

The first glimmerings of an enormous, frightening upheaval. The pattern of the past was being replicated now.

"Yes. People are taking great risks of exposure. Something's got to be urgent." Stone looked around the apartment. "M-3 is about to be maneuvered into power. Imminently." Then he added, with a sudden bolt of icy realization, "There is a deadline."

"You tell me, Mr. Stone. You're the Soviet expert. I was merely an employee."

"The summit," Stone said, and he sat in his chair, frozen in terror, like an insect in amber.

50

Moscow

The driving rain had not let up all day; the sky was steel-gray. Charlotte had negotiated the fifteen kilometers slowly and carefully. The roads were slick, and she suspected the Renault needed a new set of brakes, but she dreaded having that kind of work done in Moscow. You could never trust the Soviet mechanics, and they never had the parts anyway.

Directly ahead was the crumbling Krylovsky Monastery, just as Sergei had described it. It had once no doubt been a forbidding presence on the city's outskirts, its rugged stone masonry solid and ageless; no doubt, too, the monks that had once dwelt within had imagined the place would endure forever. In the eighteenth century, the monastery had been converted to soldiers' barracks, and then it had fallen into disrepair, and when the Revolution came, it was left to disintegrate into the surrounding hills.

She waited in the car, listening to the engine block tick, refusing to stand out in the rain any longer than she had to.

The rain was making her contemplative. She didn't know whether she could trust Sergei. You could never trust official Russians anyway, and Sergei was KGB, which often meant trouble. KGB had their own veiled agenda, their own bureaucratic tangles that made the normal Soviet bureaucracy seem, by comparison, innocent.

When the bizarre call from Charlie had come in the middle of the night, she was momentarily baffled, wondering whether he were indeed out of his mind. Then she realized he was trying to tell her something.

He had mentioned the sites of all the most recent bombings in Moscow and said, with great emphasis, something about *American* and something about *involvement.*

Were these not native acts of terrorism? Were these done by . . . *American* terrorists? This, added to the suspicions she had already made, made her more curious than ever.

The next day, Charlotte contacted Sergei.

She knew he had something to do with the KGB's Special Investigations Department, but he was hardly forthcoming about that. He was in his early forties, round, with plump dimpled hands and stubby fingers. His large head was beginning to go bald. He seemed introverted, which made her trust him more. He was not a careerist, not the smarmy outgoing type who accosted you at a banquet and then went back to the office to write a "contact report" for the files. Sergei was the first "good" KGB employee she had ever met, although "good" was still a relative term.

But meeting in a deserted monastery? Either he had something terribly important to say—

—or it was a setup. Was that possible? "Receiving state secrets"—would that be the charge?

She got out of the car and found her way into the front of the ruin, pushing open a heavy wooden door that creaked on its hinges. She entered a small stone hallway, so dark she could barely see. When her eyes adjusted, she found the narrow corridor Sergei had described, and pushed open another wooden door.

The room, illuminated irregularly by shafts of gray light from jagged holes in the ceiling, had once been the refectory. She turned around and saw the dark shape that was Sergei.

"*Privyet,* Charlotte," he said, his hushed voice echoing.

"*Privyet.*" She came closer, sat down on a stone bench beside him. "*Nu?*"

"*Vy byli pravy.*" You were right. He seemed tense, and he kneaded his pudgy hands together.

Charlotte waited.

After a time, he spoke again, still hushed. "Where did you get your information?"

Charlotte shook her head. No.

"Do you plan to broadcast a story?"

"Perhaps."

"Please don't. Not yet. Wait."

Charlotte turned and looked at him sharply. His features were distinct now. He looked terrified.

"That's my decision to make, Sergei. You know that."

He nodded slowly.

"What was I right about, Sergei?"

"The bombs *were* CIA. I checked the results. They are made from CIA materials. Your CIA is up to its old tricks. You should look into this. You should rip the lid off this scandal. In time. Your CIA is out of control."

She felt her mouth dry out suddenly, and she could not turn her head. "Why are you telling me this?" she managed to whisper.

"Please," he said. "You don't know how much courage it took for me to meet with you. If I'm caught . . ." His voice trailed off. "Yes, things are much better in my country. But in KGB, well, things are not so much different from the old days."

"But why are you telling me this?"

A long pause. "I wish I knew."

Sergei Abramov sat on the bench for a long while after Charlotte had left. He shivered from the cold, and from his fear of being caught. His problems with his daughter Zinaida seemed so distant now. Was he doing the right thing in leaking this shocking news to a reporter? It had seemed shrewd when he first thought of it. Terribly risky, yes, but sound. He knew that Harper would not report anything until she'd begun to dig around with her sources in the CIA. Maybe she'd uncover another CIA scandal, which would discredit the American government. That would help Abramov's career enormously, when his role was revealed. Yes, he had used her, but if she helped expose the CIA's involvement in trying to destabilize the already unstable Soviet government, the result would be good. He rubbed his hands together, and after twenty minutes or so he went out to brave the rain.

Charlotte didn't believe him. Sergei was planting a story, that had to be it. The theatrics, the meeting in the deserted ruins of a monastery. It all smacked of melodrama, and she refused to buy into it.

Why was he leaking this information about the CIA? True, he'd leaked before, but this was precisely the sort of thing a KGB investigator would keep secret until his higher-ups could decide how to handle it.

Was the KGB trying to manipulate her?

Yes. It had to be. They were trying to use her.

That was all it was.

51

Paris

At a café on rue de Buci, on the Left Bank, not far from L'Hôtel, Stone sat drinking an espresso, taking methodical notes in a small notebook he'd just bought.

He knew that at this moment Fyodor Dunayev was working on acquiring a gun for him. The old Russian had his sources, of course, and he recognized that it was close to impossible for an amateur to buy a gun on the black market anymore, especially in Paris. Even if Stone managed to find the right bar in the sleaziest part of town—in Pigalle, say—and managed to find someone who had the wherewithal to get him a gun, there would be no deal. No one, in this age of terrorism, would risk a sale to somebody who might later be linked back to the seller. It wasn't worth it.

No, Dunayev would have to get it, and fortunately he had the connections to do it easily.

The only problem was that Dunayev's knowledge of weaponry did not extend much beyond the mid-fifties, and automatic weapons had gone through significant changes since then. Most important, perhaps, was the development of the "plastic"—a high-impact-polymer semiautomatic pistol.

Only the grip is plastic, actually, but these guns had one chief advantage over all-metal ones: they could be smuggled onto airplanes, even past metal detectors. Or so Stone had been told; he had only the faintest idea of how to do it himself, if it became necessary.

If he was going to Moscow, he would probably need a gun he could slip into the country.

But he hoped to God he wouldn't have to use it.

At a pay phone at the back of the café, he sent a telegram to Paula Singer: ALL WELL. But how to sign it? They'd agreed upon HASKELL, but for all its cleverness, that seemed too risky. If his ruse in Haskell had been uncovered by now, Haskell would be too obvious. He signed the telegram simply A FRIEND. Paula needed to know he was all right.

Then he returned to the small round table, ordered another espresso, and resumed taking notes.

Soon he had an explanation that made some sense.

Winthrop Lehman had had a daughter during his years in Moscow—Sonya—who had taken her mother's name so that she would never be connected with her famous American father.

So far, so good.

Sonya had been a hostage, a tool who had been used against Lehman to force his cooperation. *The Soviets had once had a powerful hold on one of the most influential men in America, an aide to several presidents*.

Yet this same man had been given a document by Lenin, something powerful and explosive that, if released, could have caused the Soviet state tremendous damage.

A document that, for some reason, might also reveal the identity of the mole M-3.

So Lehman had something of a *counter*-hold on them.

And his daughter was dead.

For some reason, still unclear, Lehman had once cooperated with a number of American officials, and at least two Soviet ones, to overthrow the Soviet government and install Beria. It made sense that Lehman had once gone to great lengths to try to free his daughter. Yet . . . Beria?

But that was the past.

The pieces of the puzzle—of the *present* puzzle—were at last coming together, and the questions that remained loomed larger than ever.

Haskell, Michigan

Chief Randall Jergensen of the Haskell, Michigan, police was just about fed up. Most of the night, he'd been out on the lake with his deputy, Will Kuntz, and a handful of volunteers, dredging the Haskell shore of one of the goddamn hugest lakes in the entire U.S. of A.

As if dredging wasn't bad enough, he had to endure the nonstop yapping from the feds who insisted on coming along, somehow thinking he could maybe do a better job if they were around to ask moron questions and flash their three-piece suits and generally act important. When all Jergensen wanted to do was say, All right, you win, the goddamn accident was a goddamn hoax, and be done with it. Tell the goddamn feds to write up their little reports and go back to their motels, and he could go home and get some sleep. "You just lay off," he wanted to tell them, "and let me do my job."

By half past four in the morning, he finally let them have it.

"All right, you sumbitch," he said, "the guy set it up. He's gone." Jergensen turned and stormed off for his cruiser.

On the way home, he stopped by the dark station

house and put a quarter in the vending machine around back. A can of Grapettes grape soda, icy cold, came tumbling down to the chute. He popped it open, took a long slug, and walked back to the car wearily.

That sly bastard, he thought as he drove home, smiling to himself. Whatever the hell the guy did, you gotta admire the smarts.

He pulled into his driveway, and remembered that his ex-wife, Wendy, wasn't there, and he smiled again.

Paris

Lehman, Stone knew, had visited Paris countless times in his long life, on business and on pleasure. Two of those times, Stone realized, it had been to visit the daughter no one knew he had.

Suddenly an idea occurred to him. Stone went through the Paris Yellow Pages looking for the names of photo archives, companies that would have extensive photographic files—of historic personages and the not so historic, of events and moments captured on film by news photographers through the years. New York had quite a few of them, on which magazines, newspapers, and publishers relied heavily.

He came up with a list of four of the largest photo archives in Paris and visited them one by one. He was looking for photographs of Winthrop Lehman in Paris taken during two specific years.

Once Beria allowed her to visit Paris. . . .

Sonya Kunetskaya.

When was that?

In 1953 . . .

Was it possible that Lehman's daughter had been photographed? She had been buried *in Paris,* her name prominently displayed, engraved in gold. If Lehman, or Beria, had wanted to keep her existence secret, then why bury her in Paris's most prominent cemetery?

The woman must have been seen in Paris.

Yet, after several frustrating hours, Stone had come up with nothing.

Finally, he walked into the fourth archive on his list, a small storefront on rue de Seine with the name H. ROGER VIOLLET painted on the window.

The walls were lined, floor to ceiling, with green binders, no doubt filled with photographs.

"I'm looking for a photograph of someone," Stone told the young female clerk in French.

"Historical, diplomatic, scientific . . . ?"

"Well, none of those, really. She's the daughter of an American statesman. Her name is Sonya Kunetskaya."

"Let me check."

The woman consulted a large card file. A few minutes later, she looked up. "Born 1929, died 1955?" she asked.

"That's the one."

"One moment."

She got on a small stepladder against the wall and located a large green album marked HISTOIRE ETATS-UNIS, K–L. She placed it before Stone, and opened it to a page. The photographs were affixed neatly and captioned with typewriting. Touching one page with her index finger, she said, "I believe it's that one."

It was Sonya.

The picture had been taken by a well-known French society photographer at a party at the Soviet Embassy in Paris. She stood talking to someone who was not Winthrop Lehman, while a few feet away several dour-looking men watched her.

"Oh," the woman said abruptly, "I'm afraid that's not the right one."

"Yes, it is."

"No, I don't think so. This picture is dated 1956." She laughed nervously. "That would be a year after her death. This can't be the same person."

Nineteen fifty-*six*? Her gravestone had said April 12, 1955.

It made no sense.

Unless the very public gravestone, the date chiseled in the marble, was false. *If it was a cover-up.*

"Ah, here's another," the woman said, turning the page with a moistened finger.

Stone, his mind reeling, for a moment could not hear the woman.

"Monsieur?"

Could Sonya Kunetskaya still be alive?

"Monsieur?"

Stone looked up slowly, unable to think. "Yes?" he said thickly.

"Monsieur, if you like, here is another one. It is dated Paris, December 16, 1953. This one is three years earlier."

Stone examined the second photograph, and his astonishment grew still further. He could scarcely believe his eyes.

It was a picture shot on a street outside the Soviet Embassy. Sonya was, as before, surrounded by menacing-looking guards, but this time her father stood nearby. It was unmistakably Winthrop Lehman.

And standing next to Lehman, only a few months out of prison, was the gaunt figure of the young Alfred Stone.

52

Moscow

Yakov Kramer sat in his cubicle at Progress Publishers, having done with his editing for the day. He was tired and saddened.

Stefan had now set off three bombs in the heart of Moscow, and still Avram was not free. There was no reply.

They had made a terrible mistake.

He had sent two letters to the Kremlin, both of which made it very clear that the destruction would continue, and that they would soon be forced to go public with their demands. He knew the Politburo could not want such a public humiliation, with the Moscow summit so near.

And his beloved son Avram remained in a mental hospital, his brain deteriorating by the day.

The office was almost deserted, and Yakov knew that Sonya was still at work in her cubicle across the large room. Any minute, she would come up to him, wearing her coat and a weary expression, and announce it was time for them to go. He straightened his desk, and got up to find Sonya.

She was already coming toward him. He took an irrational satisfaction in the innate sense of timing they shared. Somehow she always knew when he'd be ready to leave.

They did not like to kiss each other in the office, because they weren't married, and Russians have a Victorian prudishness about public displays of affection; better not to offend people. But when they left, he grabbed her hand and felt a warming surge of affection for Sonya. He loved her, and he loved her increasingly, each day.

They had met here, at Progress, years ago. Yakov had recently been released from the gulag; Sonya was a fact-checker and researcher, a beautiful woman who kept to herself, shunned friends, a loner. Yakov, who was valued for his skills but ostracized because of his face—because of *fear*, really, the horror most people have of physical deformity, he knew that—used to fantasize about this small, dark-haired woman whose eyes were flecked with green. She was a Woman with a Past, he was sure. Why else would someone so beautiful act like a nun? In passing her desk one morning, Yakov said something to her, something reasonably clever, and she looked him directly in the eyes, and smiled, and his heart caught, and he was stuck.

At lunch that day, she appeared at his desk with a sandwich, cheese on thickly cut black sourdough bread, and asked him to share it with her—she wasn't hungry. The gesture of a child who wanted a friend. Did she feel sorry for him? he wondered. They talked, she laughed at his jokes, they argued about literature, and that night, when he walked her to her apartment building, where she lived with her widowed mother, he kissed her in the middle of a torrential rain, and she didn't flinch! What was wrong with her? he wanted to know. As they got to know each other better, she would talk, once in a while and always sketchily, about the traumas in her past, broken love affairs, that sort of thing. He wanted to know everything about this woman, and he would interrogate her—*Who were these men, these bastards, who could possibly have left you?*—but she would smile wanly, and say nothing. It seemed to Yakov, in the years that they had lived together—as lovers, not as man and wife—that both of them were, in a way, wounded, and that this was the bond between them.

Now Yakov wanted to tell her everything about what he and Stefan were doing to obtain Avram's freedom, but that was out of the question.

Maybe she'd approve of what we're doing, I don't know, he thought.

No. The most selfish thing he could do would be to tell her. She must never be hurt by what he was doing, he'd resolved. She must never know.

He thought about that American reporter who had come to see her, and wondered what the secrets were that Sonya kept from *him*. Sure, they had talked about her past, but the way she told it everything seemed so normal that Yakov could not help wondering whether she really might be concealing something. Was that any way to think about the one you loved?

After work, they had to do shopping, wait in line for bread and then for milk and then for chicken (the chickens in the store looked pale and scrawny) and then for vegetables. The whole fucking ritual, Kramer knew, was intentional. Keep the peasants so busy working and then scuttling around to feed their faces that by the end of the day they'll be so tired they won't even think of revolting.

Then there was the long subway ride, and at last they were traversing the muddy courtyard, into the urine-stained building lobby, and home at last.

Yakov and Sonya dropped the groceries on the kitchen table and looked at each other, mouths agape with frustration and exhaustion.

"Yakov, I don't want to cook right now," Sonya said.

"Don't. I'll cook. You sit down."

"No, don't you cook, either."

"What are you talking about?" he asked, and then he saw what she was hinting at. "Sonya, I may be too tired."

"No," she said, coming up to him slowly and kissing him. She kissed both sides of his face, the good side and the bad, and then his lips.

Although her looks had faded somewhat with age, there remained something irresistible about her, something poignant, even tragic, in her dark eyes. He found her amazingly erotic. He wasn't a young man; he could no longer make love with the old frequency, but he invariably found her arousing. There was something about her that made him feel tremendously virile. They didn't rut like teenagers; they made love less urgently, more tenderly.

They got up slowly, went into the bedroom, and removed their clothes. Sonya took hers off neatly and folded them and put them on her night table, beside the photograph of her and her father that she loved so much, and they made love.

When they were done, and they lay in a loose embrace, she began stroking his neck and one of his shoulders.

"It's always there, isn't it?" she asked softly.

"Hmm?" he grunted.

"The anger. Even if they let Avram go free, you'll carry it with you."

There was no use in fighting her, so he didn't reply.

"I want you to be careful."

"What are you talking about, Sonushka?"

"Sometimes I think they watch me carefully, and so they might see."

"You're not making sense." He sat up and took hold of her shoulders.

"Please, Yakov. You don't have to tell me any more than I know. But I want you to be careful."

"Sonya . . ."

"I found an envelope on the floor. An empty envelope, addressed to the Kremlin."

He stared into her eyes, terrified. How had she found it? He had been so careful.

"Sonya, I want to explain . . ."

"No, Yakov. Don't explain. Please. I don't know if you're doing a good thing or a bad thing, but I understand why you're doing it. And I'm scared." Her voice cracked, and she spoke now through tears. "I don't want anything to happen to you. Someday I'll tell you something about my life before I met you, but right now I can't. I've made a promise. I just want you to be very, very careful. For both of us."

As she cried, tears sprang to his eyes, too. He could not stand to see her unhappy; it tore him up. He wanted to ask her, How can you love me so much? I'm so ugly, inside and out, I'm such a monster, how can you love me? But instead he said nothing and looked at her sadly through his tears, the way you look at something that might be taken away from you at any moment.

Washington

Early in the morning, wracked with tension, Roger Bayliss was attempting to relax in the Jacuzzi in the Executive Office Building, next to the White House, when the phone buzzed. He reached up to answer it.

It was the Director of Central Intelligence.

"Call me from a secure line," Templeton said.

Bayliss got up, wrapped a towel around himself, and walked into the adjoining restroom, where the urinals were equipped with heat-activated flushing devices, installed during Nixon's time. The heat sensors rarely worked.

Fifteen minutes later, he was dressed and back in his office, where he returned the director's call.

"Yes, Ted," Bayliss replied. "We've got a pretty good sense of the general direction he's taking. I'd say this report about the murder of the Sekretariat guy in Paris is pretty definitive. More or less places it."

He listened to Templeton's reply, and then said: "Yes. Let's keep up the passport-customs search plus the normal police fugitive search in the half-dozen or so target cities. But I'd say we should step up Paris."

He listened again, and said, "The odds are pretty high he'll turn up before long. We'll have him. The stakes are too high to let him live."

53

Moscow

Sergei F. Abramov of the Special Investigations Department of the KGB had never actually met the chairman. He was, he knew, just about to do so, and the thought of it made him nervous. Forty minutes earlier, his secretary, Dusya, had run up to him, her eyes wide, to tell him that the chairman of the KGB himself had actually, personally, sent for Abramov. What did he make of *that*? A car was sent round to pick Abramov up and take him to Pavlichenko's office at the Lubyanka.

Standing in the chairman's anteroom now, watching his feet and kneading his hands and listening absently to the secretaries answering the telephones, Abramov did not know what to make of it at all.

Was it possible the chairman himself had read his report, about how the bombs were made from American plastique? No, it hardly seemed likely, and, besides, why would the chairman himself want to talk to a mere technician?

The horrible thought crossed his mind fleetingly that somehow someone had discovered that he had leaked highly classified information to an American reporter, and that the chairman of the KGB was calling him in for interrogation . . . but why would the chairman himself be involved? Wouldn't internal security handle it, swiftly and without a ruckus?

Please, he thought. Let it not be that.

But there was no time to think further, because suddenly he looked up and saw Andrei Pavlichenko standing in front of him. He was surprised at how dignified the chairman seemed. Pavlichenko was a man of sixty, but he had a head of thick brown hair that was probably colored.

"Tovarishch Abramov," Pavlichenko said, shaking hands.

"Sir. It's an honor."

"Please." The chairman led the way toward a white-painted double door. He walked with the springy step of a much younger man.

Abramov found himself babbling from nervousness. "I'm surprised to find there's a door here," he said as the two men entered Pavlichenko's office.

Pavlichenko laughed. "You know, before I set foot in this office, in the days of Beria, I had heard the same stories. Everyone said Beria's office had no doors. And then one day I was summoned to Beria's office, much as you've been today."

"And found there was no truth to the rumors," Abramov ventured, a little more at ease. What did the chairman want? Please, I have a wife and two daughters at home who depend on me. Why did I ever meet with that American reporter? What did I think I was doing? At the time, it seemed like a good idea.

"And found the rumors were true." Pavlichenko seemed a soft-spoken man, and an intelligent one, which was quite a divergence from the long line of brutal, brutish men who had always ruled Soviet state security. "I showed up at midnight, which was when Beria preferred to conduct meetings, and I was guided by one of his secretaries into a *shkaf*, what appeared to be a free-standing oak wardrobe closet against a wall. The secretary reached a hand into the darkness and pressed a button, and the back of the *shkaf* opened into the chairman's office. Beria had a mania for privacy and protection. Well, years later, by the time I got this job, I was distressed to learn that Yuri Andropov had had the *shkaf* taken away and replaced with a conventional set of doors. So I'm sorry to disappoint you."

"I'm not disappointed, sir," Abramov said.

Pavlichenko had walked to his simple mahogany desk and had seated himself. Abramov sat, discreetly glancing around. The legendary office of the chairman of the KGB was even more plush than he had imagined. It was quite big, imposingly so, and ornately decorated. The floors were covered in large, beautiful carpets from Central Asia; the walls were wainscoted in lustrous mahogany, above which was wallpaper of ivory silk and just one portrait, of the founder of the Soviet secret police, Feliks Dzerzhinsky. There were off-white brocade sofas and mahogany end tables. The room looked like the library of a baronial manor.

Looking closer, Abramov saw that Pavlichenko was actually not a handsome man. His face was plain, with massive cheekbones and chin. Yet he cut a striking figure, with his fine English suits. It was joked around Moscow, especially among his detractors, that Andrei Pavlichenko looked like a star of the cinema—except from the front.

The chairman was also, Abramov knew, possessed of an extraordinary mental acuity, an ability to reason at lightning speed and to see the panorama where others could see only a few trees. He was blessed with a genius for politics, a talent for making allies that had catapulted him to the top—or so the scuttlebutt had it.

Which was not to say that the new chairman of the KGB—he had been in office less than a year—was not genuinely impressive. Everyone in the Committee had by now heard tales of Pavlichenko's feats. Unlike most KGB chairmen before him, Pavlichenko had actually spent time in the West, having done tours of duty in London, Paris, and Washington. In the mid-fifties, he had been assigned as control for Sir Anthony Blunt, the Queen's curator, who was also the "fourth man" in the spy ring of Burgess, Maclean, Philby, and Blunt. He had masterminded several false defections of KGB officers to the United States, operations that appeared to have successfully poisoned the CIA's well. Abramov was awed to be chatting with him.

"I read your report," the chairman said.

Abramov silently expelled a breath. Thank God, that was it. "Sir?"

"I'm impressed you took it upon yourself to request the samples from the recent terrorist bombings. You were admirably thorough, and I wish we had more like you around here. Unfortunately, we don't."

"Thank you, sir."

"I want to tell you, this is not the first report I've gotten indicating that the CIA has been supplying the terrorists."

"Is that right, sir?"

"Tell me, what made you requisition the samples? Were you dissatisfied with the way things are being done in Forensics? If you are, I need to hear it."

Abramov could not tell the chairman the truth, that an American correspondent had asked him about it—had actually planted the idea in his head—so he said instead, "Just a theory, sir. Pure instinct."

Pavlichenko leaned back in his chair. He looked weary suddenly. "I'm told you're one of the best."

"No, sir, I doubt it."

"From now on, I want you to be in charge of this matter. If Moscow is hit again, I want you to be the only forensic investigator. If you need to put together a team— and only if it is absolutely necessary—then I want you to be the sole authority. And you will answer directly to me."

"But, sir . . ."

"Don't worry about lines of authority. I've taken care of that. My friend, I know all about bureaucracy, and how governments can topple in a crisis because a single clerk chooses to oversleep one morning. Now, I can't tell you precisely what sort of internal security investigations are going on, but let me just say that they are of enormous possible consequences. Nothing you will ever do will be of greater urgency. Is that clear?"

Abramov swallowed, astonished. "Of course, sir."

"If we don't track down the source of the terror, Tovarishch Abramov," Pavlichenko said, getting up from his chair, "I'm afraid we're all in grave trouble."

54

Paris

"Here," Dunayev said, laying down a pistol on the coffee table in Stone's hotel room. "The best my friends could do was an outrageous eighteen hundred francs for this thing."

"Thank you," Stone said, picking it up. It was a 9mm Austrian-made Glock 17, small and lightweight because its receiver frame was high-density plastic. He loaded the seventeen-round cartridge and heard it click in. "Good. Well made."

"Yes, it is. Use it in good health."

Stone laughed as he removed cash from his belts and bookbindings, gathering much of it in one pile, which he placed on his person. He shoved another pile toward Dunayev. "I need you to keep this for me," he said. "Put it somewhere safe. A bank safe-deposit box, perhaps. And take some of it for yourself."

Dunayev scowled. "I wouldn't think of it."

"For a man who used to kill for a living, you're pretty moral," Stone said genially.

"Kill for a cause," Dunayev said slowly. "In that, we are not so different. You, too, have killed."

"Yes." Stone shook his head slowly. "Once, in Chicago. Maybe again." He got up and checked the closet, making sure he had taken the vital necessities. The rest, the clothing he didn't need and so on, he would leave with Dunayev, so as not to provide his pursuers with any more traces than they already had.

"It's not safe for me to stay here," he said. "Not after what happened at Père Lachaise."

Dunayev sighed, wearily and almost musically. "My friend, the *gendarmes* are already looking for you."

"How do you know?"

"They are going from hotel to hotel showing a photograph of you. It is a slow process, but hotel managers will certainly cooperate. You're not safe anywhere. If I hid you in my apartment, they might find you."

"I just need a few hours. There are no flights at this time. If—"

"There is a place," Dunayev interrupted. He beamed with triumph. "You can find shelter with the woman who met you at the café."

"That redheaded woman?"

"Yes. For the time being, she is safe—they do not connect her with me."

"But what *is* her connection with you?"

Dunayev shrugged and spread his hands, palms upward. "I am not a fool, Stone. If you think that when I defected from Moscow I did so without protection, you underestimate me."

"*What?*"

"Like most clandestine operatives, I kept records to protect myself from my employers. Encrypted messages, onetime pads, payment records. Lists of Soviet agents-in-place in French and West German ministries. Even decades later, those lists are more valuable than platinum— some of those agents have now attained quite high positions. Every time I was in Paris, I squirreled away another scrap of paper, another shred of microfilm."

"And this woman has them? This prostitute?"

"Yes, she is a prostitute. And, yes, she keeps them for me, in her flat in the Marais. My life insurance."

"Why the hell would she—?"

"Loyalty. Gratitude. The reason many human beings do things for others. She was a fourteen-year-old prostitute during the Second World War when the Nazis discovered she was working with the Resistance. She was lined up on a roof with others, about to be shot. I had infiltrated the Nazis' organization in Paris. I was one of the Nazis up on the roof that evening, and I saw this unfortunate girl, and I was able to spare her life. I told them I wanted her for myself. Yes, Mr. Stone, she keeps my files for me. The safest place for them. Do you know Paris?"

"Somewhat."

"In the Marais, there is a small street, rue Malher." He drew out a dog-eared map of the city and pointed with a stubby finger. "Here. For me, and for her, do not stay long. Where will you go next?"

"Moscow."

"*Moscow!* That's insanity. You are putting your head into the lion's mouth!"

"Yes, maybe. But I have no choice. If I do not go, I will certainly be killed. If I do go—well, that's my only hope. If I can connect with this network, perhaps I can draw upon their resources, to stop this conspiracy, and at the same time to protect me. In the interests of the Soviet state, they will *have* to."

Dunayev nodded solemnly. "They will have to," he echoed. "Yes."

"Who *are* they? What do you know about them?"

"I hear they are called the Staroobriadtsy, the Old Believers."

The Old Believers . . . Stone had heard the term before—where?

"I've heard it began in the last days of Stalin, when good, loyal people were being slaughtered indiscriminately. You hear talk about the Staroobriadtsy's reach into the very Kremlin itself. When Nikita Khrushchev was about to be thrown out of office, he got advance warning: a phone call from a bodyguard working for one of the men conspiring against him. They say that was the work of the Old Believers, who saw Khrushchev as the Motherland's last hope in those days."

The Old Believers. Now Stone remembered. It was a passing reference in Alfred Stone's letter in the safe-deposit box back in Cambridge. Was it possible he, too, had heard—that he knew something about this network? "Any underground network like this must have a head, a leader," Stone said. "You have to help me here. Who is it? Who are these people?"

"Yes, there is a leader. A man whose name is secret."

"There *must* be a way . . ."

Dunayev had been nodding very slowly, his face drawn in concentration. "I know some," he said. "You must have heard—you are an expert on the politics of my godforsaken country—of one of the worst atrocities of the Second World War, an unspeakable horror only outdone by the Nazis, a mass slaughtering perpetrated by my very own people, the NKVD. The Katyn Forest Massacre."

"Of course I've heard of it. Thousands and thousands—what was it, four thousand?—fifteen thousand?—officers of the Polish Army were killed in 1940. One of the most brutal episodes of the war."

"Ah, my friend, you don't even know the half of it. For years afterward, the affair was skillfully covered up by the Soviet government. The great Winston Churchill did not want the details revealed, for fear of what it would do to the war effort. Even now you in the West know very little about it."

"If it's relevant in some way . . ."

"On a spring day in 1940, fifteen thousand Polish officers suddenly disappeared. Professional men, engineers, doctors, professors, and generals. The Soviet government had taken them prisoners and then, because Stalin was afraid Hitler might think the Russians were trying to steal the elite of the Polish Army, Stalin had to get rid of them. These men were packed up in trucks and buses and, load after load, taken to the edge of a giant, freshly dug pit."

Stone nodded, unwilling to interrupt Dunayev, puzzled about what this had to do with the Old Believers.

"And then each one was shot in the back of the neck. Day after day, and it took weeks, there were so many of them. Bodies were piled on top of bodies, thrown in the pit. It was grotesque—a nightmare so unbelievable that even a few of the NKVD men, hardened and ruthless killers, later went out of their minds. As the days went on and the pit became a rotting, decomposing mess, the prisoners would look down into it just before they were to be executed and bellow in terror, struggling, wild. Mostly the work was done by NKVD, as I have said, but they were assisted by some infantrymen from the Red Army, a special detachment of troops who did not know what they had come there for. And on the sixth day, when the stench had become unbearable, some of the troops—vomiting, dazed—finally had had enough. They carried out a mutiny: their regiment commander led them in the rebellion against the NKVD sadists. They were arrested at once and sent back to Moscow for a court-martial." Dunayev paused and closed his eyes.

"And?"

"And, my friend, the court-martial never happened. Suddenly the trial was terminated."

"Stalin would not allow it?"

Dunayev laughed bitterly. "Stalin never got word of it. It was the work of one very brave, unknown man, someone powerful but most of all brave, who risked his career to save a few good soldiers."

"And he's the head of the network? Who was it?"

"I don't know his name. Somehow he managed to survive. But, yes, he was the founder of this network of Party faithful who could no longer take what Stalin had done to a good nation."

"He is alive?"

"So they say."

"How can I get to him?"

"I wish I knew that. I wish I could help you."

Stone was silent for a long moment. "Can you help me to get to Moscow?"

"If you're so foolish as to go to Moscow," Dunayev said, shaking his head, "I may be able to help. I hope you don't plan to enter the Soviet Union illegally."

"Only a fool—or a professional field operative— would try that. No, I need to get there legally, and to do that I need a visa to enter. But there's no time. These things can take weeks."

"Not always. When a great and powerful German industrialist decides on the spur of the moment to go to Moscow, the Soviet Embassy is always happy to arrange the paperwork for him."

"But do you know of any way *I* can . . ."

"There is a man in the Soviet Embassy in Paris. A good, decent man—one of the network. He can arrange it."

"That's—that's terrific. But I can't wait even a few days."

"I can probably get it for you in a few hours. If I can convey the urgency, he will do it at once."

The squat, gray-haired Russian in the black leather coat came down the stairs that wound around the center atrium of the hotel, watching above and below. As he descended, however, he saw something that unnerved him.

Two French policemen were talking to the night concierge. It was too late at night for a casual chat; these policemen wanted something. Dunayev knew at once what it was. Their body language gave it away: they were showing a photograph, demanding the room number of a man they said was wanted for murder.

They were here, and they were seeking Charles Stone.

He turned and walked deliberately back in the direction of Stone's room. Now he understood. Everything was out in the open. The French police had been drawn into the search for a fugitive American who had violated U.S. treason laws.

Dunayev knocked rapidly on the door. "*Otkroi, tovarishch,*" he said in a low voice. "*Eto ya.*"

Stone opened the door, bewildered, and saw the alarm on Dunayev's face.

"*Get out!*" the Russian hissed.

55

Within a minute, Stone had finished gathering all the essentials, his passports, money, tape cassettes, checking to make sure that he was leaving behind nothing that could positively identify him.

"I'll find a way to contact you, my friend, and get the visa," he said, clasping the old Chekist's hand as he left the room and headed for the back stairs. There was, he knew, a *cave* in the hotel, a cellar in which were a bar and various hotel utility rooms. He had inspected the hotel shortly after arriving in Paris; increasingly, he understood the importance of knowing one's surroundings completely. This was the best, least-observed, way out.

He made it to the *cave*, glanced around swiftly, and found the laundry room. Its door was, as it had been earlier in the day, open. At the far end of the small chamber was a short set of steps leading to a door, which, he calculated, opened onto the tiny rue Visconti, behind the hotel.

Stone unlatched the lock and pulled the wooden door open to the dark, narrow street, which was barely more than an alley. A baby was crying somewhere nearby. He ran as quietly as he could, past a building marked VILLE DE PARIS CRÈCHE MUNICIPALE, then past several small art galleries, in the direction of rue de Seine.

"Au voleur!"

The cry came from a policeman who had suddenly spotted him. Now the Frenchman was running toward him. Stone put on a burst of speed. The policeman was shouting as he ran, calling out to others to join him. They had him ludicrously outnumbered.

He made it to rue de Seine, rounding the corner at great speed. The late-night street was almost deserted.

He saw it at once: a red Peugeot motorbike leaning up against a wall, a delivery vehicle with a yellow metal strongbox marked ALLO POSTEXPRESS affixed behind its seat. Its owner, who had evidently just gotten off, had crossed the street. He yelled when he saw Stone jump on it.

"Sorry," Stone said, turning the key and starting it up. "Right now I need it a hell of a lot more than you do."

The bike emitted a fearsome roar as Stone took off down rue de Seine, leaving the enraged deliveryboy running after him, the two policemen not far behind.

But now there was a police vehicle following. Stone

saw it in the bike's right rearview mirror, coming up rue de Seine, gaining on him, its blue light flashing, the siren wailing.

The little Peugeot accelerated remarkably well. Stone shifted into second, toward the river, to the Quai Malaquais, and pulled into traffic. *The wrong way!* He barely missed a Renault, and veered out of the road into the circular lot in front of a French Renaissance building with a columned portico, the Institut de France, and then up on the sidewalk. He had lost them!

At the Quai des Grands Augustins, he crossed the Seine over the Pont Neuf, and went into the Ile de la Cité. Behind him, though at quite a distance, he could just make out police sirens. Had he lost them? He turned right onto the Quai des Orfèvres, toward the Palais de Justice. My God! he thought. The goddamned place is full of *gendarmes*. The sirens were closer now, he realized. A second police car—which must have been radioed by the first—suddenly pulled away from the curb, heading toward him.

Stone turned the accelerator on the handgrip and made a right turn at the Pont au Change, the wrong way up the Quai de la Corse. Thank God, several cars were coming. He heard the squeal of brakes as the oncoming cars sought to avoid hitting the police car, which was then forced to pull over momentarily. He heard a crash and saw that one of the police cars had collided with an oncoming Volvo.

He had not lost them; one police motorcyclist was especially adept, and he was closing in.

Across the street, he maneuvered the Peugeot onto the narrow rue des Archives, up a slight hill, then swung around the block. He had lost his pursuer—for the time being, at least. Then he took a hard right at a brasserie called La Comète, onto rue de la Verrerie. There, on the right, was a parking garage, its vertical lettering in English. He pulled in, shut off the motor, and shoved the bike against the wall.

In a booth at the front of the garage sat a night watchman, a pudgy middle-aged man in worker's clothes.

There was no time to lose. It could be a matter of

seconds. Stone pulled two hundred-franc notes from his wallet and waved them at the man. "Get me out of here," Stone told the man in French, "and there's another two hundred in it for you."

The trunk of the car was filthy, overwhelmingly redolent of some kind of animal manure, and coated with a sludgelike grease. The watchman had grumbled, but when Stone had added another two hundred francs to the upfront price, he had acceded. Stone gave him the address, and the watchman opened the trunk of an old Renault and pointed; Stone got in. The watchman closed it after him. Crouched in the darkness, Stone heard and felt the engine start. They were moving.

But the sirens . . . !

The wail of police sirens was suddenly loud, loud enough to be heard over the roar of the old car's motor. It had to be only feet away. He felt the car grind to a halt.

The car was idling now, and there were voices.

The wait was too long. Had the police stopped the car, realizing that Stone might be inside?

With enormous relief, Stone felt the car move again, bumping over the uneven asphalt.

A few minutes later, the engine was turned off. Then there was a knock on the metal of the trunk, a few inches from his ear.

"You want out," came the watchman's gruff voice, "you give me another five hundred."

"All right," Stone said. "You've got the fucking five hundred. Just get me out of here before I pass out."

The trunk was opened, and Stone saw that he was in the courtyard of a building. He squirmed around to extricate himself but was stopped by the watchman's hand.

"Jesus Christ!" Stone said. He pulled out his wallet and fished out five hundred francs. Thank God I changed a lot of money, he thought. After handing it to the worker, he lifted himself out of the trunk and jumped to the ground. As the watchman started up the car again and pulled out of the courtyard, Stone found the stairway and walked to the third floor. To the right of the stairs, in the dim corridor, he found the apartment door he was looking for.

He pushed the doorbell, but there was no answer.

"Shit," he said aloud. It was past midnight. Would anyone be home? He glanced at the address, checking it again: 15, rue Malher. The right address; the right apartment. And what if . . . ?

He pushed the bell again, and held it in for several seconds.

The door opened. Standing in front of him, in a blue dressing gown, was Dunayev's friend the prostitute. He was surprised to see that even at night, even in bed, she wore makeup.

"Hello," Stone said.

Moscow

Shortly after midnight, Charlotte Harper was in the editing room, trying to select a "sound bite" from a lengthy interview with a soporific Soviet official on the significance of the U.S.-Soviet summit meeting in an era of such rapid changes, when the phone rang.

She was startled, because the phone rarely rang so late at night at the office. When she picked it up, she realized at once, from the static on the line, that it was long distance. Rapidly she calculated that in New York it was four o'clock in the afternoon; probably it was her editor.

"Is this Charlotte?" The hoarse female voice was immediately familiar.

"Yes. Who's this?"

"Charlotte, Jesus, I can't believe you're there so late at night. What is it, like midnight or something?"

Sometimes you can hear the voice of an old friend even after years, and it takes but an instant to recognize it. "Paula?"

"Yeah. God, I thought I'd try to reach you there. I can't believe it."

"How're you doing? I can't believe it, either. Long time."

"Charlotte, listen, I can't really talk. This is kind of complicated. I mean, it's scary."

"What's the matter?"

"It's about—well, you know who I mean if I say it's about a good friend of yours."

"I don't think I . . ." Could she mean Charlie? But what the hell would Paula know about that?

"Look, it's kind of a long story, but I don't have any way to reach this—close friend of yours. I mean, I'm guessing he might try to contact you. And if he does, I need you to give him a message."

"Paula, I don't think—" *I don't think you should be talking on the phone!* she wanted to shout. Charlotte's mind reeled, not knowing how to react, whether to listen or to keep her from talking.

"If he talks to you, can you tell him something? Can you write this down?"

"Of course—"

At her end of the line, Paula was nearly frantic. How much could she say over the phone? "Write down—that I ran a trace."

"A trace."

How much was too much? How to indicate that she'd traced the phone number on the ID card Stone gave her to an organization called the American Flag Foundation in Washington?

"Tell him—oh, Christ, Charlotte, I'm really scared for the guy."

"Paula, *please* be careful what you say," Charlotte whispered urgently.

"Charlotte, look, tell him that the guy who attacked him is connected to this group in Washington that— Well, when I ran a check on them, it turned up that it's a sort of a cat's-paw for . . . an American intelligence consortium." Oh, God, Paula thought. Was that clear? Will Charlie understand? Did I say too *much*?

Charlotte felt short of breath. "Paula, I'm going to

have to hang up. Yes, I'll tell him if I can. But we can't talk anymore. I'm sorry."

And she hung up, and for a long time she stared at the blank video screen, feeling leaden with fear, listening to the faint ticking night sounds of the empty office.

56

Moscow

Andrei Pavlichenko's black Zil limousine entered the main gate at the side of the Lubyanka, the headquarters of the KGB in Dzerzhinsky Square. The gate was opened by two soldiers in the gray-and-blue uniforms of the KGB internal-security troops. Another glanced into the limousine, confirmed that it was indeed the chairman, and saluted.

This evening's work was to be done not in his third-floor office but at another, far more secret location, deep within the bowels of the Lubyanka.

The forensics scientist who was now solely in charge of the investigation into the terrorist bombings in Moscow had asked to meet with Pavlichenko urgently. Evidently he had found something of great importance.

Pavlichenko was met at the side entrance by his aide-de-camp, who nodded and then wordlessly accompanied him to a newly installed German elevator a few hundred feet away. In front of the elevator stood a guard.

When the elevator closed, the assistant spoke. "He says it's a very serious matter."

Pavlichenko nodded and leaned against the elevator wall. The strain of the past few weeks was beginning to tell on him.

The elevator had descended several flights, and it opened onto a windowless corridor whose concrete walls had been freshly painted white. The floor was of white stone. The aide led the way, opening the second door he came to.

The room was bare except for a copper-topped bar against one wall and a white metal conference table around which were four comfortable-looking chairs. The forensic technician, Abramov, was already seated in one of them, looking extremely worried. Pavlichenko noticed that the pudgy little man was wearing a cheap gray suit that was too short at the arms and legs.

"*Tovarishch*," Pavlichenko said, walking over to him and shaking Abramov's plump hand. "What is it?" His assistant hovered close behind.

"I need to see you alone, sir."

"Certainly." He turned and said, "Thank you, Alyosha. I'll call you when we're done talking."

When they were alone, Abramov spoke. "Comrade Chairman, I'm becoming extremely concerned about what my investigation is turning up. Things are becoming more complex. More—disturbing."

Pavlichenko was alert. "Yes?"

"I had a chance to do a thorough analysis of each of the last several bombs, sir. Really did a complete run-through of the data. And I kept coming up with the same thing: the explosives are CIA-supplied, whether plastique or dynamite."

"Yes, yes, we know that," Pavlichenko said impatiently.

"But then I began to examine the other fragments from the bombs, especially the detonators, the blasting caps, the chemical pencils, and so on. And, sir—I'm sorry to say this, but the equipment is entirely of KGB manufacture."

"What do you mean to say?"

"That the bombs, sir, may have been constructed by someone within our organization. Using American explosives."

"Who else knows of this?"

"No one, sir. As you asked, I was careful to be the sole authority. Because it may turn out to be the work of one of our own. I wanted to talk to you first."

Pavlichenko stood up abruptly. "I want my assistant to debrief you fully. We need to compile a thorough file of names, of possible suspects." He pressed a button on the underside of the table. "I'm grateful," he told Abramov.

The door opened, and Pavlichenko's assistant came in. "Please come with me," the colonel said. Abramov got to his feet awkwardly and walked with the chairman's man through the door.

Pavlichenko sat alone in the room, waiting. As he went to the bar to fix himself a Laphroaig straight up, his favorite single-malt Scotch whiskey, he reflected that it had been wise to encourage and isolate this man, the only one in the KGB who had an inkling. Only in such a way could Pavlichenko be sure that rumors did not spread, that he learned who else had ideas, that no one else could get on to this. He could hear the gunshot, muffled, through the concrete wall of the adjoining room. He felt a pang of genuine remorse, hating what he felt compelled to do, what justice in fact *required*, and, grimacing slightly, he poured two fingers of whiskey.

57

Paris

The building in which Stone had found sanctuary was located in the Marais district of Paris, the old, heavily ethnic area that had recently, during the wave of renovations of the 1980s, become a highly desirable place to live. It was five stories high, a small, free-standing triangular structure, an old beige stone island surrounded on three sides by narrow streets: rue Pavée, rue Malher, and rue des Rosiers. In addition to the three entrances to the building's apartments, there were several commercial enterprises located on the ground floor, including a funeral-memorial store, an Italian restaurant, a small antique-store, a café-bar, a *boulangerie-patisserie*, and a Félix Potin convenience store, the French equivalent of 7-Eleven.

But Chief Commissioner Christian Lamoreaux of the Paris police did not know that this was the building. He knew only that the American had disappeared in the immediate neighborhood, an area heavily populated by Orthodox Jews. And so the search had begun.

Lamoreaux had been contacted by his superior, René Melet, the chief of police, who had in turn been contacted by American intelligence—the very top of the Central Intelligence Agency, Lamoreaux was led to believe—who were urgently interested in apprehending this American, who was, they learned, a rogue agent. Melet had placed Lamoreaux in charge of the investigation, urging him to use all assets at his disposal. With that sort of mandate, the assets could be considerable.

But the American bastard had eluded them, taking off down the streets of Paris like a maniacal daredevil. It would not be long, though, before they found him. The American had made the mistake of trying to disappear in the Marais.

There were a limited number of doorbells to ring, apartments to search. With the men out in full force, they would have him in a matter of hours.

"What did you do?" the prostitute asked suspiciously. "You are on the run from something. I hear the sirens."

"What is it, Mother?" A gawky teenage boy, wearing a soiled T-shirt and a pair of sweatpants, came out from behind a curtained-off room. "Who are you?" He approached Stone menacingly.

"No, Jacky," she said to the teenager. "This is a friend." She turned to Stone again. "What did you do?"

"I'm being accused of a crime I didn't commit."

"In Paris?"

"In America. It's complicated. Dunayev thought you could shelter me for the night," he said, and briefly explained what had happened.

"Why don't you turn yourself in?" asked the son, who

was trying, unsuccessfully, to grow a beard. "If you're really innocent, you should have nothing to be afraid of."

"Jacky," the prostitute said warningly.

"It isn't that simple," Stone said. "May I please come in?"

More than seventy-five police officers, reassigned for the night from the forces of the twenty *arrondissements*, were combing the neighborhood, searching the alleys and storefronts, the trash dumpsters and parks and garages. Each had been ordered to let no one pass without questioning. Two-thirds of the *gendarmes* had been instructed to visit apartments, conducting searches if there was even a slightly reasonable suspicion.

"I would do anything Fyodor asked me to do," the woman said, pouring Stone a cup of strong black coffee. "But this building is tiny. Eventually they'll get to us, and then they'll find you right away."

The telephone rang, its abrupt, piercing bell making all three jump. The woman got up to answer it.

She spoke rapidly for a minute, arching her plucked brows, and then hung up. "It's my neighbor across the street," she explained. "She says the police are searching her building for a fugitive. They've searched her apartment!"

"I need somewhere to hide," Stone said.

She drew aside the diaphanous curtains at the nearest window and peered down into the street. "She said our building is surrounded, too. I see she's right."

"What about the roof?" Stone asked, directing his question at the boy, who seemed incongruously young to be her son.

"No," the son replied, "there's no access to any other roof. Bad luck for you—the building isn't next to any other."

"You can't think of any other way?" Stone prompted. "There must be tunnels, passages—"

The son's face suddenly broke into a wide grin. "I've got an idea. Let's take the back stairs."

Stone, carrying his things, followed the teenager down a dark, narrow set of stairs and back into the enclosed courtyard. They ran as quietly as they could, knowing that any commotion could attract immediate attention now. Within a minute, they had reached the ground level.

"We have something that the nicer buildings don't have," the son explained, walking into the center of the courtyard.

"What is it?"

"Look."

Stone looked at the ground and saw a large round disc of concrete, set tightly in a round frame of steel, within a large square. It was a manhole cover.

"My friends and I sometimes go down there."

"The *sewer*?"

"I don't think you have much choice."

"No, I don't," Stone agreed. "But what's down there? Does it lead anywhere?"

"Didn't you ever read Victor Hugo? *Les Misérables?* Jean Valjean making his great escape, after stealing a loaf of bread, through the sewers of Paris?"

"No," Stone admitted. "I couldn't even get tickets to the musical."

The boy walked over to a door off the courtyard and opened it. It was a storage closet of some sort. He pulled a large iron hook from the floor and carried it over to the manhole cover, then inserted the hook into the hole at the lid's side. "Give me a hand, will you?"

Stone helped him pull back on the heavy concrete lid, which, after considerable effort, finally popped open. The two of them shoved the lid aside. A foul odor wafted from the dark opening. Stone could make out a metal ladder—actually, he realized, a row of steel handgrips that led straight downward.

"The only problem is, we can't close it after us. You can only do it from outside. We can pull it closed, but not all the way. Maybe the police will just figure it was hooligans, like me and my friends. Can you deal with the smell?" the teenager asked, a trace of defiance in his voice.

"At this point, I can deal with just about anything,"

Stone replied, as he followed the boy down into the opening.

58

The stench got progressively worse as the two descended the fifteen-foot drop. The boy had a flashlight, which he attempted to direct at the wall and the handgrips, but he succeeded mainly in illuminating the bottoms of Stone's feet. The grips were slimy and covered in rust; it was hard to get a decent hold. Stone's foot slipped from the bottom rung, plunging him without warning into the murky water.

Water it was, mostly. They had entered an *égout élémentaire*, a primary sewage-and-drainage line leading to the *collecteurs secondaires*, which are broader tunnels through which all the fluids sluice. This tunnel, about five feet wide and barely six feet high, was used to catch runoff from the gutters in the street. Floating in the water—it was so dark that Stone could not make out any hues—was street trash, empty cigarette packs, a plastic bag from Yves Saint-Laurent, a gnarled condom. The stone walls dripped with water and were webbed with pipes.

The two ran on one of the narrow concrete banks beside the wide, malodorous stream. "I'll take you as far as the main juncture," the teenager said, "so you can see where you're going. Then I'm taking off."

"I appreciate it." They were wading through the thigh-high water. "Do you have a name, by the way?"

"Jacques. Jacky."

"Nice to meet you, Jacky."

"My friends and I used to climb around in here. It gets a lot easier once you get out of the *égout élémentaire*. You can start walking on dry land when the tunnels broaden."

"You did this for fun?" Stone grimaced. The smell of excrement came in waves, as if from a neighboring tunnel.

As they walked, glimmerings of light came in through street grates and manhole covers, fluorescent light from the crowded streets above.

"Yeah. Sometimes. There's more than a thousand kilometers of canals, but it's easy to see where you are. See?" He pointed up at the wall, shining his flashlight on a plaque set in the wall: the name of the cross streets above. "You can learn it pretty fast. Make a left here."

The narrow tunnel suddenly met another, much broader one, a river with concrete banks four feet wide on either side. Jacky leaped up onto the bank, and Stone followed. "It'll be a lot easier now. We can walk on this for quite a while. Not so long ago, I heard, you used to be able to get around on boats down here, but the cops outlawed it—bank robbers used to use them for getaways."

Stone reached into his jacket pocket and fished out a pack of cigarettes. "Kill the smell," he explained, lighting one and then offering one to Jacky, who took it. He coughed. Probably he'd never smoked before.

"What'd you do, really?" Jacky asked.

"I told you. I was set up."

"Set up," the boy ruminated. "That means you've got an enemy."

"I suppose so."

"Who?"

Stone paused to inhale, and answered truthfully. "I don't really know. I've got some theories."

Jacky considered that for a moment, and then asked, "You married?"

"I don't know. I think so."

"You *think* so?"

There was a rustling sound, and a dark shape came toward them, along the concrete walkway. "Cat?" Stone asked.

"Rat."

The rat, which was larger than any rat Stone had ever seen or even imagined, scurried by, brushing up against Stone's wet pants leg. "*Jesus,*" Stone said, giving a powerful, involuntary shudder.

The boy let out a whoop of terror, and then quickly

regained his poise. "They get a lot bigger than that," he scoffed, laughing nervously. "Wait. What's that?" He froze.

"I don't hear anything," Stone said.

"Shh. There's someone else down here."

They stood completely still for a moment. There was something, faintly, a hollow noise quite unlike the periodic distant thuds from above.

Jacky shut off the flashlight, plunging them into almost total darkness. The noise became louder: Footsteps, the scrape of metal against stone. Then muffled voices.

"Can you see?" Jacky asked.

"A little bit." Stone's eyes were gradually adjusting to the dark.

"Let's walk. Keep to the wall. I think they found the open manhole cover. Damn it—now I'm stuck with you."

As they walked, Stone could hear the voices, quite distinct now, and then a flash of light played against the tunnel wall not twenty feet behind them.

"It's them," Jacky said. "This way."

They ran, each of them moving as stealthily and silently as possible, their hands raking against the tunnel wall as they went. "Turn here," Jacky whispered.

They entered a narrow tunnel, which descended at a sharp angle, wading in water that was now up to their waists. Stone felt for his passports and cassette tapes, which were in his breast pocket, still dry.

The voices grew fainter. Jacky led the way to another broad tunnel, and they pulled themselves up onto the bank. There was a splash as the water drained from their clothes. Another sound came, a few feet away: the rustle of a rat. "Shit," Stone said.

Jacky flashed his light briefly against the wall and picked out the street signs. "As long as we're quiet, they may never find us." They ran along the tunnel, which bent a few times.

After they had been running for almost fifteen minutes and hadn't heard a sound from the police, Stone said, "Let's find an exit."

"That's no problem. We need another *égout élémen-*

taire that leads to a quiet street. If we listen, we'll know which one is safe. The last thing we want is to get out on some boulevard."

"Where are we, anyway?"

Jacky flashed his light against a wall, searched for a moment, and found a sign. "Montparnasse. Intersection of Boulevard Raspail and Boulevard du Montparnasse. Right near the Montparnasse Cemetery."

This time it was Stone's turn to hear footsteps. "They've caught up to us."

"No." Jacky shrugged dismissively and glanced around. "Wait."

"You hear it?"

"Shit," the teenager said, imitating Stone's cadence.

"Let's find another *égout élémentaire*," Stone suggested.

"There's one around here. There has to be."

Now the voices were loud and distinct: several male voices, shouting to one another, "Over here!"

"I know a way," Jacky said.

"Let's *take* it already," Stone said. "Come on."

"It's near here."

"*Move!*" Stone started running along the walkway, feeling his way, his hands outstretched.

"No, wait. Over here. I know a way that I think the cops don't know."

"Bullshit."

"Maybe some of them. Not many people do," Jacky said proudly.

"Well, let's go already."

The voice came from the tunnel they had left five minutes ago: *"Do you hear that? Over there!"*

Jacky leaped off the bank and into the foul sluice; Stone followed immediately. They swam across to the other side, then got back up on the edge and ran around to another narrow tunnel.

"This is it!" Jacky whispered triumphantly.

"Where?"

"Up there. Do you see?" The boy flashed his light at a grating on the wall a few feet above their heads. "Help me up." Stone locked his hands together and used them to hoist the boy's feet. Jacky grabbed at a pipe and pulled himself up, his feet now lodged against an indentation in the wall.

"That way!" The shout was perhaps fifty feet away.

The teenager grabbed at the top of the steel grating and pulled. The top came open with a metallic squawk. The bottom of the grating was hinged; now it lay open like a trapdoor. He shimmied his way in, and Stone, taller and stronger, was able to pull himself up on a water pipe. In a minute, he, too, was in the opening. The passage was less than three feet by three feet.

"Close it!" the boy ordered.

Stone awkwardly swung his torso around, grabbed at the grating, and pulled it back up until it closed. "Do you know what you're doing?" he whispered.

"Shh."

The voices now came from the tunnel directly below. Stone followed Jacky through the passage, his knees scraping against the damp stone. They did not have to go far. After they had moved about twelve feet, there was another iron grating directly ahead. The boy pushed at it, and it came open. "Careful," he said. "Getting out is the hard part. There's a pipe just on the other side of the hole. Grab that, and you can swing yourself down." The boy reached his hands through the grate and patted them against the wall, searching. "Here." He grabbed at it, curling his hands inward, and then dangled his feet out of the hole. They had reached a cavelike place, which could not be the sewers any longer, Stone realized: no water, no odor. Something else.

Stone swung himself down easily, landing on the ground beside the boy. "Is this your idea of an exit?" Stone asked. "Where the hell are we?"

The boy clicked on his flashlight and shone it against the wall.

Stone gasped.

Straight ahead of them was a doorway that led into a chamber of some sort whose walls, on first glance, were brownish and uneven. Stone's eyes focused on the walls, seeing with terror what they were: human bones. The walls were constructed of human skulls and tibias, packed densely but neatly in gruesomely regular rows. A sign, carved in stone in the lintel at the top of the entrance, explained:

ARRETÉ!
C'EST ICI L'EMPIRE DE LA MORT

Stop! it said. Here is death's empire. They were in the Catacombs.

59

Chicago

Paula Singer was not expecting anyone.

The doorbell rang around fifteen minutes before midnight. She was watching the Johnny Carson show. There was a guest host, a comedian, and he was much better than Johnny usually was. Also, she had begun to nod off, so she had not noticed the bell until the third ring.

She tied her robe closed and looked out the front-door peephole.

It was a large man in a suit, a respectably dressed man. He had a round, fleshy face and long muttonchop sideburns.

"Yes?" she asked. Jesus, it was almost midnight. She refused to open the door unless he identified himself to her satisfaction.

"I'm sorry to disturb you, Miss Singer."

So he knew her name. "Who's there?"

"I'm a friend of Charlie Stone's," the man said. He had a foreign accent of some sort. "He asked me to give you a message."

"Go ahead."

The man laughed and shrugged. "It'll take me more than five seconds," he said. "It's cold out here."

She hesitated, and then unlocked the door. "All right," she said, an instant before the man shoved his way in toward her, knocking her to the floor.

He had a gun.

"*Please* don't," Paula said. She began to cry at once. "Please." She tried to get up, but he directed the gun at her face.

"Don't move, Paula." He closed the door behind him.

"What do you want? Please."

"Where did Charles Stone go?" The man was tall and powerful-looking, and definitely not an American.

"I don't know," she keened softly.

"Take your time. You *do* know. Please don't lie to me."

What had happened? Had she and Charlie been seen in Toronto? Maybe at the airport. Then what—

The phone calls. From her office. Was it possible— had they somehow *traced* them? Did this have something to do with the American Flag Foundation?

"Now you can get up, Paula. That's right. Walk straight ahead, slowly, slowly."

Her back was to him, and she was so frightened she could not speak. He would shoot her in the back of the head. "Why do you think I know?" she managed to blurt out. "Please, I have no idea." She walked, her knees barely able to carry her, toward the bedroom. He was going to *rape* her! Jesus Christ, she thought. Please don't let this happen. Please. Oh, God.

"Lie on the bed, Paula."

"No. Please, *no*!"

"I just want to know where he went. He was with you."

She could no longer stand it. "He left the country!"

"That's not true. Please tell me the truth." He pulled from the pockets of his suit several long leather restraints.

"Oh, God, *please* don't do this!" Why wouldn't he believe her? And then she remembered: Charlie hadn't used his real passport. What was the name he had used?

"All you have to do is be honest with me."

"*Please* believe me, he left the country. He flew out from Toronto. He—he didn't use his own passport."

The man stopped for a moment, the leather straps dangling from his left hand. He seemed intrigued.

"Where did he go?" he said again.

A thought occurred to Paula now, and her heart leaped. The gun. Charlie had given her a gun, and she had put it in the end table beside the bed. "Let me think," she said, to gain time. "I have . . . I have a copy of his itinerary. His travel-agent thing, his voucher," she faltered. "Would that help?"

The man gave a grunt.

She reached down and pulled the drawer open, her fingers sliding past the papers to the back, to the . . . There it was. She felt the cold steel, and she rejoiced.

With lightning speed she yanked it out and pointed it. The man flew at her, tackling her, and the gun *would not fire*. What was wrong with it? Oh, please, Jesus, *fire*, damn it! *Go!*

And she remembered now something about releasing a safety, but the man was on her, and she flung her knee forward, catching him directly in the groin. The man doubled over, howling in pain. He was a big, powerful man, and Paula had no doubt he was an expert, but he hadn't expected meek, cowering Paula to use a self-defense expert's blow, and that had given her a momentary advantage.

The man came back at her, but she grabbed his leg and flung him, hard, to the floor, cracking his head against the floorboards, and then ran out of the bedroom, into the kitchen.

The man was unstoppable. She had thrown him with a violence from which few people would recover, but this guy was an ox, nightmarishly strong. He came after her and slammed her against the stove, but apparently he was still weak from the kick to his groin. In the tussle he had dropped his gun; now he was using his giant, powerful hands, but Paula had him, for a moment, slamming his head against the iron top of the stove with all of her weight, his head now locked in a grip she had perfected, and just as he reached around to grab her neck, squeezing with his enormous left hand, an inspiration flashed in her mind, an inspiration born of great anger.

She remembered the rapist who had tried to violate her a year ago, and she almost trembled with the adrenaline surge. In an instant, she slammed her elbow against the burner control at the front of the stove, turning it all the way on, and the gas flame in the rear burner, against which her assailant's face was pressed, shot up. She never used the burner, because something was wrong with it, something that made the blue flame almost seven inches high.

Could she keep the hold? The man was far more powerful, and now he was an enraged bull, thrusting his body with great lurches. It took all of her strength, and she knew she could not keep this up for more than a few seconds.

The first thing she noticed, as she kept the man's neck wedged against the top of the stove, was the distinctive, sweet, unforgettable odor of human hair burning, and then a peculiar, horrifying little crackle of the man's hair, a human torch, and then, just before he overpowered her, the sight of the man's facial skin singeing and crackling, and the man roaring in unspeakable pain.

His face and head still afire, the man slammed Paula to the floor and, with an almost inhuman strength, cracked her neck. It was the last killing he would ever do.

60

Moscow

Deep within the Lubyanka, which was once, before the Revolution, an insurance company, there is a private dining room used only by the chairman and his invited guests. It resembles a cathedral: its ceiling is high and slanted, its walls constructed of oak panels and stained-glass windows expropriated from a Russian Orthodox church during Stalin's antireligious campaign of the 1930s and reassembled here in a flourish of irony.

The chairman of the KGB, Andrei Pavlichenko, was holding a private meeting with his personal physician. The doctor, who was not much older than Pavlichenko but looked ten years older, his face deeply lined, was the most eminent neurologist on the staff of the Kremlin Clinic, the hospital that treats members of the Politburo and Central Committee. The clinic is run by the Fourth Administration of the Ministry of Health, which is in turn run by the KGB.

But the physician's loyalty to Pavlichenko went much deeper than the mere lines of authority suggested. Years ago, he had gotten a woman pregnant, the daughter of a high Party official, and the resulting scandal threatened to expel the doctor from the clinic and even the medical profession. Pavlichenko had personally intervened to save his career and have the matter expunged from official records. Ever since, the physician had remained unswervingly loyal to Pavlichenko, throughout Pavlichenko's rise to the chairmanship of the KGB.

Now the two were speaking quietly, yet the tension between them was palpable.

In this very room, Pavlichenko remembered, he had once had dinner with Beria. It was March 9, 1953. He remembered the date well. He had been a young official of the secret police, and he had been taken aback when Beria had asked him to dinner in the cathedral. Especially on such a day.

Earlier in the day, Stalin had been buried. Beria had given a eulogy, and throughout his speech Stalin's son Vasili, who was drunk, had cursed at Beria, calling him a "son of a bitch" and a "swine." But Beria had been implacable. He had summoned his own forces that day, surrounded the city, and paraded his own strength, letting the rest of the leadership know who was in charge.

Pavlichenko had been integral in organizing the security forces that day, and he remembered thinking: Beria, Stalin—they're the same thing. The day will come when I will command these tanks and machine guns and troops.

At dinner that night, as the young Pavlichenko almost shook with excitement, Beria had first told him about his plans for a coup d'état. Beria wanted Pavlichenko to serve as a conduit between a Russian woman and a very rich and powerful American. There was a document Pavlichenko must get, a piece of paper that, once released, would throw the Soviet leadership into disarray, turn it inside out, pave the way for Beria. Pavlichenko listened with fascination to the details of the plan.

Beria had failed. Pavlichenko would not.

For no one—not Beria, not anyone now in the Soviet leadership—had endured what Pavlichenko had endured.

His parents had been peasant farmers in the village of Plovitsy, in the Ukraine. Their farm was tiny, consisting only of a horse and a cow and a small plot of land, but it was the time of Stalin's great collectivization campaign and his war against what he termed the "kulaks," the rich peasants, in the course of which seven million Ukrainians—a fifth of the Ukrainian nation—starved to death.

His parents were not rich, but they were classified as kulaks all the same.

And very early one morning, when he was only three years old, he, his two sisters, and his parents were carted off and loaded onto a train, all their meager belongings confiscated by the authorities. What little was left in the house was taken by the villagers. They were to be sent to a camp in Krasnoyarsk, Siberia. They were crowded into a train that teemed with other deported farmers, whose anguished cries almost deafened the young Pavlichenko.

On the way, the train stopped at a small town in the Ukraine for provisions. And there Pavlichenko's parents somehow, swiftly, abandoned him and his sisters in a crowd at the station.

The train departed without them, and the authorities, who could scarcely keep track of all their adult prisoners, took no notice of the missing children. For hours, Pavlichenko and his sisters didn't know what had happened.

Scared and miserable, they walked along a roadside, not sure where to go, asking help of passersby.

Within a few days, they found their way to a neighboring village, where an uncle took the trembling children into his house; later he adopted them.

It was not until years later that they learned that their parents had perished in the camps at Krasnoyarsk.

The young Andrei Dmitrovich, who nurtured a growing hatred for the system that had done this to his parents, remembered particularly one day in the hot and rainy summer of 1934. A terrible rain had eroded the topsoil from the graveyard where, just the year before, hundreds of villagers, who had died of starvation, had been buried. The flood washed the cadavers up into the streets and yards. Pavlichenko opened his uncle's front door and saw the ghastly corpses strewn about, seeming to reach for him, and he screamed until he lost his voice.

He had not communicated in any way with the Sanctum in several years, not since he was named head of the First Chief Directorate. This had naturally infuriated the Americans, who quite understandably salivated at the prospect of having their own man at the very heart of Soviet intelligence, but Pavlichenko had insisted upon it. It was far too risky, he told them.

He had been M-3, as Sanctum had dubbed him, for decades. Since 1950—which was virtually all of Andrei Pavlichenko's adult life—and it made his life peculiarly shadowy, for he was always looking behind him, never knowing if he would be found out.

It had all begun when, as a newly married graduate of the KGB's training school, the Vysshaya Shkola, he had made a foolish mistake. He had met secretly—or so he had thought—with an anti-Soviet Ukrainian activist in Kiev, a young man whose views he privately shared, and then suddenly an American intelligence official had snapped a photograph. He was caught. His first reaction was terror, then resentment, and then he thought it over calmly and knew it was the right thing to do.

He remembered his first meeting with his control, a man named Oliver Nyland, who was for years the chief of the CIA's counterintelligence division. They had met in London, furtively, in a location Nyland had arranged with considerable care to attract no attention.

The young, ambitious Pavlichenko had been surprised at the American's appearance: he looked like a disheveled college professor, in a poorly cut tweed suit, one button missing from his shirt. He had long shaggy gray hair that spilled over his ears, and tired hazel eyes. Not at all the image of a CIA master-spy, but, then, the reality so rarely lived up to the fantasy.

"We've had our eye on you for some time," Nyland had explained. "Ever since a relative of yours from the Ukraine emigrated and we learned the story of three children whose parents were killed by Stalin's people during the collectivization campaign in the Ukraine. Adopted by an uncle who was so thoughtful and so careful as to change your names, so that the Russians wouldn't come after you children later."

Pavlichenko had just listened, amazed at how much they had learned. Not even the KGB, which had done the standard background check before hiring him, had managed to uncover the secret of an adoption, the changing of a family name done under the table by means of a bribe. In the turmoil of the Ukraine in the early thirties, records had been lost; the KGB's internal-security operatives had naturally found nothing suspicious.

"We have the ability," Nyland had told him at the safe house in Hampstead Heath, "to smooth your way to the very top of the KGB. To provide you with secrets that will look like brilliant insight, information that will make you seem even shrewder and more farseeing than you are."

The Americans hadn't disappointed.

As soon as he agreed, they had given him detailed instructions, as well as the equipment he would need to stay in clandestine contact with his control. They supplied him with onetime pads, secreted in loaves of black bread that he bought from a certain assigned bakery on Gorky

Street in Moscow. Each page of these onetime pads, a sophisticated type of codebook, consisted of a random five-digit sequence of numbers, which he would use to encipher messages, using a matrix that was then destroyed. The code was virtually unbreakable, since the only other copy of the onetime pad was in Washington.

At first, he furnished the Americans with KGB payroll sheets or personnel records, which listed every employee in a particular subsection. Gradually he gave them intelligence assessments, and then larger secrets. He photographed these documents with a small German camera they had provided.

He transmitted the material to the Americans by means of a dead drop, leaving the film cassettes behind a loose brick near a *gymnasium* that his oldest son attended. Or he would attend a certain showing of a movie, choosing a specified empty seat and placing his coat over the seat in front of him; when he left the theater, his pocket would be one item lighter. There were, too, brush contacts on crowded buses. He would be notified that the transfer was successful by means of chalk marks on telephone poles, or sometimes fresh black tar smudges on white interior walls of the *banya* where he went to take the steam.

He was even given a telephone number, which was routed through a private Moscow apartment and rang in the office of his case officer. This number, exclusively for Pavlichenko's use, was for emergency purposes—a danger signal he had never had to use.

"It is all set, sir," the physician said. "What you will have is not a stroke per se but a TIA, a transient ischemic attack."

"Explain."

"When the day comes, you can't get out of bed in the morning. You can't speak. You can't move your right side. Naturally, you are brought to me, at the clinic. I do a CAT scan on you—that's normal procedure—and it reveals, let's say, an infarct of the left hemisphere. This is because you have a dysfunction in one of the arteries that supply your brain with blood, perhaps cerebral emboli, plaques in the vertebral or carotid arteries. You have always had this condition."

"Very good," Pavlichenko said, nodding slowly. "I shall depend upon you to make this condition known to the right people, immediately. A few words here or there; let it be known that you are treating me. Words spoken out of pride, or immodesty. I want the rumors to spread."

"As they have about your alleged heart trouble," the doctor replied.

"Exactly. But is there any way to forge the results of such an examination?"

"Yes, sir, quite easily. In the last few years, we have treated quite a number of people who have had strokes. I can take a CAT scan of someone else we've treated here, who's actually had a stroke, as well as someone else's computer-generated NICE studies—noninvasive carotid exam, an ultrasound examination of the carotid arteries—and I can simply change the dates."

"After such a stroke—is it *believable* that I would recover quickly?"

Pavlichenko's physician paused for a moment. "Yes, sir. Such a person could recover within days. It is entirely credible. The dead, sir, shall rise."

"Ingenious," the chairman of the KGB murmured.

He gazed around the dining room, at the stained-glass windows, and he knew now that his dream, and that of his people, was about to come true.

61

Paris

Stone sat on the rough gravel in the Empire of the Dead, reclining against the damp, russet bones. The air was dank, the smell acrid. He had been able to sleep for a few hours, and he awoke with a great stiffness in his back and neck.

He was waiting for Jacky to return.

The teenaged son of the prostitute was now imbued with a sense of adventure. This was his hideaway, late at night, the hideaway of his friends. Occasionally they would break into the Catacombs through the secret passage, and party for hours: drinking and scrawling graffiti on the stone walls. They found the ossuary exciting, morbid and illicit. As they got drunker, Jacky explained, some of them could even see the ghosts. The only rule they all observed was that the remains were never to be defaced.

Fortunately, none of the teenagers had decided to come in tonight and disturb Stone's sleep. Fortunately, too, he could seek refuge here for part of the next day: the Catacombs did not open to the public until two o'clock.

There would be just enough time. Stone would require Dunayev's assistance, if Dunayev was willing and if he thought it was safe. He gave Jacky his soaked Robert Gill passport and the set of three extra photos in a glassine envelope that he'd slipped into the passport's last page.

With this, Dunayev could arrange to get him a visa to the Soviet Union.

Jacky had agreed to help. He told Stone he'd spend the rest of the night at the apartment of an old girlfriend, call his mother and let her know everything was all right, and call Fyodor Dunayev. While he waited for Dunayev to procure the visa, Jacky had agreed to go on a shopping expedition. The list Stone had given him was a long one. It included such disparate items as a metal pocket comb, an inexpensive suit in Stone's size, a blazer and pair of pants, a pair of American hiking boots, a men's carry-on garment bag, a leather shaving kit, a metal tape measure, a bar of soap, a can of shaving cream, a tube of toothpaste, an assortment of toiletries, and razor blades.

It was five in the morning. If his luck held out, the Catacombs' guard would not return until after noon.

He got up, walked around, his feet crunching on the gravel. He shone his flashlight around the ossuary, admiring the morbid fastidiousness with which the skeletons had been packed. The perfectly symmetrical rows of skulls glistened by the lantern light, tight rows perched atop bundles of femurs, a mournful, deathly chorus line. In places, crossed tibias had been arranged in a skull-and-crossbones formation.

Plaques told of when the skeletons had been moved from which Paris cemetery, a process that was begun in 1786, when the Les Innocents cemetery was deemed over-crowded and unhealthy. Millions of skeletons, mainly of paupers, were transferred over the decades to the under-ground compact-storage burial ground, stacked neatly. OSSEMENTS DU L'EGLISE ST.-LAURENT, one sign pro-claimed. Another: OSSEMENTS DU SAINT-JACQUES-DU-HAUT-PAS. Here and there were inscribed quotations about death and eternity.

The Catacombs, he remembered Jacky telling him, had once been the secret headquarters of the French Re-sistance during World War II, unbeknownst to the Nazis who swaggered about Place Denfert-Rochereau above them. Compared with the brave Resistance fighters, he felt laughably insignificant. He remembered his grandiose schemes of exposing it all, forcing powerful men to co-operate in exonerating him and his late father. Dashed—all of these hopes.

The thought of going to Moscow was terrifying. The American fanatics would no doubt be able to get to him there as well. But he had no choice.

He returned to his resting place, against a column of skeletons, and before long he was fast asleep.

Moscow

Charlotte had been pacing back and forth in the corridor next to the teletypes, thinking about the dispatch she'd been working on, thinking about Charlie, thinking about the upcoming summit. Thinking about dozens of things, which meant she couldn't concentrate on anything.

For want of anything better to do, she tore off the telex printout from the Associated Press wire, and scanned it.

A name caught her eye.

Paula Singer.

A Chicago resident found dead in a fire in her apartment . . . apparently a cigarette fire . . .

She gasped and gave a shriek. The others in the office—the cameraman, the producer, the Russian employees—looked up, and the Russian woman, Zinaida, dashed over to see what was wrong.

Paula Singer, Charlotte knew, had never smoked.

Paris

A light was shining on Stone's face. He opened his eyes, blinked a few times, and, to his relief, saw that it was Jacky.

"What time is it?" Stone asked, rubbing his eyes.

"About noon. We'd better get out of here soon."

"Well?"

"Got it. The Soviet Embassy doesn't open until ten, and he was able to get a visa by ten-thirty. Whoever this guy Dunayev is, he's got—how you say?—clout."

"That he does."

"I bought you Timberland boots," Jacky said uncertainly. "Good, yes? I hear they're very good."

"Just fine."

Jacky had managed to get everything on the list. All of the smaller items he had stashed in the garment bag.

There was very little time now, and Stone worked quickly. First he would have to field-strip the gun, disassemble it entirely. He moved the slide release at the rear of the trigger guard and slipped out the magazine.

Always better to be thorough. He checked to see that there were no rounds left in it. There weren't. He decocked the gun by pulling the trigger, dry-firing it; grasping the gun by the barrel, he pushed the slide assembly back until he heard a slight click. The square breech block had dropped.

Good; Dunayev's brief tutorial had been useful.

Without releasing his pressure on the slide assembly, he gripped the slide lock, two inset pins on either side of the barrel, and pulled it down. The whole top of the gun now slid right off. He liked the feel of the Glock; it was well engineered and extremely lightweight. The whole thing was not much more than seven inches long.

In a matter of seconds, he had the gun apart. He laid the components carefully on the ground in front of him: the steel oblong that constituted the barrel, slide, and spring; the magazine, which was mostly plastic with some metal in it; and the dense-plastic receiver frame.

He picked up the plastic frame and examined it. He knew it wasn't one hundred percent plastic; the manufacturer had in recent years begun to impregnate the polymer with some steel, as a precaution against terrorism. But the metal content was so slight it would register on metal detectors as nothing more than a ring of keys. Probably, in fact, less than one key.

If it were placed in the garment bag, it would show up on the airport scanners, however, as a gun frame. Stone slipped it into the breast pocket of his suit. They didn't X-ray the passengers, of course—just the luggage.

The steel components of the gun were a much greater challenge, but the old Russian spy had provided Stone with some ideas. He placed the barrel-and-slide assembly end to end next to the magazine, which he knew held seventeen rounds and two extra 9mm Parabellum cartridges. Getting the cartridges had been much easier for Dunayev than getting the gun, since most European small arms—from handguns to machine guns—take 9mm Parabellum cartridges, and have done so since before the Second World War.

He wrapped the line of metal objects several times with aluminum foil until the package looked like a long, flat bar. This he inserted into a seam at the bottom edge of the garment bag, which he had opened by means of the razor blade. He slipped the metal tape measure between the suit and the blazer.

Next he took the bar of soap and unwrapped it. Against one of the catacomb walls he had earlier noticed a small puddle of water, which had probably seeped in from the surrounding earth. He carried the bar over and floated it in the water for a few minutes, while he uncapped the toothpaste, squeezed some of its contents out, and placed it into the shaving kit, along with the metal can of shaving cream, the razor blades, the steel cordless shaver, the metal comb, and the toiletries. When he picked up the slippery, now soft bar of soap and added it to the bag, he mushed the soap around the toiletries and the toothpaste. He inspected the goopy, unsightly mess with a proud smile, and zipped it up.

They left the Catacombs through a different way, briefly passing through the adjoining *égout élémentaire* and out through a manhole on a side street, rue Rémy Dumoncel, in front of the large illuminated green cross of a homeopathic pharmacy. Several pedestrians, startled, watched them come out.

"What the hell are you looking at?" Jacky shouted at them. "Mind your own business!" They turned away.

A block away was the car that Jacky had borrowed from his friend, a gigantic black late-1950s Chevrolet with sweeping tail fins. Placed on the back seat was an old suitcase Jacky had picked up for him and packed with clothes. The Chevy roared to life, and they were headed for the airport.

"The cops are all over," Jacky said. It was clear he was enjoying playing the coconspirator. "You can see them. Train stations, Métro stations. All over."

"Doing what?"

"Watching. Once in a while, they stop people."

"Who look like me."

"I guess so." He smiled. "Your suit is a wreck."

"The sewers can do that. Do you have any idea where you can buy wigs around here?"

"Wigs?"

They stopped at a phone booth, where Jacky made a few calls and finally located a place in the Ninth Arrondissement, Les Costumes de Paris, a large and well-known store that rented clothing and accessories to film production companies. There Stone found a men's wig, light brown with a very natural-looking sprinkling of gray. It fit perfectly. Worn over his brush cut, it altered Stone's appearance entirely; he now appeared to be a well-groomed businessman. From a wardrobe rack he selected a dark-blue American naval uniform that was somewhat baggy but respectable. He glanced at himself in the mirror.

Jacky stood by, watching. "Pretty good. But anyone who looks closely will know it's you."

"True. But the naval uniform might gain me a few valuable seconds—they'll be looking for anyone *but* a military man. In any case, it's better than nothing. What about a mustache?"

"Why not?"

He added a grayish mustache to the order, and paid the rental fee and the deposit. A lot of money for a bad suit and an ugly head of hair, he thought.

On the street, he found another phone booth and placed a call to Air France, where he inquired about the schedule of flights to Washington and, using his Charles Stone credit card, booked a flight for the following afternoon, out of Orly Airport.

He was careful to book the flight under another, false name. If he was lucky, the ruse would work. They'd believe that he had made the mistake of an amateur—clever enough to book a reservation under a false name, but forgetting that a person could be traced by means of his credit card. And they would wrongly believe that he was returning to Washington.

Or perhaps they wouldn't believe the trick at all.

He preferred not to think about that.

Then he called several of the airlines that had flights departing from Charles de Gaulle Airport.

Stone had been careful not to use the name of Robert Gill in Paris. The French police would be looking for a Charles Stone, who went by any of several aliases. Not for a Robert Gill.

At Charles de Gaulle Airport, Stone said goodbye to Jacky and, with a quick handclasp, gave his thanks. "Hold on a second," Stone said, and withdrew a crumpled envelope from his pants pocket.

"What?"

It was a wad of bills, probably more money than the boy had ever seen.

"No," Jacky protested, refusing to take the envelope. "Your money's no good here." Where had he picked that up? Stone wondered, amused. Studying B-movies?

"You risked a lot for me," Stone said. "You probably saved my life."

Jacky scowled in dismissal, but he was unable to hide a slight smile of pleasure. "I think you are out of your mind."

"Maybe," Stone said, pushing the envelope at him again. "Look, it's for your mother," Stone said. "Tell her to take a couple of nights off—tell her thanks for the help."

There was a beat of silence, and then Jacky said, "I hope things go good for you."

Stone shook his hand firmly, putting his other hand on the teenager's shoulder. "Thanks."

Then, after another long moment of silence, Jacky turned wistfully and was gone.

There were no signs of heightened security as he entered the terminal. Looking around nervously, he saw nothing more than the usual security guards.

Odd, he thought. You'd think they'd watch the airports especially closely.

He went up to the Air France ticket counter and bought a ticket on the next flight to Bonn, which departed five minutes before the Aeroflot flight to Moscow he really wanted—and, he ascertained, from an adjacent boarding gate. He paid in cash. The sales agent affixed his seat assignment to his ticket. Then he went up to the Aeroflot counter and bought a ticket to Moscow, also paying in cash, and got his seat assignment. He found a restroom and brushed his suit off, straightened his tie, and glanced at himself in the mirror. He looked a little rumpled, but no more than a military man who'd been traveling all night.

He took a deep breath, and returned to the terminal. Now came the worst part. He slowly approached the luggage X-ray check, hearing the last-call announcements for both flights.

Stone watched the long line. He was amazed to realize

that his heartbeat had begun to accelerate, his face and hands to break out in fine drops of perspiration. There could be no holdup here. If they discovered the disassembled gun, they would immediately seize him, take him in for questioning, arrest him—and soon enough discover that the man who had just tried to smuggle a gun through airport security was the very same one whom much of Paris's *gendarmerie* were pursuing so hotly.

Once again he heard a boarding call over the public-address system.

There was no time to spare.

A large noisy family—four boys and two girls all under ten—joined the line now, the children quarreling and running around their beleaguered parents. Stone could hear German being spoken. He quickly got into the line behind them, grateful for the distraction they would surely provide to the security personnel.

When the German family reached the metal-detector gate, the confusion mounted, as Stone had hoped it would. Several of the children tried to carry their luggage in through the metal detectors and had to be told by a rueful blue-uniformed security officer to place the bags on the conveyor belt so they could be X-rayed. One of the boys rapped his brother on the head with his knuckles; the younger girl started crying and tugging on her stout mother's dress. Stone caught the eye of the young man who was operating the scanner and smiled benevolently, shaking his head. The man smiled back: what a disaster, he seemed to say.

Now it was Stone's turn. His heart was hammering again, but he continued to smile good-naturedly. He placed his garment bag casually on the conveyor belt and stepped through the metal detector.

The green light flashed on.

Clear. The plastic gun frame had made it through. Thank God the magnetometer wasn't set to pick up absolutely *everything* metallic.

Then Stone saw that the man operating the scanner was peering closely at the luggage-scanner monitor. He was seized with fear.

Watching the grayish X-ray monitor, the security officer, who was already exhausted even though five hours still remained in his day, grimaced inwardly. Something metal inside this thing. He looked closely at the X-ray image and noticed something: a profusion of opaque objects in the fellow's garment bag.

"Hold it," he said.

Stone turned to look at the X-ray operator, puzzled. "What's up?" he asked, still good-natured.

"I've got to look inside, *hein?*"

"Go ahead," Stone said, forcing his smile, feeling the tension wrack his entire body. "Whatever." He felt a rivulet of sweat ooze slowly down the back of his neck into his shirt collar.

The Frenchman lifted the bag, which had emerged from the other side of the scanner, and zipped it open. He moved aside the suit and pants and located the shaving kit, which he opened at once. Glancing inside, he saw the repellent mess of oozing soap and toothpaste, a metal comb, some razor blades, what looked like a shaver. He wrinkled his nose in distaste and closed the kit, refusing to look any closer at what was obviously nothing more than the personal accessories of a not very neat man. His fingers touched something metallic, and he lifted it out: a metal tape measure. Crazy Americans. "*Merde,*" he exclaimed to himself. Aloud, he asked, "*Vous êtes américain?*"

"That's right."

"I'm going to have to put it through again, *je vous en prie,*" he said, fastening the bag and placing it at the entrance to the scanner.

He looked again at the image on the monitor. Just the filthy shaving bag and that damned tape measure. The only other metal that showed up opaque was the garment bag's steel reinforcing bar at its perimeter. Nothing suspicious; the American businessman's only crime was his slovenliness, and he let the man pass. The guy obviously was no terrorist.

As Dunayev had predicted, the barrel-and-slide-assembly-and-magazine package, wrapped in foil and inserted in the garment bag's seam, appeared merely a part of the bag's construction. Airport security personnel are trained to look within the bag's outline, and not at the outline itself. The profusion of metal objects inside the garment bag had served as distractors. Stone slowly let out his breath, and walked on.

Passport control was a series of glassed-in booths at the entrance to the gates. *If only my luck holds*, he said silently, getting in the line. Just a few minutes left now.

The ritual at passport control, as it seemed to be everywhere in the West, was perfunctory. The guard scarcely glanced at him, caring not at all that his appearance differed radically from the photograph on the passport. He stamped Stone's passport with a French visa mark to indicate that he had left the country, and then slid it through the window, smiling briefly. *"Bon voyage, monsieur."*

As he walked away from the booth, he felt the tension ebb from his body. He had made it.

He noticed a man in a blue blazer and tie, standing at the end of the passport-control area, glance at him for a few seconds too long. Am I being paranoid? Stone wondered frantically.

In the next brief, sickening moment, Stone understood that the man, who seemed to be an airport-security officer, was indeed looking at him. Too closely: examining his face with more than passing interest.

Stone had been recognized.

He was sure of it.

Don't move quickly, he told himself. Nothing is out of the ordinary. Only a scared man would run at this point. Walk with the normal hurried pace of a man late for a plane.

The man had turned to follow him. He had left his station at the passport booths and had begun to walk behind Stone.

Stone caught the reflection of the man in the plate-glass window of the corridor as he walked. Normally. Walk normally. Nothing is out of the ordinary.

There it was, the gate. It was empty; the flight to Bonn

had already boarded, and the airline personnel were lingering at the gate, waiting for any last-minute stragglers, laughing and talking among themselves.

The man was still behind him. Why didn't he catch up with him? Why didn't the man just *grab* him, get it over with?

The airline employee at the gate watched Stone's approach, shaking her head with disapproval. "It is very late, sir," she called out. "The plane is about to depart."

Stone waved his boarding pass at her. "I can make it," he said, pushing his way past her. "I'm a fast runner."

"Hey—sir!" the woman shouted as Stone ran past her, through the tunnel into the airplane.

Now!

He shoved his boarding pass into the flight attendant's hand as he entered the jet, which was full. He ran through the length of the plane, shoving aside a man who was placing a suitcase in the overhead compartment, and to the back of the plane.

Yes! They had not closed the rear exit yet; they were about to.

"Sir!" One of the flight attendants, a man, gestured toward him. "What are you doing?"

But Stone was already descending the metal stairs, clutching his suitcase, now running onto the runway. The noise of the engines was deafening. He had timed it right. The next plane on the runway was, sure enough, the white-and-blue Aeroflot, the Soviet Ilyushin 62 jet that sat there preparing for takeoff, which would be in something like two minutes. He could just make it.

Stone had lost his pursuer, running in a direction he would not anticipate. From the terminal building, he knew he was not visible, blocked as he was by the plane's girth. Mounting the exterior, service steps to the Aeroflot's jetway, he saw the surprised look on the face of the plump Soviet stewardess as he entered the plane and handed her his boarding pass. The surprise turned to disapproval.

"*Izvinitye,*" he told the woman. "*Prostitye. Ya ochen' opazdivayu.*" Forgive me; I'm running terribly late.

He took his seat, watching tensely out the window.

He was safe. The airport-security guard thought he was on the flight to Bonn, and had almost certainly called in reinforcements to delay and search the plane; by the time it was discovered that he had left it, the Aeroflot plane would be in the air.

Stone felt the engines increase their pitch, and two minutes later the plane was moving down the runway. When, another minute and a half later, the plane lifted off, Stone sank back into his seat, closed his eyes, and breathed a sigh of relief.

PART FOUR

LENIN'S TOMB

To the north of this Kremlin is the Red Square, called so, as I have said, long before the days of the Bolsheviks, however appropriate it may seem now. Against its southern border, formed by the north wall of the Kremlin, stands the comparatively humble tomb of Lenin, to which nightly march the faithful, almost a thousand strong, to view his body. Already by the ordinary Russian mind he has been canonized. And I was told by many that his embalmed corpse—quite the same in looks to-day as the day he died—is enmeshed in superstition. So long as he is there, so long as he does not change, Communism is safe and the new Russia will prosper. But—whisper— if he fades or is destroyed, ah, then comes the great, sad change—the end of his kindly dream.

—Theodore Dreiser, *Dreiser Looks at Russia* (1928)

62

Washington

The President had assembled his chief foreign-policy advisers in the Cabinet Room to make the final preparations for the Moscow summit.

Present, along with Secretary of State Donald Grant, Director of Central Intelligence Theodore Templeton, National Security Adviser Admiral Craig Mathewson, and Roger Bayliss, were sixteen staff members of the National Security Council.

Only about half of the people in the room had been invited to Moscow—a list the President had drawn up with Admiral Mathewson—and so there were, of course, some bruised egos. The hierarchy had become clear early in the administration. There were those who were going to Moscow, and those who weren't. To Bayliss, it was that simple.

And then, about halfway through the meeting, came an unexpected remark from the President concerning the outbreak of terrorism in Moscow, a remark that instantly filled Bayliss's stomach with acid.

"I'm told by some pretty reliable sources," the President said casually, "that there's more to this terrorism than meets the eye."

Bayliss's glance moved from the President to the Secretary of State to the Director of Central Intelligence. Oh, Christ. Was it out?

There was a beat of silence, until it became clear that the President was addressing Ted Templeton.

Bayliss felt momentarily dizzy.

Had the President somehow learned—impossible as it seemed—about the existence of the Sanctum? The possibility was always there; presidents always had their own private networks. If he did, there was little doubt he'd hit the ceiling. An intelligence operation of this magnitude kept secret from him! No matter that the *result* of the conspiracy would be greeted by the President—and the world—with jubilation. He'd certainly disapprove of the committee's conspiratorial methods, and then it would all be over. Decades and decades of work, of careful preparations—obliterated.

But he couldn't possibly know. No committee in the history of American intelligence had ever been as invisible as Sanctum.

"As you know," the President said, "I'm hardly a coward. I've traveled places, taken risks that made my Secret Service people go out of their skins."

The working group, knowing how gregarious and outgoing the President was, murmured appreciatively.

Trouble, Bayliss thought.

"Well, I got some information this morning," the President continued, nodding toward CIA Director Templeton, "information that frankly concerns me. About the terrorism in Moscow. Ted?"

Bayliss understood at once. Templeton looked embarrassed, chastened—like a schoolboy caught by the teacher passing a note. Somehow the President had gotten information from the CIA that didn't come from Templeton. The President must have another channel. And Templeton was no doubt embarrassed that there was information he was withholding from the President.

Yes. The President had somehow learned that the bombs in Moscow weren't just homemade things cooked up in a couple of dissidents' garages. They were made of American explosives, American plastique. Understandably, the President found that alarming.

"Yes, Mr. President," Templeton said, clearing his throat and brushing back his gray hair from his large square forehead. His face was flushed. "One of our assets in Moscow managed to turn up a few fragments of two of the bombs that went off recently. Our forensics people have determined that the plastique was American in manufacture."

Anxiously, Bayliss watched. Templeton was squirming. Sometimes Bayliss wished Sanctum had found it acceptable to inform the President of their maneuverings. Times like this, especially, when there was a risk that the President might just call the summit off. But of course that mustn't happen. Nothing at all must be allowed to alert M-3's Politburo colleagues. Nothing must make them suspicious.

The President nodded. He was in his silent, uncommunicative mode, which all of his aides found most baffling—did it signal anger? boredom? contentment?

"Mr. President," Templeton continued, "I'm not concerned."

"You're not?"

"No, sir. It's clear that the Russian terrorists must have gained access to American material. Maybe some of them are ex-soldiers who served in Afghanistan and managed to get their hands on American materiel captured during the war."

The President nodded.

"If I thought there was anything of serious concern," Templeton said, "I would certainly have brought this matter up sooner."

"Remarks?" the President suggested to the rest of the National Security Council.

"Yes." It was the Secretary of State. "I wouldn't send the President into the middle of a war zone. And I certainly can't countenance your going to Moscow at this time, Mr. President. I have the feeling Moscow is ready to explode, and I think it would be foolhardy for you to go. I think we should cancel."

"You do?" the President said.

"I have to agree," his national-security adviser said. "I don't know how much protection we can offer over there. Maybe we should run it by Secret Service."

The President nodded and cupped his chin in his fist.

For the next twelve minutes, Bayliss sat uncomfortably in his seat, watching the debate.

"If I may, Mr. President," Templeton at last put in.

"I've already expressed my opinion that Kremlin's security has matters well in hand. But there's another factor to consider: Gorbachev's position."

"Meaning?" the President asked.

"He needs all the support he can get right now," Templeton explained. "If you cancel the summit meeting, I've no doubt his prestige within the Soviet leadership will plummet. And then—well, then we've got real troubles."

"All right," the President said abruptly. "We're going to Moscow. Now, let's move on."

Templeton had won him, and the rest of the NSC, over. He'd been brilliant, Bayliss thought. It was all over now; the President's mind had been made up.

I hope, Bayliss told himself silently as the meeting proceeded, I hope that in fact nothing *does* happen during the summit. Virtually unthinkable, though. M-3 had been extraordinarily careful for decades.

Yet the man would have to be even more careful. The man called M-3, together with the group that called itself the Sanctum, was about to change the world forever.

Moscow

At approximately the same time, a black Chaika limousine was pulling up before the National Hotel in Moscow. The chauffeur, a Russian, opened the door for his eminent American passenger, a dignified old man of aristocratic bearing named Winthrop Lehman.

"Welcome to Moscow, sir," the chauffeur said.

A little over an hour later, there was a knock at the door of Winthrop Lehman's hotel suite.

Lehman, walking stiffly, opened the door with trembling hands.

There, standing before him, was a small, frail woman of middle age, accompanied by a man in a suit of Soviet cut.

"Father," Sonya Kunetskaya said in English.

After a long moment of standing at the threshold, she moved forward to embrace Winthrop Lehman. The guard hung back in the hallway, politely closing the suite door.

"*Doch' moya*," Lehman said. My daughter. His Russian, acquired decades ago, when he was a young man, still retained some fluency.

Sonya finally released her grip on her father and, her eyes not moving from him, said, "*Skoro budyet.*" It will be soon.

"I won't be around," Lehman said, his voice cracking.

"Don't say that," his daughter said firmly.

"But I won't," he said.

And then came the knock on the door.

"Soon," Sonya said, turning to leave.

63

Stone arrived in Moscow in the early evening, shuffling into the dark Sheremetyevo Airport building in a long line of tourists, most of them German.

The airport was gloomy and ill-lit. Constructed in the late seventies by the West Germans for the influx of foreigners expected at the 1980 Summer Olympics, it was sleek and modernistic as only a German structure could be: a great, spacious expanse of black-rubber-tiled floor beneath a high vaulted ceiling made of patterned metal tubes. Had all the lights in the ceiling been turned on, the airport would have blazed; instead, the Soviets, in the interest of economy, kept most of them off.

Stone's body was stiff with tension. He knew that if an enterprising customs inspector found the disassembled gun it was all over.

He found a restroom and brought his garment bag into a toilet stall. There he swiftly reassembled the pistol and put it in his suit pocket.

Minutes later, Stone was seated in the front seat of an old black Russian automobile, a Volga, whose windshield bore a blue Intourist-insignia decal. The taxi ride from the airport to the hotel was provided by Intourist free of charge, and was not optional.

The driver said nothing as they motored down a stretch of highway lined with scrubby woods and an occasional placard marked with red-and-white Cyrillic lettering. In a little over half an hour, they were on Tverskaya Street, formerly Gorky Street, one of Moscow's main thoroughfares, and then, when the Kremlin loomed just up ahead, they turned right and pulled into a parking space in front of the National Hotel.

The hotel dated from before the Revolution, one of very few remaining pre-Revolutionary hotels in Moscow, where, Stone remembered once reading, Lenin had lived in 1918 for several months while his rooms at the Kremlin were being restored.

From the street, it was a plain-looking building of brown stone. Russians in fur hats and shapeless coats strode past briskly. The driver pulled the taxi up to the front of the hotel and shut off the motor.

"Wait," Stone said.

The driver turned around questioningly.

"Where can I change money?" Stone asked in Russian.

"The Intourist office on the next block."

"Is it still open tonight?"

"For another hour."

"Take me there, please."

The driver shrugged, started the car up, and maneuvered back around to Tverskaya Street.

When Stone had changed some of his cash into rubles, he returned to the taxi and paid him. "All right, I'm all set. I'll walk to the hotel."

The driver furrowed his brow. "Do what you want," he said, pulling away from the curb.

Stone stood on Tverskaya Street for a few minutes until a gypsy cab, no doubt identifying Stone as a foreigner, came to a halt. The car was also a Volga, but this one looked at least twenty years old.

Stone got in and gave the address.

The cab drove past the Kremlin, on Marx Prospekt,

and then on to Kalinin Prospekt, across the Moscow River at the Hotel Ukraine, to Kutuzov Prospekt. Stone looked out the window at the sights they passed: seeing Moscow for the first time, after hearing about it for so long, was somehow like visiting the set of a movie you have seen many times before.

The city had an air of unreality, larger than life, drabber and grayer than he had expected, the streets broader and ill-lit. They approached a massive ecru stone building. In front, a uniformed guard stood in a booth. He exchanged a few words with the driver, and then the driver turned around. "He says I've got to let you out here."

Stone got out and paid the driver; then, once again checking the address he had written down, he found the right entrance number, and the apartment number.

There was no doorbell; he knocked.

She opened the door.

He was not prepared for her beauty. Certainly he had thought about her quite a bit in the last few, desperate weeks, remembering what she looked and sounded like in New York, wondering whether she would shut the door on him, just as she had hung up when he'd called from Toronto.

But he had not remembered how astonishingly alluring she was. Her blond hair shone in the dim light from the hallway; her high cheekbones were even more finely sculpted than he remembered.

"Charlotte, I need your help," he said.

64

Washington

The Director of Central Intelligence, Ted Templeton, was the first to speak. He looked purposefully around the black marble table, first at the younger members of the Sanctum—his deputy, Ronald Sanders, and Roger Bayliss of the National Security Council—and then, a respectful smile on his face, at the older members: Evan Reynolds and Fletcher Lansing, the legendary ones, the best and the brightest.

"What I don't understand," he said, "is what would possess him to go to Moscow. Of all places."

Fletcher Lansing immediately raised his still-strong chin, and interrupted. Lansing's voice was hoarse, his elocution precise and mid-Atlantic. Bayliss was reminded of movie actors of the 1930s. "Out of the frying pan—" Lansing began.

"In heaven's name, why would this surprise you?" asked Evan Reynolds irritably. "It seems perfectly logical to me. His trail seems to lead right there—as if he intends to find the evidence that might exonerate his father and himself. That's not worth discussing."

"I *hope* it's personal," Lansing said. "Unless he's *really* gone rogue—defected to the Russians, selling what he knows . . ."

"If the man is in the Soviet Union," Reynolds said, "it's all the more urgent—imperative, in fact—that he be found and neutralized at once."

Bayliss found himself glancing around the chamber; he could not help thinking, even at this time of great tension, that he was overdressed. It made him feel all the more out of place. Most of these men had on the almost worn-out, fashionless blue suits of old money. Whereas Bayliss was wearing a charcoal-gray Italian sharkskin suit that looked quite as expensive as it was, a yellow-and-blue-striped silk Metropolitan Club tie, and an elegant pair of snakeskin loafers as thin as tissue paper. He was perfectly aware that he looked like a young man on the make.

And he reminded himself, as he did often, why he was there, why he'd been invited to serve on this super-secret committee: he was one of the few members of the National Security Council who received not only the NID, the top-secret National Intelligence Daily, but the far more secret PDB, the President's Daily Brief, ten pages of the choicest intelligence—which very few in Washington were privileged to see. The committee needed a man in the White House. They also needed someone to serve as a link to Malarek, M-3's man in Washington.

That they now had. And more: Bayliss had set things up so that the American Flag Foundation bugged the White House's unsecured lines (to make sure no secrets had been leaked) and, more important, kept Malarek under close telephonic surveillance. Never take chances.

Now Bayliss knew what they were about to ask. Three minutes later, it came.

Fletcher Lansing glanced briefly at Bayliss, then looked away. "Mr. Bayliss will have to contact Malarek. M-3's people can do the job."

"No," Bayliss said hoarsely.

There was a long, shocked silence. Bayliss reddened visibly. "You want me to order Charles Stone's death," he said.

"We want you to inform M-3 that Stone is in Moscow, assuming his people don't know." Lansing spoke softly. "That's all."

Bayliss could feel four pairs of eyes on him. "There's too much I don't know," he said haltingly. "I know you—we—have been running a mole. Okay. But how *sure* can we be about this . . . this M-3 . . . ?"

This was, Bayliss knew, a shocking violation of Sanctum protocol. You didn't ask questions, call into doubt the wisdom of the elders. The long silence was punctuated by the hum of the ventilation equipment.

"I don't think he needs to know the details," Sanders said, hunching his shoulders as if he were still quarterbacking his college football team.

"He's in this with us," Fletcher Lansing said. "A very valuable member of the team, I might add. Ted?"

"M-3 is the Agency's greatest secret since the days of Bill Donovan," Templeton said. "Bigger, even. Too big even to be entrusted to the Agency's own personnel. His name is Andrei Pavlichenko."

Bayliss's eyes widened. "Oh, my God."

"The Pavlichenko file is so ultrasecret," Sanders put in, "that it's not even referred to on the most highly secret, limited-access computers within the Agency."

Templeton continued: "Pavlichenko was a young, rising star in the Soviet intelligence service in 1950 when he was approached by one of our people."

"How the hell did you manage to press him into service?" Bayliss asked. "What did you get on him?"

Lansing gave Templeton a significant glance, and nodded.

Templeton nodded in return, and said: "We learned that he'd been concealing his background. His parents were deported, murdered, by Stalin's people, and he was raised by a relative. Never would have been let within a thousand yards of the Lubyanka if anyone knew it. So this guy works his way up, I mean fast, and soon he's the chief assistant to Beria, Stalin's boss of the secret police. With our help, obviously."

"That means he's secretly a Ukrainian sympathizer," Bayliss said. "In essence, an enemy of the state."

The elderly Evan Reynolds replied: "It's not the first time someone like that has made it into the upper echelons of the Soviet leadership. Don't forget about Petro Shelest, who masqueraded as an unshakable supporter of Russian dominance over his own Ukrainian people, a dedicated member of the Politburo. Only later was he uncovered as a secret Ukrainian nationalist."

"But, Ukrainian or not," Lansing interjected, "the point is that he's fiercely opposed to the whole damn Soviet system—a system that murdered his family. That's what we can count on."

"And you gave Pavlichenko chicken feed," Bayliss said, using the intelligence jargon for genuine but minor secrets provided to nourish moles.

"Morsels, table scraps here and there," Templeton said. "Not so much that it would draw suspicion to him, but enough to make him look awfully impressive. We'd tell him how a president was thinking on something, as long as it didn't harm our interests. And, once in a while, bigger stuff, too. Advance warning on several air strikes in Vietnam. We've even had to blow some of our intelligence operations. Even Bay of Pigs, when we saw it was destined for failure . . ."

"Enough to give him a boost up the ladder," said Fletcher Lansing, "without damaging our own interests in any serious way. Just enough to make him seem terrifically shrewd."

"And how do you know this guy isn't going to turn out as bad as Beria?" Bayliss asked.

Lansing interlaced his fingers and made a tent. "We don't assume the power struggle will be bloodless, Mr. Bayliss. It's not like electing a president, you know. But we admire his vision: we have, in the past, been in touch with him through intermediaries. In the last few years—since his elevation to the Politburo—Pavlichenko has evidently deemed it unwise to allow any communications whatsoever."

"His *vision*?" Bayliss asked.

"Do you know about Kievan Rus'?" Lansing said. "You are a Soviet specialist, are you not?"

"I was a Soviet-affairs specialist in graduate school," Bayliss said. "Not Russian."

Lansing shook his head in mild disapproval. "It's hard to know anything worthwhile about the Soviet Union and not know Russian history intimately. In the eleventh century, what is now Russia was then a political entity, a nation-state, known as Kievan Rus', ruled by Prince Yaroslav, also known as Prince Yaroslav the Wise. It was the first Russian state. Kiev, in those days, was the seat of Russian power—you know, of course, that Kiev is the capital of the modern-day Ukraine."

"That I do, sir," Bayliss retorted.

"Well. Kievan Rus' maintained close and friendly ties with the heads of the European nations; it was a decentralized, loosely held federation of areas. There was much trade. It was the birthplace of the Russian enlightenment."

"I see," Bayliss said, as the significance of Lansing's history lesson began to dawn on him.

"Pavlichenko," Lansing resumed, "as a fervent Ukrainian patriot whose parents were taken away from him and murdered by Stalin's forces, has all his life cherished a vision of tearing down the old and starting over. He sees himself as—well, I suppose, a modern Yaroslav the Wise."

"But Gorbachev's already making serious changes," Bayliss objected.

Templeton spoke, sighing petulantly as if Bayliss were a tiresome child. "Gorbachev, as we've discussed a thousand times, is short-term. He can't last—*won't* last. And then—a matter of months, maybe weeks—his enemies do away with him, and we've got a right-wing, neofascist Soviet leadership that will be dangerous. We can't take that chance. We can't put our eggs in that basket."

Bayliss nodded, transfixed.

"But if we give Gorbachev a chance—" Bayliss began.

The Director of Central Intelligence cleared his throat. "Roger, Gorbachev has had it. It's time to put our man in. If we wait any longer, history will pass us by. And then we're back to the Cold War."

"But *how*, exactly, does Pavlichenko plan to seize power?" Bayliss asked.

"We don't know, Roger, and frankly we don't care. But all the signals are that it will happen soon, probably within six months. Sometime after the Moscow summit. Now, some of us will be going to Moscow in a matter of hours. While you're there, get a good look around you, because things are going to be different when you return on the TWA Washington-Moscow shuttle. Next time our President goes over there, I predict, he's going to be negotiating with a different man."

Bayliss nodded. "I'll contact Malarek," he said, "the moment I leave." He nodded again, swallowing, and smiled at the rest of the Sanctum. "Thank you. I appreciate it." He shot his cuffs, felt his chest tighten. "Thank you."

65

Moscow

Charlotte gasped.

"What are you *doing* here?" she whispered harshly, her face burning with anger. "What's *happened* to you?"

"I need you, Charlotte."

"*God damn you.* God damn you. What did you do? For Christ's sake, what did you *do*?"

Stone tried to take her hand, but she pulled it away, glowering.

"The place looks great," Stone said gently, looking around at her living room. The apartment was furnished in her simple but elegant taste, spare but neatly arranged, the pale-peach couch and chairs complemented by the ocher Oriental rug. "Sort of like the place where we spent our honeymoon. Only you forgot the heart-shaped bidets."

Charlotte didn't laugh. She looked back at him, forlornly.

"Why did you hang up on me?" he asked.

"*Jesus!* We can't talk here!" She pointed a finger toward the ceiling. He watched her, taking in her fragrance, her poise.

He found himself marveling, as he so often had in the past, that he was married to this woman. He felt a spasm of guilt, too, that he could ever have hurt her.

"Where can we talk?"

"Let's go for a walk," she said icily.

She put on her coat, and they walked out of the building, toward the street, passing the stout uniformed guard, who nodded at Charlotte without smiling, looking closely at Stone.

She strode confidently. This was, in many ways, her

city, and Stone could sense it immediately in the way she navigated purposefully, yet unthinkingly. The time apart had done good things for her. She seemed to possess an inner calm, a confidence she'd never had before. He wondered whether she had closed him out. Whether it was too late.

The streets were cold, with a few drifts of discolored snow, remains of a recent snowfall that had melted and then refroze. Several of the buildings were festooned with long red banners proclaiming the Revolution Day ceremony that was to take place in two days.

"You must have a million things going on," Stone said as they went down the street. "With the summit, I mean."

She seemed relieved to be able to talk about her work: it was safe, neutral. But at the same time, she seemed reserved. Was it resentment? Or something else? "The President's party arrives tomorrow," she said. "There's really not much to say about that—we'll shoot tape of the arrival at the airport, I'll do a stand-up. There aren't that many press conferences or briefings. Then, the day after tomorrow, we'll get some footage of the whole she-bang, the President standing next to Gorbachev up on Lenin's tomb. Great photo opportunity, as the politicians say."

Watching her, he was momentarily overcome with affection, and he slipped an arm around her. She seemed to stiffen.

"Charlotte, why did you hang up on me?"

"Come on, Charlie. They tap correspondents' phones."

"You were protecting me."

She shrugged. "Least I could do."

He told her what had happened, virtually everything—from Alfred Stone's murder to the frenzied chase in Paris. Charlotte interrupted only to tell him about Sonya.

Stone stared. "So she *is* alive." He shook his head, smiling, elated to see his hunch confirmed.

"And now I know what she was concealing," Charlotte said. She felt alternating waves of love and anger. He had a claim on her, knew her as no one else did, and yet he seemed impossibly distant. Even in a few short weeks, he had changed: he'd become weary, scarred, cautious, constricted.

He told her about Dunayev, the NKVD defector in Paris, and the defector's story about the Katyn Forest Massacre and the network of Old Believers. Charlie was exhausted, but the story tumbled out, urgently and even coherently.

They were at the deserted banks of the Moscow River. Charlotte had listened for twenty minutes, occasionally interposing a question.

She took his hand and gave it a quick squeeze; he held on with a strength and firmness that she found comforting. She felt something down below, a surge, a warmth and a weakness that arose, she knew, from aching to make love to him, and that confused her hopelessly.

Now she turned and faced him. "I didn't believe you at first, you know."

"I understand. It sounds crazy, I realize."

She stared ahead at the Stalin Gothic hulk of the Hotel Ukraine. "It really did. First your father. And then, yesterday morning, I read a news item that came across the Associated Press wire." She paused, not knowing how to say it, and then she blurted: "Charlie, Paula Singer is dead."

Stone was leaning against a low concrete wall, and for a moment, Charlotte thought he hadn't heard her, or maybe didn't understand, but then he seemed literally to crumple, to slide to the ground, his head buried in his arms.

"No," he said, his voice muffled. "I was so goddamned . . . careful. I was . . . She must have done something to . . ."

And Charlotte, unable to stand there any longer, sank to the ground and put her arms around him.

Stone watched, as if through a scrim, Charlotte cross the street to a phone booth.

He felt a lump rise in his throat, a rush of love for her. Some minutes earlier, Charlotte had told him about what Paula had discovered just before her death.

Her information was vital. Now everything was beginning to make sense.

His attacker in Chicago was connected to an organization that did the dirty work the intelligence agencies were prohibited from doing. Did that mean that the Agency had gone after him, one of their own? What else could it mean?

And then Charlotte had revealed the leak she'd gotten from a source in the KGB that the CIA was behind the bombings in Moscow.

Another piece of the pattern. But now she needed to know more from Sergei. Was there anything else her source had discovered?

She had to contact Sergei directly. A terrible risk—a quick phone call very late at night—but she'd be as careful as she could be. They had no choice.

He could see her hang up the phone and make another call, gesturing as she spoke, her motions agitated, distraught. Then she hung up again, this time with great force.

And called out to him.

"Charlie!" She was now running across the street toward him. Her voice was high and frantic. "Oh, God."

"What is it?"

"*He's* dead."

"Who?"

"Sergei. Oh, God. My source. I called his private number at work—he works late at night. Normally I only have to say a word or two, so it's safe—but someone else answered the phone. So I did something I've never done before: I called him at home. And his wife answered. I told her I was a colleague of his from Latvia, to explain my accent, and she told me he was *dead*. Killed in an explosion at the lab."

"*When?*"

"I don't know." She had begun to cry. "It must have just happened. But I said I wanted to go to the funeral, you know—I didn't know what else to say—and she said the body had already been cremated without her knowing.

One day he was there; the next day she had his ashes in an urn."

"Executed," Stone said tightly.

Charlotte suddenly threw her arms around Stone, squeezing him tightly. He could feel her tears hot against his neck, her breathing heavy. "He was *caught* in it," she said. "The same thing that killed Paula."

Stone held her for a long time. At last he spoke. "I don't want you involved."

"Do I have a choice?"

"Yeah. Yeah, you have a choice. I'm cornered; I have to fight. And, sure, I want your help, your contacts, your brain. But I don't know what I'd do in your place."

"Oh, hell, sure you do," she shot back angrily. She gripped his shoulders as if to shake him, but only stared intently into his eyes. "No, Charlie. Damn it, I don't think I do have a choice. After what happened to your father— well, that changed everything for me. Everything's changed. What kind of person do you think I am, that I could possibly turn away from you now?"

He moved his face close to hers, and then kissed her.

"I love you," he said.

She looked at him, startled. Then she pulled away from him and dabbed at her tears with the back of her hands. "So what are we going to do?"

He bowed his head, and then looked up at her. "Listen, Charlotte . . ."

"Charlie," she said brusquely, suddenly all business, as if the moment had not passed between them. "What are we going to do?"

After a pause, he replied: "Lehman's daughter is one of the keys. I may be able to force her to reveal more than she wants. More likely, I can use her to get to *others* who can help."

She nodded.

"But the first order of business is to try to get to whoever's the head of this Old Believer network."

"For what?"

"Because we—I—need help. I can't be in this alone any longer."

"But you don't have a name. You don't have anything."

"That's why I need you."

"But you can't just walk around talking to Russians and asking them if they *happen* to know anyone who was sent up for a secret court-martial during World War II, and then, if they do, if they *happen* to know the name of the man who terminated the court-martial. Charlie, that's the sort of thing that's not public. Sure, Moscow's admitted its guilt in the Katyn Forest Massacre—but I'd be shocked if the records aren't locked up. This is a nation where just about everything is a state secret."

"There has to be some way."

"Who do you think this guy is? Some sort of dissident, maybe—someone like Andrei Sakharov was, who's well connected? Maybe a Party leader who was once thrown out of office, now in disfavor, nursing his grudges?"

"Anything's possible. But there have to be records. At Parnassus, they always kept us insulated from sources and methods; I wouldn't know. But you know this city better than anyone, and if you can't—What?"

Her eyes were wide, and she was suddenly smiling broadly. "Records," she said under her breath. "Yes." She reached over and kissed him briefly on the cheek. "I think there's a way. I can try tomorrow, first thing."

"Charlotte, if you can, that's tremendous. But there's just no *time*."

"I'll do my best."

"If anyone can do it, you can."

"Well. Tomorrow afternoon, the President's arriving. I can ask my producer to attend the briefings for me; there's not going to be anything big happening, anyway. It's unusual, but she'll do it."

They had turned around and were heading back in the direction of Charlotte's apartment building.

"We need to put together the pieces," Stone said. "What do we know? That the CIA, or maybe some faction of it, is involved in backing, or initiating, a wave of terrorism in Moscow. Linked to an impending coup, in which their asset, M-3, will seize power. Yes?"

Charlotte nodded, listening intently. "Yes. And the wave of terrorism is causing the same sort of havoc that the release of the Lenin Testament might have done a few decades ago."

Stone spoke rapidly now, his words flowing into hers. "We know this M-3 was linked to Beria and to Lehman, through Lehman's daughter somehow. But I still don't get it."

"So what's being planned? What sort of *incident*, if there's going to be an incident?"

"Maybe it's some sort of armed action, a military assault. Every indication tells us it will take place on Revolution Day, during the summit."

"When the President of the United States is there, right?" Charlotte said. "So that, if something happens, maybe it will be seen as directed against the President? Is that *possible*?"

"Yes. That makes a lot of sense."

"If there's an attack on the Soviet leadership, it will have to be coordinated by someone who's got the power to do so, right?"

"Of course. Someone in control of the army, maybe, or the air force. A general."

"Like who?"

"M-3 could be any one of twenty or thirty people," Stone said quietly. "Any of whom is in a position to coordinate a seizure of power. Could be anyone, from the Politburo to the army to . . . yes."

"Huh?"

"In 1953, Beria planned to be absent on the day of his planned coup, probably to marshal his forces. If he was on the scene, he couldn't seize the others, so he *had* to absent himself."

"So?"

"Okay. What if M-3, whoever he is, really *is* planning a coup on Revolution Day. Wouldn't he, too, be absent?"

"Possibly, Charlie, but by the time we see who's absent at the ceremonies, obviously it'll be too late."

He smiled. "Maybe not. Listen to this. Revolution Day is the biggest state ceremony the Soviet Union has.

The biggest deal by far. You don't miss it unless you're on your deathbed. I remember seeing footage of Leonid Brezhnev up there on Lenin's tomb, about to totter over. People say he was out in the cold so long up there that he caught a cold and died. If you're absent, it's a sign that you're out of power, so no one just happens to stay home."

"So far I follow you."

"Okay. If the Politburo gets wind that someone important isn't at the ceremonies, they've got to be suspicious, maybe send someone to check on the man's whereabouts. Right?"

"You're the expert, Charlie. I just report the stuff."

"So what would you do if you wanted to be absent on such an important day believably?"

"Get sick. Really sick."

"Suddenly?" Stone prompted.

"Probably not. Ah, I see. God, you're good. I'd have been sick for a while, so when I sick out, no one blinks an eye."

"Exactly."

"And how does this help us?"

"You're the reporter. All I ever did was analyze the information. You tell *me*."

"Medical records," Charlotte said.

"Yes!" Stone almost shouted. "Do you remember when Yuri Andropov was dying, only the world was told he had a cold?"

"And he really had kidney failure," Charlotte said. "But the word was out on that."

"This is a city of rumors; rumors is how information is spread."

"Yes, Charlie. Yes, I have a source."

"Who?"

"One of my predecessors had a source in the Kremlin Clinic. A doctor who treated Yuri Andropov. And—because he believed that openness was the only right thing— he leaked information about the state of Andropov's health."

"And this source has access to the medical records of

the leadership," Stone whispered. "But how do you get to this guy?"

"Come on, Charlie. Give me credit. I'm not the best-connected journalist in Moscow for nothing. Do you think I wouldn't get to meet the guy?"

"You're amazing."

"You know I want to do whatever I can to help," she said. "For the memory of your father. And, damn it, for you, too."

He bent toward her and kissed her, and, to his surprise, she kissed back. Then abruptly she stopped.

Stone spoke first: "Someday you'll find it possible to forgive and forget."

She looked at him penetratingly and did not reply. Her eyes had filled with tears.

His words were now choked and awkward. He moved his face slowly, slowly toward hers, and all the while he looked directly in her eyes. Softly and tentatively he touched his lips to hers, waiting for a response, and when one came, after a moment's hesitation, he was instantly aroused, and his heart felt like it was being squeezed.

"Hey," he managed to whisper, "you need a little sugar?"

The feeling of making love to her after so long! It was as if she were both a stranger and his oldest friend. Her body felt completely different, and then, just when he was forgetting how long he'd known her, he'd feel something, she'd move in a certain way, murmur something that brought it all back. Her resistance of just a few hours ago had been so erotic: she had pushed him away. Once, years ago, she had folded her arms against her breasts as if she were embarrassed by them, although they were beautiful; now she lay back on the bed, arching her back in pleasure, and her breasts were firm and erect and almost perfectly rounded, and she seemed to have lost all her inhibitions, everything. He ran his hands over her, cupping her breasts and sucking them, biting gently on her nipples, exploring her with familiarity, yet unfamiliarity: immediately he remembered all the secret places where she liked to be touched, the rhythms she liked in lovemaking.

In the early days, Charlotte thought, he made love like a boy: a quick, urgent penetration, a rapid copulation, explosive ejaculation, and it was all over. But now there was such a closeness, an understanding between them, in the way they caressed and sucked and kissed. Through a rush of blood, a roaring in her ears, she could hear Charlie moaning softly, the vibration of his deep voice rumbling against her stomach. She moved, as if intoxicated, trying not to give in, resisting, and then she felt an orgasm that started as a wide, hot wave cutting into her thighs and then widening until she gave in to it and it took her over. For the first time in years, she felt completely safe.

For a long time, they lay there together, spent. Later they got up and shared a bottle of wine. At first their conversation was awkward. Stone kissed her; she slid her hand down his chest. "I forgot what your chest feels like," she said. With her other hand, she massaged the back of his neck. "I wish your hair weren't so short." She looked at him for a long while and added, "I'm glad you're here."
Stone kissed her. "So am I."
"But I'm kind of confused."
He laughed. "I know. That's good."
He felt her warm, soft body beneath his; she felt the hard strength of him, pressing against her. And then she felt him beginning to stir, and he was in her once again, moving agonizingly slowly, teasingly, and she was suffused, for the moment, with a delicious contentment.

In the early morning, Stone awoke from a dream—a terrible, disturbing, guilt-wracked dream about Paula Singer—and saw that the bed was empty. Charlotte was gone.
He felt a dull thud of fear, and then recalled that she had gone out to place a call to another of her sources. He rolled over and lapsed immediately back into his troubled sleep.

A short time later, Stone awoke again, and felt Charlotte climbing in bed next to him. He wrapped an arm around her waist, felt her warmth.

"Charlie," she whispered. Her lips were practically against his ear; she spoke almost without exhaling. "I know a guy we could talk to."

"Mm-hmm?"

"I think he's probably a Company man. If Saul Ansbach was right that at least some of the Agency's involved, maybe it's worth the risk to talk to him."

Stone, no longer sleepy, nodded, his eyes alert.

"Use him as a conduit, maybe," she continued in the barest of a whisper. "Lay it all out before him. If he's involved, we'll know it at once."

"Yes," Stone whispered back. "Only, to be safe, we'll lay out just enough to determine that he's *not* involved." Was the place bugged, really? he wondered. And could electronic bugs pick up whispers? He picked his watch up from the bedside table and looked at it. "We've got thirty, maybe thirty-two hours, I calculate. But I think . . ." He hesitated, not wanting to scare her. "Given the resources of the people who've been after me, it won't be long at all before they track me to Moscow."

"If they haven't already."

"Yes," he whispered. "If they haven't already."

66

November 5

The Kremlin Clinic, a five-story classical building of red granite adorned with fake Greek columns and a cupola, sits behind a high iron fence in the center of Moscow, near the Kremlin and across the street from the Lenin Library. It is here that members of the Soviet *nomenklatura*, the elite, receive medical treatment. Everything is high-security here, and the doctors are carefully vetted—so carefully, in fact, that many of the most talented specialists are disqualified on the grounds of ethnic background or suspected unreliability. For this reason, the Kremlin Clinic, which is run by the Fourth Administration of the Ministry of Health, may have the best and most expensive equipment and pharmaceuticals but often doesn't provide the best health care. Many of the physicians are in fact of mediocre talent.

But there is the occasional exception. Aleksandr Borisovich Kuznetsov, a specialist in internal medicine at the Kremlin Clinic, was in his late forties. He was skilled and quick-thinking, and that was more than the majority of his colleagues were, but at the same time he was self-effacing, so he rarely excited enmity.

A mere ten years after finishing his internship at a hospital in Leningrad, he had been chosen to serve at the Kremlin Clinic, to minister to the most powerful men in the land. He knew this was an enormous honor, and his generous salary reflected that—because privilege always went hand in hand with money in Russia. He also knew that he had been selected not for his medical expertise but for what people thought was his political reliability—his father had served in a minor position in the leadership under Stalin, and the mere fact that he had survived for so long was testimony to his father's orthodoxy.

But Aleksandr Kuznetsov was not quite who his Party comrades thought he was.

He loved the practice of medicine, and although his friends and colleagues looked upon him as a good Communist, he had nothing but contempt for what remained of Soviet Communism. For reasons of pure science, and because he believed in doing one's best to cure even the loathsome, he was an outstanding doctor in the clinic, really above reproach, but there were days when he would not have been unhappy if the Politburo and Central Committee oafs he looked after all perished at once.

And then there would be days when he'd joke with the frail, aging men, sitting naked on the examination table, and feel nothing but pity for them.

Kuznetsov had been in this hospital, across from the Lenin Library, for eight years, and before that he had been at the more gracious installation at Kuntsevo, where he had been among the team of doctors who took care of the dying Yuri Andropov. Through close and trusted friends in whom he had confided his dissatisfaction with things—although even with close friends he was circumspect—he had met a few Western correspondents, and when Andropov's kidneys first began to fail, he had gotten the word out to them.

He had thereby, quietly, become one of the foreign correspondents' "sources" in the Kremlin Clinic, though probably not the only one. He did it not because he wanted to hasten Andropov's death, far from it, but because he deplored the secrecy that shrouded the health care of men at the very top. The Russian people, he felt, must always know what was going on with their leaders. Far too often they were kept in the dark, and this only gave rise to awful rumors. He remembered when Konstantin Chernenko died, and the Politburo—desperate to select a leader and settle the succession issue—withheld the news for three days. Secrecy was for the birds.

But, even so, Charlotte Harper's request was a little unusual. Late last night, after midnight, she had called, pretending to be his cousin Liza from Riga. She had called him by his nickname, Sasha. This prearranged signal was intended to explain, to anyone who might be listening, the origin of her non-Russian accent. She spoke Russian excellently, almost as a native, but there was still a trace of an accent. No matter; there were dozens of accents in the Soviet Union. "So we're going to meet tomorrow at five at the Tretyakov Gallery," she had said. It was a signal that took him a few moments to remember: it meant they would meet at seven in the morning near the Leninsky Prospekt metro station, which was remote and safe enough.

This time, she wasn't asking him to find out the status of some leader who was dying. She wanted him to look through the medical records of each of the members and candidate members of the Politburo, nineteen men and one woman, to see if any of them had a history of some serious medical condition that wasn't publicly known. It was an odd request, but it would not take much time, and so he had agreed.

Yes, he said, he could do it safely, without arousing too much suspicion, if he had a good enough pretext.

He would try.

Every floor in the Kremlin Clinic has three computer terminals at each nurse's station, which are used to retrieve laboratory values. In addition, there are two terminals in small conference rooms for the use of the physicians, but since most of the doctors dislike using computers, these terminals generally sit unused.

Kuznetsov wondered how all the other hospitals in the Soviet Union, which have no computers, were able to function. Computers, so often associated with George Orwell's Big Brother and so on, are if anything the nemesis of the totalitarian state. They make information widely available, instead of concentrating it in the hands of the rulers. Information *is* power. Kuznetsov was glad that any of the clinic's doctors could use the hospital computers freely; he wondered how long it would take for some smart hospital administrator to find a way to restrict the flow of medical information. For these computers held the private medical files on the very top leaders.

He found a vacant terminal room and entered his access code.

In a few seconds, the screen went blank and then another prompt appeared. Kuznetsov typed his hospital identification number, followed by the eight-digit number that corresponded to his date of birth.

A few seconds' pause, and then a menu appeared. Kuznetsov selected DATA BASE SURVEY and directed the computer to call up the charts of each member of the Politburo. Incredibly easy.

He would not be asked, but in case he was, his explanation was unimpeachable. He was examining the medical records of these very important men, auditing the quality of their care, to see who might be summoned in for a checkup, who should be paid closer attention and who didn't need it, how often they saw their private physicians. A routine procedure; he would be commended for his thoroughness.

He began to pore over the most intimate health records of the men who ran the Soviet Union.

On Bolshaya Pirogovskaya Street in the Lefortovo district of Moscow, not far from the Novodevichy Convent, the main military-historical archives of the Soviet Union were located in an off-white classical-style building. Charlotte went to the side entrance and picked up a pass, which a friend at the Foreign Ministry had arranged for her, and then went around to the front of the building. A police guard inspected the pass and admitted her. The staircase before her was large and sweeping; at the top of it was a spacious reading room. Charlotte spent forty-five minutes looking around, chatting amiably with the librarians, and locating one particular archive.

It was, as she had expected, a *spetskhrana:* a locked, secret collection. There was no way to gain access to it.

She smiled pleasantly, and after chatting a few minutes with the militiaman at the main entrance, she left.

Working quickly, Dr. Aleksandr Kuznetsov jotted down serious illnesses on a pad. Vadim Medvedev, Nikolai Ryzhkov, and Lev Zaikov each had conditions he thought worth noting, ranging from heart murmur to severe gastric ulcers.

He next came to Andrei D. Pavlichenko, and something was peculiar. The message came up:

ACCESS DENIED.

Odd, he thought. Why would one file be restricted when the others were not, not even Gorbachev's? Perhaps it was that Pavlichenko was the chairman of the KGB, and secrecy was a way of life over at the Lubyanka. That was probably all.

He tried again, and still:

ACCESS DENIED.

Well, there had to be a back door to the data. There

always was. He drummed his fingers on the desktop in front of him and thought. And then it came to him: blood. All the files were contained in a separate data base by blood type, a filing system designed to enable monitoring of the clinic's blood supplies, to make sure there were sufficient quantities of each Politburo member's blood type at all times.

He entered DATA BASE SURVEY/BLOOD TYPE, and drummed his fingers again.

One after another, the files came up on the screen, and he cursored down each one. Then one came up whose name had been deleted. He scanned the information, the age, the physical description, the personal history, and he saw at once that it was Pavlichenko's chart.

Success.

Glancing at the screen, moving the cursor downward, he saw that Pavlichenko's private physician was, naturally, the director of the clinic, Dr. Yevgenii Novikov. Of course. But the last time Pavlichenko had been in, he had seen the eminent neurologist Dr. Konstantin Belov, a man twenty years older than Kuznetsov, whom Kuznetsov respected greatly. Of course—why should the head of the KGB see anyone who wasn't the best?

Well, well, he thought. Add the head of the KGB to the list of Politburo members with noteworthy medical conditions. But why was the head of the KGB seeing a neurologist?

The first thing that came up on the screen was Pavlichenko's X-ray report. It was normal; no acute infiltrates.

Then, surprisingly, a carotid angiogram. Obviously Dr. Belov had suspected some sort of problem; maybe Pavlichenko had even had a stroke. Was it possible? The angiogram showed that the right-sided system was patent, fifteen percent plaque. . . . All right . . . Ah, but the left side was bad news. The left side of Pavlichenko's blood supply to the brain was significantly obstructed—which meant a stroke on the left side could be imminent.

Someone walked by, and for a moment Kuznetsov glanced up nervously from the screen. It would be very hard to explain why he was examining Pavlichenko's chart if he had nothing to do with the KGB chairman. But the person kept on walking, and Kuznetsov returned to the screen.

The next thing he viewed on the screen was a preliminary CAT scan, which showed just about nothing. No infarcts or mass lesions, and just a mild cortical atrophy. So Pavlichenko had not actually *had* a stroke. That much was clear.

But why had Pavlichenko come in in the first place?

Kuznetsov called up the patient discharge summary, which included Belov's notes. Belov reported loss of vision in Pavlichenko's left eye.

But how could that be? How could the vision go out or be diminished in the left side if the lesion was also on the left side? It made no sense. Something was terribly wrong.

Maybe the CAT scan was mislabeled, Kuznetsov thought. Maybe it wasn't Pavlichenko's CAT scan at all, but someone else's. Mistakes like that happen all the time.

Kuznetsov had a few idle minutes, and he decided to be thorough about the whole thing. He'd go downstairs to the file room and locate the hard copy of the CAT scan, the film. Again, this was a routine matter; the hospital technical staff rarely asked questions of someone with Kuznetsov's standing.

When he got to the file room, he found that the film jacket was empty—checked out to Dr. Belov. No, it wouldn't do to go asking Belov. That would be the end of his career at the Kremlin Clinic. He'd be inspecting prostates in Tomsk in no time.

One more place to look.

The scanning room, where they do CAT scans in the clinic, was two flights down, in the basement: a cold white room run by a technician named Vasya Ryazansky, a young guy whom Kuznetsov knew casually. He had once given Vasya a dose of antibiotic for the clap without noting anything in his record, and it was time to get the favor returned. It was worth it to solve this mystery, which seemed more suspicious every moment.

"What is it?" Vasya asked slyly when Sasha asked

him how his clap was doing. "What do you want? *Yob tvoyu mat'!*" he said, employing the standard Russian epithet that translates: Fuck your mother. He laughed.

Kuznetsov returned the laugh. "All right, Vasya. Do me a favor, will you? I assume you have CAT-scan records on your computers here, right?"

"Where else?"

"I need to take a look at one."

"Make it easy on yourself," Vasya said. "Go up to the files and look at the film."

"I did. It's out. Do me a favor."

"What do you want, Comrade Doctor Professor?"

When Kuznetsov told him whose scan he wanted to see, Vasya's eyes widened. He nodded his head slowly and mock-bowed. "Well, well. Nothing but the best for you, eh?"

Let him think I've been assigned Pavlichenko, Kuznetsov thought, as Vasya punched out the name on his computer.

"Scan records are kept on computer about a month before they're erased," Vasya said. His tone had gotten much more serious. "Lack of tape and all that. Got to keep reusing it, of course. Any idea how long ago the scan was done? I don't remember doing it; must have been someone else."

"Within the last month, I'd say."

"Okay, here it is," Vasya announced. "Take a look."

Kuznetsov was even more bewildered by what he saw.

"Vasya, I want to see each slice, one by one. Can you do that?"

"Of course."

After Kuznetsov had finished viewing each brain slice, there was no longer any doubt. There was a huge, obvious infarct on the left side of Pavlichenko's brain.

But how could that be? The records he had looked at upstairs had said that the preliminary CAT scan was normal. Now he was seeing evidence of a massive stroke. How could anyone have missed it?

Something was definitely screwed up here.

Then he noticed the date of the CAT scan on the upper left-hand corner of the screen.

November 7.

According to the screen, the CAT scan had been performed on November 7. That was two days from now.

In a communications room at the KGB's First Chief Directorate headquarters on the outskirts of Moscow, a computer terminal gave off a rapid beeping. The warning system was connected to an intrusion detection system designed to provide silent notification if any of several computer networks around the city was penetrated.

The monitor flashed a sequence of terse messages:

> SECURITY VIOLATION
> CENTRAL KREMLIN CLINIC
> DEPARTMENT OF INTERNAL MEDICINE
> TERMINAL 3028

There was a pause as the mainframe's memory collated a user access code with a list of hospital personnel, and then there was another message:

> ALEKSANDR KUZNETSOV

67

The restaurant was an austere, even ugly place furnished with small tables at which people ate standing up. It was crowded, and it smelled powerfully of hot grease. The plate-glass windows were fogged with large ovals of condensation. They stood in line, neither speaking, moving past cups of sour cream and bowls of dumpling soup to the serving area, where two gray-haired women unloaded trays of crisp golden-brown *pirozhki* into a bin.

The dumplings, or *pelmyeni*, turned out to be a plate of pallid dough-covered balls of grayish meat, steamed and then garnished with sour cream. They were not as bad as they looked. The *pirozhki* were crisp and almost appetizing. Stone washed them down with a cup of steaming hot café au lait, which was certainly not genuine coffee at all but some sort of poor imitation liberally blended with hot milk.

"I can't stay at your place again," Stone said ruminatively as they ate. He took a swallow of the ersatz coffee. "For your sake as well as for mine."

"I know."

"Do you have any ideas? Any friends, maybe?"

"My cameraman, Randy. My producer, Gail. Both out, because they're neighbors, and they'd be prime suspects. But I know a Russian—an artist who has a pretty big apartment, something like a loft, where he paints. He might have room."

"Great." They ate for a while in silence. When he'd finished his plate of *pelmyeni*, he said, "The Old Believers."

"What about them?"

"We're no closer to learning anything."

"Give me until tonight."

"*Tonight?* By then it might be too late!"

"Well, look. The place I need to get into, I can't in a normal, straightforward way."

She glanced at her watch. "It's just about time. Our source usually takes an hour or so off for lunch, and the . . . clinic is just a block from here. Since the guy's not only a physician but a scholar, it's totally plausible for him to stop by the Lenin Library."

They crossed the street, then walked up the front stairs to the columned portico of the library, left their coats at the cloakroom, and descended a flight of stairs to a lounge lined with hard stone benches. Scholars, taking a break from their work in the reading rooms, sat smoking. Charlotte and Stone sat at one end of a bench.

A few minutes later, they were joined by a man who looked to be in his forties, wearing a suit and tie under an expensive-looking sheepskin coat. He sat beside them, and shortly pulled out a pack of Belmorkanal cigarettes.

He turned to Charlotte, and spoke in Russian. "You got a match?"

She nonchalantly handed him a pack of matches. He took them, wordlessly, and lit his cigarette. When it was lit, he began speaking, rapidly and quietly.

From a distance, they appeared to be nothing more than a man and a woman who happened to strike up a conversation, the man perhaps harboring designs on the attractive blonde. No one in the lounge paid them any attention.

"I think I might have found what you wanted," Kuznetsov said. He exhaled a lungful of cigarette smoke and looked around, smiling abashedly, play-acting a spurned suitor. The act was forced; Kuznetsov was terrified. Sitting to one side, pretending to examine a copy of *Sovetskaya Kultura*, Stone stole a glance.

"There are only a few people who have conditions of any gravity. But there is one that I found baffling. Apparently, the chairman of the KGB is about to suffer a stroke."

"Pavlichenko?" Charlotte asked. "*About* to . . . ?"

"That's what I said. You see, it hasn't happened yet. If the records I looked at are accurate, on the seventh of November he plans to have a stroke."

And at long last Stone knew, with a sudden jolt of terror, that he had found the mole known as M-3.

Washington

Roger Bayliss steered his black Saab turbo along the Beltway, periodically checking his watch. Aleksandr Malarek, Pavlichenko's man in the Soviet Embassy in Washington, would already be waiting at their rendezvous spot.

Bayliss chewed his third Maalox tablet. It placated his sour stomach, but his nerves were still jittery; he didn't want to take a Valium so early in the day, when Air Force One was to leave for Moscow in a matter of hours, and he wanted to stay as alert as possible. With him in it. Perhaps the highlight of his White House career.

Ever since the Sanctum meeting, he had been in a state of almost unbearable anxiety.

It was because he had become convinced, bit by bit, that Sanctum—that agglomeration of wise men—was committing a grievous error.

How was Pavlichenko planning to seize power? They did not know. Yes, it made a certain sense that the wise men would want to remove a Soviet leader who couldn't last, in favor of our mole. An agent-in-place as ruler of what remained of the Soviet Union. Yes, that made sense.

But Bayliss had become convinced that the coup was about to take place—*during the summit.* Nothing else could explain the schedule, or Malarek's urgency. All of the preparations pointed to it. There would be bloodshed in Moscow during the summit.

And Bayliss knew that any American implicated in such an action would face untold dire consequences.

He was, in a very real sense, covering his ass.

He had to tell his superior. He had to inform the President's national-security adviser, Admiral Mathewson, who knew nothing about Sanctum.

Without Mathewson's support—well, if the coup failed, Bayliss's fate was sealed. It would not be a pretty sight.

He had to tell Mathewson.

He got out of the car and walked right into the highway, the morning traffic dangerous and loud, cars slamming on their brakes, swerving to avoid him, drivers hurling abuse. There was a telephone booth there, on the other side of the road. He could not go through with this. He had made a mistake. He could fight the guerrilla war in the National Security Council, figuratively stabbing rivals in the back for the best office, for rank. He'd found himself capable of consenting to the murder of Alfred Stone. But this he could not do.

He fished a quarter out of his pants, fed the telephone, and stared at the cars passing by.

His heart was pounding, and a wave of acid washed up into his throat. He chewed another Maalox tablet.

Then he punched out the phone number of Admiral Mathewson.

Mathewson would know what to do.

68

MOSCOW

The young man spoke as if wrenched by emotion. He spoke directly at the camera. The unseen KGB technician had pulled in for a tight close-up.

From this close, the men watching the screen could see that the young man spoke under extreme duress.

"I furnished the terrorist groups with equipment," the man was saying. He paused often. There was a twitch in one of his eyes.

"How did you get this equipment?" The voice came from off-camera.

"The American Central Intelligence Agency and the National Security Council," the man replied. His left eye twitched uncontrollably. "They provided me with the explosives and other equipment."

"So you were working as a pawn of American intelligence?"

"Yes."

"Why did you agree to such a heinous crime against the peoples of the Soviet Union?"

The young man's face was wracked with indecision, his left eye twitching madly, his eyes watering. Finally, he shouted: "It's a lie! You made me do it! I followed your orders! I will not be party to this horror, this deceit. You will not force me to speak untruths!"

He broke down crying, bowing his head, and then

looking back up at the camera, his eyes red and swollen. Now he spoke quietly: "I am not a criminal."

The voice came from off-camera, metallic and brusque: "Do you remember what Czar Ivan the Terrible did to the architects whom he commissioned to build Saint Basil's Cathedral?"

The man had now turned his head and was looking at his unseen inquisitor. "I don't—"

The voice came back sharply: "You don't remember the history of your own country. Ivan did not want his architects ever to build anything to approach the beauty of Saint Basil's."

A dreadful realization came over the young man. "Oh, God, no. Please, God, no."

"You remember."

"No. *Please*, no!"

"Ivan had their eyes gouged out. You remember now."

"Please, *don't*. Please, *please*!"

The men watching the video screen were transfixed.

"Would you like to repeat your confession more persuasively now?" the off-camera voice said. An unseen hand gave the young Russian a tissue. The man dabbed at his eyes, and looked up, swallowing. "Yes."

He spoke his confession again, this time with far more conviction.

"Thank you," came the voice.

The young man began to weep. Suddenly, however, there was a loud *crack* and a red spot the size of a coin appeared on his forehead. The blood began to stream out: the confessor had been shot through the head, from behind. He slumped to one side, grotesquely.

And the video monitor went dark.

"Excellent," Pavlichenko called to one of the twelve men who sat around the table in the subbasement of the Lubyanka. "I want this edited immediately. Just keep the confession."

The head of the Fifth Chief Directorate was the first to speak. "This man, Fyodorov. Do we have footage of him meeting with the terrorists?"

"Yes," replied another voice, that of the chief of Moscow's police force. "He met them in a deserted garage we provided for him, where he stored the plastique and so on."

"And the terrorists," came another question, "which of them are alive?"

"The ones who killed my friend Sergei Borisov," said Andrei Pavlichenko. "A decision I had to make, incidentally, to be sure I was seen as uninvolved. Who also set off the bombs in the metro and the Bolshoi. When it is all over, they will be put on trial, blamed for the final act of terrorism, which they did *not* commit, and then executed. We will have our scapegoats, and they will not be alive to contradict us."

Pavlichenko did not need to explain that one of the terrorists, an old zek named Yakov Kramer, had been known to KGB for some time, ever since friends of his had, in the early 1960s, set off a bomb on Gorky Street. Ordinarily, Pavlichenko—then a ranking KGB officer—would have ordered the men rounded up. But instead he decided to do nothing, knowing that the day would come when they could be useful.

As they had been. One of the zek's sons was arrested and put in a cell at Lefortovo with the unfortunate fellow Fyodorov. The recently deceased Fyodorov, the bomb expert who taught young Kramer all about the manufacture of bombs, and planted the idea in his head. Then the zek's other son was placed in a psychiatric hospital. The scheme worked as Pavlichenko's people had determined it might, based on a thorough psychological profile. The Kramers were turned into terrorists. And, of course, it was a simple matter to intercept their notes to Gorbachev.

Terrorists linked, all of them, through the daughter of the American aristocrat Winthrop Lehman. The powerful and wealthy Winthrop Lehman, desperate to have his beloved daughter released from Russia before his death. And thus driven to cooperate with American right-wing fanatics bent on destroying the leadership of the Soviet Union.

Or so Pavlichenko wanted it to appear.

"Sir?"

The men looked up and saw a KGB internal guard standing at the doorway.

"Yes?" Pavlichenko said.

"Comrade Bondarenko," the guard announced.

"Let him in."

Ivan Bondarenko of Department Eight, Directorate S (Illegals) of the First Chief Directorate, charged with responsibility for "direct action" or "wet affairs," entered the room.

Without taking a seat, he said, short of breath: "I have reason to believe the American rogue agent is in Moscow."

"*What?*" gasped Pavlichenko.

"The Soviet visa office in Paris checked photographs," Bondarenko said, and stopped to catch his breath before he went on. "It seems that, incredible as it may sound, Stone has entered Moscow under a false name, using a visa he managed somehow to get quickly. The laser-optical scan of immigration documents, collated with the prints Sanctum supplied us, confirms it."

"Probably connected in some way with the arrival of the Americans," Pavlichenko said levelly, getting up from the table. "Now, I want all of you to call upon all of your resources to stop this man before he unravels our plan. Alive or dead, I don't care. He's come right into our backyard. We will find him. The fool probably doesn't realize that he's stepped into a bear trap."

69

Charlotte and Stone raced into the old U.S. Embassy building's main entrance, flashing their passports at the burly Russian guards, and then ran into the courtyard. They took the first left, into the entrance to the offices, and mounted the stairs to the press office.

Frank Paradiso, the embassy's press attaché, was seated, speaking on the telephone, behind a desk piled high with papers. He was stout and swarthy; his balding pate was partially obscured by thin strands of hair combed over from one side.

"Well, hello, Charlotte," he said when he'd hung up the phone. He shifted his glance toward Stone, and got up. "I don't believe we've met."

Charlotte put in quickly: "Frank, I realize you're probably raked, with the President showing up in a matter of hours. But we need to talk to you. It's urgent."

Paradiso nodded uncomprehendingly and gestured to the chairs in front of his desk, like an expansive host welcoming long-awaited dinner guests.

"Not in here," Charlotte said. "In the bubble. I know you have access to it."

"Charlotte, is this supposed to be a joke?"

"I'm dead serious, Frank."

Dr. Aleksandr B. Kuznetsov returned to the clinic immediately after meeting Charlotte and her friend, apprehensive about what he had found, wishing he hadn't found it at all.

He walked down the corridor to his office, passing the nurses' station. "Hey, darlings," he called out. The nurses liked him a lot, he knew, because he was one of the few physicians who bothered to talk to them. "Why so glum? Don't tell me your husbands are neglecting you! The fools don't know what they've got, right?"

He flashed an endearing smile, and knew something was wrong. The two nurses looked at him differently, fearfully.

"Buck up, kids," he said.

They smiled wanly.

Puzzled, he rounded the corner to his office and opened the door. When he saw the uniformed KGB guards, he suddenly understood.

The "bubble" is the safe room in the U.S. Embassy, the only place in the embassy structure believed to be secure from Soviet bugs. It consists of a Plexiglas chamber, a room within a room, taken up by a long conference table.

Paradiso led them in and switched on the air-conditioning to provide the necessary ventilation. Stone, knowing that there was a serious risk that Paradiso had received a cable from Langley concerning one Charles Stone, had refused to introduce himself.

And he was carrying, concealed in his jacket pocket, the gun; by coming into the embassy through the press entrance, from the courtyard, they had bypassed the metal detectors. Paradiso would be unable legally to place Stone under arrest—assuming he identified his visitor as Stone—without requesting federal marshals from Washington. That was the law. But if Paradiso decided to break the law and attempt to detain Stone—well, then there was the gun.

"All right," Paradiso said, sitting down at the table. Charlotte and Stone sat on either side of him. "What the hell is this?"

"Frank," Stone said, "we need your help."

"Go ahead."

"Frank," Charlotte said, "we need you to serve as a conduit to Langley."

"We're both Agency men, you and I," Stone said. "That doesn't mean you have to believe what I'm about to say. But have you heard of a group in Washington called the American Flag Foundation?"

"Sorry," he said.

"That's what I expected you to say." Quickly, and as lucidly as possible, Stone explained the fragments of what they knew about the American mole M-3, about the conspiracy he had become entangled in.

Paradiso looked genuinely amazed.

"Please listen carefully," Stone continued intently. "If I walk out that door and drive over to *The New York Times* office, they may or may not laugh me out of their office, but I don't think your superiors will like the result. The U.S. government will suffer permanent damage when it's revealed that certain groups in Washington are involved in covert action inside the U.S.S.R. Moscow will certainly break off diplomatic relations. The summit will be wrecked. I'd hate to extrapolate further, but you get my drift. It will all be on *your* head, all hung on *you*. It will be your own very *personal*, as well as very *public*, failure for allowing this to happen. And I shudder to think what might happen if this thing goes through. Do I make myself clear?"

Paradiso looked imploringly at Charlotte, his eyes wide in disbelief. "I don't know what the hell this guy's talking about."

"Frank," Charlotte said, "I just talked to someone who's in a position to know: Andrei Pavlichenko has prepared a false CAT scan, in preparation for a 'stroke' he's going to have tomorrow."

Paradiso snorted derisively.

"It's undeniable, Frank. He's behind this, on the Russian end. But if our information is right, he's not an American mole pure and simple. He's not the *Agency's* mole."

"What the hell, Charlotte . . ." Paradiso said.

"There's something more, Frank. For the last several weeks, the KGB has been investigating all the terrorist bombings in Moscow, and they've turned up some interesting evidence."

"Are you telling me you have a source in the *KGB* as well?"

Charlotte shrugged. "Their forensics people examined the bomb fragments and deduced that the explosives used were manufactured in the United States and supplied by the CIA."

Paradiso's mouth dropped open. "*Jesus Christ!*" He looked at Stone. "So what are you two alleging? I still don't understand where this is leading."

"All I can put together is this," Stone replied. "There's likely going to be some sort of action, perhaps military, probably disguised as terrorism. Presumably tomorrow, at the Revolution Day parade."

"Likely . . . probably . . . presumably . . . What am I supposed to make of all of this?"

"I want you to contact Langley. Send an emergency cable. If I'm wrong, Frank, you'll have done the right thing by reporting it. If I'm right . . ."

"I know," Paradiso said softly. "I'll have made the biggest intelligence coup in American history."

"Frank," Charlotte said, "do you understand how important it is that you move immediately on this?"

"Charlotte," he said, shaking his head slowly, dazed, a man who had been won over. "You don't have to tell me."

Washington

"I need to talk with you," the voice said desperately. In the background Malarek could hear traffic sounds. *"I'll be in in about forty-five minutes. It's urgent."*

Malarek had waited for Bayliss for ten minutes, then, deciding Bayliss must have had a good reason for missing the rendezvous, returned to the Soviet Embassy, where his aide presented him with this recording just made from an unsecured White House line. Malarek had at once recognized the voice of Roger Bayliss.

Malarek listened to the remainder of the phone conversation. Then he switched off the tape recorder, picked up a secure phone, and called a rarely used number at a small bookstore in Washington that specialized in foreign books. The phone was answered right away.

"This is a friend of yours from the Soviet Embassy," Malarek said. "I want to order two sets of the *Great Soviet Encyclopedia*. In English, please." Then he hung up and waited.

The man at the bookstore, who was a Soviet-born American citizen who had emigrated fifteen years earlier, was one of quite a few "blind-transfer" stations in and around Washington. He was paid a small retainer by the KGB for his services, which largely consisted of making, through an elaborate telephone system, untraceable calls. The bookstore employee did not know who had called him, nor whom he was calling. This was a method Malarek had developed to circumvent normal embassy and KGB channels.

Thirty seconds later the phone rang.

"There's been a ChehPeh," Malarek said, using the Center's slang for *chrezvychainoye proisshestviye*, an extraordinary incident.

He furnished the specifics, then hung up.

He pulled a Balkan Sobranie from the small white metal box on his desk, and lit it. He leaned back in his chair and thought about Roger Bayliss, who would do anything to advance his standing with his President. It was fortunate—extremely fortunate, in fact—that Bayliss had been so foolish as to make the call to an open line. Bayliss had not been specific with the national-security adviser, so there had been no hemorrhaging of any secrets. There would be just enough time.

He had never liked Bayliss.

Roger Bayliss wondered whether he was being followed.

The car behind him was trailing too closely, and so Bayliss moved over to the right lane, alongside the metal railing. He glanced into the rearview mirror and saw that it, too, had changed lanes. It was right behind him again.

He glanced nervously at the steep incline just beyond the railing, and then he knew what was happening. He instantly remembered something Malarek had once told him, about how good his people were at making "accidents" look real.

He shouldn't have called an unsecured line at the White House. After all, anyone could eavesdrop electronically on those lines.

He slammed on his horn, but now the car was at his bumper, and it was forcing him off the road. He could hear the squeal of metal scraping against metal.

He saw the license plate on the Ford, saw it was registered in the District of Columbia, and then he spotted the little maroon sticker on the Ford's windshield, at first just a little glint of purple, that decal that would mean nothing to anyone who hadn't heard of the American Flag Foundation.

No. The call . . . They'd bugged the call. . . . My own arrangements to bug the lines, Bayliss realized, aghast, knowing the irony, and then of course there was no doubt, the moment he felt the impact, about how he was going to die.

70

MOSCOW

The night had gotten frigid, the roads slick with ice. Stone, driving Charlotte's Renault, had found the driving difficult. Moreover, many of the roads were blocked in preparation for the next day's ceremony, which had taken over the city entirely, as do all state occasions in Moscow. Much of the center of the city had been cordoned off for security reasons. Banners were going up all over the city, large triumphal posters of larger-than-life socialist workers boasting of factory quotas overfulfilled.

After meeting with Paradiso, Stone and Charlotte had returned to her apartment, where together they drew up a plan. They agreed it was important that Charlotte go about her work normally, partly to avoid attracting any suspicion, which might expose Stone's presence in the city to anyone who was looking.

Charlotte had gone over to her office to put together a story, to which she would have to add only footage of the President arriving at Vnukovo Airport. Later, as soon as she could, she would finish her search for the name of the man who was said to lead the Old Believers network. Perhaps there was a way, she said, refusing to tell Charlie exactly what that way might be. But Stone could call her later, and learn what she'd found, if anything.

Stone had spent several hours unavailingly searching Charlotte's books on Soviet history, desperately looking for a name connected with the Katyn Forest Massacre, the name of a lone hero, but there was nothing.

He could not sit still, and soon he set off to confront Sonya Kunetskaya. Lehman's daughter, whom Charlotte had found. The woman Alfred Stone had met once, briefly, on a subway platform in 1953.

Stone found Sonya Kunetskaya small and unprepossessing. She wore a plain dress and steel spectacles, which concealed a pretty, delicate face. When she opened the door, she looked perplexed.

"*Chto takoe?*" she asked: What is this?

"We must talk," Stone replied, also in Russian. "Now."

Her eyes widened in terror, glinting with tears. "*Who are you?*"

"If you won't let me in to talk," Stone said, "I'll have to take measures you may not like."

"*No!*"

"It's urgent. Come *on*." He forced his way past her into the apartment. *This is the woman for the sake of whom my father was sacrificed,* Stone thought. *This is the one.*

Sonya Kunetskaya followed him into the living room, where a man was sitting. Stone would later learn his name: Yakov Kramer. He was badly scarred on one side of his face, a powerful-looking middle-aged man who would, but for his deformity, have been handsome.

"You met my father," Stone said slowly.

She seemed about to laugh. "You confuse me with someone else."

"No, I don't. I have the pictures to prove it. One day a long time ago—in 1953, to be exact—you met with my father on a platform in the Moscow metro. He gave you a package."

Now suddenly her face registered alarm, and it betrayed her. "I don't know what you're talking about," she protested.

"I know who you are," Stone said. "I know who your father is."

"Who are you?"

"Charles Stone. You met my father, Alfred Stone."

She gasped, her mouth open as if to scream, her eyes wild.

Then, oddly, she reached out a trembling hand and touched Stone's arm. "No," she said, shaking her head, choking out the words. "No. No."

Yakov Kramer watched, astonished.

"We must talk," Stone said.

Sonya's face was frozen in an expression of the sheerest terror. Tears sprang to her eyes. "No," she whispered. She looked at him closely, then reached out both of her hands to touch his. "Oh, God, no. Why are you here? What do you want from me?"

"I know whose daughter you are. Your father is here to take you out of the country, isn't he? But you should know that I'm prepared to interfere. Make no mistake about it. Unless you help."

"No!" the woman shouted, her eyes fixed on Stone. "Please, go away. You mustn't be here with me!"

"Who is this man, Sonya?" Yakov asked. "What is he saying? *Get out of here!*" He began to move menacingly toward Stone.

"No!" Sonya said to Yakov. "Let him be. I'll talk to him." Crying now, she removed her glasses and wiped at the tears with the side of her hand. "I'll talk to him."

At seven o'clock in the evening, Air Force One landed at Vnukovo Airport, some twenty miles southwest of Moscow. The tarmac was illuminated brightly by klieg lights and adorned by rows of Soviet and American flags, which rippled crisply in the wind.

The first to emerge from the plane were the President and his wife, then the Secretary of State and his wife, and then the rest of the American delegation.

Standing in a cluster to greet them, the moment captured on film by a Soviet camera crew, was a small group of Soviet officials, including the Politburo.

After a brief welcoming ceremony, the President was taken to a waiting American limousine, a bulletproof black Lincoln, with an American chauffeur at the wheel. The rest of the official party were put into Chaikas, and with a great roar of engines the cars took off at top speed down the middle lane of the road to Moscow.

The President's chauffeur at first seemed nervous about driving as fast as the Soviet drivers; then he relaxed and seemed to enjoy it. "Mr. President, I've never driven this fast in Washington."

"Don't get any ideas," the President said, looking a little queasy.

The cars in the motorcade followed one another breathtakingly closely, almost tailgating, the sirens screaming. They were moving at such a speed that the President, a cautious man, felt sure there would be an accident. Several cars, occupied by Soviet security agents, cruised on the outside of the motorcade, darting in and out deftly, dangerously.

When they had gotten into the city, the President looked out of the window with fascination.

Two cars behind, in a Chaika limousine, sat the President's national-security adviser and a few of his aides.

Craig Mathewson was crafting a statement, to be released at the U.S. Embassy the next morning, in which the President expressed his heartfelt condolences upon the demise of one of his most loyal White House staff members, Roger Bayliss. ". . . And I regret that Roger cannot be with us," the statement ended, "at this time of triumph that he did so much to bring about."

Mathewson was deeply grieved at the loss of the young man. Bayliss had been as ambitious as anyone Mathewson had ever met in government, a touch too slick for his own good, but still fundamentally a decent person. How had the accident happened? What was Bayliss doing, driving around on the day he was to leave for Moscow? Was it excitement about the summit, perhaps, that might have caused him to be so fatally unattentive?

But why had Bayliss called him, just before the accident, going on about having "something really urgent to tell you"? What could Bayliss possibly have wanted to say that was so urgent, and—here Mathewson's speculations grew dark—could there have been some connection between whatever Bayliss wanted to say and the accident?

Mathewson was suspicious, even a little afraid.

He watched Moscow racing by. Even at night, when so many cities look magical, this was an oddly unbeautiful place, he thought, and it was disquietingly still, devoid of people. Strange, for so populous a city, the day before its biggest holiday.

Then he saw that the streets were not quite devoid of people: every few yards stood militiamen in gray uniforms, in a line that never ended, from the airport all the way into the city. There must have been thousands of them.

It was clear that the Soviets were taking every precaution to protect the life of their honored guest.

Four cars behind Mathewson rode Mikhail and Raisa Gorbachev, and Gorbachev's close friend and adviser, Aleksandr Yakovlev.

Gorbachev sat silently, staring straight ahead, lost in thought, until Yakovlev interrupted: "He's a personable fellow."

"Hmm?"

"The President. I've always thought he's a personable fellow." Yakovlev, who had studied at Columbia University and spent years as ambassador to Canada, felt he understood the Western temperament. "Reasonable as well."

Gorbachev nodded, his eyes unmoving, steely.

"He's overtired," Raisa Gorbachev said, looking at her husband.

"Well, get your rest," Yakovlev said. "Tomorrow's a long day."

Then Gorbachev turned his head toward his adviser. "Do you think they know?"

"Know what?"

"Know," Gorbachev replied hotly, "about the—

about whatever or whoever the hell it is that's trying to pull off a coup."

"I don't know. No doubt they've got *some* kind of intelligence on it. Which means they'll try to exploit your weakness. The whole idea, you know, that you're not going to last. The way Brezhnev played Nixon when Nixon was facing impeachment, you know—"

"I don't mean that," Gorbachev shot back, turning back to face the road. "I mean, do you think they know what we've learned? About CIA involvement?"

"If you mean, do the President and his people have a hand in what's going on here, as Pavlichenko seems to think—well, it seems preposterous to me. I can't see it."

Gorbachev nodded again. He ran his tongue absently along the inside of his cheek and did not reply.

In the car immediately behind his sat Andrei Pavlichenko, alone except for his driver. He wore a pair of reading glasses and looked without interest through a thatch of digested intelligence reports from Germany, Poland, and Bulgaria.

Mentally, he ran through once again what was about to happen.

He knew that only a swift decapitation of the Russian leadership would be effective. It would plunge the nation into turmoil. The lawmaking bodies—the Supreme Soviet, the Congress of People's Deputies—would be gripped with fear, unable to act decisively. They would call for emergency measures.

After the destruction in Red Square, martial law would be declared by a few survivors—ranking officers in the Red Army and in the Ministry of Internal Affairs, each of whom belonged to the Sekretariat, yet who would not be standing atop the mausoleum or even near it.

To the world, the destruction of Lenin's mausoleum would seem the culmination of a campaign of terrorism that had so bedeviled Russia of late. When the remains of the explosion were examined, the CIA-produced plastique would reveal clear, irrefutable evidence of American involvement in the tragedy.

Why, there would be little doubt of it. Especially when Pavlichenko—once he recovered from his stroke—unveiled the evidence of attempts on the part of a small group of American conspirators that called themselves the Sanctum to eliminate the Soviet leadership from within.

But before that could happen, what remained of the uppermost Soviet leadership—that is, the Sekretariat—would charge the Americans with conspiring to destroy the Soviet Union at a time of great instability. Just when Moscow was loosening the chains, unlocking its gates, opening itself to the West.

And they would swiftly move to rectify the situation.

The Sekretariat, believing that they were about to make the Soviet empire whole again, would issue orders that the foolish and dangerous policies of Mikhail Gorbachev were to be terminated at once. That public safety required order. And then . . .

And then Andrei Pavlichenko would carry out his life's dream.

He would liberate the Ukraine.

It was the one thing that would never happen under Gorbachev or any other Russian leader. The Ukraine, the breadbasket of the Soviet empire, the wealthiest hostage republic, would at last be free.

And in short order, what little remained of the Soviet empire would be ruled by a Ukrainian whose parents had been murdered by Moscow. A Ukrainian, the master of Moscow.

And the Kremlin, as history knew it, would cease to exist.

Pavlichenko turned his attention back to the sheaf of documents, but he could think of nothing other than the coup d'état that would change the face of the world.

"You were," Stone said, "a hostage here, weren't you?"

She nodded, biting her lower lip. She had asked Yakov to leave the two of them to talk alone. Later she would have to tell Yakov everything. It would be terribly difficult, and she didn't know how to begin. "Yes," she said. "By 1930, Stalin forced my father to leave. Without his wife. And without me."

She drew her arms around herself in a tight embrace, as if she were cold, a gesture that seemed to be warding off the outside world. "He had to return to America, where his future was. The worlds of high finance and politics. But now, the woman and the daughter he loved so much— he could not bring out with him. Do you understand? *They wouldn't let him.* My father says the orders came from Stalin himself. My mother was devastated. She was a single woman with a small child. Without her husband.

"Oh, she was a beautiful woman, you know. She had worked in my father's house as a servant—she had no education, but my father loved her for other things, her beauty and her kindness. And, you know, I think they really were in love.

"Well, he kept in touch with my mother and me through letters he sent in various secret ways. He later told me he didn't trust the Russians, that they—he meant the GPU, which is now the KGB—would surely read his letters, and so he concealed the letters in fur coats he sent my mother with friends who were traveling to Russia. My father was a great figure to me, all the more because I saw him so seldom."

Sonya explained that she and her mother, who was to die in the early 1970s, moved to a tiny apartment in the Krasnaya Presnya district, and her mother managed to find a job at the Moscow Underwear Factory Number 6 of the Textile Trust. She made 159 rubles a month working at an ancient Singer sewing machine. People assumed that they had been abandoned by the American, and in the mood of anti-Americanism that dominated Moscow in the 1930s, people at once felt sorry for the mother and child and feared them, as people feared anyone who had been connected in any way with foreigners.

"But you were permitted to see your father," Stone said.

"He was never allowed to come to Moscow, but twice

I was allowed to see him in Paris. Only me; never my mother. Two terribly short visits, and always under guard."

"Yes. In 1953 and 1956. And Lehman couldn't have you kidnapped because your mother was still alive, in Moscow."

"Yes."

"Have you always wanted to leave this country?"

"Oh, yes," she cried. "Oh, God, yes. My mother desperately wanted to leave, all her life. And so did I. And then, when I met Yakov—well, I knew he wanted to emigrate."

"Does he know about you?"

"No."

"You kept that a secret from him?"

She bit her lip again, and looked down.

"Why?"

Her reply was anguished. "He couldn't know. No one could know. If I ever wanted to see my father again, I had to keep silent."

Stone considered a moment. "Stalin had something on your father, and your father had something on him."

"How much do you know?" she asked warily.

"Your father had a very damaging document, and Stalin had *you*. A standoff."

She said nothing.

"You have the document, don't you?"

"What makes you say that?"

"That was what my father handed to you, wasn't it? That was what your father was so concerned about getting to you, so concerned that he would do anything to get it to you, even if it meant having my father discredited, his career destroyed."

"Please, I don't *know* anything about that!"

"What is it? I want you to tell me what it is!"

"I don't know anything," Sonya said, in tears.

"But you do. Your father—through *my* father—gave you a file, didn't he?"

She shook her head, too emphatically, unconvincingly.

Stone was nodding. He knew now. "Once I thought it was something called the Lenin Testament. But it's more, it has to be. It has to be some kind of evidence of a secret attempt, years ago, to seize power. Names, specifics—which would blow the *present* plot out in the open . . ."

"Why are you *saying* all this?"

"Your contact at the Lubyanka," Stone said. "A man named Dunayev, am I right?"

"Please. I know so much less than you think. There were so many go-betweens between me and the Lubyanka. Maybe yes. I don't know. . . ."

Stone stood up, pacing, thinking aloud. "There's about to be an exchange, isn't there? How is it going to be done? *Where?*"

"I can't—"

"Tell me! *Where is the exchange going to take place?*" Stone stared out the window.

"Please," Sonya whispered. "All I've ever wanted to do is to get Yakov and his sons and me out of the country, and if you interfere—*please!*—you will end my last hope."

"Your father is in Moscow now, isn't he?" Stone said, turning around to face her. Things were falling into place. He was beginning to understand.

"I don't—"

"You have no choice, my friend," Stone said sadly, feeling for this woman's immense unhappiness. "I need you to tell me how I can get to your father—*now*."

And suddenly Sonya Kunetskaya got up from her chair, came close to Stone, and embraced him. "No," she pleaded. "Soon everything will make sense to you. Please don't interfere."

Stone held her tightly, comforting her, realizing how desperately miserable she was. "I'm sorry," he said. "We really don't have a choice."

The middle-aged Russian man, his face veined from a life of consuming vodka, mounted the broad marble stairs, weaving from side to side. He was visibly drunk, a bottle of Stolichnaya *pertsovka*, or pepper vodka, shoved in the pocket of his blue workingman's coat. It was past midnight, and Bolshaya Pirogovskaya Street was dark and empty.

"Oh," he said, entering the building and spotting the *vakhtyor*, the night watchman, who sat at a desk by a telephone. The *vakhtyor* appeared to be absorbed in an issue of *Za Rulyom,* the Soviet Union's version of *Car and Driver.*

"What the hell are you doing here?" the *vakhtyor* yelled. "Get the hell out before I throw you out."

The drunk threaded his way across the lobby, toward the desk. "Regards from Vasya."

"Vasya?" the *vakhtyor* asked suspiciously.

"Hey, is your head up your ass? Aren't you a friend of Vasya Korolyov? Vasya the Bandit?"

Now the guard's curiosity seemed to be piqued. "What do you want?" he asked, a shade less hostilely.

"Vasya said I should come talk to you. I lost my job today. The damned car factory booted me out on my ass. Vasya said you might be able to help me get a job here as a cleaner." The drunk sat down clumsily on a chair near the guard. "Mind if I sit?" he asked.

"Look," the *vakhtyor* said tentatively, shrugging. "I don't know what the hell . . ." His eyes greedily spied the neck of the Stolichnaya bottle. "Looks like you've had about one liter too much, comrade."

The drunk cast his eyes around the empty lobby, toward the deserted street, as if afraid someone might come by at any moment. He pulled out the bottle and set it on the watchman's desk, jarring the phone slightly. He extended his hand. "Zhenya."

The watchman, his spirits buoyed by the sight of the vodka bottle, took the man's hand, shaking briefly. "Vadim. Where the hell you get that?"

"Stolichnaya?" The drunk grinned as he divulged his secret. "My cousin Lyuda works in a *beryozka*," he said, referring to a hard-currency store. He twisted the bottle open. "Be my guest. I don't have a glass."

Vadim took the bottle and held it to his lips. He took a healthy swig and shoved it toward Zhenya.

Zhenya grinned again. "If I put any more in this stomach of mine," he said, patting his ample belly, "I'll mess up this beautiful floor. Be my guest. Ten minutes, I'll join you."

Vadim took the bottle again and drank deeply, then belched. "Now, how did you say you know Vasya?"

Yakov Kramer, who had returned to the apartment five minutes earlier, could not believe what he was hearing. It was turning his life inside out, altering the meaning of the last fifteen years of his life. He didn't know what to say or how to respond or how to begin to understand it. His shock turned into anger and then sorrow.

"You poor thing," he said, holding her shoulders.

"No," Sonya said. "Don't feel sorry for me. But accept my apology."

"Don't say that," he said. "In this life, things happen for reasons we can't always understand."

He felt her warm breath on his neck, felt her tears rolling down his cheek, and then he knew that they were all in terrible, terrible danger.

Everyone in the U.S. Embassy in Moscow knows the place is bugged. With the exception of the ambassador's office, and the "bubble," both of which are regularly swept for electronic listening devices, the embassy's offices are not used for any significant conversations pertaining to national security. The walls were peppered with electronic radio transmitters, some buried deep in the masonry, which are monitored from a KGB station across the street.

But, unknown to the CIA station, even the bubble is not safe.

Although it, too, is swept for radio-frequency emissions, sweeping cannot pick up a species of bugs that emit no signals and yet are easily activated from hundreds of feet away. In mid-1988, despite the previous year's uproar over a few marines' having admitted female KGB officers to security-classified rooms in the Moscow embassy, the bubble was penetrated. Several passive transmitters were installed into the legs and under the top of the only piece of furniture in the bubble, the conference table.

As a result, Frank Paradiso's entire conversation with Charlotte Harper and Charles Stone was transmitted and recorded at a KGB monitoring facility across Tschaikovsky Street.

The woman who monitored the transmission had received strict instructions from her superior, the head of the Second Chief Directorate, Pyotr Shalamov: the transcript was to go directly to him.

Within two hours, the transcript, typed in triplicate, had gone from the listening post across the street from the U.S. Embassy to the headquarters of the KGB's Second Chief Directorate, an anonymous five-story building less than half a mile from the embassy, and then to the Lubyanka, where Shalamov presented it personally to Andrei Pavlichenko.

The head of the KGB looked up when he had finished reading the document. He looked neither pleased nor displeased.

"Find Stone," he said simply.

Stone drove a few blocks away from Sonya and Yakov's apartment building to what looked like an American-style bar. He hadn't seen a legitimate bar in his entire time in Moscow—just the café where he had phoned earlier, and the dreary nightclubs that seemed to be peopled by Russian prostitutes. This bar had a plywood counter, a seedy-looking bartender. It served lousy Russian beer. Four Russian men in dark-gray, padded workingman's jackets sat at the counter blearily drinking and at the same time talking loudly, flashing a few metal teeth.

Stone entered, and saw that there were a few others, who also looked like laborers—factory workers?—sitting at small tables. As he walked to the telephone on the back wall, every eye in the bar was on him. Everything Stone was wearing, the clothes Jacky had purchased for him in Paris—his dark wool overcoat, his jeans, his heavy Timberland boots—seemed to be an advertisement for Western manufacturers. Everyone in the bar knew that, and the stares were not altogether friendly: this was a crowd that generally feared foreigners. You get a foreigner around and then you get the cops and the Gebezhniki— the KGB—and there's trouble.

He dropped a two-kopek piece in the phone and tried Charlotte again. He had tried from Sonya's apartment, knowing that using her phone was a risk, but he had to hear her voice, know she was safe. She hadn't answered at her apartment or her office. It was after midnight. Where the hell was she?

The phone rang and rang at her apartment. He hung up and dialed her office.

Nothing.

Please, God. If anything's happened to Charlotte . . .

A slender woman slowly climbed the marble staircase of the official-looking Soviet government building. She wore a tattered overcoat, her blond hair covered in a *babushka.*

Entering the building's lobby, she saw the two men.

"Well done, Zhenya," Charlotte said.

Zhenya was sitting with his hands folded over his stomach. The night watchman was fast asleep, snoring loudly, his face pressed into the desk blotter.

"Go home, Zhenya. I'll be awhile. And thanks." She gave him a peck on the cheek, then walked over to the desk and pulled out a key.

She unlocked the main interior entrance and climbed the grand staircase to the reading room. The building was dark, but she made her way without lights, clutching the banister.

Zhenya was indeed a hard drinker, but he was also an unemployed actor who had once performed at the Moscow Art Theater. Charlotte had met him and his family shortly after moving to Moscow, and he, who harbored no deep affection for Soviet bureaucracy or night watchmen or the police, had easily agreed to help her.

The bottle of pepper vodka he had so generously offered the night watchman was laced with a few tablets of Halcion, or triazolam, a sleeping pill Charlotte occasionally took. She knew alcohol exacerbated its effects but wouldn't make the drug deadly. She also knew that Halcion took effect quickly, often inside twenty minutes, and that it would wear off by the next day.

Earlier in the day, asking around, she'd learned that the watchman was excessively fond of booze, and so the spiked vodka seemed the best strategy. The guy might have an unusually deep night's sleep, but he would be okay.

And she was in the military-historical archives.

When she reached the reading room, she opened the door and saw that it, too, was dark. It wouldn't do to put the main lights on, which would be visible from the street, so she switched on a small table lamp behind the reference desk.

She knew exactly where to look: the microfilm records of the Soviet-Polish front, 1939–1945. Many of these records were kept in the open shelves, available to all scholars. The ones she wanted, however, were stored in a locked cabinet. During her morning visit, she had inquired where these would be. The librarian, who was unusually helpful for a Soviet archivist, had pointed at the cabinet but shook her head: you had to get *special permission*, she warned.

Or the key. The same key opened four of the cabinets, and Charlotte had glimpsed where it was kept.

In short order, she had opened the cabinet and pulled out an arm's length of microfilm spools. She found a microfilm viewer and switched it on. The glow gave the entire dark reading room a grayish tinge.

The work did not go as quickly as she'd hoped. After an hour, she was still lost in a tangle of Soviet-Polish military records. She rubbed her tired eyes, took a deep breath, and pulled out another reel.

The Investigation into the Crimes in the Katyn Forest Region.

Her heart leaped. She turned the spool faster and faster, her eyes skimming over the documents, searching for one in particular. Half an hour later, nothing. A lot of records, some grisly, some dull.

At two-thirty in the morning, she found it.

Proceedings in the Court-Martial of the 19th Company of the Infantry Division of the 172nd Regiment on the Polish Front Under the Command of Major A. R. Alekseyev.

The documents, which went on for page after page, listed the accused. Captain V. I. Sushenko, commanding officer. First Sergeant M. M. Ryzkhov, squad commander. She squinted at the screen, trying to make sense of it. Eighteen men, all soldiers of the Red Army, had rebelled against the instructions of the NKVD to descend into the pit and, with their four-sided bayonets, stab anybody who had miraculously survived the massacre and appeared to be moving. It was horrible. It was inhuman, and the Russian soldiers had fought back, cursing the NKVD men.

The prosecution had taken testimony from seventy-three NKVD officers, in preparation for the court-martial of the eighteen men.

And then, on the last page, was—just as Charlie had been told in Paris—an order to terminate. It was a brief form that decreed the proceedings unnecessary, other satisfactory arrangements having been made.

She skimmed the page, her eyes moving to the signature at the bottom, and for an instant she thought her eyes had gone. It could not be. She let out a short, breathy cry that filled the dark, vacant room.

It could not be. She squinted again and moved her eyes closer to the screen.

The name at the bottom of the page was that of Valery Chavadze, one of the legends of Soviet politics. An old Georgian, now retired, who had been one of Stalin's henchmen. A Georgian, like Beria, like Stalin himself. An elderly man by now, living in grandeur somewhere outside of Moscow. He had been a deputy commissar, later minister, of foreign affairs, a member of the Politburo, and—so Charlotte had always believed—an unswervingly loyal Stalinist.

Chavadze had stayed at the top of Russia's leadership, serving in Khrushchev's Presidium, Brezhnev's Politburo, only deciding to retire in 1984. Chavadze's was the longest-running, most successful, most illustrious political career the Soviet Union had ever seen. He was one of the country's grand old men, a figure who—despite his reputation as one of Stalin's men—was widely regarded with reverence, almost awe.

And—if Stone's information was right—this hard-line Stalinist was the leader of the underground movement called the Old Believers.

Valery Chavadze was the only man who could stop the terror.

71

Stefan arrived at his father's apartment out of breath, still wearing his ambulance technician's uniform. He had been summoned by Yakov urgently, and his father's expression indeed seemed grave.

"What is it?" Stefan asked.

"I am very afraid for us," Yakov said. His voice trembled.

"We have been found out," Stefan said, his stomach turning over.

"Worse, I think. Much worse."

"What?"

Hunched over, Yakov smoked a Stolichnye cigarette. "I learned something today about Sonya, something that is tearing me apart. My Sonya—" He broke off and compressed his lips, trying to gain control of his emotions. After a moment he continued: "My Sonya has been living a lie. She has lied to me. She—she is not the person I thought she was."

"I don't know what you're talking about," Stefan said, wondering what it was about Sonya that could possibly be so terrible.

"She—she has a father. A very well known man, an American. Winthrop Lehman."

Stefan had heard the name Lehman, read about him

in Soviet history books. He laughed, quite sure his father was joking, and then, seeing that he was laughing alone, stopped abruptly.

"Yes," Yakov said. "I found it hard to believe, too."

"But I don't—"

"Stefan," Yakov said, his voice suddenly sharp. "This man who gave you the explosives. This cellmate of yours at Lefortovo. Who is he?"

Stefan looked puzzled. "A car mechanic, a petty thief of some sort."

"KGB," Yakov said.

"*What?*"

"Stefanchik, listen to me. You were arrested by the KGB, placed in a KGB prison—"

"Who the hell do you think arrests people in our country?" Stefan responded archly. "The World Court in the Hague?"

"*Damn* it, listen to me! Why do you think it was that you alone of all your friends were singled out for a jail sentence? Pure coincidence?"

"Papa, what are you talking about?"

"Your cellmate, who *happened* to be an expert in terrorism. Do you think that was an accident, too? Who *happened* to have access to a store of explosives? And your brother, Avram. He happened to be arrested, happened to be thrown into the *psikhushka*? Stefan, *we were set up!*"

"No—"

"There's been no word, nothing, on Avram," Yakov said with bitter triumph. "It's as if they were unaffected by our attacks. As if they wanted us to keep on doing what we were doing! They knew how we would respond." His voice cracked.

"How is it possible?"

"The American told me a number of things," Yakov said wearily. "He told me that the bombs we set off used explosives supplied *by the CIA.*"

Stefan listened in shock.

"Fyodorov," Yakov continued, "was using us, playing upon our anger, upon our ignorance. This American thinks we are pawns, just like he is a pawn. He thinks the KGB plans to seize us all, arrest us for a great act of terrorism that may take place tomorrow."

"During the parade?"

Yakov nodded.

"Then what are we going to do?"

"The American says he has an idea. I told him we will do anything to help him now. Maybe we will need the help of others, I don't know. But we must move very quickly."

72

Driving Charlotte's Renault, Stone pulled out onto Prospekt Mira, the great broad highway, with the spire of the Exhibition of Economic Achievement looming on his right. Two cars passed him, weaving between the lanes: drunkards. The highway was ill-lit.

A large drop of water splashed on the windshield, and then another, and then another. Shit, Stone thought: the snow has turned to rain. Bad for visibility, bad for driving conditions, and the time remaining was dwindling away. It was vital to reach the Old Believers, and with each hour, the possibility receded that he ever would.

Charlotte had said she thought there was a way to discover the identity of the leader of the Old Believers, but now she had unaccountably disappeared.

He hoped she was safe.

The only possibility that remained was Winthrop Lehman himself. Sonya had finally broken down and revealed that her elderly father had indeed arrived in Moscow a few days earlier. As Stone had suspected: Lehman would be an honored guest of the Soviet state, but with an additional, secret mission of his own, to obtain the release of his adult daughter. Sonya, who had lived her entire life in Moscow.

Stone would have to face down his old employer, the man who had betrayed his father years ago, and compel him to help—if for no other reason than to protect Sonya. He was staying, Sonya had said, at the National Hotel. The same place where Stone had originally booked a room.

Lehman was the last hope.

In a few minutes, he would reach the hotel, and face Winthrop Lehman.

As Stone thought, he stared through the raindrops, mesmerized by the windshield wipers, keeping his eyes on the white divider lines on the road. Suddenly he became aware, as a message from somewhere in his subconscious crossed the barrier into the conscious, that a pair of round headlights had been following him for some distance.

The rain got heavier, and Stone felt himself reflexively begin to accelerate. A surge of adrenaline, of fear, was forcing his foot down onto the gas pedal, and he had to force himself to lift his heavy boot a little.

The lights got closer.

There were *three* sets of headlights now coming out of the blackness. Not the militia car—these were different, two very large trucks.

Jesus Christ! They were closing in on him.

The two sets of headlights belonged to two large squarish trucks, and now one was in the left lane and one in the right. Stone was in the center lane.

As soon as he realized what was going on, he frantically tried to swerve the car into the right lane, the shoulder, off the road, but it was too late: the truck on the right was coming up on him too fast.

One of the trucks was labeled "bread," a solid closed-back truck, and the other was even larger but looked like the kind of thing you only saw in rural America: its sides were slatted, and beneath the slats was chicken wire, and the truck's bed was full of live chickens.

The two trucks were now fully abreast of the Renault, and they were beginning to squeeze in.

There was a horrifying metallic crunch as the truck on the right smashed into Charlie's car, and then a scrape from the left as the chicken truck cracked into him.

Stone was already in overdrive, and he pressed the gas pedal all the way to the floor, but as fast as the Renault went the trucks were able to keep up, slamming into him with increasing frequency. He knew they were trying to kill him.

Where was the tunnel? Somewhere around here, half a mile away or so, the three lanes were supposed to merge into two and go through a long tunnel. He could just make it out, up ahead maybe a mile. A mile: sixty seconds. In sixty seconds, the drivers of the trucks would be faced with a road-maneuver decision, and there was little doubt they would smash into him, decisively, before they got into the tunnel and its two lanes.

The trucks were pummeling the Renault, slamming the car back and forth, like a Ping-Pong ball. With each slam Stone was jolted, and then one crash from the chicken truck on the left cracked a deep gash into the side by the backseat.

Crack! The right rear window smashed. He felt a spray of rain hit his neck.

Stone felt his panic change into an eerily calm determination. Something within him took control, banishing terror. Forty-five seconds away from the tunnel's opening, with one hand on the wheel, he unrolled the driver's-side window all the way. The wind roared in, carrying with it a torrent of rain, and he reached out a few inches until he grasped a grimy slat on the side of the chicken truck. Tugging at it, he realized it was sturdy: the slats on the truck could function as a ladder.

The truck on the right slammed into the Renault with awesome force, forcing the car into the truck on the other side. Stone swung the wheel in the opposite direction. The wind whistled past his head.

Wham!

The chicken truck had crashed into him again, this time with enormous force, mangling the Renault's left fender, its own giant fender now locked. The Renault had been jammed into the left-hand truck, wedged into it, and the two vehicles screamed along, inextricably connected.

He reached down, swiftly grabbed at the laces on his boots, and loosened them. Then, using his left boot, he eased the right boot off his foot and wedged it against the gas pedal. It stuck. The accelerator was jammed down, and the car would continue to move ahead on its own, locked into the truck's mangled fender.

The mouth of the tunnel was just ahead. Maybe twenty seconds. Steering with his right hand, he reached over with his left and grabbed a slat. He pulled himself out of the car, supporting himself with his feet on the windowsill. His bloodstream was full of adrenaline now: his strength was enormous. He would need a tremendous surge of energy, and it *came*.

He swung himself upward, and the slat came off in his hand.

The only chance. The only alternative was certain death within seconds. He jumped into the air and grabbed the slat above.

Sturdy.

It was sturdy, it held, and he was on the truck now. Glancing down momentarily, he saw that his car was propelling itself ahead like a bottle rocket, and the trucks continued to pummel the Renault—was it possible they hadn't seen him climb out?

The chickens were clucking, seeming to shriek with nervousness. Stone inched himself along the length of the truck, toward the front.

There was a deafening crash of metal below, and Stone glanced down to see Charlotte's car veer off under the high wheels of the right-hand bread truck, its top shearing off horribly. Then, just as the tunnel came upon them, the car slammed into the concrete abutment at an angle and exploded instantly into a fiery ball.

At that moment the trucks entered the tunnel, and everything was plunged into darkness.

Now he had reached the truck's cab, and, peering into the right side, he could just make out a bull-necked man wearing a flat cap, blissfully unaware that Stone had survived the grisly crash.

The rain made it almost impossible to get a grip on the top of the cab, but by lying flat Stone was able to slide himself over the top, and around, and—

The window was open.

Stone reached around and pulled out the Glock, wedged in his waistband. He released the safety, holding on to the top of the cab with his free hand, shivering with cold.

The driver didn't know he was only feet away. Stone angled the gun around until it was pointed directly at the driver. The man who had tried to murder him.

"*Privyet,*" he said—greetings—and pulled the trigger. The bullet struck the man cleanly in the forehead, with a sudden spit of blood against the windshield. The driver's head flopped down to the wheel grotesquely, almost comically, as if he had suddenly decided to take a catnap. His blood continued to jet forward, into his lap.

Stone twisted his body around and, with a tremendous exertion, forced himself into the cab. Momentarily he faltered, then desperately he shoved the driver aside and managed to grab the steering wheel just as the streetlight at the tunnel's end became visible. With one hand he slipped the cap off the dead man's head and put it on: the silhouette would make the difference.

As the truck emerged from the tunnel, the light from a carbon-arc lamp illuminated the cab's interior, turning the fresh blood a sickly green. The other truck followed behind. Stone took the old-fashioned, long-handled gearshift and eased it into a lower gear and accelerated. The other truck honked out a tattoo, signaling victory—we've done our job, congratulations—and Stone honked out a response. Throwing the truck into fifth, he turned off Prospekt Mira onto the streets of Moscow.

73

Podolsk, U.S.S.R.

The three Spetsnaz munitions experts stood on a vast field of dirt, watching a stone pyramid a quarter of a mile away in the darkness. It was a small building constructed of large blocks of granite. This was the fourth trial, and each had been completely successful.

"An amazing replica," the first said.

"Yes," the second replied. "Precisely the same exterior and interior dimensions. Even the stone has been chosen to duplicate the weight of the original."

The field the three men stood on was about twenty-five miles directly south of Moscow, just outside of Podolsk: a military proving ground that had been taken over from the Red Army by the Spetsnaz in 1982. Once it had been a military airfield; now it was used exclusively for Spetsnaz testing of explosive devices.

All three had flown down on a GRU helicopter, and all would return to Moscow as soon as the final test was completed, in the early hours of Revolution Day. They stood in silence, watching.

Then there was a terrific, dreadful rumble, a great thunderstroke, a flash of white light, a whoosh. The stone structure was blown apart from within, and in a split second nothing was left standing. The ground shook, but there was nothing to be seen except a pattern of grayish rubble scattered for hundreds of feet.

"Our man does good work," the third one said, and the tiniest smile lit up his face.

74

Revolution Day. November 7. 12:36 a.m.

Bone-tired, scraped and bloodied, Stone drove the truck as far into the city as he dared, for a chicken truck in the center of the city was sure to be conspicuous. He had pulled off Prospekt Mira onto the ring road, Sadovaya-Spasskaya, and from there managed to find a telephone.

No one seemed to be around; in fact, the streets were completely deserted. No, not quite deserted: there was one militiaman patrolling.

He closed the booth's door, inserted a coin, and dialed Charlotte's apartment number. No answer again.

He tried the office number. It rang five, ten times.

"Yes?" A male voice.

"I'm looking for Charlotte," Stone said. "This is a friend."

There was a long pause.

"I'm sorry," the man said. Her cameraman, perhaps? "Charlotte was supposed to be back here six hours ago. I have no idea where she is. Which is a bitch, because we've got a whole hell of a lot of work around here."

Stone hung up and leaned against the glass side of the booth. They had gotten her; they had probably come to get him, and taken her instead.

It was half past midnight, but it was time to wake up a very old man and force him to help.

The alley gave Stone an idea. Every hotel he'd ever seen had a service entrance, and Russian hotels could be no exception: they could hardly unload sacks of potatoes and crates of eggs in the front.

At the back of the National Hotel was an alley where

great dumpsters of trash were kept, stinking messes of decaying food. He saw at once that the kitchen workers in the hotel had to walk by the dumpsters on their way into what the Russians would call the *chyorni khod*, the back entrance. Even at this hour of the morning, the door was in use, and it banged loudly as night-shift employees came in and out.

Stone walked briskly, angrily. If you can't look like a Russian, at least look like a foreigner so purposeful that no one would dare to question you. Wearing only one boot, Stone knew he could not help attracting attention.

Yet no one did question him; who would enter a hotel through the kitchen?

Once inside, Stone saw that the lobby was out of the question, but, like all hotels, the National had a back stairway, used mostly by the maids and the *dezhurnaya*s, the women who keep the keys on each floor. Outside of one room, someone had left a pair of shoes to be polished overnight, and Stone, feeling a bit guilty, took them. The fit was not great, but it would do.

On the second floor, he easily found the Lenin Suite, marked with a brass plaque. In recent years, the Lenin Suite has been given to honored guests of the state not quite august enough to be housed at Lenin Hills or within the Kremlin.

There didn't appear to be a guard in sight.

The old man, wrapped in a silk robe, had been sleeping. He opened the door after Stone had knocked for quite a while, and stared at the younger man.

He did not seem to register surprise.

Frank Paradiso, press attaché of the United States Embassy in Moscow and officer of the CIA, had recognized the man as Charles Stone. Once, during his brief affair with Charlotte Harper, he'd found a picture of Stone among a pile of things in one of her drawers, and he'd asked her about him. She'd been curt and dismissive.

He knew who Charles Stone was, knew from the moment he had gotten the coded cable from Langley. It had come, marked code word ROYAL, which signified an especially sensitive operation, known to fewer than a hundred people. The cable, which accompanied a description and biography of Stone, an Agency employee who had committed murder and was believed to be attempting to defect to the Russians, was from the office of the DCI, Ted Templeton. It was unattributable, but the marking on it clearly indicated it had originated with the DCI and thus had the highest authority.

The Director of Central Intelligence wanted Stone apprehended immediately.

Paradiso had sent an urgent cable the instant Stone and Charlotte had left his office, and the Agency had sent personnel to Moscow almost immediately. The men from internal security had accompanied the presidential party under the cover of State Department employees, and had arrived just minutes ago.

"How credible is this information, Frank?" asked the CIA operative. His name was Kirk Gifford, a blond, brawny forty-six-year-old.

"Very," Paradiso said.

"What's the source?"

Paradiso hesitated. "Forget the source for now. We've got just about—"

Paradiso sagged suddenly to the table as Gifford clipped him swiftly at the back of the neck with a heavy metal object that resembled a blackjack.

Gifford next jabbed a needle into Paradiso's forearm: a short-acting benzodiazepine central-nervous-system depressant called Versed, more reliable than the Agency's old standby, scopolamine. Versed, or midazolam hydrochloride, is a hypnotic as well as an amnesiac. When Paradiso came to, disoriented and foggy, he would have forgotten everything that had happened to him in the last day or two. Everything except for vague details that would seem like a dream.

The door to the bubble opened, and two men entered, bearing a stretcher. Each had the legal authority of United States federal marshal.

"I want him on the next plane out," Gifford said. "I don't care if you send him parcel post. Just get him out of Moscow."

"Do you know why I came here?" Lehman said, sitting in a large wing chair. He seemed small in this big room, dwarfed by the grand piano.

"Yes. For Sonya. You hand over a piece of paper to Andrei Pavlichenko's people—or is it a file?—and in return you get your daughter released. At long last."

Lehman seemed not to have heard Stone's reply. "So, you came to Moscow expecting to exonerate yourself," he said, "is that it?"

"Something like that."

Lehman seemed to find it very amusing. "Well, don't interfere now, Charlie. You have interfered in things far more significant than you know."

"You're not really in much of a position to refuse me," Stone said softly. "For your daughter's sake."

Lehman's eyes widened ever so slightly. "Please don't resort to threats."

"I don't want to have to say anything to anybody that might disturb your arrangement."

Lehman barely hesitated before saying, "I think you're the one whose position is untenable."

"Charlotte and I want safe passage out of Moscow. You have the connections and the visibility to make the necessary arrangements."

"No, I don't think so."

"You don't think you have the connections?"

"I don't think, Charlie, that you'll leave Moscow alive."

Stone paused. He could not help admiring the old man's finesse, even at such a difficult moment. "Will you?" he said, half-smiling.

Lehman returned the smile. "Very good." His eyes were watery, and he seemed enormously amused. "You don't like me, do you?" His voice was reedy, yet powerful, with the mellow tones of an oboe.

Stone said nothing.

"Things are seldom what they seem," Lehman said archly.

Stone watched the old man, pensively. "Did you set my father up? In 1953, I mean."

"I did what I could to help him." He coughed violently, the sort of cough that can easily become a retch. "Is that why you're here, Stone? History lesson? Is this what you wanted to know?"

"In part. He was innocent, wasn't he?"

"Of course he was," Lehman said derisively. "Jesus Christ, Stone, what do you think? You're his son. A son's got to have faith in his father."

Stone was nodding. "You allowed his career to be destroyed, didn't you?"

Lehman shook his head slowly. His mouth opened and closed a few times wordlessly. "I didn't think—"

"You know, once upon a time I was proud to know you," Stone said. He knew that the room was bugged, but it was too late now to make any difference.

Lehman, who could not stop shaking his head, was lost in some dark and private corner of his mind.

"Now, let me see," Stone said. "They've had your daughter for all of her life, yes? And you have something."

"It's very late. . . ."

"A *number* of papers, am I right? An old woman who was once Lenin's secretary told me about a 'Lenin Testament' that the world never knew about. Something that might have destablized the Kremlin a few decades ago—"

"Very old news—"

"—but more. Other bits of evidence. Proof that Beria tried to pull off a coup, with Western help."

"*Decades* ago. Please don't waste my time now. I don't have much of it. And neither, I'm afraid, do you."

"But that, too, is old news, as you put it. No, not entirely."

Lehman's attention seemed to be drifting.

"Not entirely," Stone resumed, "because in those papers were names. Names of Beria's aides. Young men who would later make illustrious careers for themselves, and who would scarcely want to have anyone know that they once conspired against the Kremlin. At least one person, yes?"

"Get out of my room—" Lehman said, but he was cut short by a rattling cough.

"So, you have proof that the new chairman of state security is an enemy of the state. Well, now, of course you have something on him." He gave Lehman a fierce, blazing stare. "*So why did you have to come to Moscow?*"

"Anyone who knows . . ." Lehman began.

"Anyone who knows about Pavlichenko."

"I know too much. . . ." Again his mind appeared to wander.

"But you just walked right into Pavlichenko's trap!"

"*No*, damn you!" Lehman spoke with a sudden anger. "I've known the Soviets for almost all my life. Obviously I have papers in the hands of my attorneys in New York, detailing Pavlichenko's past, our relations with him, our help in creating his career. The release of which would . . . If—if I should die before my Sonya was freed, I've left instructions that upon my death my attorneys would be required to make public certain papers unless my daughter Sonya were allowed to leave Russia."

"And now? What about now?"

"I know Pavlichenko won't allow me to leave. He can't. I'm the witness. But I provided for that, too. My attorneys have received instructions from me that all my papers on Pavlichenko are to be made public on November 10 unless their release is stopped *by either me or Sonya.*" He had summoned up the energy to speak with great emphasis, and his expression was triumphant, though his words had become slurred. "And Pavlichenko knows this. He knows. It's my failsafe. Only Sonya will be able to stop the release of this damaging information. So Pavlichenko will *have* to free my daughter. Only Sonya can stop the release of information he won't want out."

He doesn't know, Stone suddenly realized. He doesn't know the enormity of Pavlichenko's plan. He doesn't know that information made public by some white-shoe law firm in New York can have no effect on a man who has seized power the way Pavlichenko is about to. *Lehman doesn't know!*

But Stone only said, "What do you mean, only Sonya?"

Lehman coughed again. A gut-wrenching cough.

"I'm dying, Stone."

"But even if you only live for a few more years . . ."

"I'm dying now, Stone. Right now, before your very eyes."

And so he was. His face was ghostly white; he had begun to fade. But it was strange: he spoke with such pride.

"They call this a 'mercy cocktail.' You're too young to think about such things. They've used them in England for over a hundred years." He smiled. "Liquid morphine and liquid codeine. Some other things—sugar and water and a bit of gin. The way my father died. Instead of subjecting us to a long decline. I packed the vial before I left. I knew this would happen."

Stone only stared in amazement, speechless.

"I swallowed it shortly before you arrived. I knew when I came here I'd never leave. And with the legal mechanism already set up, as long as I didn't allow them to take *me* hostage—they could do that, you know—and killed myself instead, I knew I could save Sonya. *They have to let her go!*" He was almost shouting now, and his eyes were afire with triumph. "For years, I couldn't help my dear Sonya. And now . . . now . . ." He smiled, broadly, again.

Stone didn't have the heart to tell the dying old man about what would happen, in a matter of hours, in Red Square. He couldn't tell him that the materials in the safe-keeping of his lawyers in New York were of little importance now to Pavlichenko. How could he tell the man that his dying gesture—the greatest, most unselfish gesture of his life—would be a failure?

"Lenin was murdered, wasn't he?"

"All true," Lehman repeated. "So he was. You know about Reilly, Sidney Reilly?"

Reilly, the British superspy who tried to overthrow

the Soviet government in 1918. What did he have to do with anything? "Yes."

"Then you know that a year after the Russian Revolution the Allies were furious at the Bolsheviks. For signing a separate peace with Germany. Decided they had to topple the Bolsheviks. Strangle the Bolshevik infant. Only way. They saw the beginnings of a Lenin cult, and they zeroed in on the only way to destroy the leadership. Eliminate the charismatic leader. The Brits sent in Reilly to assassinate Lenin, but the plot failed."

"And you?" But Lehman ignored him.

"Warren Harding and Churchill and a whole lot of other people thought if Lenin was gotten out of the way the Bolsheviks would fall."

"I don't believe it," Stone said aloud, to himself.

Lehman heard this. "Don't believe it." He laughed dryly. "Harding and Churchill *thought*, I said—they didn't do. Stalin *did*. Sonya was born into this world a little, lovely hostage, and Stalin was able to secure the cooperation of the only foreigner Lenin trusted. Otherwise my daughter would die. That sort of thing happened often then—people would just disappear. . . ."

"Foreigner?" Stone said, not understanding.

"Embalming didn't take. Not in someone whose body was loaded with poison. Body was cremated. They made a wax dummy out of a life mask Lenin had had made for a sculpture. Stalin knew. He wanted Lenin out of the way as soon as possible—he saw the Soviet state paralyzed, and it was his chance to seize the throne. He knew that I was one of the very few people Lenin would see, even when he was terribly ill," Lehman gasped. "Lenin saw me. Served me tea, both of us. Lenin—Lenin drank his tea extremely sweet. Stalin gave me lumps of sugar treated with a sophisticated, fast-acting poison. All I had to do was switch sugar lumps."

"*You?*"

"Krupskaya wouldn't let her husband see Stalin. I was the only way. I knew Lenin was dying anyway, after his stroke, and to hasten it would mean nothing. And Stalin would protect me—he had to, because I had his little secret: he provided the poison. So, without planning to, I facilitated the rise of the twentieth century's greatest tyrant. He made me do it—he threatened all manner of reprisals, and I was too young to face up to him. But once you're in with thieves, you're in, and he always had a hold on me. Honor among thieves. For the rest of his life, and even after."

Lehman was rambling again, his eyes almost closed. "Your father brought the papers to Sonya. The Lenin Testament and the other things. Lenin Testament . . . an attack on the Soviet state . . . by its creator . . . meaningless today, but probably a collector's item . . . worth a lot of money. That, and a few pieces of paper that implicated Stalin . . . Beria . . . Pavlichenko, the whole lot. Folded and sealed and . . . dry-mounted right in behind the picture of Lenin. Then your father found out. He would have ruined everything. If I died, I wanted her to have life insurance. Had to be secret, or else Sonya would be harmed. I couldn't let your father destroy my Sonya's life insurance. My Sonya . . . Now they'll let her go."

"So—so you have nothing with you. No documents."

"Sonya has them. The trade—the trade is—Sonya—for me."

Stone got to his feet, and pulled from the pocket of his coat the Nagra recorder. The thing was still working, amazingly, even after the truck nightmare. It had been recording, and he clicked it off. Lehman stared at the machine as if he didn't understand that their entire conversation had just been taped.

But then his eyes flickered open. "Keep your machine on," he said. "I have one more thing to tell you."

And for the next ten minutes, Lehman spoke; and by the time Lehman had closed his eyes for the last time, Stone had sunk deep into his chair, speechless, overwhelmed by the confirmation of something he had for so long suspected. For a very long time, Stone sat, unable to cry, unable to think clearly, unable to move.

At a phone outside the National, Stone dialed Charlotte's home number once again.

"Hello?"

"*Charlotte!* Oh, thank God. I'd thought—"

"Things took longer than I thought they would, but I found what you wanted. You're not going to believe this. The head of the . . . network."

The head of the Old Believers network, she meant. The tension was making her indiscreet; she was speaking on the phone too freely.

"Yes?"

"It's Valery Chavadze."

75

3:10 a.m.

Driving a rusty white stolen Volga, which he had hot-wired near Manezhnaya Square, Stone left Moscow's city limits and headed southwest, in the direction of Vnukovo. He recognized the area's name: it was where many of the Soviet elite had their dachas. He left the highway and entered a dark, densely wooded area, poorly lit, and then pulled into a narrow road that had been cut into a deep forest, a winding road beside a ravine. The Soviet elite's dachas were in some of the most rugged, unspoiled terrain in the Soviet Union.

That Valery Chavadze was the head of an antigovernment network boggled the mind. He was one of the old guard, a bulwark of the old order. Even until the 1980s, this old Stalinist holdover had still been attending Politburo meetings. There were unsubstantiated rumors that he had been influential in ousting Khrushchev.

That was what he wanted the world to think.

The world considered Valery Chavadze the very essence of the long-lived, recalcitrant Soviet leadership. But could it be that at the same time this man was a secret traitor to his own government, a dissident within the inner sanctum?

And would Chavadze have the power to block whatever it was that was surely about to happen in—what was it?—maybe eight hours?

He thought again, as he had done constantly in the last few hours, about what Lehman had told him, and he did his best to banish it.

He thought, too, of what he could not tell Lehman. The old man, dying by his own hand, would not want to hear the ultimate irony: that, after decades of careful preparation, he would not free his daughter. Pavlichenko's final masterstroke was a cruel and devious one.

He remembered Yakov Kramer's enormous fear.

"We need to talk, you and I," Yakov Kramer said. *"You spoke of the terrorism. The bombs—the conspiracy, you called it. I—we—must speak very openly with you. Can we trust you?"*

"Yes, of course," Stone said edgily. *"What about?"*

"I want to tell you about some terrorists," Yakov began. *When he had finished, Stone could barely speak, so filled was he with rage.*

"Do you understand why?" Stone said, almost shouted. *"Do you understand the perverted logic of this whole thing? With Sonya's connection to Winthrop Lehman, everything is in place. It will look like an American plot orchestrated by a very powerful member of the American establishment. I must talk to Sonya. I know her father has arrived in town, and I need to talk to him. I need your help."*

Yakov sat in his armchair, cradling his scarred face in his hands.

"Now!" Stone shouted.

The night was cold and dark, illuminated faintly by a crescent moon. He downshifted, and headed along the ravine, the headlights piercing the gloom, the tall pines grotesque in relief against the dark forest to one side. He drove as fast as he dared; the unguarded ravine on his right made any real speed dangerous. But there was no time.

When the pair of headlights of the oncoming car momentarily blinded him, at first he thought nothing of it, lost in frenzied thought as he was. And then he was grabbed by fear just as the windshield exploded, shattered by a bullet from the fast-approaching car.

Stone spun the wheel, turning in the direction of the other car. He could hear the oncoming car's brakes squeal loudly. He jabbed his fist downward at the door handle, flung it open, and dove out against the brush.

The white Volga spun wildly out of control, finally slamming into a birch tree and coming to a halt on the very edge of the ravine. The other car, Stone now recognized, was also a Volga, but a black one—an official car, he knew at once.

No. They had come for him. He had no protection, no bulletproof vest, nothing but the gun.

There was a moment's silence, but only a moment's, for then suddenly came a volley of shots, which slammed into the pine tree against which he had landed. He was behind it now, using the narrow tree trunk for protection, and he pulled out the Glock and fired once, twice, a third time.

Amid the staccato bursts of gunfire, Stone heard a human cry, a roar of pain cut short. One of the attackers was either dead or seriously disabled, Stone thought, his heart hammering.

His whirling mind allowed only the briefest coherent thoughts: *This was a setup,* his mind shouted. *Chavadze—maybe even Dunayev—had set me up for a trap I just walked into like a forest animal.*

There was the metallic click-*click* of an automatic pistol being reloaded, and then another series of shots slammed into the ground, mere inches away.

Only one of them was left now, but he was a professional, Stone was sure, and Stone didn't stand a chance.

He had to conserve his shots. There were how many left? Thirteen? Thirteen shots to fire in the darkness against an invisible foe who was undoubtedly far more skilled than he.

Stone grew cold when he heard the powerful engine of another vehicle speeding up the narrow road from the direction Stone had come.

This was it. Reinforcements. There was simply no way he could withstand several more. He looked around wildly at the wood behind him and saw that it was impassable, the brush and trees were so dense. He would have to leap out into the road and find another exit. He would have to run.

"Viktor!" the new arrival shouted, greeting the first attacker. Only one reinforcement. Good. "Where is he?"

"Over there!" the first shouted. "Hurry!"

"I'll take care of this," the new arrival said.

"My orders said—"

"Your orders," the new one said, and there was a gunshot, followed by a gagging sound. He had shot the first one, Stone saw, not comprehending.

"You!" the new arrival shouted up toward Stone. "Staroobriadets!"

Old Believer.

"Please, this way."

The chauffeur, a gray-haired man in his early sixties with the florid complexion of a hard drinker, led Stone into the brightly lit house, which was luxuriously appointed: low, dark furniture and Oriental rugs on the floors, prayer rugs on the walls. In the entrance hall was a large grandfather clock, and seated beside it was a frail old man in a neat, dark-gray suit.

Chavadze himself.

He rose unsteadily and gave Stone a dry handclasp. "I'm glad you're here," he said. "One of my people told me you had met with the old spy in Paris, Dunayev." He spoke in Russian, with a guttural Georgian accent, the sort of accent Stone had once heard in an old documentary film on Stalin. "I'm sorry about what happened to you, and most of all I'm sorry it took my man so long to get to you. Almost too long."

"Your man," Stone mused aloud. "But he was wearing a KGB uniform."

"The KGB is not free of us," he said. "Please, come in."

"I apologize about the lateness of the hour, but this is an emergency."

"Late? You forget about the hours we kept, all of us who worked and lived with Stalin. He worked throughout the night, because he *preferred* the night, and we did the same. At my age, it is too late to change. I always work late into the night."

"Work?" Stone could not help asking.

"I am writing my memoirs, memoirs that will never be published, at least not in my lifetime. Oh, maybe in ten or twenty years, if things keep changing at the rate at which they are now." The old man pursed his lips. "Gorbachev is doing good things for our country, but he is also consolidating his power, Mr. Stone. There is always a danger that we will have another Stalin. If it is not he, it will be another. And that is why *we* are here."

"It was your people, I take it, in the cemetery in Paris."

Amusement played in Chavadze's eyes, the barest wisp of a smile animating his lips. "Yes. We had somebody waiting and watching. We heard you were meeting with Dunayev, and we knew there would be violence."

"That was the second shot I heard."

"It was important to protect you."

"I don't understand."

"Let me explain."

"What does the password mean, 'Staroobriadets'?"

"Will you sit down? Come this way." They moved into a small but comfortable sitting room, furnished with low, overstuffed chairs. "You do not know who the Staroobriadtsy were? They were members of the Russian Orthodox Church who felt betrayed by the traumatic changes taking place in the church three hundred years ago. They spoke up, and they were hounded out, and they disappeared into the woods. Many burned themselves alive. But surely you know all this."

"And some still exist," Stone said. "But am I missing

your point? You're Old Believers. But you don't believe in Stalinism, do you?"

"Oh, no, quite the opposite. We want to make sure Stalin never happens again."

"And who is 'we?' "

"We are simply the old guard. Nothing organized, nothing elaborate. An organization of dying old men who have friends still in power, a widespread network. We watch, we listen. We warn and counsel, but never directly intervene, because we have no power to do so even if we wanted. You Americans have your foreign-policy establishment, your Council on Foreign Relations; we have only the Staroobriadtsy."

Staroobriadtsy. The word Alfred Stone had alluded to in his note. " 'We' again. Who the hell is 'we'?"

"We're patriots. Lovers of the Soviet state. It's imperfect, but it's vastly better than under the czars. You Americans forget that we Russians are very different. We do not want democracy—we wouldn't know what to do with it."

"Come on," Stone said with a snort of derision. "You're the old guard all right—Stalin's old guard. You and your cohorts were responsible for administering the world's longest-playing tyranny, were you not?"

"One of the longest-playing ones," Chavadze agreed. "Do you know that Khrushchev was asked much the same thing once, at a Party congress? He was as guilty as any of us. There was a voice from the back of the room, asking why didn't he speak up when he was in power, tell Stalin off? He responded, 'Who said that?' And there was silence. Then he said, 'Now you understand.' "

"You secretly terminated the court-martial of a few heroic men who refused to participate in the massacre in the Katyn Forest."

Chavadze was silent a moment. "Then you know. I thought that was lost deep in the Soviet archives. But, yes, I did once. You see, what happened there—the sheer brutality of the massacre—was a powerful influence on me. It completely changed my way of seeing the world, seeing my own country. I knew that true bravery in Russia means not speaking out and acting loudly but maneuvering secretly. One can do so much more."

"Why did you agree to see me?" Stone asked abruptly. "How much do you know about what is happening?"

"That your Central Intelligence Agency has been interfering in the affairs of our state? That much is plain."

"And M-3. You know about M-3."

"Certainly. Our esteemed head of the KGB. We orchestrated that."

"What? *Orchestrated* it? He was a source, wasn't he? A mole? Wasn't he—*isn't* he—controlled by us?"

"The reverse, Mr. Stone. The reverse. We controlled *you.*"

"*What?*"

"That was the genius of it. We had to control the secret about Lenin, and to do that, we played upon the American government's hopes and fears. Pavlichenko had been approached by an officer of American intelligence, and he agreed to cooperate. I don't know why, but it was a good thing. We were thereby able to manipulate your intelligence, leach it of secrets. You wanted to believe you had a mole, we gave you a mole. You were in the midst of the reign of Senator McCarthy, and the more you tore yourself apart, ate yourselves up, the gladder we were, because we were weak. When Stalin died, we were in turmoil, so we welcomed the opportunity to use J. Edgar Hoover, use McCarthy, use Winthrop Lehman. In order to protect himself, Lehman had to convince Hoover that he was 'running' an agent highly placed inside Stalin's Russia. It was all a great deception. I'm sorry your father had to be a casualty of that war, but he might have undone all our careful work. If McCarthy had known"—Chavadze gave a dry chuckle—"that he was saving the Kremlin from great devastation . . ."

The words echoed horribly. *I'm sorry your father had to be a casualty of that war.* . . . After what Stone had learned from Winthrop Lehman, who was also a casualty of that war . . .

Stone nodded slowly, dumbfounded. Everything

seemed so far away for an instant, Moscow, his father's house on Hilliard Street . . .

Chavadze continued speaking. "You know, it's ironic, isn't it?"

"Hmm?" Stone responded, a million miles away.

"That your father was caught in the spasms that began the Cold War. And you—you're caught in the spasms that are ending it."

"Then of course you are aware," Stone said slowly, "that Pavlichenko is about to stage a coup, are you not?"

Chavadze shook his head. "What do you base this on?"

Stone told him, ending with the details of the CAT scan. "If Pavlichenko is following Beria's plan, then he plans to suffer a stroke in a few hours, if he hasn't already. Tomorrow—today—he will be absent, and then something—some sort of catastrophe—will take place."

The old Georgian looked as if he had been struck across the face. "*No*," he said. "There have been signs . . . the murders, the maneuvers. Things have been happening that seemed, at first, only puzzling. There was talk of reassignments that seemed to make no sense, new people brought into our embassies and consulates by Pavlichenko. Talk in our listening posts abroad of a network of émigré-killers who did not answer to the normal KGB channels—as if a separate channel were set up."

"There's so little time," Stone said urgently.

Chavadze was nodding. Stone found that in his terror he was involuntarily holding his breath.

"And the deaths of people who seemed to be connected only to Pavlichenko. Lenin's former secretary in America . . . Men who were present at one certain dinner at Blizhny, Stalin's dacha. All murdered. And—"

"And what?" Stone asked, knowing from the old man's strange expression what was to come. His stomach turned inside out.

"Your father."

"Who killed him?" Stone asked, very quietly.

"This I know. One of our people, who serves on Pavlichenko's house staff as a cook, managed to tap his phone line at his dacha in Vnukovo. That's all we managed to learn. Pavlichenko ordered it."

There was a long silence, and then Chavadze continued. "Pavlichenko was Beria's closest, most trusted aide."

"Yes," Stone said. "And like Beria, like his mentor, he, too, plans a coup. But unlike Beria, Andrei Pavlichenko is extremely shrewd, extremely measured."

Chavadze's next words came out agonizingly slowly, as if they pained the old man. "I don't imagine you know the method by which Beria planned to seize power."

"Specifically, no. I don't."

"Oh, my Lord."

"What?"

"I was a candidate member of the Presidium then, and so I was privy to Beria's plans, revealed after he was executed."

"*What were they? They were the prototype, weren't they?*" Stone whispered hoarsely.

"Beria used funds that Lehman had provided him, which were therefore untraceable, to purchase a large order of high-powered explosives," Chavadze said. "Do you know that inside Lenin's mausoleum in Red Square there exists an empty chamber that is sometimes used as an arsenal? Stalin insisted upon this when the mausoleum was designed. . . ."

"*It can't be. . . .*"

"In many ways it was an ingenious stroke. The explosives piled high within the small mausoleum structure, while several meters away, on top of the thing, stood all of Beria's rivals. Sitting ducks in a sense, and all of them would be blown up."

"*Pavlichenko is using* CIA *plastique to accomplish the same thing!*" Stone said, leaping to his feet. "*A mass assassination. With not only the entire Politburo up there, but the American President as well!*"

Chavadze reached for a telephone next to him and dialed a number. After a moment, he spoke into the receiver: "Who is assigned to security for Lenin's mausoleum this morning?" He began shaking his head in disbelief.

Then he cried out, slamming down the phone furiously.

"The lines have been cut! Pavlichenko must have put his people on me, his employees at the main telephone banks in downtown Moscow!"

"So they know what you're asking about."

"But they did not cut me off before I learned that the regular personnel have been replaced, suddenly and at the last minute, by the KGB chairman's private guard," he said, his eyes wide and glistening with terror.

"I need your resources now," Stone said, "if this is to be stopped."

"My resources!" the old man said bitterly. "I have people throughout Moscow, even in Europe. Yes, in the KGB, even in the KGB's guards directorate, are young men who swear allegiance to the Old Believers. Family traditions are passed on to the sons and daughters. But we are powerless to fight the concentrated power of the KGB. My reach is not that great, Mr. Stone. Without my telephone, without time to summon my people, I can be of no help. Pavlichenko has contained operations so precisely that there is pitifully little we can do. My servants—my chauffeur—can take you into Moscow; maybe you and he can make the necessary connections. But now it's a matter of sheer speed, and I'm afraid we are almost out of time."

76

3:55 a.m.

It is extremely easy to construct a bomb. That most people are ignorant of the technique is testimony not to its difficulty but to the simple fact that few people are so inclined.

The explosives expert from the GRU had begun to

make the bomb that would, he believed, avenge the murders of his parents. How strange were the twists of fate!

He labored, in the small laboratory that the Sekretariat had provided for him, late at night, for reasons of secrecy: he wanted none of his colleagues to have an inkling of what he was working on.

At this hour, much of the Aquarium was dark. He worked at a black-topped counter, without emotion.

What was peculiar was that all of the equipment with which he had been provided was American-made. The GRU's explosives technology was every bit as sophisticated as anything made by the Americans; there was no need to use imported technology; but he did not question his orders.

Using an array of jeweler's tools, which he took from cases on the counter, he carefully connected two lengths of wire to a small black electronic detonator, manufactured by a California company. Next he began to attach the detonator to an electrical blasting cap and a nine-volt transistor-radio battery.

Electrical blasting caps contain small charges that are detonated by means of an electrical current. Emanating from the cap were two wires, six feet long. He screwed one of the blasting cap's wires to the detonator; the other wire he connected to one terminal of the small battery. He pushed the blasting cap into a two-and-a-half-pound block of plastic explosive. It was not critical where in the block the blasting cap went.

The explosive, he noticed, was a white C-4, manufactured in the United States. He recognized the label and the serial number: it was made by the Holston Army Ammunition Plant in Kingsport, Tennessee. He wondered idly how the Sekretariat had managed to get its hands on CIA plastique. And why.

The other wire emanating from the blasting cap he did not connect to the unused battery terminal; that would have detonated the explosion right there and then. No, this would happen when the time came, when he was ready to set the timer.

When the plastic bomb went off, the pressure in the

chamber beneath Lenin's mausoleum would instantly increase to such an extent that the three grenades he would place around the room would go off, thereby detonating the cloud of gas. He had determined that three grenades would be enough, but they would have to be a special sort of grenade that creates an explosion at an extraordinarily high temperature.

He needed white-phosphorus grenades. These, too, had been provided for him, and they were American-made. For unfathomable reasons of bureaucracy, the Soviet Army does not make them. The Sekretariat had, however, gained access to a significant supply of American M-15 grenades, smooth-bodied cylinders a bit smaller than beer cans.

He unscrewed the normal grenade fuses and then replaced them with snap-diaphragm concussion-detonation switches to which he had affixed blasting caps. These concussion switches, which are shaped like small orchestra cymbals, go off when subjected to great pressure.

Finally, he attached to the valve of the ten-kilogram cylinder of propane gas a second valve, a time-release one. Valves like these are sold through catalogues by any number of industrial-controls companies. A time-release valve may be used, for instance, to turn on a gas furnace in an office building at five o'clock in the morning, so that the place is warm by the time the employees arrive at nine.

All he would need was about two minutes in the basement of Lenin's tomb. He would turn on the propane cylinder and set the time-release valve to begin releasing the gas at eleven in the morning on Revolution Day. Within ten minutes, the gas cloud would be big enough, rich enough with oxygen. Ten minutes, he calculated, was the proper interval. If the plastic bomb went off five minutes too soon or five minutes too late, the whole scheme would fail.

He finished making the bomb at exactly twenty minutes past four in the morning. The whole assembly fit rather neatly in the satchel, and he was quite proud of his handiwork. It would, he was certain, do the job.

77

6:32 a.m.

Slumped in the car, Stone would not allow himself to rest. Charlotte was gone. She was not in her office, not in her apartment. Stone had called repeatedly from phone booths. No answer.

And then he knew where she would be, if she had not been arrested.

During their many talks in the last few days, she'd mentioned a hiding place in Moscow, a hotel called the Red Star in the center of the city where someone she knew worked at the desk. Once, she said, she'd met there with one of her sources who needed absolute anonymity. He knew intimately how her mind worked. If she had to hide, Stone felt sure, that's where she'd be.

Chavadze's driver pulled the black Volga into a side street very near Dzerzhinsky Square, and Stone cautiously got out. He entered a small, dimly lit building whose peeling sign was marked with a simple red star.

A middle-aged man with gray-peppered black hair and large pouches under his eyes was working at the front desk.

"I'm looking for someone," Stone said.

The man looked at him sternly for a moment, then smiled. "Ah, I think I may know a friend of yours," he said.

"*Charlie!*" It was Charlotte's voice. She appeared from a side room, running toward him, her arms outstretched.

"Oh, thank God," Stone said, embracing her.

As the chauffeur drove seventy miles an hour, Charlotte sat in the backseat of the Volga, clutching Stone.

"When I left my apartment to go to the office," she explained, "I saw a paddy wagon, one of the white vans that had once taken me away, and I knew it was no coincidence. So I wheeled around and ran as fast as I could. The Red Star was the only place I could think of to hide."

Stone was sitting next to her, and he kissed her. "I'm glad you're all right," he said. "We need you. *I* need you. Badly."

"Thanks," she said softly. "But Lehman—"

"He's dead."

"*What?*"

"He knew he was never going to make it out of Moscow. I went to see him, asked his help. He took something."

"*Took* something? What are you saying?"

"He killed himself. He died right in front of me."

"Lehman's *dead?*"

Stone took Charlotte's hand and squeezed hard. "Once he meant a great deal to me," he said, and stopped, but something in his voice indicated to her that there was something else.

"What is it, Charlie?"

"Later."

Charlotte suddenly looked up at the road and addressed the driver: "I know a shortcut that'll save us ten minutes. Ten minutes we're going to need."

The driver shook his head, unused to being ordered about by a woman. "You want to drive?" he asked.

"No," she said. "Just do what I tell you, okay? I know all the side streets of this goddamned city." More quietly, she added: "I knew someday it'd come in handy."

The limousine pulled up a deserted side street in what Stone could see was a poor neighborhood of southern Moscow.

"That's it," Stone said, and the car came to a halt. He kissed Charlotte quickly and got out. "Hurry," he said, and the Volga was gone.

"Careful," she called out.

As Stone walked closer to the garage, he saw Stefan Kramer. "What are you waiting for?" he asked the young Russian. "Let's go in!"

"I'm afraid that's going to be impossible."

"What's the matter, Stefan? What is it?"

"It wasn't here before," he said, leading Stone to the side door of Fyodorov's garage. The garage in which his old cellmate had stored the explosives.

The paint on the door was peeling, and what little paint was there was dark with engine grease. Glinting against the doorjamb was a large, sophisticated steel padlock.

"This is new," Stefan said. "They must have put it on just recently."

Stone looked at the lock, and then back at Stefan. "I'm pretty good with locks," he said.

78

6:57 a.m.

Shortly before seven o'clock on the morning of Revolution Day, two men from the GRU were driven to the side of Lenin's mausoleum.

Red Square was dark and deserted, with a lone militiaman walking across the cobbled expanse, several more sentries scattered at the perimeter. The two uniformed honor guards stood unmoving in front of the entrance to Lenin's mausoleum.

The younger man, carrying the bomb apparatus in a green military-issue gym bag, was wearing the vivid blue uniform of the Kremlin Guard. As he and his senior officer walked around to the rear entrance, the guard saluted. A security check, the guard would think. That was all.

"Good morning, sir," the guard said.

"Good morning," the older GRU man said. "Is the basement arsenal open?"

"No, sir. You gave orders that no one be allowed in. It is locked."

"Who has the key?"

"Solovyov, sir."

"He's downstairs?"

"Yes, sir."

They entered, and one level down came upon the next guard, who bolted to attention.

"Please give me the key to the arsenal," the senior man ordered.

"Yes, sir," the guard said, and removed a key from a large ring attached to his belt.

The two men entered the arsenal, closing the door behind them.

"Get to work," said the colonel general. His voice echoed against the concrete walls. The explosives expert set down the bag and removed its contents: the plastic bricks, the canister of gas, the blasting caps and grenades and batteries, and the many yards of wires. His face betrayed no emotion as he put the canister upright on the floor in the center of the room and began placing the grenades along the periphery.

He adjusted the gas-release valves. Finally, he switched on the black electronic detonator and punched in 11:10 a.m., then made the last electrical connection.

"It's all ready," he announced. "Right now it's twelve minutes after seven. The Politburo assembles atop the mausoleum at ten o'clock. At eleven, the gas will begin to be released from the tank. It will slowly fill the room with an oxygen-rich, highly combustible cloud. At ten minutes past eleven o'clock precisely, the plastic charge will be detonated, and the cloud will explode. And the structure will be destroyed."

"Very good." The older man walked across the room, inspected the wiring closely, glanced at the connections to the plastic explosive, a grayish brick wrapped in clear plastic, and paid particular attention to the time-release valves attached to the propane tank. At last he looked up.

"Everything is perfect," he said. He looked around the chamber for one last time. "Everything is perfect."

It was seven-fifteen.

By seven o'clock in the morning, the chairman of the KGB had been rushed, in his Zil limousine, to the Kremlin Clinic on Granovsky Street. He could not move his right side, he complained, and he was attended to immediately by the esteemed neurologist Dr. Konstantin Belov. After a hurried examination, Dr. Belov confirmed that the chairman's vital signs indicated a stroke, and ordered Pavlichenko transferred to the high-security clinic outside Moscow.

When the ambulance orderlies arrived to take him to Kuntsevo, two pleasant-faced young men who surely had no idea what was about to befall their country, Pavlichenko looked up from his hospital bed and smiled.

He knew that if he remained too long at the Kremlin Clinic he would be vulnerable, a sitting duck. That was why he had come up with this ruse: like a pea in a shell game, he would not remain in one place too long. At Kuntsevo he had arranged to be met by a small convoy of his forces. And in four hours or so, security precautions would be of no concern.

The orderlies lifted him gingerly from the bed and eased him onto the folding gurney they had brought in, apparently awed by the responsibility of wheeling the chairman of the KGB down the clinic's hallway, into the elevator, and into the ambulance. They seemed nervous and, for people who did this sort of thing all the time, even awkward. Pavlichenko was always amused by the effect his eminence had on ordinary people.

He wondered whether these two men would be among the hundreds of emergency medical workers who would soon be called to Red Square, sirens screaming, to carry the burnt remains of the members of the Politburo. Would anyone survive? He thought it unlikely.

The elevator stopped at the ground floor, and Pavlichenko was wheeled out into the cold, bright morning of Revolution Day.

9:00 a.m.

Miles of red bunting lined the streets, punctuated by giant portraits of Lenin and placards with the defiant, hortatory rhetoric of official Soviet propaganda: DEMOCRACY, RESTRUCTURING, SPEED-UP! and LENIN IS MORE ALIVE THAN ALL THE LIVING! and TOWARD THE RADIANT FUTURE OF COMMUNIST SOCIETY, WIDESPREAD WELL-BEING, AND LASTING PEACE!

Preparations for the anniversary of the Russian Revolution had begun weeks in advance. Posters had gone up in all public buildings, and red flags were everywhere, even on some cars; workers had struggled with pulleys and ropes to raise giant posters pasted onto wooden frames—fifty-foot-long banners of enormous supermen and superwomen exhorting Russians to fulfill the decisions of the latest Party congress.

By nine o'clock in the morning, an enormous crowd had assembled near the Gorky Park metro station, the last stop on the subway, after which people had to walk toward Red Square. University groups waving red flags filed past athletes in uniforms and others pushing rubber-wheeled floats. A delegation of workers from the Red Proletariat Ball Bearing Factory marched alongside workers from Watch Factory Number 1, carrying good old-fashioned, hard-line banners that read WORKERS OF THE WORLD, UNITE, ALL EFFORTS TO THE BATTLE FOR PEACE, and ONWARD TO THE VICTORY OF COMMUNISM. Outside the perimeter of Red Square were Uzbeks wearing black-and-white skullcaps, Gypsy women with cloth sacks on their backs, and little girls with stiff white ribbons in their hair.

A giant map of the world hung on the Kremlin wall above Lenin's mausoleum. Icons of Marx, Lenin, and Engels had been placed on the side of GUM, the state department store that faced the square. The redbrick Victorian structure of the Historical Museum, on another side of the square, was covered with portraits of the Politburo members, and a banner that read HAIL THE LENINIST FOREIGN POLICY OF THE U.S.S.R.!

In the center of all this, of all the commotion and all the triumphal posters, stood the dark-red mausoleum, looking tiny and insignificant, a child's toy.

Soon, Pavlichenko thought as he lay on the ambulance stretcher, the Politburo members, wearing their red ribbons, would be climbing the mausoleum. In just over two hours, the tomb would be a ball of fire, hurling chunks of porphyry and labradorite, granite and concrete into the dense crowd, killing hundreds of people.

He lay strapped in the stretcher, being hoisted toward the ambulance—play-acting, as he knew he must. He hoped he was convincing.

He remembered the ailing Konstantin Chernenko standing atop the tomb in February of 1984, presiding at Yuri Andropov's funeral. The day was ice cold, and you could see clouds of frozen breath coming from the leaders' mouths. Pavlichenko, not yet ascended to the Politburo, watched from the privileged guests' section as the Spassky Tower bells chimed noon and Chernenko, not terribly bright and emphysemic on top of it all, looked around, uncertain what to do, and then Pavlichenko—and thousands of others—could hear Andrei Gromyko's voice over the loudspeakers instructing the new leader: "Don't take off the hat."

What fools the Russian rulers were!

The orderlies lifted Pavlichenko into the back of the ambulance and locked the gurney and the intravenous stand into place. A minute later, the ambulance was moving, its siren wailing shrilly. The driver and his assistant looked back at him nervously, probably wondering what had happened to the KGB leader. Pavlichenko lay on the stretcher, seemingly napping.

Their destination, Kuntsevo, was fifteen miles outside Moscow, on the Minsk Highway. Once it had been Stalin's dacha; it was where Stalin had died. But in 1953 it wasn't a hospital and had no medical equipment whatsoever. The Great Leader had died with virtually no medical technology to sustain his life. They had even put leeches on his temples.

Kuntsevo.

For a week or so, he would rule the Soviet Union from his hospital bed, just as Yuri Andropov had done for six months in 1983. For much of 1983, Kuntsevo *was* the Kremlin. With the rest of the world ignorant of the state of Andropov's health, he spoke to his fellow Politburo members on the phone, seeing only the KGB chairman, Viktor Chebrikov, using him as a messenger boy to the outside world.

This time, Pavlichenko would have the assistance of forty or so trusted assistants, poised throughout Russia, ready to do his bidding. The Sekretariat was prepared to release immediately the irrefutable evidence that would link the U.S. National Security Council with the attack.

It would all happen in a few hours.

The ambulance screamed down the middle lane of the highway and soon came to a halt.

Had they arrived so soon? The ambulance had made a turn and had stopped.

Pavlichenko strained to see the stone walls topped with barbed wire that surrounded Kuntsevo, but the windows of the ambulance were too high. All he could see were streetlights.

Streetlights.

They weren't in Kuntsevo at all—there were no streetlights in Kuntsevo.

9:20 a.m.

The black Volga had driven around for almost an hour, searching for a way to penetrate the heavy security that surrounded central Moscow. The headquarters of the GRU, the Soviet military-intelligence branch, was inaccessible. Every ten feet there seemed to be KGB guards; the normally tight Revolution Day security had gotten even tighter, with the presence of the American President and his party.

Only those who were part of official delegations were permitted into the square, whose entry points were overseen by rows of grim-faced KGB guards in gray uniforms with the red letters "GB" on their shoulders. They were called the VV soldiers, the Vnutrennaya Voiska, or internal troops, harvested not from Moscow but from Russian villages, and they were one hundred percent Russians—not a Moslem or Mongol face among them.

There was no way to get to the commandant of the mausoleum; it was impossible. They were left with one strategy: the driver would have to negotiate with one of the guards, if they could find one who was not KGB: Red Army, perhaps, or GPU, for they were all out in force this morning. If he could persuade one of them of the urgency—persuade a soldier to talk to his superior officer, and maybe one would have the good sense to *listen*.

"Over there," the driver said. He pointed at a small gaggle of Red Army soldiers.

"Go," Charlotte said.

He accelerated, the wheels squealing, until they were abreast of the soldiers. He rolled down the window and said, "Where is your commanding officer?"

A voice replied, but it was not one of them. It came from the other side of the car: a KGB guard was fast approaching. "What is your business, comrade?"

"I need to talk to one of these fellows' commanders," the chauffeur replied.

The guard arched his eyebrows. "What is your business?"

"Let's get out of here," Charlotte said. She sat in the front seat, instinctively slumping down as the guard approached and peered into the window.

There seemed to be a spark of recognition in the guard's eyes, and he looked even more closely. "Stop this car, officers," he told the others. "Arrest them."

"*Now*," Charlotte whispered to the driver. "Up ahead. That group of MVD *militsiya*. *Do* it!"

With a bewilderingly swift motion, the driver slammed the car into gear and barreled ahead, knocking the KGB guard to the ground. A bullet was fired into the back windshield, but only the surface of the bulletproof glass cracked. They had made it the hundred feet or so to the next checkpoint, which did not seem to have any KGB guards in attendance. Charlotte rolled down her window and, quickly glancing at the epaulets on the men's uniforms, knew these were indeed MVD, Ministry of Internal Affairs.

"Arrest me," Charlotte called out.

79

9:40 a.m.

The chairman of the KGB reached for the pistol he had concealed in the large front pocket of his hospital robe. "Where are we?" he asked the driver warningly.

The orderly sitting next to the driver answered. "Outside Moscow, sir."

"What's going on?" He curled his forefinger around the trigger. The charade was no longer necessary, so he struggled at the straps, trying to free himself. "We're not in Kuntsevo," he said, drawing the gun from his robe and pointing it at Stefan, "and I suggest you take me there immediately."

But Stefan Kramer and a close friend, Zhenya Svetlov, the son of one of Yakov Kramer's fellow prisoners, swung themselves out of their seats and were immediately joined by a third, who leaped out from beneath a stretcher behind the front seat: Charles Stone was out of the ambulance, slamming the doors behind him.

Pavlichenko sat up and fired a shot, spiderwebbing the windshield.

"I don't suggest you fire again," Stone spoke in Russian, in a clear, strong voice. He and the two others had spread themselves out at a distance around the vehicle: Stone aiming his Glock on one side; Stefan on the other, aiming a revolver his father had kept since World War II.

The chairman of the KGB could see at once that he was outnumbered, and for a moment he froze.

Stone watched Pavlichenko, who seemed relaxed and confident, his gun casually pointed, as if this whole thing were but a brief interruption that would soon be over.

Of course it had been a simple matter for Stefan to get the ambulance and the uniforms, but Stone had been stunned at how simple it had been to go right into the Kremlin Clinic with no security credentials at all, just an ambulance operator's uniform. Even in the Soviet Union, hospital security was lax: speed in saving lives displaced the Soviet instinct for security.

Stone had picked the dead bolt on the garage with improvised tools selected from Stefan's medical-assistance bag: a long metal curette which he bent to simulate a torsion wrench, and a long steel pin used for testing "pin-prick sensation." Quite an assortment of explosives and detonators had been left there, obviously in order to implicate the Kramers in the Red Square bombing.

Knowing that Pavlichenko had readied a room at Kuntsevo for later that day, and that the CAT scan would *appear* to have been done at the central Kremlin Clinic on Granovsky Street, Stefan had theorized that Pavlichenko would have put in a call for an ambulance. This was confirmed by Chavadze's information: a bed was being readied for a Politburo member this morning at Kuntsevo.

And Stone and Stefan, joined by Stefan's friend Zhenya Svetlov, had managed to arrive first, before the real ambulance.

"Who are you?" Pavlichenko asked tranquilly. "A *foreigner*, it must be; I can hear that. Let me urge you to surrender at once. Do you realize the gravity of what you're doing? I think you may not know that you've abducted a member of the Soviet government. Please be thoughtful and put down your weapons."

From the right side of the ambulance came the voice of Charlie Stone. "And not just any member. A traitor within the government."

Pavlichenko shook his head and laughed gently. "You are dangerous, crazy people, and I am afraid you are terribly deluded. I urge you not to speak such nonsense to me." So close, so very close to the end, and *this*. Who were these people? Not ordinary MVD, probably not GRU.

Pavlichenko had not fired a gun in years, even decades, not since KGB Vysshaya Shkola arms instruction. But he knew that combat drew upon not just weapons but also psychology. These men were young, and they seemed not to be professionals. If they could not be intimidated by the enormous power of Pavlichenko's office, they could certainly be outthought, outmaneuvered. He was strong; they were weak.

"If you insist upon going through with this charade," Pavlichenko said, shaking his head sadly, "please be my guest and do so, but I warn you that the might of the entire Soviet Union will be massed against you. You may harm one man, but you will not survive." The three men had not shifted their positions; two guns remained leveled at him from either side, and he kept his pointed at the foreigner to his right. "Terrorism is a seductive thing, I imagine. You three no doubt think that by taking a member of the Politburo hostage you will change the world. But please understand that taking my life will make no difference in the end."

"I know about M-3," Stone said. "I know about how a young aide to Beria was propelled to power. With the help of some cynical Americans. Who didn't know how naïve they were being."

"You are quite mad," the KGB chairman said. "Who are you? CIA? Don't make a mistake your Agency and your country will surely regret."

"Interesting," Stone said, "to meet you after such a long journey. A long journey for both of us, I imagine. Now, lower your gun. You're outnumbered now. It's that simple."

Pavlichenko did not lower his gun. He watched, his eyes moving slowly back and forth, assessing the situation, probing for the weak spots. The idiots had to be taken seriously, talked down. One was foreign, probably American. But the others—Russians, surely? Were they CIA?

Or—yes. The CIA employee Stone. Of course. "I admire your bravery," he said gently. "But come now. Kidnapping the chairman of the KGB? I don't know what goals your service wants to achieve, but you must understand, now that you have done it, how foolish you're being. Brave, yes, but foolish."

"Put down the gun," Stone said. "We know about the mausoleum. We can get you to a telephone so you can countermand the orders—there's still time, I believe. Or we can get you to Red Square right away, if you prefer."

An edge of desperation had crept into the chairman's voice, despite the gentle, confident tone he was now assuming. "I can offer you amnesty. I will allow the CIA to arrange your removal from the Soviet Union. That is a very generous offer."

"Please don't force me to kill you," Stone said. "I've been forced to kill before, and I'm quite willing to do so once more."

Stefan began to say something, but was silenced by Stone's glare. Not a word, Stone had instructed him. Neither Stefan nor Svetlov was to speak. This was to be Stone's operation entirely.

"There is an old Russian saying," the chairman said. " 'A man who is buried before his time will live longer.' " As he talked, he slowly, *slowly*, turned the gun directly at the American and got the man's head within his sights.

"All right," Stone said. "Place your gun down on the seat in front of you. Carefully. Know that if you make any sudden moves you can only hit one of us, and then you will immediately be killed. At the same time, we will place our weapons down on the hood of the car. Agreed?"

Pavlichenko nodded. "What do you want?"

"We want to take you into Red Square," Stone said. "As simple as that. You will issue the proper instructions, and then we will release you."

"Fair enough." He extended his gun on the flat of his hand, moving it slowly toward the front seat, leaning forward as he did so.

"Carefully," Stone said. "Remember, there are *two* guns trained on you. You have one. We want to be fair about this." He, too, placed his pistol on his palm and moved it toward the ambulance's hood.

"Drop both of them," Pavlichenko ordered. The men were not murderers, he realized with relief. They had assessed the odds, knowing that they would never escape. They were being foolish, of course, but they could not know how foolish.

"*Now,*" Stone said. Stefan let his revolver fall to the ground. Stone dropped the gun onto the car, and at the moment it clunked onto the metal, bouncing once, Pavlichenko dropped his on the front seat, and leaned back.

"Well, then," the chairman said. He smiled, knowing what would soon happen to these three men, and he glanced at the American. For a moment, he thought he saw a pinpoint of red light.

He looked again: yes, a red pinpoint of light.

And then he saw what the American was holding aloft: a remote transmitter, the sort of thing one used to detonate a car bomb.

"What do you think you're doing?" Pavlichenko asked. His composure was shot through with fear; his voice had actually begun to tremble. The American was edging his thumb over to the white button on the side of the device. "Who gave you that?" he asked. "Was it someone within my organization? That's a KGB-issue device, isn't it?"

"We're all chess pieces to you, aren't we?" Stone asked, his thumb millimeters away from the detonator. He watched Pavlichenko sitting on the edge of his stretcher in the ambulance, saw the chairman's powerful body, his unnaturally dark hair, his pasty, coarse complexion and sturdy features. So this was the man. What did it take to claw your way to the top of Moscow's slipperiest pole? And then to plot to bring it all down around you? "The Kramers, me, my father—we're all part of your plan, isn't that right? You never knew my father, did you?"

"Whoever gave you that must surely be the person who wishes to bomb Lenin's mausoleum," Pavlichenko said. "Do you know who he is? We can find him. I'm a sick man, but you can help me. Get me to a phone and I

can call some people. We can stop this thing together."
He smiled. "No, my friend, I have no idea who your father
was."

Yes. Pavlichenko knew Alfred Stone was dead. *Pavlichenko had ordered Alfred Stone's death.*

Everything came together. The anger was almost ka-
leidoscopic, the flash of emotions hypnotic. Stone felt a
sudden calm, remembering his father's murder, remembering Paula. He remembered Lehman, feeling a newfound compassion. This man, this very ordinary man in
the back of the ambulance, this madman . . .

Pavlichenko was now speaking directly to Stefan.
"You can help your Motherland in a time of need," he
said to the Russian. He suddenly leaped forward and
snatched his gun, firing at the Russian behind him, but the
shots shattered the side and rear windows of the ambulance
and cut through the air, harmlessly. He whirled around
and grabbed the handle of the ambulance's back door.

Locked.

"How did you know we meant a bomb in the mausoleum?" Stone said, his voice calmly inquisitive. "We said
nothing about a bomb."

Pavlichenko aimed his pistol at the American and listened for a moment, overtaken by curiosity.

Stone clutched the live transmitter and moved his
thumb over toward the white button. His voice was choked
with emotion. "This is for my father," he said, and pressed
the button, detonating the bundle of dynamite affixed to
the underside of the ambulance's gas tank, setting off a
colossal, thundering explosion, leaving a roaring ball of
fire where the car had been a moment before.

It was 9:55.

9:56 a.m.

Sonya Kunetskaya, half mad with apprehension, returned
to her apartment building. She had gone out to make a
call from a pay phone, a call to her father. To tell him
what she'd just learned from Charlie. But there was no

answer at his hotel room, and she wondered whether he had left to go to Red Square for the Revolution Day ceremony. He had said he was not going to go. Where was he?

She had to talk to her father once more; and she had to talk to Charlie, to tell him face-to-face what she had been afraid to tell him.

A green van was parked in front of the building, its license plates unmistakably belonging to the KGB.

Sonya knew. They had come for Yakov, Stefan—and her. No, please. Her knees felt weak; she could barely walk; but somehow she got herself to the entryway, and then stopped.

She heard voices from the stairwell. Men's voices, echoing.

She turned and walked out of the stairwell and across the courtyard, concealed herself behind a column, and watched.

A cluster of figures emerged. A KGB soldier, and another one, and—and Yakov. Handcuffed. And another KGB soldier.

She wanted to scream. All she wanted to do was to run to him, to save them, but even in her crazed grief she knew that was impossible.

They will arrest me, she thought, and then it will all be over.

If I want to help Yakov, I must run. I must not let them get me, too.

Did they get Stefan?

No, she thought, as she edged her way along the apartment building. No, please. Protect us all.

On the two occasions a year when the Soviet Politburo reviews parades in Red Square from atop Lenin's tomb, they normally emerge from the Kremlin through a door just behind the mausoleum and mount the porphyry steps outside. There have been times, however, when, for reasons of inclement weather or the ill health of a leader, the members have instead chosen to take the underground passageway from the basement of the Council of Ministers building. In his later years, Leonid Brezhnev favored approaching the tomb this way, because the several underground passages that lead to the mausoleum are heated, and one of them even contains a toilet, a grave necessity when one is standing in the cold for four or five hours.

This day, for reasons not of poor weather or poor health but of security, the members of the Politburo, joined by the American President and Secretary of State and their wives, assembled in the Council of Ministers building and descended to the underground passage.

There had been too many incidents of terrorism in Moscow, and the Politburo was determined to see that nothing whatsoever happened today. The summit had officially begun, and the meetings would begin in earnest tomorrow. The Politburo wanted everything to go off without a hitch.

The twelve Politburo members, the ten candidate members, and the four Americans were accompanied by five security officers from the MVD, dressed, like the others, in heavy woolen coats and karakul or sable hats, with large red ribbons pinned to their left breasts.

It was nine-fifty-seven.

There is no elevator in the mausoleum itself; the group climbed the interior staircase, which led to the outside parapet of the tomb. They filed up the stairs and around to the front. Gorbachev and the President of the United States, the foreign minister and the Secretary of State took their assigned positions in the center of the line, before the five microphones.

At ten o'clock exactly, the Spassky Tower bells rang, followed immediately by a loud, metallic, recorded voice that proclaimed: "Glory to the great Lenin! Glory! Glory! Glory!"

And with a chorus of cheers from the thousands of assembled spectators, the ceremony had begun.

10:25 a.m.

For a moment, the MVD guard almost laughed. He saw a small, bespectacled middle-aged woman running toward him, waving her hands, shouting something. The *militsiyoner* stood with nine of his comrades at the entrance to Red Square by the redbrick Historical Museum.

Now he could make out what she was shouting: "You must stop this! There is going to be a bomb! You must help!"

The man grabbed the middle-aged woman just as she tried to break through the barricade. "How did you get this far?" he asked her roughly, shoving her away. "Get out of here before you get killed."

"No!" Sonya said. "I need to talk to someone in charge. It's important—you have to listen!"

The *militsiyoner* was tapped on the shoulder by one of the KGB guards. "What is it, comrade?"

"This crazy woman keeps shouting something."

"Let me talk to her." He approached the woman. "Tell me what the problem is."

"There's a bomb in the mausoleum. It might go off any minute. I'm *not* crazy. Listen to me!"

"Come with me," the guard said. "I want you to talk to my commander." He pulled her by the elbow toward the far side of the Historical Museum, signaling to his comrades that it was all right, and brought her to the narrow passageway between two buildings. "Now, tell me what you've heard."

"Oh, thank God," Sonya said, and then she saw that the KGB guard had drawn his revolver and was pointing it at her chest. "No, please—"

She looked plantively at him, then felt a flash of anger. Please, God, save me, she thought. Save me, save Yakov, save Stefan.

Please don't shoot.

She stared, unable to speak, shaking her head slowly. And the guard fired, once, into her heart. The noise of the shot was drowned out by a momentary crescendo of the marching music that came from Red Square.

At exactly eleven o'clock, the valve timer on the small tank of propane that sat in the center of the arsenal beneath Lenin's mausoleum clicked, and the gas began to jet forth with a hiss that filled the room.

80

11:02

Ilya M. Rozanov, a Kremlin Guard, would have greatly preferred to be out there, in front of the mausoleum, taking part in the changing of the guard. But he had done his time a few months ago, changing the guard in the dark of night, marching in the bitter cold and standing ramrod-straight before the tomb's entrance for almost an hour and not flinching.

It was too bad he could not have had that proud assignment today. It was the anniversary of the Russian Revolution, the biggest holiday of the year, when all of Russia—all of Stavropol, his hometown—would be watching Lenin's mausoleum on their TV sets. And the world, too: for the first time ever, the news said, the President of the United States of America would join the Politburo atop the tomb to pay honor to the Revolution.

But there were worse assignments than patrolling the back of the mausoleum.

It even had its thrills. He was able to see the members of the Politburo emerge from the bowels of the mausoleum and march around to the front to take their places on the reviewing stand. He even thought he might have glimpsed the American President!

True, he had hoped to see them walk right by him,

through the door in the Kremlin wall, past all the graves, but for some reason they had chosen to take the underground route. Still, he was able to make out some of the dignitaries standing in the Important Persons area on either side of the tomb.

The Kremlin Guard, of which this man was a member, was sometimes known straight-facedly as the Palace Guard, the Okhrana. In their smart, well-pressed blue uniforms and karakul hats, they were the cream of the crop, the guards in the position of highest trust in the nation's capital.

It was bitter cold, and Rozanov would have liked to warm up in the basement arsenal of the mausoleum when his shift ended, but for some curious reason the arsenal had been off-limits for the last few days.

There had been a lot of talk about it, and his superior officer, the Kremlin commandant, who was a KGB man, was furious. Why in hell had Pavlichenko gone and done such a thing as ordering the arsenal closed? Security precautions, Pavlichenko had said! But his boss, the Kremlin commandant, had lasted through four KGB chiefs and far more general secretaries, and he resented this intrusion into what he considered his domain. The arsenal was always in use on these state occasions—for gathering and giving orders, for storing ammunition, all that sort of thing. And now the guards had to gather to receive their orders outdoors, next to the Kremlin wall. It was unheard of.

But the guard cared for one reason: it meant that the only place he could warm his hands was in the bathroom several levels below ground, under the mausoleum. An inconvenience. The politics of it he couldn't care less about.

He waved at another guard to signal that the next shift was up, and he walked to the back door of the mausoleum. He could hear the endless speech of whoever was talking, followed by the unison cheers, echoing in the square.

And then, as he entered the mausoleum and walked toward the staircase that went down to the bathroom, he noticed something peculiar. The odor of gas: an overpowering stench. The farther down the stairs, the stronger the smell got. It seemed to be coming from the arsenal, and he wondered if anyone else had sensed it. It smelled like the sort of gas that was highly flammable.

In front of the arsenal's closed doors stood a guard brought over from the KGB, not one of the Palace Guard.

"Hey," Rozanov called to the KGB mannequin. "You smell that?"

The guard turned, took note of Rozanov's uniform, and ventured: "You think it's poisonous? I've smelled it for the last ten minutes or so."

"Gas," Rozanov said, coming closer. "It's coming from inside there." He pointed.

"Stay back," the guard said, suddenly menacing.

"It's probably poisonous," Rozanov said. "Could kill you. Let's take a look." He came closer still.

"Back," the guard said. "My orders are not to let anyone in."

"Look, comrade," Rozanov said more stiffly. "Your orders are not to stand there like a moron if there's a gas leak."

The guard seemed to consider this.

"Let's take a look. Who knows, you find a gas leak, you get a commendation. Maybe a promotion, right? Pavlichenko admires a little initiative in times of crisis."

The guard relented. "All right, but quick. Someone else could come by, and I'm dead. Our orders are to shoot anyone who enters the room on sight." He turned around and slowly unlocked the double metal doors. "Shoot first, ask questions later," he elaborated unnecessarily.

The arsenal was dark, illuminated partially by the light from the outside corridor. The stench of gas was overpowering, and the air in the room was hazy. Rozanov could hear a distinct, loud hiss.

"Don't touch that!" Rozanov shouted when the KGB guard reached for the light switch. "This place is full of gas! A spark from the light could set this off."

And then he noticed the tank, in the center of the

room, from which the hiss was coming. And then the wires that ran throughout the room, and the blocks of plastic explosive, and the grenades. A *bomb*? Here?

"What the fuck—?" was all he had time to say as he wheeled around and was bayoneted in the throat by a second KGB guard, whose form was suddenly framed in the arsenal's doors.

So much seemed to happen in unison at the Revolution Day ceremonies in Red Square, Admiral Mathewson noticed.

Squeezed into the dignitaries' section, he had an unrivaled view of the mausoleum, maybe ten yards away.

Everything was synchronized. A man in a gray suit, a parade marshal, stood on one of the lower balustrades of the mausoleum, directing the crowd, instructing it when to cheer. Two open limousines careered through the square, one carrying the commander of the Moscow district, the other carrying the minister of defense, and as they passed, the serried ranks of soldiers chanted *Ooorah! Ooorah!* The troops, thousands of them, turned as a man, mechanical as robots.

Then the tanks moved in, the missile launchers with their thick rubber tires, the machine-gun carriages, drawn by four horses—a homage to the old days, surely—all rattled across the cobbled square, which was filled with blue-gray exhaust fumes.

The crowd, chanting agitatedly but joylessly, red ribbons pinned to their breasts, were unaware of the extensive security precautions, Mathewson knew: the squads of soldiers with automatic rifles gathered in the underground passageways outside the square, the plainclothesmen standing in the bleachers astride the mausoleum, wearing earplugs and bulging guns beneath their coats. Security for the summit was tight.

Mathewson watched his President up there, waving and smiling broadly, and felt a flush of pride. For the first time, a president was paying respects to the Russian Revolution. The Cold War was definitely over.

At shortly after eleven, several little girls with bows

in their hair climbed the mausoleum steps to hand cellophane-wrapped bouquets of red carnations to the members of the Politburo, bouquets supplied by Gorbachev's office staff.

Mathewson watched the Politburo members, looking bored atop the tomb, their right hands extended in a weary salute. A nearby mother—clearly the wife of an important official—was holding up her child and whispering excitedly, "Can you see Gorbachev? That's Gorbachev! And there's the President of the United States!"

Colonel Nikita Vlasik of the MVD watched Charlotte Harper with sad gray eyes and decided that maybe he believed her extraordinary story.

This was the man who had once—it seemed long ago, though it was mere weeks—arrested her. The man who had given her advice on how to stay out of trouble. Charlotte felt a strange kinship with him.

He nodded without smiling. "You know," he said, as he gestured to his chief lieutenant, "you remind me even more of my daughter. Only you and she would do something as foolhardy as you've just done, breaking through a KGB barricade.

"Vanya," he said to his lieutenant, "we have not a second to waste."

It was 11:03.

By 11:05, the KGB guard had locked the arsenal door once again, leaving the dead body crumpled inside. He had orders to follow. Everything smelled like gas, the arsenal and everything outside it, and as the guard stood watch to make sure no one else intruded, he thought he was going to be sick.

Inside the arsenal, the digital numbers on the electronic detonator indicated that six minutes remained.

The propane continued to hiss loudly out of the cylinder.

At 11:07, a team of MVD militiamen, bearing axes, chemical fire-extinguishers, and the assorted other equipment of the bomb squad, emerged from the door in the Kremlin wall directly behind the mausoleum. In order to avoid attracting too much attention, they had swung around into the Kremlin and entered from this side, but even so their presence caused a stir in the reviewing stands on either side of the tomb. There was a line of them— nine militiamen, to be exact—and they ran toward the mausoleum.

When they reached it, they split up to search.

But they were not diverted for long. The smell was overpowering now. All of the mausoleum stank of propane, and within forty-five seconds, seven of the militiamen had located the source.

The KGB guard saw the militiamen running toward him, and he raised his pistol and fired, but he was overwhelmed by gunfire.

The electronic detonator read 11:09.

With the aid of an ax they were able to sever the lock and force the arsenal doors open. The place stank.

The militiamen, experts in their work, at once saw the bomb apparatus and trod over the bodies in their haste to find some way to disconnect it.

The men coughed, overcome by the fumes.

There was no time!

Several of the men collapsed on the floor from inhaling the propane; they hadn't all brought masks—who could have known? There were seconds remaining, literally seconds, and the wiring was such a mess, such a tangle, that even tearing at it as they did seemed to do nothing to stop the maddening, terrifying, hypnotic reddish flashing of the digital readout, the numbers that rushed toward 11:10. They could see the target time on a separate readout, the precise time at which the small black detonator would click the circuit open, and the plastic explosives—

Tear the wires out of it! Pull the plastique away from the electrical current! But there were too many blocks of explosive.

It couldn't possibly be done in eight seconds. The

whole thing would detonate and they and the mausoleum and the world leaders who stood unawares, mere yards above, would be incinerated. . . .

At 11:09:55, one of the militiamen spotted the connector and dove for the wiring, wrenched the leads apart, end from end.

Would it . . . ?

"Stand back!" a voice shouted.

The clock's digits froze. Lying on the floor, surrounded by a tangle of wires, the militiaman gave a deep sigh. The bomb had been dismantled.

And it was over.

One of the militiamen spotted a face he recognized, and the two men drew close for an instant. They shook hands, and the first one said under his breath one word: "Staroobriadets."

Atop the mausoleum, the President of the Soviet Union and the President of the United States waved at the crowd. On either side of them stood members of the Soviet and the American leadership. Most of the Americans, cold and uncomfortable, their legs weary, wondered how much longer they'd be able to stand it up there. Their Soviet counterparts, more accustomed to very long public ceremonies, gave stiff little waves and stood still to conserve body heat.

Unnoticeable to observers in Red Square, a small slip of paper was passed from a military guard standing next to the mausoleum, to a civilian security officer, and eventually to the Politburo member Aleksandr Yakovlev, who handed it to Gorbachev.

Gorbachev glanced at it briefly, then looked back to the crowd.

The President turned to him. "Urgent business?" he asked genially.

"No," Gorbachev said. "A little problem, but we've taken care of it."

Charlotte stood, protected by two guards from the MVD, behind a checkpoint near the Historical Museum, just outside Red Square. The cheers and martial music of the parade were overwhelmingly loud. At last the car pulled up, a rusty Lada, looking like a squashed bug. She'd hoped the MVD would be able to find them, and they had.

The first face she saw was Stefan's, then Svetlov's. She craned her neck, terrified, trying to read their expressions. Was he—?

And then Charlie got out of the car, crawled out, really, from the backseat, a wounded, very sick-looking man. *What happened?* his anxious face asked.

She wanted to jump across the iron railing, hug him, tell him everything was all right. She found herself swelling with emotion, relieved tension, love, fear—a hundred different feelings—and then what little remained of her poise dissolved and she was crying.

Charlie Stone struggled to cross the cobblestones toward Charlotte, and then he saw the answer, her smile, the *yes,* and he began to see concentric circles around everything, doubles and triples, everything getting lighter and brighter, everything becoming wonderfully, comfortingly, white.

EPILOGUE

New York: Six Months Later

Only afterward did things come full circle.

The first thing Stone became aware of, as he slowly awakened, was the warmth and velvety softness of Charlotte's naked back, nestled tightly against him. Then: the morning light from the strong May sun, flooding the bedroom.

Her nearness aroused him, and he slowly reached a hand around to the warmth between her legs. With spread fingers he massaged her downy pubic hair gently and slowly, then closed his fingers and increased the pressure. She was, though not awake, moist. His other hand stroked her breasts; the nipples were erect now. He kissed her neck, nuzzled her shoulder. She stirred and gave a throaty moan.

Even months later, the mysteries remained.

They knew that Sonya had died on Revolution Day, and that Yakov and his sons had been permitted—by direct order from the Politburo—to emigrate to the United States.

Avram Kramer's mental health remained tenuous; for him, things would never be normal again.

They knew that the U.S.-Soviet summit had ended with more promise than substance, as is often the case with summits, and that neither the American leaders nor the Russian leaders, with one great exception, were harmed. The vast majority of American press reports called the summit "bland and uneventful"—the sole exception being the unfortunately timed death, by stroke, of the chairman of the KGB. But the reports, of course, were decidedly wrong.

Frank Paradiso had been reassigned to the U.S. Embassy in Lisbon. The Director of Central Intelligence, Ted

Templeton, and his deputy, Ronald Sanders, both announced their resignations shortly after the summit, each for various family reasons, each announcing that he had wanted to wait until the Moscow summit was over.

Each of them also found lucrative employment in the private sector. Of course, the two officials had little choice but to resign, faced with the possibility that their role in the illegal covert operation might someday be revealed, the most damaging evidence being contained in a package that was found in Andrei Pavlichenko's office safe after his death.

Unbeknownst to Stone, the extraordinarily secret group that called itself the Sanctum disbanded itself, a mere memory in the minds of its prominent members, who of course said not a word when they ran into one another at parties in Georgetown or panel discussions at the Council on Foreign Relations.

He was unaware, too, that at this very moment a nurse in a psychiatric hospital in Moscow was, as she'd been ordered, injecting one of her latest patients with a solution of halperidol and a colloidal suspension of sublimed sulfur, which she'd done for several weeks' running. This solution, the nurse knew, causes the patient to run an extremely high fever and to suffer unbearable discomfort in whatever position he assumes. The nurse knew only that the patient was afflicted with criminal schizophrenia, having been arrested, by Politburo order, in the Soviet Embassy in Washington on November 7 and flown at once to Moscow.

The patient, a former high-ranking diplomat named Aleksandr Malarek, once an aide to the late chairman of the KGB, was being administered a little lesson designed to impress anyone so foolish as to attempt what Malarek had done. Malarek now suffered a side effect of the medication: he had little more intellectual capacity than a parsnip.

Charlie refilled their coffee cups and sat down next to Charlotte at the breakfast table.

Both of them were enjoying the energizing glow of having just made love. Charlotte, who was rapt in the Arts

& Leisure section of *The New York Times,* looked up after a few moments. "Charlie, we need to talk."

He groaned. No one ever "needed to talk" about happy, pleasant things.

"How committed are you to teaching at Columbia?" she asked.

Immediately after Stone returned to New York, Columbia University had offered him a tenured professorship in Soviet studies, at a respectable academic salary—which wasn't much. But Stone had plenty sacked away from his days at Parnassus and from the money his father had left in his safe-deposit box, and besides, the apartment and his mountain-climbing equipment were already paid for. And then there would be the Lehman inheritance . . .

He was about to publish another book, on the future of the Soviet empire, and was teaching a class on the Soviet empire, or what little was left of it.

"Committed?" Stone asked, getting up to retrieve the toast, which had just popped up. "Now what are you talking about?"

"I mean, do you like it? Would you ever consider leaving?"

"Do I *like* it?" Quite a bit, he thought. He'd turned away requests from several intelligence agencies, the NSA, and the DIA for his expertise. Intelligence, he'd come to believe, was a little like a snake: slimy, though deceptively dry and inoffensive, even agreeable, to the touch. He said: "Teaching in a university would be wonderful—without the backbiting colleagues and the undermotivated students. And the academic politics—which are so fierce because the stakes are so small, as someone once said. Charlotte, what are you after?"

"The network's offered me a job in Washington I can't pass up."

"Really?"

"Covering the White House."

"Seriously?" Stone stepped forward to throw his arms around her, and then stopped. "Oh, no. Washington."

"I knew you wouldn't be thrilled about going back there."

He rolled his eyes toward the ceiling. "The land of the white sky in the summer. The land of pedestrian malls. The city that teems with lawyers and congressional interns."

"Charlie—"

"But, then, I suppose I could manage to get a job at Georgetown."

"Charlie, they'd hire you in a second."

He turned to face her. "Yeah," he said. "I guess I could do it. Why not?"

There was a sadness in both of them, but especially in Stone. In some sense, he had found two parents and lost them both. He had learned to kill and knew that he had within him the ability to take a human life, just as so many had been taken from him.

On the anniversary of his father's death, he made a pilgrimage to Boston and placed flowers on the grave, in Mount Auburn Cemetery. The epitaph was the verse from Boris Pasternak, bleak and yet at the same time hopeful, that Alfred Stone had liked so much:

> YOU ARE ETERNITY'S HOSTAGE
> A CAPTIVE OF TIME.

And it had always meant little to Stone, until things came full circle. It was the key to the final mystery, the astonishing revelation that Winthrop Lehman had made in the last ten minutes of his life.

Keep your machine on, Winthrop Lehman had said, gesturing weakly at the tape recorder. *I have one more thing to tell you.* And then Stone had known.

"You saw the gravestone I had put up in Père Lachaise to conceal the fact that Sonya was alive," Lehman said. "She was allowed to come to Paris twice, in 1956 and in 1953. You see, your father was always grateful to me for selecting him to serve in the White House. He looked upon me as a surrogate father of sorts, and so he went to Moscow for me uncomplainingly. And when he was photographed by FBI agents in Moscow, he knew he had to go to prison rather than reveal the truth."

Stone, watching Lehman struggle to keep his eyes open, nodded. His head whirled; he could barely speak. "I know," he said. "I think on some level I've always known, although Dad never said anything. My father wanted to protect my childhood. He didn't want to take from me the one immutable thing. I could never understand why he felt so close to you, so loyal, against all reason. But I think I always had an inkling."

Lehman, who was almost dead, could not contain a small, pleased smile. "My daughter was a beautiful woman. I shouldn't—shouldn't have been surprised when your father fell in love with her. He would do anything—he was even willing to suffer a great indignity in silence—to get Sonya out—Sonya, who was now pregnant with his child. But he didn't know that Sonya could never be let out, that she was a hostage. And Sonya—poor Sonya—refused to let her child grow up in a land of oppression. This was 1953, remember, and the terror was at its peak. She made the greatest sacrifice of her life. She said—she said she didn't want her child to be a slave."

"You couldn't get her out," Stone said tonelessly. "But you were able to get me out. That was why my father went to Paris in late 1953. To see Sonya one last time, and to take his newborn child. But why—"

"I had to lie to him. I had to tell him that Sonya had remarried. Otherwise he couldn't have faced it. A few years later, I told him she had died. But I did everything I could for him."

"Yes."

"I got a forged birth certificate for him—for you. I helped him, with money, whenever he'd allow me to do so—"

"I know. I'm—grateful."

"When I saw you in my archives, I was terrified you'd find out, and I didn't know what you'd do, how you might disturb the delicate arrangement—as much as you had the *right*. . . ."

"Before he died, my father wanted to tell me, but he

never got the chance. But I knew." Somehow Stone had suspected something like this all his life; in the way children can sense things that have no logical explanation: that Margaret Stone was not his real mother. What was it that Alfred Stone had said in a moment of rage, years ago? "You're the only mother he has!" Yes. The cry of someone who feels at once angry and guilty: I need you to be his mother, since his *real* mother . . .

"Some of us—some of us—we're caught in traps that aren't of our own making," Lehman whispered. "In the Cold War between two superpowers. I was; my Sonya was. At least you are not, Charlie."

And the old man closed his eyes.

Traps. Hostages.

"You are eternity's hostage," Alfred Stone liked to quote. "A captive of time."

Charlie had misunderstood. His father hadn't been referring to his very public tragedy. He'd been referring to his own, private tragedy. To Sonya. To the mother of his son.

Washington

Almost a full year after that Revolution Day, Stone received in the mail a registered and insured letter from Yakov Kramer, who was by now living in the Brighton Beach section of New York. He found a comfortable chair and opened the package. Charlotte, her hair tied back with a paint-spattered bandana—their new apartment in Georgetown was a disheveled maze of paint cans, spackling, ladders, and drop cloths—stood over him and gasped.

The package contained several yellowed sheets of paper.

Stone pulled them out carefully and, with a peculiar mingling of elation, puzzlement, and shock, examined the documents. They seemed, after all this time, after such a long search, oddly familiar.

On top was a letter. "To the Politburo of the Central Committee," it began. It was signed "V. I. Lenin."

About the Author

Joseph Finder is also the author of *Red Carpet: The Connection Between the Kremlin and America's Most Powerful Businessmen*. He is a graduate of Yale College and Harvard's Russian Research Center, has been a member of the Harvard University faculty, and has written extensively on Soviet affairs and other subjects for *The New York Times*, *The Wall Street Journal*, *Harper's*, *The Nation*, and *The New Republic*. This is his first novel. He lives with is wife, Michele Souda, in Boston, Massachusetts.